THE LONG JOURNEY TO CLEVELAND

Rudolf Ruder

2-15-2015

Rudolf Ruder

ISBN: 0-9909161-0-3
ISBN 13: 978-0-9909161-0-9
Library of Congress Control Number: 2014916050
Phoenix Bookworks, Clinton Township, MI

ACKNOWLEDGEMENTS

As with most worthwhile endeavors such as writing a book, there are people and organizations that provide assistance and support. This book is no different, and so I would like to acknowledge their efforts.

First and foremost were my parents whose courage, devotion and love through their perilous journey through the war and holocaust and afterward provided the inspiration for the book.

The Holocaust Memorial Museum in Farmington Hills, Michigan was extremely helpful in terms of historical information and their willingness to put up with my frequent visits. I owe a special thanks to Distinguished Professor Emeritus Guy Stern of Wayne State University who is also the Director, International Institute of the Righteous at the museum for his enthusiastic support for the book and especially for his quick wit and humor. Remarkably active in his early nineties, Guy is one of the celebrated World War II 'Ritchie Boys' whose heroism and operations interrogating German POWs saved countless lives. Professor Stern provided continued inspiration and support for the book.

Another scholar whose assistance I'd like to acknowledge is Christopher R. Browning, Frank Porter Graham Professor of History Emeritus at the University of North Carolina at Chapel Hill whose graciousness and support for the book in its early stages provided incentive for me to continue.

As a survivor herself, Marianka Zadikow May's story was featured in a documentary called "The Defiant Requiem" describing the events at the Theresienstadt concentration camp. I had the honor of meeting Marianka and her enthusiasm for and support of my story in its early stages gave me great inspiration to continue with the book

Additionally, instrumental in solving some of the story's mysteries were documents and photos from the Stadtarchiv Mühldorf a. Inn, Germany, my mother's hometown and where I spent my younger years before coming to the United States. Mr. Edwin Hamberger was kind enough to provide some rare photographs that I think added significant interest to the story.

Along those same lines, information graciously provided by Bill Neutzling from his website contained in "Anatomy of a Mission: Mühldorf, Germany 19 March 1945" provided detailed photographs and information about an important event in the lives of my mother, father and grandfather.

Similarly, the Yad Vashem organization in Israel provided some chilling photographs that helped communicate some of the more somber events my father experienced in Poland.

Finally, I'd like to acknowledge the unwavering support of my siblings, sisters Elfriede, Jeanette and Doris, my brother Manfred and cousin David.

FOREWORD

This is a book that had to be written, and it took sixty-six years to do so. It is both a tribute and a memorial to my parents, who both survived the horror that was World War II and the Holocaust, but each on polar opposite sides, one a Jewish Holocaust survivor from Poland, the other a young German girl in the Hitler Youth who later worked for the Nazi government. This is a true story of how, against all odds, they met, married, and came to the United States with three small children. It is an inspirational story of love, hate, and prejudice, but above all, survival. It chronicles my father's life before the war in Lvov, Poland, as a successful tailor with a wife and two children. It follows his imprisonment by the SS in the infamous and brutal Loncki Prison in Lvov and his experience in several forced labor and extermination camps at Plaszow, Gross-Rosen, Auschwitz, Dachau, and several of its Mühldorf sub-camps at Waldlager V, Thalheim, and finally at Ampfing where he was rescued by the US Army. The book tells the true story drawing on historical facts, birth and death records, family records and photographs, declassified US Army Air Forces mission documents, oral stories from other survivors, and most critical, documents from various historical tracing services, some in handwritten form, painstakingly identifying individual work records and prisoners' transfers from camp to camp. It is truly remarkable that these records survived and are available. The book contains copies of these records and photographs to augment the story.

The book also follows the life of a young Catholic German girl growing up in the Nazi era, where she actually presented a bouquet of flowers to Adolf Hitler and was a member of the Girl's Hitler Youth. Her father, my maternal grandfather, was a Nazi Party member and a train engineer who took cattle cars full of Jews to Dachau and other camps. Several of my mother's uncles were in the German army, the *Wehrmacht*, including one who was in the elite First Mountain Division. In all, two of her uncles and a half brother died fighting the Russians.

My mother, too, had a close call with death. During an Allied bombing raid on her town of Mühldorf, three of her friends were killed taking shelter in a church. My mother decided not to follow them into the church, running home instead. I had a conversation with one member of the bomber crew who shared his recollection of the event, corroborating the hit on the church.

While researching for the book, I discovered several hidden, unknown connections between the families before my parents ever met. Things like my great-uncle being an *Obergefrieter* (lance corporal) in the *Wehrmacht* First Mountain Division and taking part in the German capture of Lvov in 1939 and again in 1941, his unit actually rounding up Jews. Another great-uncle was killed in June 1944 during the first day of a strategic Russian offensive that resulted in the liberation of my uncle and cousin.

It should be noted that the map of Europe changed several times before and within the time span of the book. Lvov, Poland, for example, was called Lemberg up until 1919 following the collapse of the Austro-Hungarian Empire at the end of World War I. It was renamed Lvov/Lwow after it became part of Poland. In 1941, after the German attack on Russia, it was again called Lemberg. The Jewish ghetto was called the Lemberg ghetto, but was also referred to as the Lvov ghetto. After the Germans were driven out, the town was called Lviv as part of the Ukraine. While it would have been easier to use a generic name throughout, I chose to use the name of the town within its historic time frame and context, hence Lemberg, Lvov, Lwow, and Lviv all refer to the same geographic location but under different masters.

It should be understood that I am not a historian, nor is this book intended to be a comprehensive history of the Holocaust. The book does not attempt to explain the genesis of the Holocaust; that would take uncounted volumes, many not yet written. I leave that to eminent scholars like Christopher R. Browning, Yehuda Bauer, and others. It is, however, a microcosm of the tumultuous events that took place in Europe during and immediately after the reign of the Third Reich.

In writing the book, I used actual historical facts as the canvas upon which to paint the story. These historical facts provided the hard dots that had to be connected. As noted earlier, I used actual copies of German/SS documents to trace my father's hellish journey through the Third Reich. While the records seized after the war were far from complete, I was able to reconstruct the dates and places with reasonable accuracy. For example, records from Dachau were remarkably complete to the extent of showing work assignments, detailed and summarized lists of prisoners and their occupations, transfers in and out of various Dachau sub-camps, and liberation dates. In contrast, Auschwitz records were far less complete, probably due to SS destruction of many records. I was able to find transfers in and out of Auschwitz, for example, a list of prisoners transferred to Dachau via Gross-Rosen, the dates of transfer, and the prisoners' tattooed prisoner numbers, but little else. My father, normally reticent to talk about his experience, did communicate some of the Auschwitz experience, including a guard who saved his life and his encounter with the infamous Dr. Josef Mengele. In addition, I was fortunate to be able to talk to other survivors who spent time with my father, and their recollections proved instrumental in showing a more personal side of the events.

It is also important to understand that various conversations, thoughts, and opinions of the people in the book reflect what I believe are logical based on the time, place, and circumstances, but are obviously not quoted verbatim. Some minor characters are fictional but represent various personas during the period. These characters are based on conversations with my parents, other survivors, and other historical sources indicated in the appendix. The names of some actual people in the book were changed out of respect for their privacy, even some seventy years after the events took place.

Finally, the destination of the long journey of my parents, uncle, cousin, and several other survivors is Cleveland, Ohio, where this group of Holocaust survivors and war refugees found a new life. Until the very end, none of us knew where we would go or when. We had never heard of Cleveland, and while some of the survivors arrived in Cleveland years before our family finally came over, all were instrumental in assisting our family in completing the long journey and settling in a new land.

1938

LVOV, POLAND

Thirty-one-year-old Simon Ruder was busy working at his tailor shop at Legionow Street 41 in the Polish city of Lvov, once known by its former Austrian name of Lemberg. Simon, like many of the Jews living in Poland and Eastern Europe, was an Ashkenazi Jew, descended from the medieval Jewish communities along the Rhine in Germany, from Alsace in the south to the Rhineland in the north. Located in the Galicia province of Poland, Lvov was an industrial, though very cosmopolitan, town with a large Jewish population of some 110,000 out of a total population of 330,000. The number of Jews would soon swell dramatically to over two hundred thousand. Lvov was a classically beautiful city, its architecture reminiscent of Florence. Its museums, opera houses, and many coffee shops attested to its charming atmosphere and reputation—that is, unless you were a Jew.

"Your suit will be ready next Tuesday, Dr. Zalewski," said Simon as the Polish doctor prepared to leave the shop. "You will look superb in it, I'm sure," he added as the doctor left.

"Thank you, Herr Ruder," said the good doctor. "I'm looking forward to another outstanding work of art from you."

Simon smiled at the compliment. "Thank you, Herr Doctor. It is a pleasure to be of service to you."

It was almost six o'clock, and it was beginning to get dark as Simon locked the door to his shop and made his way upstairs to the small apartment he shared with his family, wife Lola, age thirty, daughter Hanna, age seven, and one-year-old son Artur.

Lola, nee Sternberg, came from a well-to-do family. She and Simon had been married as part of an arrangement between their families. Lola was an attractive woman, with surprisingly vivid red hair, and was a few years younger than Simon, whose charisma and success as a businessman and tailor had attracted the attention of the Sternbergs; their match had been negotiated in 1931. The bride's family, as was customary, provided a bridal dowry, which had enabled the couple to establish the tailor shop on Legionow Street in Lvov. Lola also had an impressive collection of jewelry, furs, and other valuables. Simon considered himself a lucky man to have made such an outstanding match.

The couple's first child, Hanna, was a pretty little girl. She showed promise as a musician and was a top student in her class, excelling in arithmetic. She was one of the only Jews in her class, and while no clear hostility had been directed toward her, she understood that she was somehow being treated differently than the Polish and Ukrainian children. She had definite musical talent and demonstrated those skills on the violin that Simon had purchased for her at a secondhand store. The Polish teacher, Mrs. Karpinski, was proud of Hanna, but could not acknowledge her success publicly, whether in or outside the classroom, but especially in the classroom in front of the mostly Polish and Ukrainian students. This, her teacher feared, would fan the flames of resentment even more than the already simmering anti-Semitism lurking just below the surface.

The Ruders' apartment was small but comfortable and reflected the middle-class Jewish furnishings of its occupants. Simon's tailoring business was successful, and he was well known and respected in the Jewish community.

Simon was a man of medium stature, with dark hair and penetrating eyes. Perhaps that was why he was a successful amateur actor in many plays. He also played soccer on one of the local teams and was active in Jewish politics, as well as being an assistant cantor at the synagogue. He was born in 1907 in not-too-far-away Obertin, where, as a youth, he had survived the ravages of World War I and the 1918 influenza pandemic. Both Obertin and Lemberg were part of the Austro-Hungarian Empire until 1919, but since then, they had become part of Poland and had been renamed Lvov. That, too, would change dramatically in the near future.

Simon's parents, father Mordko Fischel and mother Chija Frima, nee Leiner, had a large family in Obertin, which had hosted a small Jewish community from the late seventeenth century that now numbered about eleven hundred or so. Simon had three brothers: Abraham, born in 1898, who, in 1930, had fled to Cuba with his wife Balbina; Izak, born in 1900, who was living in Krakow; and younger brother Mendel, born in 1909, who was currently living in nearby Zloczow. Rounding out the family were sisters Dobrysza, born in 1893; Frieda Ryfka, born in 1896; Miriam, born in 1903; and Fani, born in 1910. Many years later, brother Izak would be part of a story and subsequent motion picture that would forever immortalize the monstrous evil and good that took place during the Holocaust.

Simon was typical of the ethnic makeup of the Jews in Lvov who were involved in trade and professions, such as tailors, hat makers, jewelers, and opticians. In fact, 80 percent of the tailors and 70 percent of the barbers in Lvov were Jewish. Furthermore, in 1921, 74.1 percent of merchants were Jewish. Eleven hundred fifty of the seventeen hundred were practicing doctors, 41 percent theater workers, 43 percent dentists, and 45 percent nurses. There were twenty-two hundred Jewish lawyers in comparison to the 450 ethnic Ukrainian lawyers. These numbers in Lvov and elsewhere clearly demonstrated the disproportionate percentage of Jews in the upper economic strata and in positions of influence. This fact was to haunt them for many, many years for the resentment, jealousy, and anger it engendered against them. The Jews had had a long history of being made convenient scapegoats, a situation that would tragically continue.

News and rumors were swirling about within the Jewish community. News of Hitler's rants against the Jews in Germany had been very troubling well before he had come to power in the 1930s. Now, in 1938, the threat of war was very real. Germany had already annexed Hitler's Austria earlier that year, and the Fuhrer's gaze had turned alarmingly westward to the area of Czechoslovakia inhabited by ethnic Germans. In October, the Sudentenland had been annexed by Germany, literally handed over by the West, in large part to appease Hitler. News of this both relieved and alarmed the Jews in Poland. They were relieved because they thought, perhaps, this move would satisfy Hitler and stop any further aggression as espoused by the British statesman Neville Chamberlain. On the other hand, many Jews were afraid that this would simply embolden further acts of domination and conquest.

Many Jews felt insecure and tried to blend in. Because of the more cosmopolitan environment in Lvov, the Jews, especially the well educated, felt this was a viable strategy. In many cases, though, this was difficult. For example, Hassidic Jews, with their beards, side curls, and black clothing, proved conspicuous and were frequent targets of abuse.

Later that November evening after Simon had come home from work and the family had eaten dinner, Simon and Lola sat at the small table in the kitchen of their three-room apartment discussing the disturbing news out of Germany describing the recent events called *Kristallnacht*, also referred to as the Night of Broken Glass. These horrific events represented a series of coordinated attacks against Jews throughout Nazi Germany and parts of Austria on November 9–10, 1938, carried out by SA Storm Troopers and civilians. Disturbingly, German authorities had looked on without intervening.

This was not a good sign of things to come. The attacks had left the streets covered with broken glass from the windows of Jewish-owned stores, buildings, and synagogues. At least ninety-one Jews had been killed in the attacks, and a further thirty thousand had been arrested and incarcerated in concentration camps. Jewish homes, hospitals, and schools had been ransacked, as the attackers demolished buildings with sledgehammers. Over one thousand synagogues had been burned, and over seven thousand Jewish businesses had been destroyed or damaged.

"This will pass," said Lola. "We Jews have endured pogroms many, many times before, and I fear we will continue to do so." Simon just shrugged. "It's not so bad in Poland. We have coexisted with the Poles and Ukrainians for a hundred years," Lola continued. She held little Artur in her arms and rocked him. He started crying, and she got up to get some baby food for him. After eating most of the food, Artur started to gurgle happily. Soon after he quieted down and fell asleep. Lola looked down at her son and wondered what kind of future awaited him. She then put him in his little bed that Simon had made for him. Aside from being a talented tailor, Simon was good at working with wood—a skill that was to play a pivotal role in his future.

Simon was deeply worried, though he tried not to show it. Despite the fact that these events and pogroms were happening next door in Germany, he worried about what would happen if war came to Poland. Maybe they would just change flags as they had done after World War I. Flags flying over a country could be changed, but the old Jewish customs would endure as they had for hundreds of years. Simon was hopeful that this would be the outcome of an expanded war into Poland but doubted it would be so easy.

More and more Jews were now streaming into Poland as they tried to escape the beatings, murders, and losses of property in Germany as more outrageous anti-Jewish laws were being enacted almost monthly. The Jews had been stripped of their citizenship, their human rights, their possessions, and in alarmingly rising numbers, their freedom and their very lives. It had become impossible to become or remain a professional lawyer, doctor, engineer, teacher, or intellectual in Germany. Jewish professionals had been summarily fired from their jobs. Jewish stores were being boycotted, then either destroyed or forced to be sold at a fraction of their value to "Aryan" owners. The news from Germany came in two varieties—bad and worse—and the news was not lost on Simon and many of the Jewish community of Lvov.

For now however, daily life in Lvov continued in a seminormal way. Anti-Semitism was still prevalent, but sometimes it was submerged just below the surface. Jewish stores were still frequented by the non-Jews, and in a cosmopolitan city like Lvov, Jews were still tolerated if not accorded a certain amount of respect, especially as professionals and artists in literature and the theater. Many Jews had Polish and even Ukrainian friends and business associates. It seemed that while the Polish and Ukrainians hated Jews in general, they made exceptions for certain individuals in their social and business spheres.

Several days later, Simon and several friends met to play cards and discuss politics at the home of a prominent Jewish doctor, Dr. Deutsch. The group had diverse ideas about the future and how it might affect their lives. However, no one at the table could conceive of the evil future that was lurking around the corner. Several of the gathered group offered their thoughts, ideas, and predictions for the near future.

Simon, always one with something to say, looked around at his friends and began his often-repeated line of thinking. "Communism is good for the Jews" he began. "I think the concepts of Communism hold the key to the path toward more power and influence for us Jews. And because of this, it is my feeling that this will result in the end of state-sponsored anti-Semitism. You all know that Jews have achieved a number of high-level positions of power and influence in the Soviet Union. Also, the Soviet government has established a system of Jewish education and culture."

Simon paused and took a drink. "Furthermore," he continued, "in both the Soviet Union and Poland, Communism is perceived as opposing anti-Semitism. Can we not say the friend of our enemy is our friend?"

For individuals like Simon, the attraction of Communism was extremely alluring, if somewhat simplistic. To Simon, it was the best of all worlds where an individual could simultaneously retain a strong Jewish identity while combining Marxism and various components of Zionism and Bundism into a significant and powerful movement.

Simon finished his conversation emphatically, replacing his empty glass on the table and saying, "Remember, too, the Polish government has recently implemented policies in which Jews have been excluded from public-sector employment and quotas have been placed on Jewish representation in universities and the professions, and there have government-organized boycotts of Jewish businesses and artisans. To this day, these policies affect each of us in this room and our children."

Jakob Lansky, the architect, had been listening intently. He decided it was time for him to chime in. "Simon, if you are so enthralled with Communism, why are you not yet a member of the party?" he asked.

Somewhat taken aback, Simon took time to frame his response and replied, "I know several party members, and most prefer to have their affiliation kept secret. Others are more open. I have attended meetings, and while I agree with many of the ideas, I'm not yet ready to join. I want to wait to see what will happen in the future. I have discussed this with my wife, Lola, and she doesn't like the idea, so we shall see. Besides, Josef Stalin himself dissolved the official party in Poland last year. Some of the officials were summoned to Moscow and were never heard from again. Maybe they received jobs within the party, but who can tell?"

Meyer Rosenthal, a successful lawyer with offices on Legionow Street near the Opera House, had other opinions. "Why make trouble for ourselves?" he asked. "I consider myself a Pole of Jewish faith. While it hasn't exactly been perfect in Poland, it has been tolerable. This is not the Shtetl. We are part of a modern country. Lvov is a sophisticated and cosmopolitan city, and we have succeeded in blending in, assimilating into the Gentile population. I have many Polish friends and clients and have built a fine reputation for trust and reliability. I even have some Ukrainian friends and clients. Yes, I admit the situation could be better, but I am not socially outcast, and I still have many freedoms. My children attend good schools and are accepted and well treated. And, Simon, you have a successful tailor shop near my office with a mixed clientele, both Jews and Gentiles. Why would you risk all of that?"

Simon thought carefully about how he would word his answer. "Meyer, my friend," he began. "I understand what you are saying. But consider that, for the most part, we Jews have been allowed to live in various societies with vastly different levels of tolerance. We have been tolerated, sometimes with more freedoms and rights, sometimes with greatly limited or no rights. The key here is the word 'tolerated'. We are not accepted, not seen as valued members of the society in which we live. The so-called freedoms and rights you now think you enjoy are an illusion. Hiding in plain sight may work for some of us, but as a people, 'assimilation,' as you call it, cannot substitute a lasting future strategy. We are continually subject to the whims of any political entity in power. Our lot can change overnight." This comment would later prove to be all too tragically prophetic.

Slowly sipping his beer, Julius Kaplan, the pharmacist, had listened carefully to his three friends. Kaplan's views were clearly different from those of Simon and Meyer. Kaplan started, "Meyer, Simon, and the rest of you, my thoughts go to a different place. Simon, I agree with you that we, as Jews, must play a more active role in our fate. We must be participants, not just observers."

Kaplan finished his beer in one last swallow and continued. "Meyer, my friend, blending in has provided some of us a measure of success in surviving. But look at Germany. Look at what that maniac Hitler is saying. Look at the rights being taken away from the Jews there. Look at what is happening in so-called civilized Germany. Can you doubt Hitler's intentions toward our people? He has made no secret of what he wants to do to us. We all feel a war brewing on the horizon. Maybe not now, but soon, inevitably. I say we Jews must have a homeland. We must establish Israel again. That is the only way we can achieve the freedom we deserve after almost two thousand years of persecution. If that brands me a Zionist, so be it."

ZLOCZOW, POLAND, 1938

Not too far away to the east in the town of Zloczow, Simon's younger brother Mendel was busy at work. Like his older brother and countless other Jews living in Poland, Mendel was a tailor and had established a fine reputation for the men's and women's garments being turned out by his shop. Mendel lived in a small apartment near his shop with his wife Zofia and one-year-old son Dolek. Mendel was a man of smaller stature, barely five feet tall and balding even though he was still in his late twenties. He and Simon kept in touch, and Mendel would sometimes make the trip to Lvov to watch his brother play soccer or act in local amateur playhouses and, of course, to play cards when the opportunity presented itself.

In Zloczow and throughout Poland, at Jewish dinner tables, the topic was war and the impact it might have on the Jews. The anti-Semitic violence directed against the German Jews foretold what was in store for the Jews of Poland, and all but the most optimistic among the Jews feared what was coming.

MÜHLDORF, GERMANY, 1938

Eleven hundred twenty-seven kilometers to the west of Lvov, five men sat at a table in the kitchen of a small farmhouse in Mühldorf on Xaver-Rambold Strasse, not far from Munich, in the heart of German Bavaria. Spirits were high, though a vague undercurrent of anxiety lingered just below the surface. Two of the men sat proudly in their crisp *Wehrmacht* uniforms. Eighteen-year-old Alois Kiermeier looked admiringly at his two uncles, Leonhard and Max, both of whom had joined the military a year ago and had been training with their respective units. Leonhard was especially proud of his enlistment in the elite First Mountain Division that had recently formed in Garmisch Partenkirchen and consisted mainly of Bavarians, like himself, and some Austrians. The edelweiss, a white flower found in the Alps, was the symbol of the division, and an elaborately embroidered circular patch with its image adorned his right sleeve. His younger brother Max was part of the Eighth Artillery, 337th Regiment. Both brothers held the rank of *Gefreiter*, or corporal. Alois was planning on enlisting as soon as possible but wanted to finish his apprenticeship as a carpenter in nearby Oberbergkirchen.

Also at the table was Ludwig Häusl, whose farmhouse was hosting the gathering. He was a tall, slim, and distinguished-looking man who fought in World War I and was decorated with the Iron Cross First Class for bravery. He was an engineer for the Deutsche Reichsbahn, the German railroad.

The remaining participant was another brother-in-law, Josef, who had not yet enlisted. Josef was a beekeeper and lived on a small farm, also in nearby Oberbergkirchen. All five men were smokers, and a miasmic haze hung over the small table. As with the vast majority of Germans, the family had been indoctrinated into the Third Reich propaganda machine and enthusiastically supported their Fuhrer and the bright future he promised for the country.

Leonhard cleared his throat and spoke first. "Things are going well. The military is growing stronger and larger every day. Just last month I was with my unit in Austria. We just marched through the country and annexed it without firing a shot. We even have a Chinaman in our unit, a Lieutenant Wei-Kuo Chiang. He is the son of Chiang Kia-Shek, an important Chinese military leader. He is proud to fight for the Fuhrer."

In fact, history would record the annexation of Austria, the *Anschluss*, as less than a war but more than a military maneuver. The so-called "union" between the two countries was announced by Hitler on March 12, 1938, and a vote was held on April 10, with the Fuhrer getting over 95 percent of the vote. Austria as a country was gone, absorbed into greater Germany.

Tapping the ash from his cigarette, Leonhard continued excitedly. "The Fuhrer is a military and political genius. We hear he has his eyes fixed on the Sudetenland where there are thousands of Germans—Germans who want to be part of the greater Reich, not part of that backward Czechoslovakia. I think maybe we will go there soon."

Leonhard's lowly opinion of and disdain for the so-called Slavic peoples living in the areas east of Germany reflected the Third Reich's concept of the *Untermenchen* or subhuman status of these people. These were people to be conquered and exploited, and in the case of the Jews, eventually exterminated.

Ludwig's expression remained unchanged as he thought about this. A veteran of the First World War, he understood firsthand the implications of another war. The defeat of Germany and the perceived injustice of the Treaty of Versailles in 1919 had had an effect on him, as it did many Germans. And, like most Germans, he agreed with the concept of *Lebensraum*, or living space for the Germans, but wondered if a war was really the best approach. So far, however, the Fuhrer had masterfully outmaneuvered the French and British, especially that simpleton Chamberlain.

This particular conversation reflected a microcosm of what was going on in uncounted numbers of such discussions in households throughout Germany in 1938. The Häusl and Kiermeier families precisely reflected the makeup and history of the typical German family, especially those in Bavaria.

Rumors of war had been spreading like a fog over Germany. The massive military buildup was growing, and Leonhard and Max were spending most of their time training with their respective army units; thus, it was rare that both men had the opportunity to visit with their relatives. Privately, the men sensed and often talked about what was coming, and while anxious, they all had a feeling of euphoria at the rightness of the war. It would be over quickly, they thought, the inevitability of victory firmly entrenched in their minds and hearts. Germany's rightful place in the world order would be restored, and they would be proud of their contributions to the Fatherland that were required to make the Fuhrer's vision a reality. Theirs was, they were sure, a destiny to be gloriously fulfilled.

The family gathering continued in good cheer as they continued their prophesies of the glorious future that would soon unfold for the German people.

"Imagine," began Leonard. "All of Europe under our Fuhrer and the Third Reich's control. A thousand years, they say. Autobahns everywhere. The Slavs will have their roles as workers and craftsmen. The Jews, well, we all know about the Jews." Brother Max and nephew Alois loudly agreed, yet an undertone of uncertainty pervaded the otherwise festive atmosphere, and each of them wondered silently if they would be together again.

Always a pensive man, Ludwig Häusl listened to the conversation at his table. His gaze turned to his two brothers-in-law. He thought they looked smart in their *Wehrmacht* uniforms and wondered how long they would be wearing them. Involuntarily, thoughts of another war twenty-five years ago intruded into his conscious, where he, as a seventeen-year-old, fought in what the West called "the war to end all wars." Visions of trenches, barbed wire, poison gas, and death surfaced, images he thought were safely locked away but had unexpectedly broke through Ludwig's carefully crafted mental barriers. He was suddenly filled with an uneasiness about the future, nothing he could put his finger on, yet the feeling was palpable, foreboding. A sudden chill worked its way through his body, like a dog shaking off water. While not particularly political, he, like the majority of the people in the area, had joined the Nazi Party, partly out of national patriotism and, in no small part, to keep his job. Ludwig joined in December 1937, amid high hopes for the future of Germany. Things were looking promising, and he wondered how the new direction would affect his family. His thoughts drifted in their direction.

His wife Maria was part of a large family, and her mother, Katarina Kiermeier, had given birth to twenty children, of which only ten had survived. Maria was the oldest, born in 1897, followed by brother Johann in 1899, sister Rosalie born in 1901, sister Kattl in 1903, and followed by another sister, Bettl, in 1907. Brother Josef, nicknamed Seff, followed in 1908, along with Leonhard in 1910 and Georg in 1911. Finally, another sister, Lotte, was born in 1915, followed by brother Max, in 1917.

The Kiermeier family, circa 1922. Marile's mother Maria is pictured in the center of the top row. To her right are brothers Leonhard and Georg; to her left are brothers Josef and Johann. Her parents, also Maria and Josef, are seated on opposite ends of the table. Standing between the grandparents is young Alois, flanked by Max on the right and Lotte, wearing a ribbon, on the left. Sisters Kettl and Bettl round out the family. Marile Häusl was born in 1928, the eldest child of Ludwig Häusl and Maria Kiermeier.

Ludwig's pride and joy, however, was his eldest daughter, also named Maria, but nicknamed Marile. She was a pretty girl, petite, with brown hair worn in two braids. Three other children rounded out the family, daughters Bette and Rosie and younger son Ludwig, nicknamed Wiggi.

The Häusl family, circa 1938, Marile (Maria), father Ludwig, Bette, and the elder Maria holding little Rosie. Note Ludwig is wearing his blue Deutsche Reichsbahn (German Railroad) uniform.

Their home was comfortable, if not large, but served them well. It was typical of the small whitewashed houses that dotted the outskirts of town. They grew some of their own food, and the farm had a number of fruit trees, with apples and plums comprising most of them. Though rationed, eggs and butter were available as was an allotment of meat, sugar, and fat. The Mühldorf town center was within walking distance to reach the school and church, to attend social gatherings, and to purchase goods not available on the farm. Marile and her siblings generally rode their bicycles the short distance to town, although there were times Marile liked to walk.

Ludwig had married the elder Maria, rescuing her from a scandal still being whispered about behind her back. Formerly Maria Katarina Kiermeier, she tended to be a bitter, angry woman whom Ludwig, at times, loved, tolerated, and feared, often simultaneously. She was a small woman, barely five feet tall, with raven-black hair and piercing ice-blue eyes. She was a dour woman, not given to open displays of affection or compliments, especially toward her children. At the age of twenty-one and unmarried, she had been working on a large farm in the area where she had a liaison with the farmer's eldest son. The union produced a son, born in 1920. Unfortunately, as Maria soon found out, a rich farmer's son couldn't marry a mere farm girl, so she and her newborn son, named Alois, were sent packing. Tainted by this scandal, Maria had been fortunate to find a husband who accepted her and her son, whom he raised as his own. Alois, however, never took the Häusl name, instead keeping the Kiermeier name. Marile, the Häusl's oldest daughter, was born eight years later, in 1928. The Häusls had moved into the little farmhouse on the outskirts of Mühldorf in 1930, and they had a good, if unloving, life together.

Mühldorf itself was a medieval town dating back to the thirteenth century. Mühldorf am Inn is the capital of the district Mühldorf on the river Inn and is situated in a beautiful part of Bavaria with many forests and the Alps looming on the horizon. It is also an important railway hub linking many major cities in southern Germany. Lurking not too far away, just northwest of Munich, like a black, festering stain on the countryside, was the town of Dachau, site of the infamous concentration camp of the same name. The Häusls knew it as a place where "bad" people went—or so that was what the children were told. It was the first German concentration camp, first established in 1933, and its purpose was to house political prisoners. Since business had been good, its purpose was to expand dramatically and more horrifically over the next seven years, a fact well known to Ludwig Häusl, whose trains often visited the site. In fact, Dachau was to branch out with a myriad of sub-camps scattered around Mühldorf like a necklace of terror and death.

Lost in his thoughts, Ludwig realized the gathering was breaking up. The two soldiers were anxious to return to their units for more training, and they were sure to be assigned to take part in some glorious future campaigns.

Leonhard and Max said their good-byes to their older sister Maria and Ludwig and turned to leave the small farmhouse. "By the way," said Leonhard, looking at his sister Maria but addressing the group. "One of my fellow soldiers, *Obergefrieter* Helmut Gruenburger, was telling me about Bad Reichenhall and how his mother, Paula, runs a small hotel for tourists visiting the spa facilities. The spa is good for your health, or so they say. She has invited us to stay with her for a few days. Business is not so good, and the rooms are available. The *Wehrmacht* also has a barracks nearby, and we will stay there to train in the mountains. Perhaps you and Ludwig may want to visit—I mean, before the war breaks out."

Maria looked over to her husband. He knew the area well from the trains he had driven there but had never visited there as a tourist. He looked unsure about what to say. Slowly, deliberately, he put out his cigarette. "Maybe. Maybe it would be good for us to get away for a day or so. We should take Marile with us. She's old enough, and I think it would be good for her before she starts her training."

Leonhard nodded curtly to his brother-in-law. "Very good, Ludwig. I will tell Helmut. You will like Frau Gruenburger. She is also a very good cook."

"Thank you, Leonhard. We look forward to it," said Ludwig as the two soldiers left.

As if waiting for the adults to leave, Ludwig's eldest daughter quietly entered the room and sat down at the table beside him. Little Marile, just a few months short of her tenth birthday, was a hero of sorts, at least in the family. Just a few months ago, she was one of only a few young girls chosen to present the Fuhrer, Adolf Hitler, with a bouquet of flowers when he had visited the town on March 12, 1938. The elder Maria was ecstatic when Marile was chosen. She had been among four or five girls chosen for the honor based on her perfect school attendance and good grades.

Mühldorf, Germany, March, 12, 1938. Adolf Hitler visits the Southern Bavarian town on his way to his birthplace of Braunau in Austria to announce the Anschluss, or annexation of Austria into greater Germany. Nine-year-old Maria (Marile) Häusl was one of five young girls (second girl from the right) to present a bouquet of flowers to Hitler. (Photo courtesy of the Stadtarchiv Mühldorf a. Inn.)

Pictures of Adolf Hitler in Mühldorf on March 12, 1938, with a cheering populace. His entourage would stop and receive bouquets of flowers from several young girls, including Marile Häusl. (Photos courtesy of Stadtarchiv Mühldorf a. Inn.)

On that day almost the entire town had turned out to cheer the Fuhrer. The area was not unknown to him, as many of the formative Nazi Party events took place in the beer halls in nearby Munich, and Austria, Hitler's birthplace, was just across the border. On this day, he was on his way back to his birthplace in nearby Braunau with an important announcement: Austria had been annexed, the *Anschluss*, and he would make a triumphant return to welcome his former countrymen into the greater Reich.

Interestingly, Hitler's entourage had left Munich that morning with a convoy of twelve Mercedes cars to carry all of the luggage, with five alone required for carrying the bodyguards. Hitler first stopped at the VIIIth Army headquarters, located in the Mühldorf Central Schoolhouse, where General von Bock was located. At that location, Hitler's flag was transferred from his black G4 triaxle Mercedes bearing army license plate WH-32290 to an army drab Mercedes.

After army business concluded, the Fuhrer's motorcade had slowly made its way to the center of the town. Cheering Mühldorfers had lined the streets. A number of older teenagers in their Hitler Youth uniforms greeted the Fuhrer as he drove by. Shortly thereafter, flanked by several Nazi officers and his ubiquitous bodyguards, the Fuhrer left his army drab Mercedes and was directed by the mayor to several pretty young girls standing in front of a small theater next to the *Hotel Restaurant Dinhuber*. Young Marile Häusl was among them. The Fuhrer positioned himself facing the street in front of his officers with the young girls facing him. Always interested in being seen in pictures with German girls, he moved down the row, accepting the flowers from the star struck and enamored young girls. He had a big smile on his face, as captured by the cameras. Marile's turn came. She held a large bouquet of flowers, including orange lilies, blue pansies, and the difficult-to-obtain edelweiss, but after all, this was the Fuhrer. She was nervous as the Fuhrer approached. Marile politely smiled and presented the bouquet to the Fuhrer to which he thanked her and patted her on her head. She was ecstatic, but what happened next would stay with her for the rest of her life. Standing next to her in the row was one of her schoolmates, a very pretty girl named Lisle, who had blond hair. The Fuhrer accepted the bouquet from Lisle and hugged her. To nine-year-old Marile, it was a disappointment, and one she never forgot.

BAD REICHENHALL, GERMANY, JUNE 1938

On a crisp, sunny Bavarian morning, Ludwig Häusl, his wife Maria, and his eldest daughter, nine-year-old Marile, boarded a train headed for the resort town of Bad Reichenhall. Arrangements had been made by Maria's brother Leonhard, and the trio was looking forward to a few days at the famous spas. Young Marile was particularly excited because it was her first time away from home. The train ride through Bavaria was breathtaking. Ludwig was amazed because he could actually view the passing scenery through the window of a coach without the responsibility of driving the train so he could actually enjoy the ride.

The resort town of Bad Reichenhall was nestled in the Bavarian Alps just across the border from Salzburg, Austria, about eighty-seven kilometers from Mühldorf. It was known for its scenic alpine landscape and, in particular, for its famous salt springs that supported a significant spa tourism industry dating back to the nineteenth century. Visitors from all over the world came to Bad Reichenhall to take advantage of the "cures" attributed to the salt springs. Located in nearby Berchtesgaden was Hitler's Eagle's Nest (*Kehlsteinhaus*), the site of many parties and conferences, and an airfield, *Reichenhall Mayerhof,* was built in 1925 for Hitler to fly in and out of the area. The little town also sported the Bad Reichenhaller Philharmonie, founded in 1858. A cable car, the *Predigtstuhlbahn*, was built in 1928 to take passengers 1,540 meters to the mountain station.

Frau Gruenburger met the Häusls at the train station. A handsome woman of fifty-five, she introduced herself to the trio. "I'm so glad to finally meet you," she said to Ludwig, Maria, and Marile. Her gaze fell to the young girl. "So, this is little Marile. Leonhard and Helmut have told me so much about you. I hear you actually met our great Fuhrer." Marile blushed, not accustomed to such accolades.

"Come, let's have lunch, and then I will show you the town. I have rooms ready for you. It's a pity you can only stay overnight."

The Häusls were treated to a whirlwind tour of Bad Reichenhall, including the Bad Reichenhaller Philharmonie, the salt museum *(Salzmuseum)* with a pump house at the Alte Saline, the salt baths, and of course, the churches. They ended the day with a ride on the breathtaking *Predigtstuhlbahn.*

After a busy day sight-seeing, Frau Gruenburger prepared a sumptuous dinner, the likes of which the Häusls had never experienced. Frau Gruenburger seemed to be particularly taken by the young girl, perhaps because she had always wanted a daughter or perhaps because of Marile's quick wit and charm.

The next day the Häusls boarded the train back to Mühldorf, and life returned to normal for them. But life as normal soon changed for the Jews who, in 1939, were no longer permitted to use the Bad Reichenhall spa facilities.

MÜHLDORF, GERMANY, JULY/AUGUST 1938

Ten-year-old Marile Häusl had recently joined the Young Girl's League, the *Jungmädelbund*, for young girls ages ten to fourteen. Membership was compulsory. The program was the first step for women in the overall *Bund Deutscher Mädel (BDM)*, the women's component of the Hitler Youth. The main purpose of the BMD was to indoctrinate the youth, in this case the girls, into the Nazi philosophy. This included the Nazi racial policies; Germany's and the Nazi Party's view of the world and the country's rightful place in it; Germany's glorious history; the greatness of the Fuhrer, Adolf Hitler; and, perhaps most importantly, the Jews and how they were the cause of the world war, the worldwide depression, and Communism. She learned that Jews were dirty and carriers of disease, that they were thieves and that they defiled German girls. Jews were not very nice people, if indeed they were people at all, she was told repeatedly. She had been introduced to the following definition of Jews as the *Untermensch* written by the Reichsfuhrer SS in Berlin in 1935:

Untermensch—Biologically apparently fully our equal, with hands, feet, and a sort of a brain, with eyes and a mouth—yet an utterly different, abominable creature, only a sketch of a human being, with humanoid features, but intellectually and spiritually lower than any animal. Within this being, a barbaric chaos of wild, unbridled passions, a nameless destructive will, the most primitive cravings, the most bestialities. He is and will remain nothing but an Untermensch![i]

Marile had never really seen a Jew, though there were many in nearby Munich but none that she knew of in Mühldorf. In fact, there were two Jewish families living in Mühldorf, the Hellmanns, who made their living buying and selling livestock, mostly horses, and the Fritz family. Michael Fritz was a World War I veteran who had won the Iron Cross for bravery and for having been wounded in action. His business had been forced to close in 1937. The Hellmanns had continued their business into 1938, when they, too, were driven out. Little Marile was sure that if there were any Jews in Mühldorf, she would certainly recognize them because of the horns they supposedly sported.

"So, what have you learned in the *Jungmädelbund*?" Ludwig asked his daughter. Marile repeated what she had been taught. Ludwig was familiar with Nazi Party philosophy but was still shocked to hear the outright, intense anti-Semitism coming from his young daughter. He was concerned about what was being drilled into the impressionable heads of the country's young children. As a party member, he agreed with most of the Nazi philosophies, especially Germany's rightful place in the world, but the party's hatred of the Jews, and especially those views powerfully espoused by Hitler himself, left him feeling uneasy. It was an uneasiness he could not share with anyone. He had heard about what happened to people who openly questioned the Nazis and unconsciously looked in the direction of Dachau.

Uncle Max was Marile's favorite uncle, perhaps due to their relatively small age difference. She was also close to her half brother Alois who had grown up in the Häusl family but had recently left to become an apprentice carpenter in nearby Oberbergkirchen near his uncle.

With Max away for extended training, half brother Alois would often discuss Marile's Hitler Youth teachings with her. He seemed amused at the young girl's ability to learn her lessons and repeat them. Max wondered if his pretty young niece really understood what was being taught but was proud of her nonetheless. Alois, who had grown up with Marile, was a fun-loving older brother who was concerned about the future and how it might affect his little half-sister, though he never shared these fears with her.

Meanwhile, as though fulfilling an earlier prophecy by his uncle Leonhard, the Third Reich had successfully achieved the annexation of the Sudentenland, the western border areas of Czechoslovakia inhabited by a majority of ethnic Germans. Through diplomacy and intimidation, Germany had begun its grab for *Lebensraum*, or living space.

"Peace in our time," said Neville Chamberlain as the West bargained away a large chunk of Czechoslovakia without consulting the Czech government or the Russians. Appeasement is what it would be called later.

For *Obergefreiter* Leonhard Kiermeier, it meant another commendation medal for his participation in the occupation. The first medal was awarded for his service in the *Anschluss*, the annexation of Austria earlier in the year. Both of these campaigns were called the *Blumenkriege*, or Flower Wars. They added considerable space and population to greater Germany and also bought front-row tickets for Leonhard and the other Kiermeier men for what was to come.

Anton Becker, born in 1925, was three years older than Marile, but as a friend of the family, he was almost an older brother to her. The young man, nicknamed Donei, had dreamed of working in the woods and wanted to be a forester one day, but for now, those plans would have to wait. As required, he joined the Hitler Youth and was being indoctrinated into the Nazi view of the world and Germany's rightful preeminent position therein. He and Marile would often discuss what they had learned in their respective Nazi Youth organizations, especially the role of the country's youth and what was expected of them. They learned about the Jews and how the ills of the world could be laid directly on their doorsteps. The two friends soon fell under the spell of the glorious Third Reich and were determined to do their part to support the Fuhrer and their glorious Fatherland.

"I can't believe it," said Donei. "You actually met the Fuhrer? What an honor! Why did they pick you? Were you excited? Were you scared?"

Marile was a smart girl, but she was not sure exactly why she had been chosen for this great honor. She was told it was because of her outstanding grades and perfect attendance in school, and she had no reason to doubt that, but she still had questions.

"Yes," she began. "I was very nervous but not really scared. I gave the Fuhrer a bouquet of flowers. My friend Lisle was also there." A frown formed on her young face. "What's wrong?" asked Donei.

"Oh, nothing. I was just thinking of something."

"I still can't believe it, but I'm sure you did just fine."

The two young children laughed and left for their Hitler Youth group meetings to continue the indoctrination that would play an important role in their future development into adulthood.

Forty-eight-year-old Dr. Ernst Loske idly scanned the day's appointments while sitting at his desk in his third-story office at 46 Statdplaz on Mühldorf's main street. "Very routine," he mumbled to himself as he examined the list of patients in more detail.

Dr. Loske was born and had grown up in this Bavarian corner of Germany, and after earning his medical credentials in nearby Munich, he soon returned to the small town and set up a medical practice that he ran with his wife Regina. Well liked and respected, Dr. Loske was pleased with his station in life but worried that the rumored war would eventually materialize. While not a member of the Nazi Party, he, nonetheless, had faith in Adolf Hitler and the direction the country was going. As a professional and educated person, however, some of the emerging policies, especially those enacted and carried out against Jews, left him feeling uncomfortable. He was not sure why, but for now he was willing to accept these actions as necessary evils to achieve the Third Reich's desired results. Still, Dr. Loske had met and indeed was educated by a number of very prominent Jewish doctors and, until recently, had corresponded with many of them, both professionally and socially. Sadly, though, and he could not openly admit it, those days had come to an end and he would miss them.

Soon, as Regina ushered in the first of a stream of patients, Dr. Loske focused on the complaints they brought with them and soon forgot the political issues with which he had grappled. But the unease was still there.

1939

During the second half of August 1939, the German *Wehrmacht* First, Second, and Third *Gebirgs,* Mountain Divisions, had established positions in the northern part of the newly created Slovakia, a puppet ally of Germany. The trek across the High Tatra Mountains on the Slovakia-Polish border was exhausting, but true to their name and reputation, the Mountain Divisions successfully negotiated the rugged mountainous terrain and assembled on the border as planned as part of the larger invasion codenamed *Fall Weiss.* Each of the divisions consisted of some fourteen thousand soldiers, fifteen hundred horses, forty-three hundred pack animals, and five hundred fifty mountain horses. The pack animals were particularly well suited for crossing the difficult mountain passes, carrying or pulling the various mobile armament, other equipment, and supplies. Additionally, some fourteen hundred vehicles, consisting of motorcycles, cross-country cars, and six hundred horse-drawn vehicles, provided transportation support. Finally, the armament consisted of various rifles, machine guns, pistols, light and medium mortars, howitzers, and antiaircraft guns and cannons.

The objective of the Mountain Divisions was the city of Lemberg, now called Lvov. Newly promoted *Obergefreiter* Leonhard Kiermeier, a veteran of the so-called Flower Wars was anxious to see some real action. Highly trained and considered an elite force, the men of the *Wehrmacht* Mountain Divisions were waiting for the real war to start. They did not have long to wait. They would cross the Polish border on September 5 and make their way toward their target objective.

Simon Ruder and his family awoke on the morning of September 1, 1939, to news of Germany's invasion of Poland. "So it's finally started," Simon said apprehensively. "Turn on the radio. Let us hear what's happening."

Lola rushed to the radio and turned it on. It hissed and sputtered with static until finally a BBC broadcast was received. It reported that hostilities started in Gleiwitz after a so-called provocation by the Polish army against the Germans. Things seemed to be in a state of confusion. The German mechanized troops poured into Poland, and there were rumors of Russian troops involved as well. Were the Russians saviors or allies? No one knew. One thing was certain: monumental changes were coming and the impact on the Jews was potentially devastating. Rumors of the Russians' involvement were, however, premature—by a little over two weeks.

In reality, Poland's fate had already been decided, at least for the next two years. A week earlier, the Molotov–Ribbentrop Pact had been signed between Germany and the Soviet Union, defining how Poland was to be partitioned and annexed into the two conquerors' territories. Poland would no longer exist as a national entity. For the three million Jews living in Poland who would soon cease to exist, exactly where one lived would have a dramatic effect on his or her future, at least in the short term.

In spite of the fact that the Polish military assured the population that it was fully prepared to repel any German attack, people were skeptical—and for good reason. While the Polish military waged a valiant, if mostly ineffective battle, it was no match for the might of the German army and *Luftwaffe*. The United Kingdom and France both had pacts with Poland and did declare war on Germany on September 3, 1939. However, neither could or actually did provide any meaningful support to its beleaguered ally.

In Lvov, Simon and his family were anxiously awaiting the hostilities to find them. They, too, didn't have long to wait. Lvov was an important strategic target, a fact of which the populous was mostly unaware. Polish military plans for the defense of the city were in place by September 7, but things did not go according to plan. There were small tactical successes for the Polish military. However, the Germans captured Sambor, some sixty-six kilometers from Lvov on September 12, and by September 13, the main forces of German Colonel Schörner arrived in Lvov. It was 2:00 p.m. when the Germans broke through to the center of the city. They were initially driven back after heavy fighting, and to strengthen the Polish defenses, General Kazimierz Sosnkowski left Lvov for Przemyśl and assumed command over a group of Polish units trying to break through the German lines and reach the city of Lvov.

During a seeming lull in the fighting, Simon left his tailor shop, which was closed for business, to attend a meeting with several colleagues to discuss the situation. On his way to the meeting at Meyer Rosenthal's apartment, the air raid sirens sounded. This had become a common occurrence with the German Luftwaffe attacking power plants, water plants, hospitals, roads, and other random targets almost daily. The main train station had also been greatly damaged.

Rushing into the apartment out of breath, Simon brushed the dust off his jacket and hat. He looked at his friends standing around the apartment. Dr. Deutsch, Jakob Lansky the architect, Julius Kaplan the pharmacist, and Meyer Rosenthal the lawyer were already there. They were not playing cards today. "It's getting worse," Simon began. "The Germans are getting closer. I hear they are surrounding the city. Those damned screaming airplanes are bombing everyone and everything. The situation seems hopeless. They were already in the city but were driven back, but how long do we think we can hold out? What are we going to do when the Germans finally get here?"

Jakob Lansky was the first to speak up. "My God, they are bombing the buildings. Destroying them. Some are over one hundred years old. I'm concerned about the opera houses and museums!"

Simon looked at Lansky with a look of frustration and anger on his face. "Fuck your buildings, you idiot! What do you think is going to happen to us, our families, our businesses? Look what's already happened in Germany. That's what's going to happen here!"

Meyer Rosenthal let out a sarcastic laugh. Always the optimist, he spoke up next. "We are Poles, then Jews. The Germans will treat us no differently than the Poles. The Ukrainians, however, are a different story. They are mostly peasants from the rural areas. They hate the Jews and Poles. How they will fare under the Germans is anybody's guess. I'm hoping the Germans will treat the Poles and Jews fairly."

Julius Kaplan was listening intently to the developing conversation with a pensive look on his face. Simon thought it reflected a bitter realization and acceptance of a fate he did not like. Kaplan put out his cigarette and coughed to clear his throat. "My friends, you all know my position," he began. "I think if the Germans come, we will be singled out. What happened and is still happening in Germany will most certainly happen here. The Germans have no love for the Poles. They consider them peasants, inferior human beings. The Poles fear, yet respect, the Germans. But the Germans hate us. We are not Poles; we are Jews, and Jews, wherever the Germans find them, are still Jews. I fear we will not escape them. There is nowhere for us to go. Yes, a small number of Jews have managed to escape to the West or to Palestine. A very small number. The rest of us are in a trap, one that is closing rapidly. I fear for our existence."

Simon considered what Kaplan had said. "I'm sorry to say I mostly agree with you, Julius. I think we will survive as a people, though. The Jews in Germany are surviving, but under some very harsh conditions. It may get worse for us here in Poland."

"So what do you suggest, Simon?" asked Dr. Deutsch.

Simon gave a self-deprecating shrug as if to reveal his frustration and reluctance to continue. He did anyway. "I still think Communism is the only answer for us Jews. The system promotes worker equality and discourages anti-Semitism, the very opposite of our enemies knocking at our door. The question is, how do we get access to this system? Do we escape to Russia? And if so, how?"

"I don't trust the Russians," said Dr. Deutsch. Most of the group expressed agreement.

Many of the group's questions were answered just a few weeks later when many surprises began to unfold for the residents of Lvov and the Galicia district.

On September 17, 1939, the Soviet Union declared all agreements and pacts with Poland null and void. The reasoning was that the Polish state had ceased to exist, so the pacts were no longer in effect. They immediately joined Nazi Germany in the occupation of the Polish territory. The end of Poland was near. On September 18, the German Luftwaffe dropped thousands of leaflets on Lvov urging the Poles to surrender. Nothing was mentioned about the 110,000 Jews still living there.

The warnings were ignored, and the final assault on the city began. In the early morning of September 19, the first Soviet armored units arrived at the eastern outskirts of the city and the suburb of Łyczaków. After a short fight, the Soviet units were pushed back. However, overnight the Soviet forces completed the encirclement of the city and joined up with the German army besieging Lvov from the west.

The Germans fell back and encircled the city waiting for more reinforcements to arrive. They achieved limited success and captured the important suburb of Zboiska, together with surrounding hills. However, the Polish forces were also reinforced with units withdrawn from central Poland and new volunteer units formed within the city. In addition, the Polish Tenth Motorized Brigade, under Colonel Stanisław Maczek, arrived and started heavy fighting over the suburb of Zboiska. The town was recaptured by the Polish forces, but the surrounding hills remained in German hands. The hills were an excellent position and provided the Germans with a major advantage from which to shell the city.

The Polish defenses were composed mainly of field fortifications and barricades constructed by the local residents under supervision of military engineers. General Sikorski ordered organized defense of the outer city rim, with in-depth defenses prepared. On the morning of September 19, the first Soviet envoys arrived and started negotiations with the Polish officers. Colonel Ivanov, the commander of a tank brigade, announced to the Polish envoy, Colonel Bronisław Rakowski, that the Red Army had entered Poland to help it fight the Germans and that the top priority for his units was to enter the city of Lvov.

The same day the German commander sent his envoy and demanded that the city be surrendered to Germany. When the Polish envoy replied that he had no intention of signing such a document, he was informed that the general assault was ordered on September 21 and that it was inevitable that the city would be captured.

Then, surprisingly, Hitler's evacuation order from September 20 instructed the Germans to leave the destruction of Lvov to the Russians. The attack planned by Eighteenth Corps for September 21 was canceled, and the corps prepared to move to the west of the Vistula-San River line. Then the Polish garrison of Lvov abruptly and unexpectedly surrendered to the German First Mountain Division on September 21. The following day General Sikorski decided to start surrender talks with the Red Army.

For *Obergefreiter* Leonhard Kiermeier, the battle ended on a hollow note. His division had fought bravely, albeit against a determined but ultimately disorganized and inferior opponent. Yet the *Wehrmacht* and the Mountain Divisions were bloodied, losing about ten thousand who were killed, thirty thousand who were wounded, and thirty-five hundred who were missing in action.

Polish and German parliamentarians discussed terms of surrender. On September 22, 1939, the act of surrender was signed in the suburb of Winniki. The Red Army accepted all conditions proposed by General Władysław Langner.

The agreement called for the privates and noncommissioned officers to leave the city, to register themselves at the Soviet authorities, and to be allowed to go home. The officers were to be allowed to keep their belongings and leave Poland for whichever country accepted them. The same day the Soviet forces entered the city a period of Soviet occupation began. The act of surrender signed in the morning was broken by the Soviets shortly after noon, when the NKVD started arresting Polish officers. They were escorted to Tarnopol, from where they were sent to various gulags in Russia, mostly to the infamous camp in Starobielsk. Most of them, including General Stanisław Sikorski himself, were murdered in what became known as the Katyn Massacre in 1940.

Following this Polish campaign, *Obergefreiter* Leonhard Kiermeier and the First Mountain Division were moved west to the Swiss border area.

Simon Ruder and his family survived the bombing and subsequent invasion by the Germans and the ultimate capture by and Russian takeover of Lvov. The city, while bombed by the *Luftwaffe* and having taken constant fierce artillery shelling for three weeks, remained mostly intact. The train station was demolished, but the tracks were repaired and made serviceable again. Power and water stations were repaired sometime later. It was still unclear to the residents of Lvov exactly what had happened and what effect it would have on their lives. A clearer picture began to emerge as news of the Soviet entry into the war and subsequent occupation of Eastern Galicia trickled in through the grapevine network and radio broadcasts from the West. It was obvious that Poland was finished as a nation and that the West had, for the most part, abandoned the country. While the British and French were now technically at war with Germany, nothing could be done for now. In the last week of September, Hitler made a speech in the city of Danzig in which he said, *"Poland never will rise again in the form of the Versailles treaty. That is guaranteed not only by Germany, but also…Russia."*

Simon and his group of friends, along with millions of Jews spread throughout what was Poland, were to learn over the next few weeks that Germany had directly annexed western Poland and the former Free City of Danzig. This territory immediately became part of the greater Fatherland and became firmly under Nazi control. Hitler decreed that large portions of this territory would be set aside for *Lebensraum* or "Living Space" for the Germans. The remaining non-Soviet-administered territory was to become part of the so-called "General Government" announced on October 10 under the leadership of Hans Frank, with its capital of Krakow. Initially included in the General Government were the districts of Warsaw, Krakow, Lublin, and Radom. Hitler and his henchmen saw this vast area as a pool of unskilled workers to be exploited, all laboring for the good of the Third Reich.

The Galicia district, of which Lvov was the capital, now under the control of the Soviets, was incorporated into Belarusian and Ukrainian republics. The Ukrainian Soviet Socialist Republic alone gained over seven million new citizens and expanded its territory by some 130,000 square kilometers. The news seemed to hold a ray of hope for the Jews in Lvov and neighboring towns under the new Soviet overlords. Sadly, it turned out to be only a short reprieve. However, the situation was far worse for the Jews still in the Central Government or directly annexed parts of Poland, and their future would prove to be particularly bleak.

As the capital of the Galicia district, Lvov was now the home of a myriad of party offices that were established there—a bureau for this and a bureau for that, according to the Soviet blueprint. Dangerous in their own right, they were bureaucratic, cumbersome, corrupt, and graft filled. But there was an even darker side to Lvov. Three prisons, Brygidki Prison, Łąckiego or Loncki Street Prison, and Zamarstynowska Street Prison, were all witnesses to torture, imprisonment, deprivation, and murder. Enemies of the state were questioned, confessions were obtained, and punishment was administered. Perhaps the most infamous was the Loncki Prison, home of the NKVD, the Soviet secret police. They were everywhere, in uniform or undercover, ferreting out "enemies of the state." Jews and Poles were their favorite targets. Polish prisoners of war were also frequent inhabitants of the dark and foreboding structure at the end of Sapiehy Street near the yellow and terra-cotta Technical High School building.

Simon's group once again began to meet on a more or less regular basis. Today they were meeting in Simon's apartment above his tailor shop on Legionow Street. The card games resumed, but concerns about their new masters overshadowed the games and dominated the conversations.

"At least it's not the Germans," said Jakob Lansky. "I'm relieved that the city and buildings still stand."

Dr. Deutsch looked at the architect and just shook his head. "You are still an idiot, Lansky. After surviving all the bombs and shellings, all you can think about is your damn buildings?" Abashed, the architect opened his mouth to say something but then thought better of it.

Meyer Rosenthal interrupted. "We know the Russians are not our friends, and their Ukrainian thugs are going to be trouble for the Jews. I heard from a Ukrainian friend that they think they will have an independent Ukrainian Republic very soon. Somehow I don't think the Russians will agree. In the meantime, what do we do?"

Julius Kaplan said, "Simon, you're the Communist. You got what you wanted. What do you suggest we do?"

Simon's wife Lola picked that moment to bring out refreshments. Simon turned to her and gave her a quick nod, as if to thank her for the diversion, giving him some time to think of a plausible answer.

Simon, like most Jews and Poles, had been surprised by the turn of events and tried to rationalize reasons for them to play out in their favor. Suddenly, the Soviet-administered area around Lvov appeared comparatively safer than those areas controlled by the Nazis.

Soon thousands of other Jews fled from the Nazi-controlled districts of the Central Government. The Jewish population of Lvov alone swelled from 110,000 to over two hundred thousand. Lvov and surrounding cities and towns had tried to accommodate the influx of Jews, but these numbers had put a strain on space and resources.

"I really don't know right now," Simon began. "I think we are beginning to see what the future is going to look like. Here in Lvov, Zloczow, and other cities in the new Ukrainian Soviet Socialist Republic, sovietization has begun. They are nationalizing the big industries and confiscating personal possessions of wealthy people branded 'bourgeois.' Many are being deported to Siberia to the gulags. Jews and Poles alike are being deported. We hear Polish prisoners of war by the thousands have been sent there. This is not what I expected, and I have many doubts and more questions. In the meantime, though, I'm watching and waiting."

Julius Kaplan took the drink he was offered, smiling at Lola. "Thank you, my dear," he said. Always the pragmatist, he continued, "I agree with you, Simon. The Russians will try to impose their system on us. Everything will be planned and run by the state. I think it will be difficult for us and for them. My profession as a pharmacist will surely be affected. There is talk about a centralized pharmacy prust being established in Lvov to control all manufacturing and distribution of drugs and medicines for the district. The pharmacies are already tightly licensed and controlled, but I think it will get much worse. I'm sure the industry will not be run as smoothly as it has been. Medicines and pharmaceuticals will be much harder to obtain, even on the black market."

Meyer Rosenthal spoke up next. "I suppose my profession as a lawyer will also be affected. There are already some Ukrainian Communist judges with no education being installed all over the district. Their judgment is final, regardless of the merits of the case. There is no real need for lawyers anymore, it seems."

Suddenly there was a series of loud knocks, almost frantic pounding on the door. Shocked, the group all turned their heads toward the door. Simon looked at Lola, who went to the door and slowly, while staying behind the door, peeked around the edge to see who it was. It was Israel Zloczower, a tailor like Simon. His shop, which he shared with his brother Shlomo, was a few streets over. Israel had been born in 1900 and was seven years older than Simon. He and Simon had been friends since Simon moved to Lvov from Obertin many years ago. Israel had helped Simon get established in the community, help for which Simon was grateful.

"Come in, Israel, come in, quickly!" Simon said, motioning with his arms. "How are you, my friend? You know Dr. Deutsche, Meyer Rosenthal, Julius Kaplan, and Jakob Lansky."

Israel Zloczower nodded to the occupants of the apartment. His gaze locked on Julius Kaplan for an instant. He looked scared, acted very nervously, and was sweating.

"What's wrong, Israel?" Simon asked, a concerned look on his face. He could see the fear and tension on his friend's face. Zloczower had several friends who, like Julius Kaplan, espoused Zionist ideas. To the Communists and Ukrainians, Zionists meant trouble and were not tolerated under any circumstances.

Lola offered Israel a glass of water, which he quickly consumed. "I need something stronger," he managed to say between gulps. Lola poured a small glass of schnapps from the bottle on the card table and handed it to the shaking Israel.

"Slowly," admonished Meyer Rosenthal. Israel finished the glass and began to tell his story. Regaining some of his composure, he started. "The NKVD. The NKVD arrested Samuel Rosner and Nathan Roth three days ago. I think they were taken to the Loncki Prison. I haven't seen them since."

Julius Kaplan understood the implications and feared the worst. The NKVD was hunting Zionists who had been pronounced "enemies of the state."

"What happened next?" he asked Israel in a calm voice, barely suppressing his underlying fear.

"I think I saw one of them entering my tailor shop earlier today, but I managed to slip out the back door into the alley. I have been hiding for several hours but haven't seen anything suspicious since then."

"Are you sure?" asked Kaplan in a suddenly less calm voice. "Are you absolutely sure they didn't follow you here?"

Israel looked around and said, "Yes, I don't think I was followed. I'm not even sure it was an NKVD agent, but I didn't want to take any chances."

Simon was worried. The last thing he and his family needed was unwanted attention from the NKVD.

Outside the tailor shop on Legionow Street, a man in a dark suit took out a small writing pad and began writing down the address.

The Russians soon made their presence known. Large parades of marching soldiers with red banners and military tanks and other assorted vehicles streamed down the major streets of Lvov. The soldiers looked clean and healthy, but through a tailor's eye, the uniforms left something to be desired. Simon didn't like the long coats and noticed threads hanging down. The Germans wouldn't do that, he thought to himself. Unknown to him, this thought would prove to be bitterly prophetic.

Other changes were starting to take place as well. The Russians in charge ordered the markets reopened and proclaimed the Russian ruble on par with the old Polish zloty. For what they lacked in style, the Russian soldiers made up with rubles, especially the officers. The Russians went through the various stores, amazed at the variety, quantity, and quality of the available goods. They paid whatever was asked and didn't bother to bargain. Luxury items such as jewelry and watches were in demand, especially the watches. It seemed the officers couldn't get enough of them. Inventories of watches soon disappeared, much to the disappointment of the latecomers. The shopkeepers asked no questions and soon figured out how high they could raise their prices for what the Russians claimed were merely "souvenirs."

Simon's tailor shop reopened, and business began to improve. Many of the Russians, both officers and the newly arrived party officials, wanted new suits or alterations to their plain Soviet-looking clothing. The wives especially wanted what they considered more Western-looking fashions. While Simon's business was more oriented to men's clothing, he did have an eye for fashion and proved more than adequate at altering or producing women's dresses and coats for his new clientele.

Most large- to medium-sized enterprises were quickly nationalized. Often, the former owners, who were not compensated for their losses, were kept on for their knowledge and expertise. They frequently played no role in the management of the firms but were encouraged to enjoy participating in the fruits of the workers' paradise.

Simon's shop, however, was apparently deemed too small and insignificant to be nationalized at the moment and was not bothered by the party. Julius Kaplan, however, was not so fortunate.

Simon and Lola had heard the rumor about the party branding well-to-do Poles and Jews as "bourgeois" and, hence, enemies of the state. The rumors were, in fact, cruelly true. Several prominent members of the social, intellectual, and business groups had been so identified. Their possessions had been confiscated, and they had been sent off to somewhere in Russia, probably a gulag or worse. That was the price of the workers' paradise.

Alarmed, Lola said, "Simon, we should hide our, you know, things, our wealth. My jewelry, furs, and silverware—anything that could be construed as 'bourgeois.'"

Simon nodded in agreement. "But we don't know what they consider as wealth. Is it anything they don't have? I just don't know. But for now, I think it's prudent to hide it all, even the china and some of the furniture."

"What about Hanna's violin?" asked Lola.

"You never know how the Russians think," Simon replied. "It's not a damn Stradivarius, just an inexpensive instrument I picked up at the secondhand store. It cost just a couple of zloty. It shouldn't be a problem. Besides, Hanna loves to play, and she is getting very proficient. Maybe one day she can go to the music conservatory when this is all over. I really hate to take it away from her."

Lola relented. "Perhaps you are right, Simon. But where can we hide the 'bourgeois' things? I thought maybe with your brother Mendel in Zloczow, but his location is no safer than ours here in Lvov. My family will face the same challenges, so we can't take anything there."

Simon had previously prepared a small secret hiding place in the basement of his tailor shop. It was mainly to hide small articles that were sometimes exchanged on the black market. While strictly illegal, much of the black market business was tolerated by the officials, especially if it in some way benefited them. It was a small space, well hidden and camouflaged. Simon thought he could enlarge and modify it to contain many of the potential "bourgeois" items. Over the years, he had somehow neglected to tell Lola of the spot, but now seemed like a good time.

"I think I may have a solution," Simon said. "Follow me to the basement." Lola remained silent and followed Simon down the narrow stairway to the dark, musty-smelling basement. Simon kept sewing machine parts, extra thread, and some old bolts of cloth wrapped in heavy paper stored down here. It was cool and a bit damp, but not too bad considering the Peltew River flowed underground nearby on its way to the Bug River.

Simon walked over to the northwest wall and moved a number of boxes containing more cloth, thread, an unused sewing mannequin, and a bicycle. Behind all of these items, the brick wall looked solid. However, if one knew precisely where to look, there were very thin seams in the brickwork. These seams had been cut into the brick and allowed a section of the brick to be removed. Simon carefully cleaned out the seams and inched out the section of bricks. The bricks themselves, in spite of appearing normal, were much thinner in diameter and were lighter and easier to move around. Once the bricks were removed, the small, concealed compartment became visible. It was no more than a meter around and perhaps half a meter deep, but it would hold the jewelry and maybe the silverware and other small "bourgeois" items. Looking closer, Lola could see several watches, some rings, and what appeared to be a small stack of American dollars.

"How long have you had this little secret?" asked Lola. Simon had a contrite look on his face, though Lola couldn't see it in the dim light. "For a number of years," he began. "I found it by accident and worked on it and made it better. I picked up a few things for, as the Americans say, a rainy day. Don't ask me where I got those things."

Lola sighed. "I understand, Simon. I think it's a good place to hide our things. Let's do it now, I'm scared."

Later that evening, Simon and Lola deposited several pieces of jewelry, gemstones, silverware, and extra zloty in the hiding place in the basement. Simon managed to stuff a fur coat, a present from Lola's parents, into the tight spot. He carefully sealed the false brick cover in place. They stepped back to examine the area. Satisfied with the results, they replaced the boxes and bicycle.

A few days later, Simon had a visitor to the tailor shop. "Hello, comrade," said Simon as the man stepped into the shop. "How can a humble tailor help you?"

The man smiled and looked around. "Do you have workers?" he asked. Simon was sure this was a party member, but he wasn't sure of the purpose of the visit. His instincts, however, told him to expect the worst.

"No, comrade, I'm afraid I cannot afford any workers right now. I work alone."

"I see," said the man. "My name is Boris Kogan. I work for the First Secretary. Is there a place we can talk? Your apartment, perhaps?"

"Certainly, comrade Kogan," replied Simon, feeling nowhere near as calm as his voice sounded. "I live upstairs."

"I know," said Kogan, emphasizing an ominous note.

Simon and Boris Kogan climbed the stairs to the apartment. Simon felt threatened but was at a loss to what to do. He unlocked the door, and the two men entered. Hanna was at school and Lola had left earlier to do some shopping with one-year-old Artur. "Please sit down, comrade Kogan," Simon began. "Is there something I can get you? A refreshment, perhaps?"

Kogan slowly walked around the room, looking at various items, including books, pictures, and china. He stopped to admire the elaborate candleholder used for the Shabbat celebration. He continued walking around the apartment, stopping here and there, seemingly taking a mental inventory. Kogan entered the small bedroom shared by Hanna and Artur. He noticed the violin resting in the open case. Satisfied, Kogan came back into the living room.

"Oh, thank you, no," finally came his belated reply. "I must ask you some questions. All very routine, you understand."

Simon nodded and prepared for the worst. "I will be happy to answer anything I can, comrade."

Kogan sat down in a comfortable chair. "Comrade Ruder," Kogan began. "It has come to our attention that a certain Israel Zloczower paid you a visit a few nights ago. He is a known associate of a pair of suspected Zionists, Nathan Roth and Samuel Rosen. Actually, they are suspects no more as both of these gentlemen have confessed to the NKVD. They were encouraged to talk, you see, and mentioned the name 'Zloczower' before they, well, before they were unable to continue. We would like to know why it is that this Israel Zloczower came to see you that night."

Simon thought quickly, trying to formulate an answer that would both save Zloczower and remove suspicion from himself. Remembering that Zloczower and his brother were both tailors like himself, Simon responded, "As you probably know, Israel Zloczower and his brother Schlomo are tailors like myself." Boris Kogan nodded slightly.

Simon continued. "They have a shop two streets over. I have known them for almost ten years. If they are like me, they are very busy with new work, especially from our new comrades. I have many orders for ladies dresses and alterations. Comrade Zloczower stopped by to see if I had any special material for some dresses he was making for an officer's wife. He did not want to disappoint the woman."

"And you gave him the material?" asked Kogan.

"Unfortunately, no. I did not have what he needed, but promised to check around for him. I wouldn't want to disappoint the officer's wife, either."

Kogan steepled his hands and took a deep breath. "I'm sure you wouldn't," he said. He took out a small paper pad and then, taking his time, wrote down some notes. Simon tried to remain calm, knowing that, quite likely, his future fate depended on the content of the notes. Kogan closed the note pad with a crisp snap and replaced it in his left coat pocket. He looked intently at Simon and said, "Comrade Ruder, thank you for your cooperation, but let us get down to business. You are a Jew. I must make a report about my visit here. I would like to give you a little word of advice. Be careful who your friends and associates are. We will be watching. I wouldn't want to see you at the Loncki Prison someday. It would be most unfortunate for both of us."

With that, Boris Kogan slowly lifted himself from the chair and, with a final look around the apartment, made his way to the door. Simon closed the door behind the Russian official and locked it. He was shaking but relieved at the same time. He was not sure this was the end of it but promised himself to be more careful with his friends and acquaintances. At least he was still at home.

Simon nervously paced around the apartment. He passed the chair in which Kogan had been sitting and noticed a small piece of paper left on the chair. He picked it up and examined it and was shocked to see a small, hand-drawn Star of David on it.

Simon went back to work at his shop downstairs. He dared not communicate with his friends today. He was sure he was being watched. He decided to wait until tomorrow when the group met informally at the Riz coffee shop. He didn't want to do anything that looked like panic on his part. Simon locked the door to the shop and headed toward the basement. He got busy with his project with a renewed sense of urgency.

Lola came home a short time later and began preparing dinner. Little Artur was tired from running around the stores and especially waiting in lines. He was soon asleep.

Hanna arrived from school shortly thereafter. "I don't like school anymore," she announced. "It's so different now. All we learn about is how gloriously the great leader Josef Stalin is leading us and how fortunate we are to be living under the Soviet system. I hate it and can't stand it."

Appalled, Lola responded, "Shh, shh, shh. Someone will hear you. Don't ever say anything like that again. Please, Hanna, for everyone's sake."

Simon arrived back upstairs at the apartment two hours later. He tried to appear normal in spite of the shock and emotions the visit from Boris Kogan had generated. He immediately went into the small bathroom and cleaned up, washing off what appeared to be dirt, before coming out to face his family. He kissed Lola and Hanna. Artur finally awakened and greeted his father. "Papa!" the youngster shouted and ran to Simon.

"Hello, my little boychik," Simon said, lifting the toddler in the air and swinging him around. Artur always loved this and laughed out loud. Simon loved the sound of his children laughing and wondered how much longer the sound would be heard.

Lola Ruder was a shrewd woman, quick of wit and sometimes quicker of tongue. She sensed Simon's mood and suspected something had happened while she was gone. She looked questioningly at her husband across the table. He looked back at her and simply said, "We will talk about it later."

After dinner, Hanna retired to her room and began to play her violin. She practiced often and was hoping to be accepted into the music conservatory next year. Simon and Lola were proud of their daughter and the many compliments she received and especially the excellent progress she was making with the instrument. Simon was thinking of buying her a better violin when conditions improved.

"So tell me, Simon, what happened that has made you so upset?" Lola asked. "You look like you've seen a ghost."

Simon related the story of Boris Kogan's visit. "First, Kogan walked around the apartment inspecting everything. I'm so glad we had the foresight to move the things we did. He seemed especially interested in the Shabbat candleholder, though he tried to hide it. Then he got down to the real business. He asked what Israel Zloczower was doing here the other night. Apparently the fool led him, or someone, right here to our house."

"*Oy vey iz mir*," said Lola. "What does it mean? Are we in trouble? What *tzures* has he brought upon us?"

"I don't know," Simon replied. "Kogan was very polite. I told him Zloczower came by to get some special cloth for a customer, a Russian officer's wife. I told him I didn't have what he needed but that I would check around."

"Why did he ask you about Zloczower in the first place?" Lola asked.

Simon continued his explanation. "Two Zionist acquaintances of his were caught and sent to the Loncki Prison. They were interrogated by the NKVD and confessed to being Zionists. They mentioned the name Zloczower during the interrogation. I didn't ask, but I assume the NKVD surmised Israel was a possible suspect and had him followed. Right to our apartment."

Lola put her head in her hands. "So what happened then?" she asked.

"Kogan wrote down some notes. He thanked me for my cooperation and warned me about being careful about my friends. Then he said something about not wanting to see me in the Loncki Prison and that it would be unfortunate for both of us. Very strange, that last comment."

Simon took a piece of paper from his pocket and handed it to Lola. "Stranger still," he said, "after he left, I found this on the chair he was sitting in." Lola took the paper from her husband. She was shocked to see the Star of David on it.

The next day, at their weekly meeting at the Riz coffee house, Julius Kaplan, Meyer Rosenthal, and Simon were having their usual coffee.

"Well, it's happened," a distraught Julius Kaplan explained. "A Russian Jew, a colonel named Leibkind who was appointed to run the 'Pharmaceutical Trust' for the Lvov Oblast District, and several staff came to see me. As I feared, my pharmacy has been nationalized, and I am now under their jurisdiction." Kaplan took out the document stamped with the official round seal of the party and passed it around.

"Very official-looking," Simon pronounced sarcastically.

"It's not funny, Simon," replied Kaplan.

"I know," quipped Simon. "I'm sorry." He motioned the group to huddle closer around the table. He then related the visit from Boris Kogan the day before and then showed them the little memento he had left. All expressed shock and disbelief. They were all perplexed by the Star of David and what it could possibly mean.

Kaplan was the first to respond. "The visit scares me. They are watching us. That idiot Zloczower led them right to us. Maybe we have a friend in Boris Kogan, maybe not. It may be a trap. We must be very careful from now on. He is obviously NKVD or working with them. Do you think he suspects anything?"

"It's hard to say," Simon answered, addressing the group. "He seems like a decent fellow, but I don't know if the paper is a threat to me or a sign he is willing to help. He may be sympathetic to us Jews or he may be one himself, like your Colonel Leibkind. Or it may, as you say, be a trap. But from now on, we keep quiet about our affiliations. Kaplan, don't be stupid. You know they are looking for Zionists, so you are, therefore, an enemy of the state. If they catch you, no one will be able to help. Remember that. We must be vigilant."

"What about you, Simon?" asked Meyer Rosenthal.

Simon looked at his lawyer friend. "I told you I would wait and see. I don't like what I'm seeing. The old Polish Communists who have approached the party are either ignored or they disappear. The Soviets seem to prefer the Ukrainians with whom they cooperate with to a high degree. I still have hope for the future in spite of the disappointing turn of events so far."

The group kept meeting in the coming weeks but took precautions to ensure they were not being watched or followed. They all settled into a routine of following the orders of their Soviets masters, proclaiming gratitude for being liberated and essentially keeping their heads down. Soviet books replaced the

Polish and American books. Interestingly, Boris Kogan was never heard from again, and his visit was never followed up on, much to the relief of Simon and Lola. Life went on, albeit not as smoothly or as comfortably as before. Food became an issue, as production often fell short of demand. The Soviet system of nationalization proved ineffective at best, at least initially. Basic necessities were sometimes in short supply, and luxury goods were not readily available, although Gastronom, a luxury store, seemed to have otherwise unavailable goods. The black market, at least, was thriving. But the Jews were patient, living day-by-day. To be sure, some well-to-do "bourgeois" Jews and Poles were arrested and deported, their possessions and wealth confiscated and distributed to the state. Intellectuals and other real or imagined threats to the state were likewise quickly and brutally dealt with. The Polish army, especially officers, were deported or murdered. Many of the soldiers, however, were smart enough to discard their uniforms and rifles and blend in with the populace. Overall, life was difficult but tolerable for the Jews in Eastern Galicia—at least for the time being.

Things were not so good for the remaining millions of Jews trapped in the General Government. The Nazis moved quickly to establish a brutal regime to control the area. In fact, the Nazis were busy for the rest of 1939 building the foundation for atrocities and crimes against humanity such as the world had never seen.

Ugly rumors started filtering into Lvov. Special Jewish ghettos were being established in the Nazi-controlled General Government. On October 12, the deportation of Jews from Austria and Moravia to Poland began. On October 19, Krakow was officially declared the capital of the General Government. On the same date, a Jewish ghetto was said to be established in Lublin, Poland. Everywhere in Nazi-occupied Poland, Jews were being murdered or uprooted from their homes and sent to ghettos. The rural areas were systematically being cleansed of Jews. They were being deported or outright murdered.

Even more frightening, it was said that special forces called the *Einsatzgruppen* followed the regular army with missions to kill Jews, and kill them unmercifully, as many as they could.

Unknown to Simon and the group, the rumors of these mobile killing machines proved all too true, but the victims were not limited to Jews. After the defeat and subsequent occupation of Poland in 1939, the *Einsatzgruppen* killed Poles, especially those belonging to the upper class and intelligentsia, such as priests and teachers. In fact, lists of names comprising the targeted groups had been prepared prior to the war. Those unfortunates on the lists where rounded up and summarily executed.

Simon, his group of friends, and Jews in western Ukraine took in the news and rumors with great trepidation and anxiety. But they were not surprised. It was clear the Nazi threat to exterminate the Jews was rapidly materializing. More refugees streamed in from Germany and Poland, seeking what they thought was relative safety in Lvov and nearby cities. The Russians were better than the Germans, they rationalized, the statement reflecting some degree of truth.

ZLOCZOW, POLAND, OCTOBER 1939

In Zloczow, life still went on for Mendel Ruder and his family. The so-called sovietization of commerce in the area began once the political situation had begun to sort its way through the chaos of the first few days and weeks after the Russian takeover. Like most Jews, Mendel thought being under Russian control was much better than what was going on in the General Government under Nazi control. Mendel's tailor shop was confiscated, but he found work at a party-run clothing factory. At least he was being paid and could feed his family. His wife Zofia, however, showed signs of discontentment. She was not happy about the situation and complained loudly and frequently.

"Mendel, you should go join the Communist Party. It will help your situation." Mendel just shrugged. He had heard this many times before.

"Mendel, go make friends with some of the party members. Go impress them. You may become one of them if you get motivated. Don't be lazy. Be more like Simon. He's a Communist and a big shot in Lvov."

Mendel just shook his head. Though he knew this was an exaggeration, he admitted there was some truth in Zofia's statement. He recalled past discussions with Simon that often ended in arguments. The Communist system did not resonant with Mendel. While many Jews fervently believed Communism was a haven of equality for Jews, Mendel thought differently, and the two brothers had debated this issue at great length. The fact that he no longer had his tailor shop merely reinforced Mendel's point of view. For now, he would keep his head down and do his job. He could still occasionally make the seventy-kilometer trip to Lvov to visit Simon, although it was getting more difficult all the time. Once in a while, the family would join him and visit with Simon, Lola, and the two children. The men talked politics while the women bragged about what prodigies their young sons were. Seven-year-old Hanna stayed with the women and demonstrated her expertise with the violin before her uncle and his family headed back home to Zloczow.

OBERTIN, POLAND, SEPTEMBER 1939

On September 9, Mordko Fischel and Chija Frima Ruder, along with approximately eleven hundred fellow Jews, watched the Red Army enter their little town and wondered what that singular event portended for their future. At least it wasn't the Germans, they thought, with some degree of relief.

1940

Life continued to deteriorate in East Galicia where the Jews and Poles chaffed under the Soviet yoke. NKVD spies were everywhere. Simon could identify many of them, but he was more afraid of the ones he couldn't. Daily life turned into a dull grind. Card playing was frowned upon, as was merriment in the streets. Citizens were turned in to the NKVD for any minor offense that was deemed subversive, and it seemed pretty much anything met the criteria. For example, telling a joke, laughing, and otherwise normal activities were cause for being reported, and this was a perfect time for settling old scores. Often, a trip to the Loncki Prison was one-way. People continually looked over their shoulders. Anyone could be a spy, official or not.

This time the group met at the apartment of Jakob Lansky. The group now rotated meeting venues and didn't meet nearly as often as it once had. Since the Boris Kogan visit, they had each taken great pains to appear normal and not draw any undue attention to themselves. While they were relieved and a little surprised that no repercussions had materialized, they maintained a high level of vigilance nonetheless.

Schnapps was harder to find, but vodka was readily available. The group sat around the dining room table looking at each other and wondering who would speak up first. The mood was very downbeat. As it turned out, Simon went first. "Any news from Poland?" he asked to no one in particular. Everyone understood that there really wasn't a Poland anymore; they were referring to the General Government.

"The news is very bad," said Lansky. "There are reports that the Jews of Lodz have been herded into a ghetto from which they are forbidden leave."

In fact, the news was late. The Lodz ghetto was had been established in October 1939 and was the first in major cities like Warsaw and Lublin. "What's next?" Lansky lamented.

Kaplan spoke up next. "My real surprise is that the Germans haven't attacked the Russians yet. When that happens, the devil will take us. We will be in the middle of a battle between an enemy we have come to know and one we can only imagine. Is it really better to have the devil that you know than one you don't?"

"Can it really be as bad as rumors suggest?" asked Rosenthal. "I can't believe the Germans have actually committed the atrocities we've heard about. It just cannot be. They are a civilized people. I have many German friends and associates."

"Meyer, Meyer, Meyer," said Kaplan, as though disciplining a child. "My feeling is that our worst, unspoken fears are about to come true. I think they are already loose on the land. How can you possibly not see this?"

"By the way, Meyer," Dr. Deutsch started. "How are you surviving these days?"

Meyer Rosenthal let out a sarcastic laugh. "I have a job as a clerk in the government legal system such as it is. For that, I am paid two hundred rubles a month. I have some items I sell on the black market to help out. Not enough that I draw attention, but enough to survive for now. I hope this Soviet occupation ends soon. I'm running out of things to sell. What about the rest of you?"

Simon responded with his usual sarcasm. "Meyer, be careful what you wish for. Me, I am surviving making *schmattes* into silk purses. The Russians want me to alter their clothes that look like potato sacks into what they consider fashionable clothing, especially the women. I can only do so much. At least they pay, sometimes in rubles and sometimes with food."

Lansky relayed a similar story. "Because of my architectural degree and experience, I have been granted a job as a janitor of a government party building. I am paid two hundred rubles as well. I have sold my watches, rings, and some books for a few rubles on the black market, but soon I will have nothing more to sell."

"By the way, Simon," started Kaplan. "How are your brothers? Have you heard from them?"

Simon hesitated then answered slowly. "Mendel is still in Zloczow with his family. I haven't seen him for a while now. I think it's too dangerous to travel, but I think he is safe. Izak, poor Izak. I think he is trapped in the Krakow ghetto. We heard the Jews are forced to wear armbands with a Star of David. Then their homes and valuables were confiscated. Later, we heard they were forcibly removed and resettled in nearby towns. Many young Jewish men have been sent to small forced labor camps. I don't know what happened to Izak, and I'm very concerned. I'm just glad we are safer under the Russians."

FRANCE AND THE SWISS BORDER, JUNE–DECEMBER 1940

Obergefreiter Leonhard Kiermeier and the First Mountain Division trained briefly for their planned landing on the English coast, but the operation, called Operation *SEELOWE*, and the planned invasion of Gibraltar, called Operation *Felix*, were both canceled, and the division was moved to the French Alps near the Swiss border.

1941

Having participated in the brief campaign in Yugoslavia, the German First Mountain Division was moved into position around a small town called Dzikow in German-occupied Poland. *Obergefreiter* Leonhard Kiermeier and his men were sure something important was in the wind, but they were waiting for instructions. They had just finished learning the Cyrillic alphabet and now had the ability to read Russian signposts, and thus they had some idea where they might be going.

The company commanders told their troops that the Fuhrer wanted to expand *Lebensraum im Osten*, living space in the East, and that Germany needed this room to grow. The concept was not new to Leonhard, who had been indoctrinated with this idea years before. The Fuhrer had stressed this often. What came next, however, was a surprise.

"This battle will be different from those you have fought before," began the commander. "We will be fighting against Bolshevism-Communism. This is a crusade the Fuhrer has sent us on, and we shall not fail. We are moving out this very day."

At three fifteen the morning, the First Mountain Division rolled across the German-Soviet demarcation line established in 1939 and advanced toward their objective, the city of Lvov. Their part of a major operation codenamed *Barbarossa* was underway.

LVOV, POLAND, JUNE 1941

In June of 1941, it was becoming apparent that something big was going on. The Russians, who had occupied the region since September 1939, were on the move eastward. The women went first, followed by officials, functionaries, and party members. Soon soldiers and their equipment began the eastward trek.

The Jews of Lvov watched this exodus with rising apprehension. They knew there was only one reason this move was occurring: the Germans were coming. This did not bode well for the them, living in the midst of the virulently anti-Semitic Ukrainians and the Poles, who were not much better, but who would soon would have their own problems.

Simon watched the continuous stream of evacuating Soviets from the window of his Legionow Street tailor shop. It ebbed and flowed as the town slowly emptied of Russians. The Ukrainians seemed pleased, even joyful. They knew the Germans would be coming soon as their saviors. Revenge, they sensed, was in the wind. In this part of the world, populations had long memories. Lurking just below the surface, everyone knew the pent-up Ukrainian hatred for the Jews was steeping from the days when Ukrainians were still Ruthenians, subjected to the authority of Kaiser Franz Josef I when Lemberg was the capital city of the province of Galicia in the former Austro-Hungarian Empire.

As the parade of Russians dwindled to a trickle over the next days, Simon noticed a group of NKVD soldiers and plainclothes agents leaving the city, but with a seemingly increased sense of urgency. Among them Simon recognized Boris Kogan, who had paid him a visit two years earlier. Simon quickly turned away from his window, but as the group passed the tailor shop, Kogan looked over and spotted Simon. *Too late*, thought Simon. Kogan left the group and quickly walked over to the shop. The smiling Russian opened the door and entered the shop, and in an attempt to allay Simon's apprehension, he smiled and spread his arms as if greeting a friend. Simon noticed dark spots on the Russian's coat that looked suspiciously like dried bloodstains.

"Hello, comrade Ruder," said Kogan. "As you see, it is now time for us to leave. Now the real war begins. I'm sorry I cannot help you more. Good luck to you and your family. I fear that, soon, you will sorely need it. By the way, did your friend ever finish the dress he was making? We were going to check out the story, but somehow, the report kept getting pushed to the bottom of the stack." Finally, Kogan shook Simon's hand and said, *"Zol zayn mit mazel."* With that, Kogan left quickly to rejoin his retreating group. He never looked back.

On June 22, 1941, the German army entered the Soviet-occupied zone as part of Operation *Barbarossa*, the overall attack on the Soviet Union. Once again, Lvov was bombed repeatedly. No one was surprised at the attack, which had been anticipated for a long time. For the Jews who imagined they were in a "lesser of two evils" scenario, the party was about to come to a brutal and tragic end to be played out over the next two years.

Eerily reminiscent of the September 1939 invasion, the Jews of Lvov scrambled for whatever safety they could find. The Lvov railroad stations, power plant, water plants, and hospitals were all targeted by the Germans. On June 30, the Germans entered Lvov, this time staying for the next three years. Lvov officially surrendered shortly thereafter. Perhaps more sinister and symbolic of what was to come, the Germans destroyed the Temple Synagogue upon entering the city. It was a Reform synagogue built in 1844–1845 near Starji Rinok Square, site of the historic fish market.

Simon, Lola, Hanna, and little Artur were huddled in the basement of their tailor shop on Legionow Street listening to the muffled explosions above. Cascades of dust filtered down on them, then slowed almost to a stop, only to start again as the explosions intensified. Just moments ago, as the bombs had begun to fall, they had rushed to the relative safety of the basement. Fortunately, the family was together at the time and was able to seek cover together. The basement offered some safety for the time being, and Simon thought it was not yet time to reveal his secret to the family, not until he better understood the developing situation unfolding above.

Simon, in addition to his skills as a tailor, was also an excellent carpenter, a *tischler*, and using those skills, he had built a so-called bunker, a place to hide from the Nazis. The bunker was cleverly constructed so as not to be easily discovered. Simon used the original hiding place he had prepared two years earlier to hide valuables from the Soviets. As he enlarged the meter square opening in the wall, he found he could dig underneath the building next door, which apparently had no basement. Working secretly at night, he had cleared a sanctuary about three meters by four meters and just short of two meters high. He had worried about how to dispose of the dirt he dug out, and he had finally decided to spread it around the back of the buildings, one bucketful at a time. He worried about the dark, fresh dirt and tried to cover it up as much as possible. He lined the walls of the bunker with wood planks, bricks, or whatever materials he could scrounge up. There was still debris from the attacks of 1939, so with a little ingenuity, Simon had found all he needed. He enlarged the entryway using the same technique as before by creating a false-brick facade door that perfectly matched the surrounding wall. This he disguised by mounting shelves across the seams that moved with the opening. When the wall opening was closed, the seams were well hidden. He also attached other items, such as boxes, to the wall section to further enhanced the disguise. These moved with the opening as well and appeared to be stacked against the wall. The bunker was stocked with canned goods, a radio, water, and other essential items. He even ran an electrical wire to the bunker, even though he realized the power would most likely be out for periods of time. If he ever had to use it, he knew it would be uncomfortable but much better than the alternative. He had even tacked a mezuzah on the inside frame of the opening.

"Papa, I'm afraid," cried Hanna. "What's happening? What's going to happen to us?"

"Sshh, sshh, my little Hannale," said Simon, trying to calm his daughter. He looked at Lola whose ashen face did not betray her fear. She looked at Simon and nodded her head toward her daugher.

"It will be fine, little Hannale," began Simon. "You will yet play your violin at the opera house. I promise. I am looking forward to it." But he didn't believe what he was saying. He and Lola both understood the implications of what was going on above them all too well and what the future would likely hold for them.

Obergefreiter Leonhard Kiermeier led his small squad of soldiers through the streets of Lvov. Ironically, he had been here two years earlier, but the city had been abruptly turned over to Germany's then ally, Russia. The squad moved methodically through the quiet, deserted streets. They were not quite deserted, for as the squad moved from street to street, the initial scenes of horrific brutality and tragedy began to unfold. All around the city, the Germans discovered the work of the NKVD secret police in and around the three Lvov prisons. Lying where they were murdered, singly or in gruesome piles, were the corpses of thousands of Ukrainian, Jewish, and Polish intellectuals, political activists, and convicted criminals that filled the basements, corridors, and courtyards of Brygidki, Loncki, and Zamarstynowska prisons.

Even as a battle-hardened soldier, *Obergefreiter* Leonhard Kiermeier was surprised by what his squad had found. The division stayed for a time to assist with the process of securing the town and to ensure the city was devoid of Russians. Some of the troops, however, played a more sinister role. While the town was handed over to the *German SchutzStaffel*, or SS, members of the *Wehrmacht* Mountain Divisions also rounded up Jews and sent them to work camps. Others were seen at the prisons where the massacres by the NKVD had taken place. Always the opportunists, the SS immediately saw a chance to take advantage of the situation and turn it to their favor. Blaming the NKVD and the Jews for the massacres, the SS allowed an infuriated Ukrainian population to take their revenge. Soon recognizing the unrestrained, tacit approval of the SS, the Ukrainians fell upon the Jews with an unbridled fury. Jews were murdered on the streets and dragged out of stores, homes, and other offices and were beaten and otherwise harrassed. Several thousand Jews were thought to be among the victims. This event would be recorded in history as *The Prison Riots*, mainly fueled by Ukrainian revenge for the NKVD and the alleged Jewish collaboration in the prison massacres. As the events unfolded, this was but the beginning of the horror that was to follow in the coming days, months, and years.

In reality, the SS utilized a specially trained force called the *Einsatzgruppen* to follow the regular army and kill any Jews they encountered. History would later show that nearly seven hundred Jews were murdered initially, with another thirty-five hundred shot by the *Einsatzgruppen* during the period from June 30 to July 3.

As things started to quiet down, the Ruder family, hiding in the basement on Legionow Street, began to breathe again. The gunshots, screaming, and shouting had died down, and a sort of hushed quiet pervaded the area. Fearful, yet needing to ascertain the situation, Simon motioned for his family to remain where they were. He then slowly made his way back upstairs. As he entered his shop, he could hear dogs barking in the distance and the faint cries and groans of those wounded or dying. As he crept to the front window of the shop, he inched his head up above the windowsill and peered out at the scene before him. Corpses littered the sidewalks and street. Blood from the victims seeped slowly into the brick-paved street.

Always a cautious man, Simon took in the carnage on the street. The moans and cries of several victims began to overcome his caution. The only other sounds he heard were the constant barking of dogs and now a few birds returning to the scene. One of the unfortunates lying almost in front of his shop tried to move but was obviously severely wounded and could only roll over. It was an elderly woman he did not recognize. A shopping bag lay nearby, its contents strewn on the sidewalk and into the street. A few food tins and a loaf of bread that were apparently crushed by tires lay in the street. Simon, feeling more secure, slowly, methodically, edged his way to the door. He cautiously poked his head out of the doorway and looked up and down the street. Seeing nothing dangerous and thinking of his family, he eyed the spilled contents of the shopping bag and what it still might contain. He slowly emerged from the doorway and crawled to the bag. He didn't look at the now dead old woman. She wouldn't need the food now anyway, he thought, and, unable to resist, he began to collect the loose tins. But as he was reaching for the bread, he heard the sound of a vehicle approaching from around the corner. Before he could react, a gray German military truck driven by an SS soldier and filled with shouting and laughing Ukrainians was speeding toward him. He had been spotted. Simon thought about his family hiding in the basement. Assuming his own life was forfeit, he sought to draw his pursuers away from the shop. He dropped the cans, got up, and started walking briskly down Legionow Street toward the opera house. The truck quickly caught up with Simon, and the band of Ukrainians jumped out and surrounded him. They pummeled him, causing minor injuries and a bloody nose. They relieved Simon of some money, but that was all he had with him. The SS soldier barked an order, and the Ukrainians abruptly stopped the assault. Simon was then put in restraints and loaded onto the bed of the truck. He noticed several other Jews, none of whom he recognized, already on the truck. They had obviously been similarly captured, roughed up, relieved of any valuables, restrained, and dumped on the truck.

Simon looked at the motley collection of Jews. While bloody, they did not appear to be any worse off than he was. The Ukrainian thugs were too busy enjoying their hunt for more Jews and paid little attention to their captured victims.

The captured Jews were all males, seven of them. Simon guessed they were between eighteen and maybe sixty years old. He quietly addressed one of the older Jews. "Do you know what's going on?" he asked.

The Jew whispered, "I am Samuel Ackermann. I thought I was a dead man, but they just beat me up and then put me on the truck. We have been driving around for an hour. They look for Jews. I think they need us for some work. Maybe they will let us go after we do the work." The other Jews remained silent, a glazed look in their eyes.

After two more Jews were spotted, roughed up, and captured, the truck turned onto Sapiehy Street and drove past the Technical High School. Simon recognized the area as a part of Lvov where few Jews lived. It was a part of Lvov for Jews to avoid. At the end of the street, they reached the infamous Loncki Prison where the NKVD had operated from 1939 until the recent evacuation. Hope started to evaporate.

The truck pulled into the courtyard of the dark, foreboding prison. The stench was overpowering. Corpses in the hundreds lay strewn across the grounds.

Loncki (also called Lonick) Prison in Lvov/Lemberg, Poland in 1941. Simon Ruder spent three years imprisoned here as a slave laborer sewing SS uniforms. Other visitors and inmates included Simon Wiesenthal and William Weiss and his father David. (Photo from Yad Vashem, file number 5138/100.)

Another view of Loncki Prison with Ukrainian SS and German guards in 1941. Interestingly, while this prison was run by the SS, the soldier on the right wears the edelweiss patch of the Wehrmacht Mountain Divisions on his right sleeve. (Photo from Yad Vashem, file number55AO4.)

Many more were inside, littering the hallways and many layers deep in the basement. The truck came to a squealing halt. "Raus, Raus, Juden," barked an SS officer. Simon and his group jumped or were pushed off the truck. They were soon joined by several other groups of Jews and were instructed to form a single, larger group of forty to fifty individuals.

The Ukrainians had left, and only German SS personnel remained. Some, Simon noticed, had movie cameras.

An SS officer, walking with an air of superiority and command, emerged from the main prison building. He turned toward the collection of unfortunate Jews, and with a look of disgust, said, "I am SS *Oberscharführer* Oskar Waltke. I run the Jewish Affairs section in Lemberg, and this is my prison. It is run by the Gestapo, for whom you now work." He smiled to himself as he continued. "You see all around you the villainous actions of the NKVD with the assistance of you dirty Jews. You filthy animals are responsible for this!

You will all pay! For now, however, you are ordered to bury these victims of Jewish and Bolshevik treachery. All of the bodies are to be removed from the basement, hallways, the prison grounds, and anywhere you find them. I want them out and buried quickly. We will be making moving pictures of your work to preserve for history to witness the Bolshevik and Jewish atrocities. Now get to work, you pigs!"

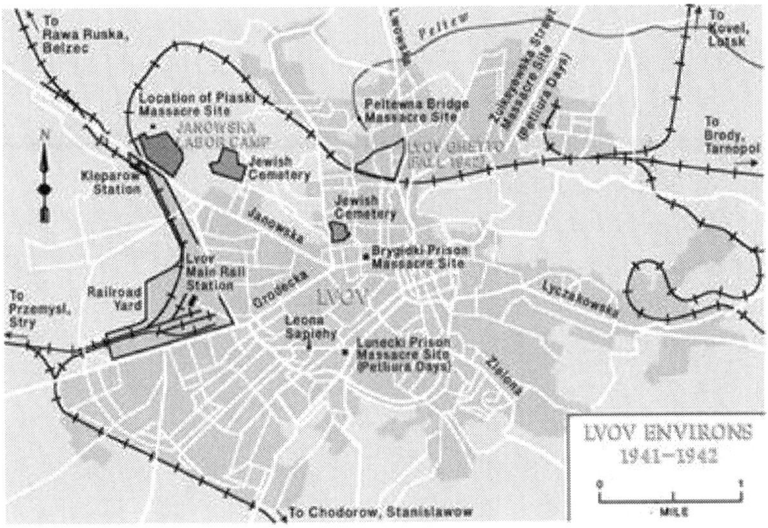

Map of Lvov, Poland, in 1941–1942, indicating locations of the Janowska labor camp, Lvov ghetto, Lunecki (Loncki) Prison, Brygidki Prison, Jewish cemetery, and railroad stations. (Map courtesy of the United States Holocaust Memorial Museum, Washington, DC.)

With that, Waltke turned on his heel and walked back into the main building. Several SS guards appeared with shovels and began to distribute them. The look in their eyes, it seemed to Simon, was the look of someone who knew a secret. It was an ominous look.

Simon was not a particularly tall or large man, but he was strong. His time as a soccer player had served him well, and he was in good physical shape. He went about the gruesome task of hauling out the bodies, piling them up for later burial behind the prison. He noticed that not a small number of victims appeared to be Jews. Most were recently murdered, probably in the shadows of the approaching German army. Simon did not recognize any of the bodies, but many were starting to decompose, and he doubted he would recognize anyone, but he was sure some of them were Zionists. He quietly thanked God he was spared, probably by the Russian Boris Kogan, who Simon was sure was himself a Jew. Simon wondered why he couldn't or hadn't helped Nathan Roth and Samuel Rosen.

After days of hauling out the corpses, stacking them outside, and finally burying them in pits already dug behind the prison, the work was finished, at least for these unfortunate Jews. The SS had filmed the entire gruesome process, presumably for propaganda purposes. These films would surely fan the flames of anti-Semitism already running amok in what was now again called Lemberg.

The group of Jews rested, some on the ground, others with their arms on their knees or leaning on their shovels. All were tired after the strenuous work they had done. They looked at each other wondering what was going to happen to them next. Maybe they would be released after all. Hope, dim as it was, still flickered in their minds.

Soon, an SS guard ordered the Jews to form a line and stand at attention. One Jew, Samuel Ackermann, panicked and tried to run and was immediately cut down in a hail of automatic gunfire. That answered any questions and quickly extinguished any hope the others may have had. Simon silently cursed himself for not showing his family the bunker he had so carefully prepared for them. What a shame, he thought. Ironically, he wondered who the Germans would get to bury their bodies. Maybe they would do it themselves, but he realized there was an almost endless supply of Jews to be captured and exploited.

SS *Oberscharführer* Waltke emerged from the prison office. He was dressed in full Gestapo regalia, including a riding crop, and with no horses in sight, he used it liberally to encourage the Jews.

The group of Jews was marched into the prison courtyard and ordered to stand at attention once more. Waltke walked among them, his SS bodyguards nearby. Anyone not at what he felt was perfect attention was made to pay with several lashes of the riding crop. Not that it really mattered, Waltke thought. He turned and looked at the group, but didn't really see them. He started walking back but stopped in front of Simon who, unlike the rest of the group, held his head high and returned Waltke's stare. The SS man raised his riding crop and viciously struck Simon in his ribs several times. Simon flinched but stayed on his feet. "Hmm," said Waltke as he stepped aside and several guards appeared with machine guns.

Simon saw the guards with the machine guns fan out in front of the group of stunned Jews. Still stinging from the blow, Simon thought of Lola and Hanna and how he would never again hear his daughter play the violin. He thought of little Artur whom he would never see grow up. As another thought was just beginning to form in his mind, it was interrupted by the sound of machine gun fire. Simon was brutally thrust backward, and he hit the ground hard. Bodies fell onto him, and he suddenly found himself at the bottom of a pile of dead and dying Jews. Yet he was still breathing and did not seem to feel the impact of the bullets. Just lucky or a perhaps a miracle? Regardless, he was uninjured and alive, and he was determined to stay that way.

The SS guards made a cursory inspection of the bleeding pile of Jews. Simon heard single shots that silenced moans and cries, but soon all was quiet, except for the noises death makes while working its way out of the corpses. Simon lay very still, partially trapped by the dead lying on top of him, but more motivated by the slight hope of surviving this ordeal. Night fell and Simon lay perfectly still. His arms and legs cramped and screamed for relief, yet he resisted the urge to move. *Just a little longer,* he thought. A dog came by and started to sniff at the bodies. This unnerved Simon, and suddenly he could wait no longer. He moved his left arm, which was heavily pinned beneath a body. Although slight, the sudden movement startled the dog. It yelped, then growled. Simon immediately froze. A light came on in one of the offices. An SS guard emerged, picked up a stone, and threw it at the dog. The dog yelped again and took off, and the guard went back inside and turned off the light.

Once it was quiet again, Simon wasted no time freeing himself from the deadly mass of bodies. Fortunately, it was a cloudy night, and the moon was mostly covered. On hands and knees, he managed to make his way to the unguarded entrance to the prison and slipped out. The next day the SS guards didn't bother to count the corpses still lying in the courtyard. More Jews would come to clean up the mess.

In the darkness of the cool night, Simon tried to work his way back to Legionow Street. He made a few wrong turns, but eventually he heard the rush of the Peltew River and headed toward it. He soon recognized some familiar landmarks and, keeping to the shadows, cautiously made his way home. He saw vague shapes of many bodies lying in the streets and alleys. They seemed to be everywhere. He was sure they had not been there on the truck ride to the prison. Suddenly, Simon felt a cold fear, a fear of what he didn't see, of what was just out of sight beyond his vision. He could feel something evil in the air. He shivered uncontrollably, but not from the cold, as he continued on his way home. His ribs started to throb where the SS thug had hit him. But he kept going. As he approached the apartment on familiar Legionow Street, the moon came out from behind some clouds, and in the light it cast, a surreal vision of corpses revealed itself, the bodies still lying in the streets and on the sidewalks just as they had been when he was caught. The cloying odor was sickening. Dogs had been at the bodies. Cloth was torn, revealing ripped flesh. The birds too had had their turn, and even now the rats were having theirs.

Simon checked his pants and was surprised to find he still had his key in a hidden part of his pocket. The Ukrainians had apparently missed the key or had decided it was of no value. He tried to brush his hair with his dirty hands and felt the stubble and dirt on his face. He realized he looked horrible, covered with blood, and even though most of it was not his, he knew he was still a frightening sight. He slowly climbed the stairs to the apartment, not sure what he would find.

He cautiously unlocked the door. The lights were out. He spotted the shape of Lola sleeping on the couch. Simon went over to her but decided not to wake her yet. Instead, he went to the small bathroom and cleaned up the best he could. He very quietly changed his clothes and threw the blood-soaked clothes in a corner. Finally, he went over to Lola and gently shook her awake. Startled,

Lola recognized Simon and hugged him. "My God, we thought you were dead! We heard you were captured. What happened? How did you escape?" she cried.

Simon told his story, leaving out the more grisly details. Lola was horrified. Then she noticed the gashes on her husband's head and arms. "That looks bad," she said. "Let me get something for it." Lola got some bandages and salve and carefully applied them to Simon's wounds. "Compliments of the Gestapo," said Simon.

Lola told Simon about the rumors of many murders in the prisons around town and how the Germans blamed the Jews. "Everyone knows the Russians did it," said Lola. "Why do they blame us? Why do they always blame us?"

Simon just shook his head and winced at the sudden pain. "Because we are here, we are defenseless, and because we make good scapegoats. They always blame us. Even though I saw many Jews among the bodies in the prison, I think some Zionists were among them."

Lola gasped and said a quick prayer for the Zionists she knew. With tears in her eyes, she looked intently at her husband. "Simon, do you know what has been happening since you have been gone?" Simon shook his head but knew it must have something to do with the scores of bodies he had seen strewn on the streets on his way back from the prison. "Tell me," he said, fearing the worst but instinctively knowing the answer.

"The Ukrainians went crazy," she began. "They just rounded up Jews and shot them. Innocent people, men, women, children, young, old, they just killed them. Some they beat to death, most were shot. There were other Germans with them. They just watched; they did nothing. We heard the Germans also killed many more Jews at the stadium. Special Germans, the ones we heard about in Poland. They are called something like *Einsatzgruppen*. We hear they follow behind the regular army and kill Jews and others with brutality and no mercy. The Ukrainians are behind this, and the damn Germans helped them. They just stood there and watched Jews being dragged off and murdered. My God, we thought you were gone, a victim of this latest pogrom. Simon, I'm so glad you're still alive."

While the children still slept, Simon told Lola, "Follow me. There is something very important I must show you." It was still dark as Simon and Lola climbed down the stairs all the way to the basement. Simon walked over to where he knew the opening to the bunker was concealed. He showed her where the release lever was hidden and how to operate it. The door slowly swung partway open. Simon grasped the edge of the opening and swung it open all the way. It opened smoothly and noiselessly on hidden hinges. Lola was astonished to see the work Simon had done, especially without her knowledge. She remembered the hours Simon had disappeared in the basement, but she had never asked. Now she knew. Simon showed her around the small space. She marveled at the ingenuity of her husband. They both left the bunker, and when Simon was satisfied Lola could find and operate the opening, even in the dark, they went back upstairs to the apartment.

Hanna and Artur had awakened and were waiting anxiously for their parents to return. Simon and Lola soon appeared and tried to reassure their children. The children looked questioningly at their parents. "Why are these bad things happening?" asked Hanna.

"Yes, Hannale, bad things have happened outside, but it's over for now," Simon told Hanna and Artur. He motioned them over to him and hugged them both. Sadly, he wondered if they would live to see the next year, much less adulthood. His close call with the Gestapo had had a sobering effect on him. This was deadly serious, and he began to see the bigger, evil picture spreading like a dark blanket over Lvov.

It was time to have a serious talk with the children. "Hannale, Artur, come here, my children. Papa has something to tell you. My Hannale, there will be no more school for you. Do you understand? It is not safe. The Germans will be coming for us. We must hide; we must survive. We have a place in the basement. I know you do not like to go down there, but it is the best place for us when the time comes. I will tell you when to go. I will show you the place. When I say go, you go. Do not ask questions and do not hesitate." Being three, Artur did not really understand what his father was telling them, but sensed the urgency in his father's voice. Hanna took her brother's hand. Tears ran down her cheeks.

Beginning in early July, Jews were required to wear white-and-blue armbands with the Star of David on them. Failure to do so came with a penalty of death. Only little Artur was not required to wear one. These armbands regularly incited violence from the Ukrainians who felt emboldened to release centuries-old, pent-up anger and hatred against the hapless Jews. The SS watched with amusement, allowing the populous to do their job. A dead Jew is a dead Jew, they thought, regardless of how they got that way.

The Germans wasted no time consolidating their newly captured territory. East Galicia, until just recently part of the Ukrainian SSR, was incorporated into the General Government and became its fifth district, the *Distrikt Galizien*. Lvov, renamed Lemberg, was to be the capital of the district.

The Ukrainians, too, were busy. More organized this time, lists of enemies, mostly those suspected of being Communists or collaborators with the Soviets, were prepared. Simon Ruder's name was on one of the lists.

Simon and his family, along with the rest of the Jews who suddenly found themselves extremely vulnerable under Nazi control, tried to cope the best they could. Major changes were coming, and they knew they would be bad. No one doubted that. Armbands we can take, they thought, but they knew more was coming. This time there was nowhere to run, no more sanctuary.

Three weeks later, on July 25, a second pogrom took place that soon was to be known as the *Petlura Days*, named in honor of the assassinated Ukrainian leader Semyon Petlura. Again, the Ukrainian militia, this time augmented by other Ukrainian militants from outside the city, participated in brutal acts of violence against the Jews. Guided by the prepared lists, and helped by local Ukrainian police, Jews were rounded up and taken to the Jewish cemetery and brutally murdered. Approximately two thousand Jews were murdered in this three-day pogrom.

However, as word of the roundup quickly spread through Lvov/Lemberg, Simon was prepared. "Go!" he said, and his family immediately evacuated to the safety of the bunker in the basement of the tailor shop. The children were very frightened but kept quiet. Lola quietly said prayers. Simon sealed the door to the bunker, and he and his family quietly awaited their fate.

The wait wasn't long. Soon afterward, they heard noises of an angry mob upstairs in the tailor shop. They heard glass shattering and then a crescendo of heavy sewing machines, bolts of cloth, and various fixtures being overturned and hitting the floor. Dust and dirt drifted from the ceiling and onto the occupants of the bunker. They fought the urge to sneeze.

More shouting. The noises intensified as the angry mob erupted into the basement. The family, holding each other's hands, their eyes tightly closed, tried by sheer will to cloak themselves from the mob. They heard more crashing sounds as the mob fanned out across the basement, overturning boxes, spare and broken sewing machines, and parts. The mob slowly quieted down, and one of them, the leader, no doubt, said something Simon could not make out. There were more noises and muffled sounds as the disappointed mob climbed the stairs and made its way back into the upstairs shop.

After what seemed an eternity, Simon managed to find a candle and with nearby matches lit it. The small flame barely illuminated the cramped refuge. The children were shaking but remained silent. Lola sighed. "Do you think it's over?" she whispered to Simon. He shook his head. "No, not yet. I think we should stay here for the time being. They may come back."

Time dragged on in the basement bunker. The air was stale, but it remained tolerably cool. They had water that they used sparingly, and they decided to conserve the food that had been stored in the bunker. Facilities for personal needs were nonexistent, and the bucket Simon had used to distribute the bunker's dug-out dirt was fulfilling the need.

Simon reckoned it had been almost two days since he and his family had entered the bunker. It was mostly quiet upstairs now, with only sporadic gunfire punctuating the quiet. The air in the bunker was becoming unbreathable, and with the added aroma of the waste bucket, it was time to leave. Very carefully, Simon opened the door of the bunker a little at a time until he could see out into the empty basement. Fresh air rushed in, much to the relief of Lola and the children. The ransacked basement was empty. It was quiet upstairs. Simon looked toward his wife and children emerging from the little sanctuary. He put his finger to his lips. "Shh," he simply said. "Wait here."

He climbed the stairs and entered the shop. Just as he expected, the shop was a mess. The glass in the heavy entry door was broken, but remarkably, the large window glass remained intact. Sewing machines were on the floor, along with unrolled bolts of cloth, thread, and needles. Papers were strewn everywhere. He noticed that the racks that two days ago had held suits were now standing empty.

Simon softly climbed the stairs to the upstairs apartment from which they had fled two days earlier. Remarkably, the door was closed and unlocked, just as it had been left when they had fled in near panic. He entered the apartment and found it was undisturbed. Apparently, rounding up Jews was more important than looting. Simon carefully crawled to a window and peeked outside. A few people were out on the street, some Jews among them. It was a sunny day. Perhaps the horror was over after all, he thought.

Simon went back downstairs to the shop and cautiously looked out the front door through the broken glass. It seemed quiet, so he stepped out onto the sidewalk. The bodies were gone, marked only by dark stains where they had fallen. Jews with white-and-blue armbands walked slowly past him, their eyes looking at him without turning their heads. Seeing the armbands, he realized he needed them for himself and his family. Luckily, a youth selling the white-and-blue armbands came walking down the street. Simon hailed the youth. "Five zlotys each," the youth said. Simon ran upstairs to the apartment and found some money. He returned downstairs, paid the youth, and took the three armbands.

He returned to his family still in the basement. "It's safe," he said. "Here, put these on," he said, handing an armband to his wife and daughter. Artur reached for his, but Simon told his young son, "Not for you, my little boychik." Lola helped Simon put on his own armband. The family then made their way up to the apartment.

For the next few days, life returned to a modicum of normalcy. Simon, Lola, and Hanna cleaned up the tailor shop. Soon they had the sewing machines back on the tables and the bolts of cloth back on the shelves. Lola picked up the papers and tried to organize them. The broken glass on the door would have to wait. Things seemed to have quieted down, but there was a palpable undercurrent of hostility in the air. Eyes downcast, no one looked at each other when passing on the street, especially those with armbands. Only the Ukrainians smiled.

The Germans became more apparent around the city and began to exert control. Patrols of the German army drove around in their Kubelwagens. The SS officials were driven around in black staff cars. One such official was SS *Oberscharführer* Oskar Waltke, the Gestapo head of Lvov headquartered at the Loncki Prison. Simon had recently met the officer, his sore ribs a reminder of the encounter. He had no intention of ever meeting the *Oberscharführer* again.

As Simon was sweeping the sidewalk outside his shop after the broken glass in his door had been replaced, he was preoccupied with the dark spot on the sidewalk in front of him. He remembered the elderly woman and wondered idly what had happened to her. Too late, he spotted the SS staff car headed toward him. He turned to run, but it was no use. He knew he would never make it to the basement bunker, and to run upstairs would certainly endanger his family.

"Halt!" shouted one of the SS men. Simon froze. Two of the SS men left the car and walked briskly toward Simon. "Hands in the air," the bigger of the two shouted. Simon did as he was told. He didn't want to be another dark spot on the sidewalk.

"Name!" shouted the big man. "Simon Ruder," answered Simon. "This is my tailor shop." The SS man looked over to one of his colleagues. "Yes, sir, that's him."

"Take him," said the SS man, nodding toward Simon.

Simon was none too gently forced into the staff car by two of the SS men. One pointed a Luger at him while they drove away. Simon knew his luck had run out. He didn't know where they were taking him, perhaps the infamous "Sands" site where hundreds of Jews had been executed. He didn't expect to see tomorrow.

From the second-floor apartment, Lola watched the scene below with horror as the SS took her husband away. She feared she would never see him again.

She broke down and sobbed. It was August 8, 1941, and her fears would prove to be all too prophetic.

Even with the Luger pointed at him, Simon could still see where they were going. He had come this way before, three weeks earlier. They were speeding off toward Loncki Prison.

The black staff car turned into the prison courtyard and stopped in front of a side entrance. Simon was roughly removed from the car and was immediately taken down a long, dark corridor and pushed into a cell. No explanation, no information. He was just locked up. Time went by slowly. The SS guards were brutal, and he was systematically beaten, not enough to kill him but enough to discourage any resistance. Food, if it could be called that, consisted of a thin gruel-like liquid with some indeterminate solids floating in it.

Realizing he might live beyond the moment, Simon started making scratches on the wall with a small stone he had found in an attempt to keep track of the days. The cell walls were thick stone, black with grime, dirt, and dried blood. It was damp and parts of the walls appeared slimy. There were no windows, and the heavy wooden door had a small port through which food was passed. Personal hygiene was not a concern to the SS, and not even a bucket was provided. From his cell, Simon could hear frequent screams, moans, and whimpers. Often he could hear unearthly shrieks, then ominous silence.

Between beatings, Simon thought about Lola and his two children. He was thankful for the time he had to show them the bunker he had built, though, unknown to him, it would serve its purpose only once more. He wondered about his God, the God of Abraham. Simon was a religious Jew and attended synagogue, at which he was an assistant cantor. He had a fine baritone voice and loved to sing. He and his family were practicing Jews and observed the major Jewish holidays like Passover, Yom Kippur and Rosh Hashanah. Mostly, though, Simon wondered why his God had not shown himself for the last couple of years. Cynically, he thought, chosen people indeed. Chosen for what? He wondered about his older brother Izak in Krakow and his younger brother Mendel in nearby Zloczow. Mendel and his wife had a small son, about Artur's age, named Dolek. "Why do we bring children into this world?" he wondered aloud to himself.

Five marks on the wall later, Simon heard the guards approach and unlock the heavy wooden door. It creaked loudly. Bracing for another round of beatings, Simon was surprised when the SS men grabbed him and raised him to his feet. The larger of the two said, "Come with us." *Here it comes*, he thought. *I hope it's quick*. The guards laughed at his obvious fear.

Simon was sure that his name was on a list, probably for his association with Communists, even though he had never joined the party. If that was the case, he knew his life was over and that he must prepare for the worst. He knew the Nazis outright killed Communists by the thousands. As to why he wasn't dead yet, he didn't know.

He was taken to a small room for interrogation and was ordered to stand at attention. He knew SS *Oberscharführer* Oskar Waltke ran the prison. His thoughts went back to several weeks earlier when he had been on a forced burial detail and faced the same SS *Oberscharführer*. He hoped he wouldn't be recognized, though the fact that he had escaped would likely cause embarrassment to the SS. The thought amused him. Waltke was known to be a sadist, often taking pleasure in torturing his victims until they confessed to whatever crime they supposedly committed, often just to stop the pain. He personally shot, knifed, or hanged many prisoners. In his future, an eight-year prison sentence loomed. For now, however, having cleared out and buried the hundreds of corpses left by the NKVD using Jewish workers, Loncki Prison was open for business once again, this time under new management.

Simon instinctively repositioned his tattered shirt to cover the bruises that had resulted from the beating he had taken from Waltke last time they met. He tried to review his situation and gather his thoughts before the inevitable interrogation began. He assumed the Germans knew about his idealist sympathy for the Communist doctrine and that his name was on a list of those to be rounded up. He had also evaded capture in the recent pogrom by hiding with his family in the basement bunker he had constructed, a fact he was hoping to deny them. Maybe they were finishing the roundup, catching anyone missed or not found.

After twenty minutes of standing at attention, SS *Oberscharführer* Waltke entered the room. He motioned to the two SS guards, and they moved off to the back corners of the room. Simon noted the Luger sidearm in Waltke's hand and the riding crop at his side. Waltke laughed. "I see you remember my little friend. I finally recognized you. I thought we killed you, yet here you stand. I must talk to my guards. I am truly embarrassed." The two guards in the back of the room looked at each other.

"However, perhaps this was an omen. I have your files, some information left by our NKVD friends in their hurry to run away. I know you are a Jew and a Communist sympathizer. We have killed thousands of you. Many more will die, here and in special camps we have set up. We are just getting started here, so we have much, how do you say it, catching up to do."

Waltke made a show of scanning Simon's file. It was three pages long, and some parts had been translated from Russian to German. He walked around the small room as he read.

"So the Russian pigs let you keep the tailor shop," Waltke said. "You must be a good tailor."

"Yes, sir, I am."

"Well, can you make uniforms?"

"Yes, sir, I can. I can make suits, coats, pants, hats, whatever you need."

Waltke considered this for a moment and finally said with a sigh, "We find that some Jews have limited value to us, skills that we don't wish to waste. I could just as easily have you shot, and maybe I should for the trouble you have caused me, but we need uniforms for our German and Ukrainian SS soldiers. You are fortunate. You have been selected to work for the Gestapo. You will work here in the prison. You will not be allowed to leave the prison grounds. This is your life now. There is no escape. If you try, you will be shot, make no mistake. You will work until, well, until the end."

For Simon, having a skill that was deemed "important to the war effort" was a blessing in disguise, albeit a well-disguised blessing, the irony of which was not fully understood or appreciated until much later. While time in a Gestapo prison was often short and always brutal, filled with beatings, tortures, prisoner selections, and quick executions of those no longer needed or just for amusement, Simon was learning to adapt to his new environment.

Simon, however, faced a moral dilemma. Serve the Nazis and survive, at least for a time, was one choice. This choice, he knew, assisted the Nazis in the overall war effort and the systematic destruction of his people. He wondered if this work could be considered collaboration with the Nazis. Furthermore, could he live with the fact that he was helping the Nazis was another question that only his conscience could answer. The other choice, he understood equally well, would result in a quick death. He could refuse to do the work, certainly a suicidal choice. Finally, he thought about sabotaging the work. This, he thought, would only result in beatings, torture, and certain execution. *No*, he thought, *I must survive. I would be no good to anyone dead. Someone must tell the world what went on here. Someone must look for Lola and the children after the war.* So Simon decided to cooperate, despite the moral objections churning in his gut.

As an experienced tailor, he knew how to make the uniforms required by the Nazis. A uniform was like a suit to him. Using existing uniforms as patterns, he was able to reproduce them in several sizes according to exact specifications dictated by the SS. These were, after all, Germans with a profound sense or order and appearances. However, Simon's job was made considerably more difficult by the myriad variety of uniforms and constant changes to them. Since the war had started, the traditional black SS uniforms were less evident. Uniforms for the Waffen SS in many variations and uses were being ordered. These included Waffen SS tunics, Waffen SS dress and officers' uniforms, Allgemeine SS (General SS) feldgrau, gray-green service uniforms, Waffen SS Panzer crew uniforms, and many others. Many uniforms were based on existing *Wehrmacht* (German army)-issued uniforms with a multitude of variations in cut, style, piping, and detailing.

Based on his past experience, talent, and compelling personality, Simon was put in charge of several other tailors and was held responsible for meeting quotas and quality standards of the products being made at the prison. Unacceptable work was not tolerated. A crooked seam or loose thread resulted in broken bones, bruises, or worse. Many workers disappeared altogether only to be replaced by other tailors so plentiful in Lvov. Though in charge of this group of tailors, Simon was not immune from the harsh methods of encouragement to improve both the quantity and quality of the uniforms and other items being produced.

Interestingly, Simon noted few, if any, orders for winter uniforms or coats. This, he assumed, was because the Germans would soon decimate the Red Army long before the harsh Russian winter would set in. Both he and the German army high command would be proven wrong.

WESTERN RUSSIA, JULY–AUGUST 1941

Having captured their objective of Lemberg, *Obergefreiter* Leonhard Kiermeier and the First Mountain Division marched eastward farther into Russia. They broke through the Stalin Line, a line of well dug in field fortifications and antitank trenches, and during the two-day battle, they lost some 105 soldiers. The Russians, on the other hand, lost about a thousand soldiers with 286 captured, along with a sizable cache of weapons.

Moving on, the division encountered fierce resistance from the retreating Russians but managed to reach the River Bug at the town of Winniza on July 18. The two bridges across the river were destroyed, ironically one by a German artillery shell that hit a previously set explosive charge. Left to defend a forty-three-kilometer front with insufficient numbers, ten thousand Russians were captured while another thirty thousand Russian soldiers escaped to fight another day.

On August 7, the XXXXIX Gebirgs Armee Korps finally successfully encircled, defeated, and captured about one hundred thousand Russian soldiers near Uman. The First Mountain Division had lost 759 soldiers during the opening two months of Operation *Barbarossa*.

Obergefreiter Kiermeier and the First Mountain Division, still part of Army Group South, continued their march through Russia. Their next objective was the Donez district and then, based on orders from Hitler, the oil fields at Baku on the Caspian Sea.

Kiermeier and several of his fellow soldiers were thankful for a rest. Still exuberant from their recent successes, the men discussed their encounters with the Russians.

One of the men, an *Obergefreiter* like Kiermeier, began. "They are just like the Fuhrer predicted. They are, after all, Slavs, peasants, just like the Poles. They are ill-prepared and ill-equipped. They might as well fight us with pitchforks. They have no leadership. Look how many we captured, hundreds of thousands. Look how they run back into mother Russia." The small group laughed and agreed wholeheartedly with the *Obergefreiter*. "This operation will be over in ten to twelve weeks, as the Fuhrer predicted."

The Russians had other ideas. Though surprised by the early timing of the attack and not prepared, they knew what the Germans, especially Hitler, failed to understand: the vast distances across Russia and the coming winter.

ZLOCZOW, POLAND, JULY 1941

Located some sixty-eight kilometers east of Lvov, the town of Zloczow was preparing for a major change of fortunes. Long rumored and nervously anticipated, the Germans were finally coming. The Russians had been running things since shortly after the onset of the war in late 1939, and while the Jews suffered continued persecution, most had survived. But that would soon change.

The Germans reached Zloczow on July 1, and the Ukrainian population welcomed the Germans as liberators. At the time, the Jewish population was approximately fourteen thousand, swelling considerably from the influx of refugees from western Poland. Tragically, within two days, that population shrank by some thirty-five hundred Jews who were executed in a place called the "Fortress." Things were looking bleak for the area, especially with the Ukrainians running wild with approval and support from the Germans.

Here, as elsewhere in Poland, the Jews suffered grievously under the onslaught of the Ukrainians. Violence against the Jews was a daily occurrence, and most families were affected in some way.

As in most Jewish cities under German occupation, a *Judenrat* was established in Zloczow, headed by Zigmunt Mayblum, a former deputy mayor and community leader. Overall, the effectiveness of these organizations was debatable and depended, in no small measure, on their composition. While some members were honest and believed they could actually help the Jewish population, many were dishonest, corrupt, and interested only in lining their own pockets. In all cases across the occupied territories, the *Judenrats* were there merely to carry out the orders of the SS. They were compelled to supply lists of those Jews for so-called "resettlement," a euphemism for deportation to forced labor camps or extermination camps like the soon-to-be completed camp in nearby Belzec.

In August of that year, the Jews of Zloczow were ordered to pay a ransom of four million rubles. The *Judenrat* was forced to put into place a variety of decrees, such as supplying manpower for forced labor and collecting valuables, furniture, and other household equipment and handing them over to the Germans. They were responsible for enforcing compliance of the curfew and regulations on the movement of Jews in and outside of the town. To ensure that the German orders were carried out, members of the *Judenrat* were taken hostage or executed and replaced with more accommodating members.

For Mendel Ruder, his wife Zofia, nee Merl, and three-year-old son Dolek, life was about to take a dramatic turn. Mendel, a well-respected tailor, had faired reasonably well under the Russians. Although he had lost his shop to the Russian economic system, he had found work as a tailor in a large factory. That work ended when the Germans arrived.

Mendel was a small man, barely five feet tall. He suffered from significant hearing loss, a probable result of being dropped as a small child by his older sister. However, he had his own problems to face in Zloczow. While not considered a well-educated Jew, his skill as a tailor had placed him in contact with some of the German SS officers who used his services to alter or repair uniforms and to make clothes for wives or mistresses. In this capacity, Mendel was able to ingratiate himself with one of the SS officers. Not as friends and certainly not as equals but on human terms.

BELZEC, CENTRAL GOVERNMENT, NOVEMBER 1, 1941

Work had begun on one of three extermination camps located in the Central Government of German-occupied Poland. This camp was located on a former labor camp at Belzec, from which it received its name. For the SS, the location was a good choice because it was within a reasonable distance of the major ghettos, and with the construction of a railway spur to the nearby station, this would facilitate the efficient rail transportation of Jews from the Lvov and Lublin ghettos. Construction of the death camp would take just three months. The gas chambers were airtight wooden structures. Buildings to house the SS and Ukrainian auxiliary personnel were also constructed. SS *Haupsturmfuhrer* Christian Wirth would be named camp commandant in December. Called the "Savage Christian," the sadist SS officer had cut his teeth in 1939 as part of the adult euthanasia program and was now ready to utilize both his skills and experience on a far broader scale.

History would later record the operational status of the camp in February 1942, and within four weeks, seventy-five thousand Jews were murdered. For most of the Jews of Lvov, it would be Belzec where they would soon meet their fate.

LEMBERG/LVOV, NOVEMBER 1941

On November 10, 1941, Lola, Hanna, and Artur were getting ready to leave their apartment above what had been Simon tailor shop on Legionow Street, though the new street signs now bore the names *Opernstrasse* and *Museumstrasse*, though a year later, both sides would be renamed *Adolf Hitler Platz*. They were allowed only what they could carry with them into the newly established ghetto. Lola had just finished retrieving as many of the items hidden away in the bunker Simon had built for them in the basement. Back upstairs in the apartment, she looked around one last time, sad that she had to leave all the furniture, paintings, china, and other items she couldn't transport. She had jewelry, coins, some pieces of gold, and a few precious photographs from happier days stashed in her suitcase. The children carried what they could. Hanna clutched her precious violin case. Two suitcases contained the remnants of their former lives, two suitcases packed with things to carry them into an uncertain future. Lola made sure she and Hanna had the required armbands with the Magen David on them properly secured and visible. Artur was in a stroller.

Out on Legionow Street, the trio encountered other Jews in similar situations. Some had carts full of possessions, though it was doubtful they would be successful in getting these items into the ghetto. The ghetto itself was across town. Lola noticed Jewish policemen in dark-blue uniforms with a

Magen David and the letters JOL (*Jüdischer Ordnungsdienst Lemberg)* on them. They herded the forlorn and confused Jews toward the entrance to the barbed wire–surrounded ghetto. People were already milling around on the other side of the fence. Lola and the children entered the confines of the ghetto under the railroad bridge on Zamarstynowska Street. Lola struggled to maneuver the stroller though the small entryway. After asking scores of people where to go to get housing assignments, they finally found one of the Jewish policemen who pointed them to a building that housed the *Judenrat*. Lola waited in a long line of people asking the same questions and looking for the same answers. After several hours of waiting in line, Lola's turn came up.

"Name?" the official asked.

"Lola Ruder of Legionow Street."

"Husband?" asked the official.

"My husband is Simon. He was taken away by the Gestapo three months ago. I don't know where he is or if he is even alive."

The official shook his head. "If the Gestapo took him, I'm afraid his chances of survival are not good. I'm sorry. Do you have children?"

"Yes, two children. Hanna is nine, and Artur is three."

The official scanned the stack of papers on his desk. "Ah," he said. "I have a small apartment available. There are only three other families sharing it, for now at least. Available space is in short supply. Here is the address. From here it's only a short distance."

Lola took the piece of paper. "Thank you," she said. She left the building holding Hanna's hand and pushing the stroller containing her young son. As she turned the corner, she saw another blue-uniformed Jewish policeman and was about to ask him for directions to the apartment. He looked familiar. He was young, perhaps in his early twenties. Lola thought she recognized him from the neighborhood.

"Mrs. Ruder," the policeman finally said with a look of recognition on his face. "I'm Josef Salzmann. I worked for your husband a few years ago. I was there a year. I was going to be a tailor but decided to be a carpenter instead.

I could never get the hang of sewing. Now I'm a policeman working for the *Judenrat*."

"I remember now," said Lola. "You have certainly grown since then. I used to feed you while you worked with us."

"I remember," he said. "You and Mr. Ruder were very kind to me. How is Simon?"

"I don't know. He was taken away by the Gestapo three months ago. We haven't heard a word since. I have asked around, but people just turn away when I mention the Gestapo. Maybe he is already in the ghetto or on his way."

Josef Salzmann shook his head. With a sad look on his face, he said, "I'm very sorry to hear that. The Gestapo operates out of the Loncki Prison and has imprisoned many Jews, mostly Communists and people they regard as enemies of the Third Reich. I have to tell you that many are tortured, many more are shot, and unfortunately, few, if any, of the prisoners survive. It is a very bad place to be. I'm afraid there is little hope for Mr. Ruder."

Lola shrugged. "I was afraid of that. You are the second person who has told me a similar story. I'm not giving up, though. Someone will know what happened. Simon is a very strong person. He will find a way to survive. I know he will do whatever is necessary."

Fighting back tears, she handed Josef the piece of paper with the address of the apartment. "Do you know where this is?" she asked.

"Yes, of course," he said. "One block down, then turn right. It's two or three buildings from the corner. I think it's on the third floor."

Josef Salzmann came from a middle-class Jewish family who had certain connections in the Jewish community. At twenty-two years of age, he had not yet decided on a career, but had tried tailoring and carpentry without significant success in either. When the *Judenrat* was looking to appoint policemen, Josef thought that was the calling for him. While not a bully, he enjoyed the illusion of power the job represented. The official-looking dark-blue uniform made him feel substantial and provided him a position of respect and power. After all, the *Judenrat* managed the affairs of the ghetto occupants, forlorn and pitiful as they would become, but in his new position, he somehow felt above all that.

Josef Salzmann, like most of his kind and many of the *Judenrat*, failed to understand the insidiousness of the Nazi psychology employed in the ghettos. By giving the ghetto-dwellers the illusion that they had some measure of control over their fate, modest as it was, was viewed as a positive development. Never mind that the *Judenrat* was forced to provide names of Jews to be rounded up and sent to work camps like Janowska located in Lvov or to Belzec extermination camp. Never mind that leaders of the *Judenrat* themselves were hanged or committed suicide when they learned the truth about the power and influence they really had and the fate of those wretched souls whose names they put on the Gestapo lists. For now, Josef Salzmann thanked his lucky stars for his position in a very bad situation. His luck, too, was to be an illusion.

As Lola, Hanna, and little Artur made their way up the stairs to the small third-floor apartment to which they had been directed, they could hear shouting coming from behind many of the doors. Most likely it was people arguing. They could also hear the clanking of what sounded like pots and pans and the moving of furniture—all noises of people trying to adapt to a new, uncertain situation and trying to find, bully, cajole, or otherwise stake out their place in it. In an ironically pitiful way, in the next six months, none of this would matter. The ghetto would be systematically eliminated. The Germans didn't care too much about the method. Starvation was the weapon for them. The daily rations allotted for the Jews in the ghetto amounted to less than 10 percent of what the Germans received. This was below subsistence level and ensured a steady number of starvation-related deaths and a thriving black market to make up for the caloric deficiencies for those who had the means. Of course, the Germans knew all this and made effective use of this diabolic strategy.

Lola soon learned the art of transforming her possessions into food or other essential items. Black marketers, heedless of the threat of death if caught, managed to establish channels to and from the ghetto to procure food for those who could pay. Lola shrewdly made enough off her jewelry and other precious commodities to obtain enough food for herself and her two children. This sustained them through the winter of 1941–1942. Soon, however, the value of her remaining items plummeted, and food was harder to smuggle in. Things were getting much more difficult for the 120,000 or so unfortunate souls living in the Lvov ghetto.

LONCKI PRISON, LEMBERG/LVOV, DECEMBER 1941

As he worked, Simon frequently thought about his family. He hoped they were surviving but was concerned about Lola's ability to cope with what was happening. They had hidden much of her jewelry and other items that could be sold on the black market. He hoped some of his friends could help her turn some of the items into cash or food. He thought of his Hanna. Would she grow up to be the woman fulfilling her bright future, so full of the promise he envisioned for her? Would he ever see her again? Would he see any of his family and friends?

News from the outside was sporadic, often contradicting, and was usually communicated by new inmates, most of whom experienced a short tenure at the prison. The news they brought was not good. Simon learned that on November 8, 1941, the German civilian administration issued orders to establish a ghetto in Lvov into which all Jews were being forced to move before December 15. All Poles and Ukrainians were to move out. The area designated to form the ghetto was Zamarstynów, which, before the war, was one of the poorest and rundown suburbs of Lvov. During this time, German police conducted so-called "selections" on Peltewna Street. Elderly and sick Jews were selected and shot, numbering almost five thousand. This "action" was called *"Action under the bridge."* By December 15, occupants of the ghetto numbered between 110,000 and 120,000 Jews. Simon also learned that in November a

Judenrat had been established to run the Jewish affairs in the ghetto. In reality, they had little power and served as the middlemen between the inhabitants of the ghetto and the SS masters. Its first chairman was the lawyer Josef Parnes, who was later executed by the Gestapo in November 1941 for his refusal to turn over Jews for forced labor. His successor was Henryk Landesberg.

New inmates told of five hundred Jewish men being captured on October 2 for forced labor for the for the German Armament Works (Deutsche Ausrüstungswerke-DAW Lemberg) constructing a work camp on Janowska Street. This camp was later to achieve its share of notoriety.

Not much news about the war trickled in other than the assumption that it was still raging further east. Rumors that Moscow had been captured had turned out to be false, but it must be winter now, Simon thought, and since they had not been making winter uniforms, the group of Jews assumed that the Germans had been victorious, and Simon wondered how the outcome might affect his future. Certainly not in a positive way, he mused apprehensively.

What Simon didn't know, but what would have undoubtedly amused him, was that the mighty *Wehrmacht* had stalled within kilometers of Moscow and had been driven back by the Red Army on what was to be the beginning of an inexorable retreat westward that would have a profound impact on both the future of the Third Reich as well as his own. Without the winter-capable equipment, and especially clothing, the *Wehrmacht* was totally unprepared for the onslaught of the brutal winter. Napoleon and his army had been victims one hundred years earlier, a lesson the Germans were about to learn. In many cases, the Germans were reduced to raiding farmhouses to obtain white bedsheets to use as camouflage in the snow. Soldiers wore what they could scrounge up to try to stay warm in frigid, well-below-zero temperatures, even resorting to wearing women's fur coats. Apparently, even in the *Wehrmacht*, style and protocol were not issues when survival was at stake.

1942

Lola Ruder, her two children, and her friends the Rosenthals, the Lanskys, and the Kaplans were desperately trying to survive in the Lvov ghetto. She had no idea if Simon still lived. Like tens of thousands of other Jews in Lvov and Central Europe, she and her friends wondered how the end game would play out for the Jews. So did the Nazis. On January 20, 1942, in a suburb of Berlin, the so-called Wannsee Conference was held to determine the implementation of what was called "*The final solution to the Jewish question*." Fifteen high-ranking Nazi Party and German government officials attended the conference, not to debate the objective, which had already been agreed to at a higher level, but rather to make plans and forge agreements with other required parties to implement the final solution. The agreements and plans created during this conference would seal the fate of millions of Jews as the plans for their systematic destruction were soon put into action. Interestingly, of the fifteen participants of this conference, eight of them held doctorate degrees.

Between March 16 and April 1, 1942, a series of dramatic events unfolded throughout the Lvov ghetto. Called *Aktion Reinhard*, the Germans deported around fifteen thousand Jews from the ghetto to the nearby Belzec extermination camp. Always with a profound sense of efficiency, the Germans rounded up those who, to them at least, represented the least productive mouths to feed, those whose further existence was of no value to the Third Reich. Clearly, with this in mind, the Germans had previously registered those Jews who were working on their behalf. These mouths provided some level of usefulness and, therefore, would be spared for now. These lucky souls would be allowed to continue to live in the abomination that was the Lvov ghetto. Those not so designated, in this case the elderly, the religious, and women with children, were ordered to assemble in the courtyard of the Sobieski School. A selection process would take place where a very few might be chosen for work at the Janowska camp, which would be, at best, a short reprieve. The rest would be taken to Kleparow railway station, near the Janowska camp, where the deportation trains, called *Sonderzüge* (special trains) departed for Belzec, a short, terror-filled, forty-six-mile train ride into oblivion.

On March 17, Lola and her two children were standing at the Kleparow railway station with hundreds of other Jews waiting for trains that would take them to what they were told were resettlement camps, places farther east where the Jews could find a new beginning.

Several JOL policemen in their impressive dark-blue uniforms were on the train platform. "Leave your suitcases and belongings over there," shouted Josef Salzmann, pointing to an open area to the left of the crowd. "They will be sent to you shortly, where you can retrieve them later." He sounded so sure of himself, so believable. Well, he was, after all, a Jew, the crowd thought. He must certainly be here to help them, they thought.

Poised in the background, watching the events unfolding, were a number of SS soldiers with guns. These were not Jews, nor were they there to help them.

The Jews obeyed and reluctantly made a neat pile of their belongings exactly where Josef Salzmann, the helpful Jewish policeman, had indicated. Some took extra precautions to mark their particular suitcases or boxes to make sure they could be properly identified and retrieved when they reached their final destination.

The group was led to the waiting train. They began to notice that the train consisted of a locomotive and a long string of what appeared to be cattle cars. The crowd began to chatter among themselves, and a rising sense of alarm washed over them. The alarm quickly escalated into near panic as the policemen herded them into the wooden cars, now not even fit for the animals they once carried.

Lola, perhaps realizing what the ultimate fate would be for herself and her two children, made an instinctive, if futile, decision. "Run!" she whispered urgently, and grabbing Hanna and Artur, she broke free of the crowd and made a frantic dash for the nearby woods. Josef Salzmann shouted for her to come back. "Stop! Come back. No one will hurt you." Salzmann began to chase them, but when he saw the SS men moving toward the fleeing mother and children, he stopped abruptly and retreated back toward the train. The two SS men laughed. They did not seem to want to catch the Jews, nor did they try. A short burst of machine gun fire brought a quick end to the escape. Little Artur, stunned but still alive, was crying as the SS men stood over the bodies of his mother and sister. He started to crawl over to his dying mother. He looked at her, then turned his gaze to the Germans, a look of "Why?" on his innocent three-year-old face. One of the men then took out his Luger handgun and finished the job. "Little Jews grow to become big Jews," he said, looking at his partner. Replacing the Luger in its holster, the SS man and his accomplice walked away from the scene and were heard laughing at some joke only they understood. A Jewish mother and her two children making a heroic escape attempt now lay dead just short of the woods near the railroad station in the city of Lvov, now called Lemberg. In an ironic sense, Lola and her two children cheated the Nazi hangmen. They avoided the horrors of the cattle cars and gas chambers.

The crowd quieted down. Many were already in the cattle cars and did not witness, but heard, the event. Others saw what had happened and passed the word. Now they all knew there were no resettlement camps. The Jewish policemen finished the loading process and locked the doors. With seventy to eighty Jews crammed into a car, the train whistle blew, starting slowly to the left, toward the extermination camp at Belzec.

Josef Salzmann walked away from the Kleparow railway station as a tear started to make a crooked track down his left cheek. He quickly wiped it away so no one would notice.

On the train platform, several other Jews scurried out of the station to the mound of suitcases, boxes, and other possessions of people who would no longer need them. People who were now struggling for air as the train slowly chugged its way to their personal encounter with the Final Solution. People who would soon wish they were lying near the trees with Lola, Hanna, and Artur.

The suitcases and boxes were emptied and the contents sorted into piles. Piles of shoes, clothes, valuables, household items, all plunder stolen from innocent victims of a brutal regime hell-bent on the total annihilation of a people. This process was to be repeated many times at many railroad stations throughout Germany and much of Central Europe. At this particular station, a Jewish worker picked up a violin case with the name of Hanna Ruder neatly inscribed on it. He opened the case and found a secondhand violin and bow inside. He looked around to make sure no one was watching. He took out the bow and put the small instrument to his chin and as if testing it and played a short piece of music he knew from better times. He sighed as he reverently put down the violin and replaced it and the bow in the case and gently placed the case on the pile of other instruments from the first, but certainly not the last, batch of Jews from Lvov to be deported to the death camp called Belzec. The initial phase of what was called *Aktion Reinhard* had begun.

THE LEMBERG/LVOV GHETTO, JUNE 1942

Jakob Lansky, Julius Kaplan, and members of their families were living in a three-room apartment somewhere in the Lvov ghetto in late June of 1942. Sharing the small space was another family of four, the Goldblatts. Izak Goldblatt, husband and former bookseller, had been fortunate to find a place to live with his friend Jakob. Izak's wife, Rifka, and children, Bela and Samuel, rounded out this family. In all, only eight people lived in this small apartment. After six months in the ghetto, living conditions were rapidly deteriorating. Food was getting scarce and harder to find. Water was being rationed, electricity was sporadic at best, and the weather was hot. Sanitation was a thing of the past. Illnesses, especially typhus, ran rampant. Tempers flared, often over the most insignificant things. Life in the small apartment reflected a microcosm of the entire ghetto. The black market was still operating, but gold, diamonds, and other precious stones brought less and less and, therefore, procured less food. Starvation increased in the streets. Small children and the old alike begged for food on the streets, and many died right there on the street where they sat all day. Desensitized passers-by merely stepped over them.

"I never thought it would be this bad," said Kaplan. "I can't believe the Germans are doing this to us."

Lansky, looking more and more emaciated, replied, "You told us, Julius. You told us it would not be good for us. You were right."

"Yes, but why is it being allowed to happen? Where are the Americans? Where are the English? How could they stand by and not help us? What about the pope?"

"I don't know," said Lansky. "Maybe they just don't know, or maybe they are busy fighting the Germans. Who knows why. In any case, when the Allies eventually win, I'm afraid it will be too late for most of us. Look what happened to Lola Ruder and the children, God bless them. Simon, he's probably dead too. Hundreds more are dying every day. This can't go on. Soon we will all be gone."

Rifka Goldblatt, a small, once attractive woman, with dark curly hair and brown eyes, spoke up. "The question is, how do we survive? We have a little food left, but it won't last long. Not for the ten of us. Where do we get more food? Bela is getting weak, and Samuel is sick."

Lansky was clearly frustrated. "We are all getting weaker. The German dogs mean to starve us. What do you want us to do? Do you have anything of value left to sell? I don't. Why don't we all just go out and get shot. That will solve the problem."

Izak Goldblatt, defending his wife, said, "Rifka is right. We need more food. We are all in this together. I say we pool whatever resources we have left and get what food we can. We can survive a little longer. Maybe long enough. Julius, let's take half of what we have left and see our contact. We should be able to get more potatoes, some bread, maybe a salami, or who knows what else is out there today."

Julius agreed. Later the next morning the pair gathered some of the remaining valuables. At first, everyone was trying to save the best pieces for after the war. As the war dragged on and food was in shorter supply, however, thoughts of hoarding those valuables began to evaporate as it had become obvious that a thing worth a fortune in 1940, at present, could only buy another week of life. It was not hard to see that if something didn't change soon, the end was fast approaching. There were just too many mouths to feed, not enough currency, real or in trade, to sustain the ghetto population. The *Judenrat* was powerless to do anything, and in the end, even to save their own lives.

Julius Kaplan and Izak Goldblatt left the small apartment with several diamond earrings secured in small bags hidden inside their pants and made their way across the ghetto to the residence of their black market contact, Rubin Gelman. Gelman was a successful middleman in the black market with contacts outside the ghetto too willing to exchange Jewish treasure for food. Though illegal and punishable by death, enough money could be made by conducting these transactions that many people willingly accepted the risk. Poles and Ukrainians alike, while hating the Jews, were still more than willing to take the Jews' valuables in exchange for some potatoes, bread, and meat. They especially liked to trade for pork because of the Jewish taboo against the meat of the pig. Another insult heaped upon the Jews.

Kaplan and Goldblatt never made it to Gelman's residence however. In large numbers, the SS stormed through the ghetto on the afternoon of June 24 and 25 and rounded up and captured unwary Jews at random.

"Run!" shouted Kaplan as the SS fanned out to capture them. But it was too late. Goldblatt had already been captured, and several SS soldiers were rounding up Kaplan and several others unlucky enough to be in the wrong place at this pivotal moment. The group of Jews grew as the SS captured more and more Jewish men. The group soon swelled to two thousand or so and was herded to the Kleparow railway station near the recently completed Janowska forced labor camp. The SS group leader called each captured Jew forward and made a cursory inspection. He asked each prisoner his name, age, and occupation. He then motioned the unfortunate soul to the right or left. As the SS man continued through the ranks, the group on the right grew larger as very few Jews were sent to the left. It was Julius Kaplan's turn. After the name and age questions were answered, the SS man shouted, "Occupation?"

"Pharmacist," answered a nervous and frightened Kaplan. The German looked at Kaplan and nodded. "Go to the right," he said. Not knowing whether this was good or bad, Kaplan followed the directions and joined the much smaller group of confused Jews who were trying not to look over to the much larger group to their left.

Soon, Goldblatt's turn came. Again, after the formality of name and age, the occupation question was asked. Izak Goldblatt did not achieve success in business by being a fool. He had been watching the proceedings very intently and realized that answering the question incorrectly would certainly not serve him well. A bookseller would be of little value to the Nazis, especially since they burned many of the books he once sold. Thinking quickly, he remembered the experience he had gained as a carpenter. Though he didn't enjoy, nor was he particularly adept at, the trade, he knew how to measure, saw, and nail pieces of wood together. This, he thought, could be useful. Besides, he had nothing else.

"Carpenter, sir," he answered. The SS man looked skeptical. "Let me see your hands!" he ordered. Goldblatt stuck out his hands, palms up, for the man to examine. The SS man yelled something over to another SS guard watching over the small group of Jews assembled on the left.

The guard put his hand behind his ear and shook his head as if he didn't hear. "Tischler?" yelled the SS leader, louder this time.

The SS guard nodded his head. "Go to the right, *tischler*," barked the SS group leader. Goldblatt, like Kaplan, was unsure what the two lines meant, but at least he was with his friend, someone he knew. Soon, however, they understood exactly what the two lines meant. Goldblatt, Kaplan, and 118 other just-rounded-up Jews standing in a group at the end of the line to the left were taken across the railroad tracks and marched into the Janowska forced labor camp. The larger group of about 1,882 Jews from the right line was marched behind the camp to an infamous place called the "Sands," an area of sandy hills in Piaski, and were summarily executed. While the dead victims were never aware of it, Goldblatt, Kaplan, and the 118 other Jews would learn they had been unwilling participants in what history would remember as the "Great Roundup" (Großrazzia).

JANOWSKA LABOR CAMP, LVOV/LEMBERG, POLAND, JUNE 1942

Kaplan, the pharmacist, and Izak Goldblatt, a bookseller recently turned carpenter, both captured in the Lvov Jewish ghetto as part of an *Aktion* in late June 1942, were being introduced into the forced labor camp (*Juden-Zwangsarbeitslager*) located at the north end of the town. The Janowska labor camp had been established in September 1941 at 134 Janowska Street and provided slave labor to support the *Deutsche Ausrüstungwerke* (DAW—German Armament Works), a division of the SS located within the boundaries of the Janowska labor camp. The entire camp complex was enclosed by a barbed-wire fence, with searchlights and watchtowers every fifty meters. Armed SS and Ukrainian guards patrolled the area. Some Russian POWs were also used as guards, having volunteered for the duty.

The overall camp was comprised of three distinct sections. The first section included various workshops, garages, offices, and separate living quarters for the camp staff, SS, SD, and the Ukrainian guards. The villa of the camp commandant was situated in the center of this section.

Another section of the camp consisted of the DAW factories where most of the inmates toiled for their SS masters. Each section was separated from the next by a barbed-wire fence.

The last section was the camp proper, comprised of several barracks, each housing two thousand inmates, mostly Jewish forced laborers.

After entering the camp, Kaplan and Goldblatt were searched and relieved of the diamond earrings both had hidden in their pants. They had planned to exchange these for food on the black market in the ghetto when they and almost two thousand other unfortunate Jews had been rounded up by the SS. Most of those rounded up were now dead, murdered behind the camp in an area called the "Sands." As part of their work assignment, Kaplan and Goldblatt would soon be reunited with those poor souls.

Kaplan and Goldblatt were assigned to the same labor brigade (*Sonderkommandos*). These brigades normally consisted of twenty to thirty workers who were constantly watched and harassed by the guards. The Ukrainians were the most brutal. Shortly after their brigade assignment, both men were severely beaten by the guards, a kind of special welcome to let them know what to expect. The pair quickly found that the conditions in the barracks were appalling. They were assigned sleeping quarters consisting of basic racks of shelves made of wooden planks with a thin layer of dirty, often moldy, straw upon which to sleep. Some prisoners slept on the ground. Too late for a work assignment, they both staggered to their beds and managed to drift off into a fitful, unconscious sleep.

Sanitation was abysmal, with many inmates disease ridden by the frequent epidemics that spread through the camp. Many prisoners died of starvation. Food, if it could be called that, was well below the starvation level and consisted of a black coffee substitute (*Ersatzkaffee*) in the morning. Rounding out the daily menu was a midday meal of a watery soup, with unpeeled potatoes and a piece of bread in the evening.

The conditions in the camp were horrific, not even meeting minimum human standards of survival needs or dignity. The SS and Ukrainian overseers were among the most sadistic, brutal, and inhumane that Julius Kaplan, Izak Goldblatt, and the other Jewish inmates were to face during the entire Holocaust era. While conditions in the ghetto had been terrible and were getting worse, no one had ever seen anything approaching the conditions in which they now found themselves.

The next morning, the prisoners assembled for the routine roll call. Kaplan and Goldblatt could barely get out of their sleeping racks. Some of the other inmates helped them up and managed to get them outside. The men could barely stand after the beating they had endured the day before.

"Quickly, stand at attention," one of the prisoners whispered urgently to the two new arrivals. In spite of the pain and with great effort, they managed to do so. An SS officer came around to personally inspect the brigade. The officer made a show of walking around the assembled group of thirty prisoners. He examined each one, but occasionally he spent a little more time examining certain individuals. He looked at one prisoner in particular, a short man of about fifty years old, who, at least to the officer, appeared a bit too inattentive. The SS officer took out his Luger handgun and calmly shot the man in the head. Shocked and in spite of his pain, Julius Kaplan winced. The SS officer instantly noticed and was quickly at Kaplan's side. With the Luger still in his hand, the officer raised it to Kaplan's head. Kaplan closed his eyes, waiting for the bullet he probably wouldn't hear. He didn't.

The SS officer laughed as he lowered the gun. "You are new here. Let that be a lesson, Jewish scum."

Before being assigned the work for the day, the brigade was given their morning ration of black coffee substitute. Both new inmates found this particularly ironic because of all the fine coffee houses they had frequented and for which Lvov was so well known.

The brigade was assigned to bury the Jewish dead, both those in the camp and those Jews executed in the sand hills behind the camp—the same hills that had just recently witnessed the execution of most of the two thousand Jews rounded up in the ghetto with along with Kaplan and Goldblatt on June 25. Adding insult to injury, the brigade had to collect and sort the clothing and any valuables that belonged to the dead.

The group of twenty-nine prisoners was taken to the "Sands" and received shovels with which to conduct their gruesome task. Many of the corpses were bloated, and most showed signs of rigor mortis. In spite of their deteriorating condition, Kaplan and Goldblatt both thought they recognized some of the bodies belonging to the Jews rounded up with them a few days ago. Why Kaplan and Goldblatt weren't among them, they didn't know, but doubted, that what they were going through at the camp was a much better fate.

Twelve hours later, working in the hot sun, the task was completed. The bodies were now soft mounds of sand, and a pile of clothing, shoes, and some valuables lay nearby. Here and there, though, a hand or foot stuck up out of the sand. Sometimes the sand moved grotesquely. The guards didn't notice or didn't care. Task completed, the group was then made to return to the camp at a brisk run.

"Keep running, don't stop," whispered someone in the group. Kaplan and Goldblatt, still weak from their beatings and fatigued from the strenuous twelve-hour workday, struggled to keep up with the group. They soon understood the warning. Several SS officers were waiting for them, watching like lions on the African plains, as if looking for signs of weakness in a herd of zebras, except in this case, the only stripes were on the uniforms of the panting Jews. One officer shouted something, pointing at a Jew having difficulty keeping up. The straggler was very thin, obviously malnourished. He appeared to be in his sixties, but it was hard to tell. He could just as easily have been in his thirties. Another SS officer and several guards intercepted the man before he made it back to the barracks. Probably too weak, the man didn't resist and let himself be led away. The guards took him to a space between two rows of barbed-wire fences and struck him in the head. With a groan, he collapsed to the ground. His arms and legs moved around for a while, and he tried to sit up. After a few minutes, he slumped over and was still.

The group, less yet another member, survived another roll call and inspection and went to their barracks for the night. Kaplan and Goldblatt began to slowly recover from their ordeal. They had not yet been weakened by the daily deprivation and abuse that had taken such a harsh toll on most of the others in the barracks.

Looking at his friend Kaplan, a tired Goldblatt said, "I told them I was a carpenter, not an undertaker." Kaplan tried to laugh but found it was too much effort. He was looking forward to his two hundred grams of bread. With his background as a pharmacist, he knew that the caloric intake his captors were providing would not sustain them very long. They could last maybe a month, but malnutrition and disease would invariably set in, then a slow, painful spiral into starvation.

After finishing with the evening meal of bread, the group began to settle down for the night. Kaplan thanked the group for the help getting them out of the sleeping racks that morning. He wasn't sure he could identify which ones helped or which ones whispered warnings to them.

Then one of the other prisoners spoke up. "Welcome to hell," he said. He was a tall man who looked emaciated but was still able to do work. "I am Felix Mendelson. I've been here for over a year. I helped build this place last year. I was a carpenter in Lvov when I was captured and brought here. I have been put to work doing many tasks. I have survived because I work hard, stand at attention, and follow orders. If you want to survive, you must do the same. They are watching you all the time. They make sport of killing us, the more brutal, the better for them. They try to outdo each other. They strangle our women, they shoot our children. We are locked in a large cage with these Nazi animals, barbarians, savages. May God strike them dead. Poor Edelstein, they left him outside between the fences. He's probably dead already. It's probably best for him. He couldn't go on. He didn't want to. Death has many faces here. He went quietly. So tell me, what's your story?"

Kaplan went first. "I'm a pharmacist from Lvov. I owned a pharmacy before the war. Then, in 1939, the Russians took it over, but I could still work there. When the Germans came in June 1941, I was thrown out, and in November, I was forced into the ghetto with my wife and child. My friend Izak Goldblatt and I were looking to buy some food when we were captured by the SS a few days ago. We were with the unfortunate Jews we buried in the Sands today. Maybe a little over a hundred of us survived. I haven't seen any of the other survivors yet."

"They kept you alive because they needed a pharmacist. You will probably be assigned to the infirmary. Not much of one, because they don't care if you live or die. Who is your friend?"

Goldblatt, lying on his shelf, had regained enough strength to prop up on one elbow. He introduced himself and said, "I'm also a carpenter from Lvov." Kaplan looked at his friend but said nothing. Mendelson made a quick assessment of Goldblatt. "I was captured with Kaplan, and I was spared too," Izak continued. "Although I can't say I'm happy about it. Who are these people?"

"The SS bastard who identified Edelstein, that's Gustav Wilhaus, the Janowska camp commander as of last month. He is a bad one. His predecessor was Fritz Gebauer, who we think now runs the DAW camp, was just as bad. They have killed hundreds, if not thousands, of Jews in the most inhumane and brutal ways. If you look at them wrong, if you don't pay attention, if you commit the slightest infraction, or if they are in a foul mood, they will kill you. Just like that. He has an assistant named Franz Warzok, and the two bastards will walk through a group of Jews and arbitrarily kill anyone they want. I have seen them hang unfortunate Jews upside down until they die. I have seen or heard that they have killed Jews by flogging, choking, hanging, crucifying, and cutting them to pieces with knives or axes. And Edelstein out there, he is not the first one to be put there to die a slow death."

Kaplan and Goldblatt looked stunned. They could not believe what they were hearing. Could such brutality actually walk the earth?

They looked at Mendelson, who continued. "You want more? On the first day of Purim, last March, six Jews were forced to spend the night outside the barracks because they looked sick and, therefore, should not be allowed to infect the others. The temperature was below freezing. We heard all six were found frozen to death the next morning. On the same day, Gebauer ordered a barrel of water to be prepared and picked out eight Jewish laborers from Janowska. They were forced to undress and were then placed in the barrel where they remained all night. These men too, were frozen to death."

"What can we do?" asked Kaplan. "How can this be allowed to go on?"

"There is nothing we can do now. These sick SS bastards do anything they want. Gebauer and Wilhaus have used Jewish laborers for target practice. Prisoners just walking through the camp. Gebauer, especially, was known for his ability to strangle people, and he would often select a Jew and strangle him with his bare hands. Then these same assholes would shoot sick Jews for fun. Quite a bunch we have here."

The next morning the barracks was short another prisoner who was found hanging from the rafters. It was just another face of death at the infamous Janowska labor camp.

LONCKI PRISON, LEMBERG/LVOV, JULY 1942

While conditions at Loncki Prison were harsh, if you did your job well and were classified as "vital to the war effort," you had a chance to survive. A slim chance, to be sure, because many prisoners were worked to death, especially those assigned to hard labor. If you were a prisoner being interrogated, your chances were drastically reduced. Most did not survive their interrogations. Fortunately, Simon successfully made the transition from being an interrogated prisoner, suspected of being a Communist, to a "vital to the war effort" prisoner, partially by luck and in no small part due to his quick wit and fluency in German. As long as quotas were being met, life in the prison moved forward in an almost predictable pattern. The myriad of uniforms required by the *Wehrmacht* and SS kept Simon and his group of tailors busy, especially lately, with an influx of orders for winter uniforms, coats, and hats.

New arrivals were often brought to Loncki Prison. Mainly concerned with real or imagined threats to the occupation of Poland, the Gestapo systematically rooted out Communists, Zionists, or anyone suspected of agitation. Few survived the intense interrogations, and no one left alive. One day, two new arrivals, nineteen-year-old William Weiss and his thirty-nine-year-old father David, were assigned to the group of tailors. Simon did not know why they were in the prison but accepted them into the group. Help with producing the SS and some *Wehrmacht* uniforms was always in demand. Unknown to Simon, the younger Weiss would play an important role in his future.

Besides his skills as a tailor and carpenter, Simon Ruder had an additional skill that most certainly made a difference in his ability to survive the Gestapo assault on the Jews. Most Jews living in Lvov spoke Polish and/or Yiddish, and a small percentage even spoke Ukrainian. However, only about 17 percent of the Jews spoke German, and Simon was among them. The Gestapo process of dehumanizing their victims was easier when communication proved problematic. Simon's ability to communicate with his captors in their native tongue gave him an edge, and one that he was able to exploit.

One day, SS *Oberscharführer* Oskar Waltke himself entered the rooms where Simon and his tailors were working. The group of tailors immediately came to attention. Flanked by his ubiquitous bodyguards, Waltke motioned to one of the guards, who called Simon over to him. The group of tailors quickly turned to their work as though their lives depended on it, and, of course, they were right.

SS *Oberschutze* Johann Lichtner, the guard, said "You, Jew. You have another job to do. The commandant and his wife are attending an important Gestapo affair. His wife wants a new dress. I am ordering you to make one for her. I don't care what it takes."

Simon was surprised but showed no sign of it. "Of course. Anything for the *Oberscharführer* and his lovely wife." Simon thought for a moment. "I will need material for the dress and a sewing dummy. One that is similar to the lady that I can use as a guide."

"Very good," said the SS man. "You have one week. Get what you need—cloth, thread. Oh, and the dummy, go find an appropriate Jewess if you must. You know what Frau Waltke looks like. Now go!"

"Scheiße!" Simon muttered to himself. His already complicated life was suddenly getting even more so. He thought about his situation and realized the ironic humor in it. After all, he was a Jewish prisoner in a Gestapo prison manufacturing uniforms for an international war, and now he was being forced to make a dress for a high-level Gestapo officer's wife so she could to attend a party. No one would ever believe this, he thought. He wondered where he would get material. Even more difficult, he wondered how he was going to get a live sewing dummy. He knew that, of the hundreds of prisoners currently in Loncki Prison, few were female, and none fit the description of Frau Waltke.

An idea began to form in Simon's mind. He might be able to exploit the situation to his own benefit. If he could obtain a pass to leave the prison, he could go to the ghetto and find a suitable Jewess to use as a pattern and maybe material with which to fashion the dress. The material could be a problem in the ghetto, so he would have to search outside the ghetto in the city proper. He remembered the inventory of cloth at his tailor shop but had no idea if it even still stood. He could also try to find Lola and the children. Perhaps too, he thought, he could try to escape.

Over time, Simon had come to be somewhat friendly with two of the SS guards. SS *Oberschutze* Johann Lichtner was a recruit from the Frankfort area, and while maintaining the SS facade of ruthlessness and brutality, he was the contact point for Simon to the SS staff, and as such, the two men had grown to tolerate each other. Reinhart Stossel, the other SS guard was a bit less friendly. Eventually, though, the senseless beatings diminished, and because communication was in German, a sort of unofficial truce between captured and captors had developed.

The next morning the two SS guards entered the room where the prisoners were busy making uniforms. They approached Simon at his sewing machine. "How is the dress coming?" asked SS *Oberschutze* Lichtner, a smile unsuccessfully attempting not to show on his face. "You do not have much time left."

"I have a design in mind, but I need some material to actually make the dress. I wouldn't want to disappoint Frau Waltke with just any fabric. I have looked around my sewing room and cloth storage closet. I'm afraid there is no suitable fabric available anywhere in the prison. Forgive me, but Feldgrau, gray-green material would not make an impressive garment, especially for a woman like Frau Waltke. I'm sure there is more fashionable fabric available outside the prison, maybe in the ghetto or in Lemberg." Simon made sure to use the German name for Lvov. "Maybe you could go out and find something suitable for this dress." The two guards looked at each other. "We'll be back," Litchner said. The pair left in a hurry. Simon smiled knowingly to himself.

About a half hour later, the two guards returned to the sewing room. "Simon, you are ordered to obtain suitable fabric for the dress you are making for Frau Waltke. Here is a pass signed by the *Oberscharführer* Oskar Waltke. It will allow you to enter and leave the ghetto and enter Lemberg. A guard will go with you to make sure you come back. You have eight hours, no more. Do you understand?"

"Yes, *Oberschutze* Lichtner. I understand. When do we leave?"

"You leave tomorrow morning. You must be back by five p.m. Do not be late. If you are late or don't come back, we will kill ten Jews and then find you and kill you. Be absolutely sure of that."

Because Simon had been incarcerated in Loncki Prison since August 1941, he had only heard about the ghetto and the conditions inside from inmates new to the prison. He had not actually seen the ghetto, and thus, he had no idea what had happened to his wife Lola, his two children or his friends.

Now, a year later, on a morning in August of 1942, Simon and a Ukrainian SS guard, whose name he refused to even try to pronounce, left the main gate of Loncki Prison. The ghetto was several kilometers to the northeast of the prison, so a small jeep, a Kubelwagen, was provided to make the short trip. No fancy SS staff car for this trip. The Ukrainian drove the vehicle across Lemberg to the entrance to the ghetto on Zamarstynowska Street. As they approached the ghetto, Simon was shocked at what he saw. The streets were full of people milling about. Beggars were everywhere, old people and young children alike. The air was filled with the stench of garbage, sewage, and too many people in too small a space. People scattered at the sight of the Ukrainian's SS uniform.

"Maybe I should go in myself," Simon said in Polish to the Ukrainian. The guard looked around at the crowded ghetto. He looked wary and unsure.

Reading the guard's mind, Simon said, "Where could I go? I cannot escape. The ghetto is like a prison. If I don't come out, they will kill ten Jews in retaliation. They will eventually find me and kill me. So let me go in, look around for what I'm trying to find, and come back. You have nothing to fear."

The guard had doubts, but after looking at the throngs in the ghetto, he thought Simon's idea made sense. Besides, his orders were to make sure Simon came back, not to follow him wherever he went.

Simon showed his pass and entered the ghetto. He asked for directions to the *Judenrat*, the Jewish organization that was in charge of running the ghetto affairs. He wanted to find out where his wife and children were. At first, no one would give him directions. They had seen him with the SS guard and instinctively distrusted him, especially since they didn't know him.

Suddenly, someone shouted, "Oh my God! Simon, Simon Ruder. I thought you were dead."

Simon turned around and watched as a dark-blue uniformed policeman with a JOL patch and Magen David star sewn on it came running toward him. The young policeman shook Simon's hand and slapped him on the back.

"It's so good to see you, Simon. We had no idea what happened to you. Did you escape the Gestapo prison? What are you doing here?"

Simon looked at the man. He finally recognized the young policeman as Josef Salzmann, a one-time apprentice who, he recalled, had no talent for sewing.

Simon showed Salzmann the pass and explained what he was looking for. First, however, Simon was eager to find Lola and the children. "Do you know where my wife and children are?" he asked the policeman. The look of pain on Salzmann's face told him everything he knew was coming. He prepared himself for the worst.

"Mr. Ruder, ah Simon," began the policeman. "I am so sorry to have to tell you that on March 17, a roundup of Jews from the ghetto took place. They took mostly the elderly, the religious people, and the women with children. Your wife and children were among those captured and taken to the courtyard of the Sobieski School and then to the Kleparow railway station, near the Janowska camp. From there the deportation trains departed for the Belzec camp. We all now know what fate awaited them there. While waiting in line to be crammed in the cattle cars, Lola, probably realizing this fate, chose to flee into the woods. The SS guards murdered them as they ran. I was there, but there was nothing I could do. I tried to call her back, but it was too late. Lola and your children are dead, Mr. Ruder, murdered by the SS."

Simon was deeply shaken by the news. He found a place to sit and wept in a state of shock and despair. The rage he felt was profound. Rage against the Nazis and the brutality they had unleashed against his people. Little Hanna was dead. Artur, his three-year-old son, so happy and always giggling, was dead. Lola, the woman he married in an arrangement brokered by their families, a woman he had grown to love, was dead. *Why, Lord, why?* he thought. *Where are you? We have done nothing to deserve this! I have done nothing to deserve this! My family certainly has done nothing to deserve what happened to them!*

Simon felt alone and frustrated. His rage slowly subsided and was replaced by a feeling of profound sorrow. He wondered if life was even worth living. *Why should I go back to help these heartless bastards?*

Slowly, Simon regained his composure. He needed to think. He knew what would happen if he failed to return to the prison. He had less than six hours left on the outside. He decided to go to the *Judenrat* for information and advice.

Salzmann had walked away from Simon to give him some privacy. Soon, though, he returned.

"I understand there is a *Judenrat* running things here. Where is their office?" asked Simon. "I must see them before I go back."

"I'll take you there," said Salzmann. "Follow me. It's on the corner of Łokietka Street and Hermana Street."

It was short walk through the crowded, dirty, and noisy ghetto. Simon was stunned by what he saw. Beggars were everywhere, even small children. The pair had to step over some bodies, a few with flies crawling all over them. Simon was searching the faces of the people he passed. Most people were gaunt caricatures of what they must have been six months ago, and he doubted he would even be able to recognize his friends.

The pair reached the building that housed the *Judenrat* offices. The policeman said something to the woman at the desk. She left and returned a short time later. "This way," she said and led them to an upstairs office. She opened the door and announced, "Herr Ruder and the policeman, Josef Salzmann, here to see you, Herr Landesberg."

"Please send them in, Rebecca," said Henryk Landesberg, head of the *Judenrat* in the Lvov/Lemberg ghetto. Dr. Landesberg was the latest of several

Judenrat leaders for the ghetto. He had succeeded Dr. Abraham Rotfeld as head of the Jewish organization when Rotfeld died of "natural causes" in February 1942. The first head, Dr. Yosef Parnes, was murdered when he refused to supply a list of Jews for work in the nearby Janowska labor camp. In March of the same year, the *Judenrat* was ordered to create lists of Jews to be transported east for so-called "work." Apparently believing or rationalizing that more Jews would be deported if the Germans did the selections, Landesberg and the *Judenrat* dutifully prepared the lists in spite of appeals from a delegation of rabbis. As a result, from March 19, 1942, for a period of a month, fifteen thousand Jews were sent to Belzec.

Henryk Landesberg motioned Simon and the policeman into his office. "Sit down, please," he said. Simon took an immediate dislike for Landesberg. His intuition told him here was an evil man, a collaborator with the Nazis. He didn't trust him.

"What can I do for you?" asked the *Judenrat* head man.

Salzmann started first. "Simon's wife and children were killed by the Gestapo in March during the Great Roundup. He is inquiring about his friends."

"Herr Ruder, I'm sorry to hear about your wife and children. May God rest their souls. I'm sorry to say, many of our ghetto residents have succumbed to the Nazi assault on the Jews. In June, two thousand more Jews were rounded up and sent away. These barbarians, they ask for lists of people, they ask for money, valuables, that we are forced to collect for them. Things are getting unbearable. As you saw out on the streets, sanitation, overcrowding, and diseases are a major problem. Our group is trying to deal with the situation as best we can. The Nazis give us little help, only more demands. Now, who are your friends? There are still over one hundred thousand Jews in the ghetto, so we may not be able to help you."

"I'm looking for Jakob Lansky, Meyer Rosenthal, Julius Kaplan, and a Dr. Deutsche."

Landesberg wrote down the names and called Rebecca. "Will you see if you can find anything on these people?" Simon eyed Rebecca closely as she left. He estimated dimensions and sizes with a trained tailor's eye.

Rebecca returned surprisingly quickly. "We do have some information," she began. She looked at Landesberg, who nodded slightly, and then looked down. "Julius Kaplan, a pharmacist, and an Izak Goldblatt, a bookseller, disappeared in late June during the Great Roundup. We think they were taken to the Janowska labor camp but have no other information." Rebecca said nothing about the other 1,998 Jews who were also captured and most murdered at the Sands execution site in late June. "We have nothing for Jakob Lansky, Meyer Rosenthal, or Dr. Deutsche. This is all the information we have. I'm sorry. We cannot keep track of everyone."

Simon decided he needed to leave this place. He began to understand the role of the *Judenrat* and how they operated. While he personally knew the young policeman escorting him, he distrusted the whole lot, nonetheless. He thought anyone with any power in such a dire circumstance was going to be tempted to use it for their own benefit. But before he could leave, he needed to do one more thing.

"Rebecca, I need your help. I need to take some measurements."

Surprised, Rebecca looked at Landesberg, who nodded. "Certainly, Herr Ruder," the secretary answered. She blushed. "What is this for?"

As a tailor, Simon always carried a tape measure in his pocket. It was a force of habit. "You don't want to know, but rest assured, you are helping your people survive."

With that, Simon quickly took the necessary measurements. He was grateful that Rebecca, who had not yet been significantly affected by the hunger lurking just outside the *Judenrat* headquarters, shared similar physical characteristics, such as height and weight, with Hilde Waltke, for whom the dress was being made.

After carefully recording the dimensions on a piece of paper and double-checking them, Simon politely thanked the *Judenrat* head and Rebecca for their help and prepared to leave.

Landesberg seemed puzzled by this little Jewish tailor, but since he was being escorted by one of his own policemen, he thought better of further inquiries. That could wait. Had he done that, however, he would have learned that Simon Ruder had been captured by the Gestapo in August 1941 and had been imprisoned in Loncki Prison ever since. But as the chairman of the *Judenrat*, he was a busy man. More valuables were to be collected and more lists were being prepared.

As it turned out, however, Landesberg would never get the chance to investigate further. On September 1, Dr. Henryk Landesberg would meet his fate at the end of a Gestapo rope, along with other members of the *Judenrat* and several policemen, in front of the building at the corner of Łokietka and Hermana Streets. Josef Salzmann would not be among the victims, not this time.

Simon and Salzmann left the building. "Why didn't you tell Landesberg about your prison?" asked Salzmann. "He might have been able to help you hide here."

"No," said Simon. "This isn't the time. Now that I know about Lola and my children, it changes the situation for me. I no longer have to worry about them. I don't know what will happen here in the ghetto, but I think my best option is to go back to Loncki Prison and take my chances there. At least they think I'm useful, and when I see what the *Judenrat* is forced to do, well, I don't feel so bad about what I'm doing there. Let's go look for some fabric, but I doubt we will find any here in the ghetto."

After an hour or so searching in the ghetto, as Simon had suspected, they were unable to find any remotely suitable material for the dress. Apparently, the former Jewish residents of Lvov, with limited time to gather their belongings before they were forced out, had decided that cloth was not a critical commodity in their future.

"Let's go back to the ghetto entrance. I have only four hours left, and I still have to find some material in the city."

Simon and Salzmann approached the ghetto entrance. Simon showed the pass to the SS guard, who called over another guard, and they both began to minutely examine the document. One of the guards was Ukrainian. The original guard who had escorted Simon to the ghetto, the Ukrainian whose name Simon refused to pronounce, walked rapidly over to the group. Much relieved to see Simon, he quickly validated the authenticity of the pass. Simon said good-bye to his former apprentice and now JOL policeman Josef Salzmann, and he and his SS escort left the appalling confines of the Lemberg/Lvov ghetto.

Speaking in Polish, Simon gave directions to the Ukrainian. "Go to Legionow Street. I left some fine material there above my tailor shop. It may still be there."

Jumping into the waiting Kubelwagen, the pair drove off into the city center to the former Legionow Street tailor shop Simon had started and owned for a decade. The vehicle pulled up to the building. Simon noticed the street was in good repair with considerable foot and vehicle traffic, though only a few horse-drawn wagons filled the major street in what was now called Lemberg again. Simon noticed the new street signs, proclaiming the renamed *Adolf Hitler Platz*. Simon entered the shop as though he still owned it. The new owner, a Ukrainian, stopped him, but when he saw the SS uniform coming in the door, he quickly retreated.

"We need some cloth," Simon began. "I think you may have just what we need. Up in the attic." The Ukrainian looked confused. Simon continued. "This was my shop a year ago. I left several bolts of fine cloth in the back. I'm sure you've found them. Show me what you have left." For emphasis, the SS guard added, "Now!"

Taken aback, the Ukrainian tailor smiled. "Yes, sir," he said. "Follow me to the back." The shop appeared much the same as it had when Simon had been captured and sent to Loncki Prison a year ago. The same shelves held bolts of cloth and other materials. Simon thought it was nice to see colorful fabrics again, not the monotonous green-gray of the uniforms he was forced to produce. The Ukrainian led Simon to a shelf that held the fabrics from the attic. Simon examined several of the bolts and selected two. He estimated there was enough to make the new dress.

"I also need some matching thread and some lace." The Ukrainian looked dejected but quickly provided the items.

"Who will pay for this?" he asked.

The SS guard smiled and in Ukrainian said, "Send the bill to the Gestapo. I'm sure they will be more than happy to pay you."

Gathering the bolts of cloth and the other items, the Ukrainian SS guard and the Jewish tailor left the shop on Legionow Street. They walked past the unhappy, but not surprisingly quiet, Ukrainian tailor and quickly made their way back to the dark confines of the Loncki Prison.

When the pair returned, Litchtner and Stossel, the two SS guards, were there to meet them. They both knew that SS *Oberscharführer* Oskar Waltke had no patience or tolerance for failure, and that also applied to those under his command.

"Get to work, Simon," *Oberschutze* Lichtner said, looking at his watch. He glanced over at Stossel and sighed with barely disguised relief.

Simon immediately began work on the dress. Using the measurements he had obtained from Rebecca, he modified a sewing dummy to represent a more feminine profile. He had only seen Hilde Waltke a few times but felt confident he could accurately approximate her dimensions and make adjustments as necessary later. He carefully laid out the patterns he made and carefully cut the material. He had to be careful because there was only enough material to make a single dress, and he left a bit more material in case he needed to make the dress larger, but he doubted he would need it. He could always trim off any excess later.

Two days later Simon told *Oberschutze* Lichtner that the dress was ready. The SS guard passed the information on to *Oberscharführer* Oskar Waltke. The next day *Oberschutze* Lichtner told Simon to come with him and bring the dress. They walked through the prison, past lines of cells, some still housing Russian prisoners of war, others holding Jews suspected of a myriad of offenses, and the one in which Simon had made marks on the stone wall counting the days. They made their way to the main office. A shiny black staff car awaited them. Apparently, the prison was no place for the delicate Hilde Waltke. They were driven a short distance to a large house, probably taken from some unfortunate Jew. *Oberschutze* Lichtner and Simon, who was carrying the dress, went into the house. *Oberscharführer* Oskar Waltke was there with his wife. Waltke felt uncomfortable with a Jew in the house, especially one fitting a new dress on his wife. Yet he knew he had no choice, so he came along to watch the proceedings.

Hilde was an attractive woman, with dark-blond hair and high cheek bones, the very picture of an elegant Aryan wife. While a cultured and educated woman, she shared her husband's views on the Jews. She had a cruel streak, which often manifested itself on the household servants, all of them Jews. Simon was worried about her reaction to the new dress he had just finished for her.

"So let me see this dress," she said. "I have been waiting for it for days."

Simon slowly and very carefully unfolded the dress and held it up for Hilde's inspection. He had some experience with these fashions two years ago when the Russians were running things and wanted clothing in the Western style, mostly French. He had changed many plain dresses into what could pass for new fashions straight from Paris or New York. So it was no surprise that Hilde Waltke actually liked the dress that Simon had so painstakingly crafted in the prison. A smile broke out on her face, and she literally tore the dress from Simon's grasp and, barely suppressing a squeal of delight, dashed off to another room, presumably to try it on. All three men, the imprisoned Jewish tailor, the SS *Oberscharführer*, and the SS guard, looked at each other and chuckled, and just for a fleeting moment, humanity broke out again.

ZLOCZOW, POLAND, NOVEMBER 1942

Things had not gone well for the Jews in the Zloczow area during the last twelve months. In their defense, the *Judenrat* had made genuine attempts to improve the lot of the remaining Jews. In April, they attempted to find jobs they thought important to the German economy or to the war effort. They were hoping this would end the deportation of Jews to the slave labor work camps scattered around the area. The plan didn't work, however, and in mid-August, the *Judenrat* was ordered to create a list of some three thousand Jews to be deported from the town. Most members of the *Judenrat* refused and warned the Jewish population of the impending *Aktion*. Undeterred, the SS conducted the *Aktion* on August 28, and by August 30, some twenty-seven hundred Jews were rounded up and sent by train to the Belzec extermination camp.

It was obvious to Mendel that times were going to get much worse for the remaining Jews in the Zloczow area. He was determined to take action to protect his family. With escape to Russia almost impossible, the only chance to avoid deportation to a death camp like nearby Belzec or a slow death at a forced labor camp was to go into hiding. Many Jewish families throughout the German-controlled areas had managed to do so, and some had been success-ful. In the future, several books would describe their ordeals. These particular Ruders found such a sanctuary on a farm outside Zloczow in a small village called Woraki. Through mutual friends, Mendel had negotiated spaces in a bunker for himself, his wife, and his young son Dolek. Mendel was just waiting for the right time to move. He didn't have long to wait.

Mendel was warned by the German SS officer he had befriended earlier the previous year that an impending *Aktion* was to take place the very next day, November 2. Now it was time to move, and he knew he and his family didn't have much time. The first of November was a cold, snowy day as the group prepared to leave for the bunker. Three carefully packed suitcases contained all they could salvage of their former lives, suitcases that stood ready to transport them to safety and hopefully beyond. Mendel left one of the suitcases just outside the apartment doorway while he loaded the first two suitcases onto the small wagon waiting outside. He made sure the suitcases were secure in the wagon and placed little Dolek on top of them. The snow turned into a frozen rainy mix as he went back inside for the last suitcase. As he approached the apartment doorway, he realized something was wrong. The suitcase containing many of the family's valuables was gone. In a panic, Mendel searched the hallway. Nothing. He knocked on doors. No one answered. He ran outside into the worsening weather. Little Dolek and Zofia were cold, shivering, and impatient.

"What's taking so long?" asked Zofia. "We must be on our way."

"I must take care of something," said Mendel, barely able to mask the panic in his voice. "You and Dolek go ahead. I will meet you there later. Hurry!"

Zofia noticed the absence of the third suitcase and feared the worst. "Where is the suitcase? What happened?"

"I will take care of it. Now go! I will be there when I can."

Soon, a middle-aged couple joined them beside the small wagon and loaded their suitcases, but Zofia hardly noticed as she looked back at her husband.

"Go, go," he shooed. "I'll be there soon. Don't worry."

Eager to start the journey, the man began to push the wagon, and the four Jews slowly left Zloczow and made their way some ten kilometers toward the hoped for safety of the farmhouse on the road toward Tarnopol on the outskirts of town. The travelers were miserable because of the weather, but the rain and snow also limited the dreaded patrols and the curious along the way. The straw on which they sat was soaked, but no one complained. Even little Dolek stoically endured the cold and wet journey.

As Mendel watched the wagon leave, he silently cursed himself for losing the suitcase. He knew it contained needed valuables if his family was to survive, and he was determined to get them back. He suspected a Ukrainian neighbor and went out to search for him. The search was short and unsuccessful. Mendel was picked up at random by a group of Ukrainian thugs in German SS uniforms. He was walking down the street from his apartment, and as he turned the corner, they spotted him. The thugs signaled each other to intercept him. Mendel realized the danger too late and tried to run from the rapidly closing trio. The three Ukrainians were on him in seconds, and he was pummeled with brutal blows delivered with fists, metal pipes, and chains.

Bloody and beaten, Mendel Ruder was taken to the forced labor camp at Lackie Wielkie established the previous year, along with similar camps at Kozaki, Korowice, Yaktorov, Pluhow, and Sasow. Mendel would not be alone in the camps as hundreds of additional Jews were deported to these camps as well.

In reality, Mendel's capture by the Ukrainians the day before the *Aktion* saved his life because the second major *Aktion* took place as planned, on November 2 and 3, resulting in another twenty-five hundred Jews from Zloczow and many others brought in from the vicinity being loaded into cattle cars and taken to Belzec for extermination.

This major *Aktion* by the Germans and their Ukrainian accomplices signaled the beginning of the end for the Jews of Zloczow, an end that would be total as the Jewish community there would not be reestablished.

Thus, on a cold, cloudy evening early in November, a small group of Jews from Zloczow, having narrowly missed the latest *Aktion*, arrived at the farm of Anna Sawicki and entered the newly constructed bunker under the stable. The bunker itself was simple, crude, and basic. It was merely a place to hide, well concealed from the SS and Ukrainians. There was nothing fancy about it. The heavy wooden planks that made up the ceiling actually served as the floor for the stable above. The planks were tightly spaced, and with a covering of straw, little light from above managed to filter through, keeping the sanctuary in semidarkness. When things were quiet in the stable, small lights could be used below. Cooking was not allowed as the telltale smell or smoke could reveal them to unfriendly noses and eyes. The bunker also contained makeshift cots and rudimentary furniture consisting of a table and some chairs. Food could be brought down through a small, secret tunnel shaft, and entrance and egress to and from the bunker was possible through a well-disguised trap door.

In the bunker with Zofia and Dolek Ruder were the middle-aged couple that had come with them from Zloczow, the Birnbaums, Regina Wurm, a woman of about forty-five, and her eighteen-year-old daughter Blima. In the future, Regina would go to Israel while Blima would immigrate to Halifax, Canada, where she would marry a man called Gutfreund. She would have several children who would later become doctors and lawyers.

Unfortunately, things would not turn out so well for some of the other occupants of the bunker.

As Zofia and Dolek entered the bunker, Regina Wurm and her daughter were already there. Regina looked around. "Where is your husband?" she asked.

Zofia had a sad look on her face. Little Dolek began to cry, and she shushed him. "I'm afraid the Germans may have him," she began. "We were ready to leave, but for some reason he came out of the apartment without the last suitcase we had packed. He was determined to stay behind. I think the suitcase was stolen when he wasn't looking, and he went to find it. He said he would meet us here."

"Oh my God!" said Regina. "That's terrible news. Is there something we can do?"

"I'm afraid all we can do is wait and pray," said Zofia.

Zofia continued in the hope that Mendel would one day return to the bunker. In the meantime, she worked with the group to make the bunker more comfortable, if that word could be applied in that situation. As the situation rapidly deteriorated in the former Russian-occupied Galicia territory, including Tarnopol, Lvov, and Zloczow, the six Jews settled into what would be their daily activities for the next two and a half years, hidden in a bunker under the stable located on the farm of Anna Sawicki.

Payments to Anna Sawicki were made periodically and consisted of valuables such as jewelry, gold, coins, furs, and other items that could be readily sold on the black market. Everyone understood that Anna was risking her life harboring the Jews, and they were grateful. Zofia assumed Anna was friends with the Wurms and sympathetic to the plight of the Jews.

News of Ukrainian atrocities in the area trickled down to the inhabitants of the bunker through their champion Anna. The group understood that the only thing they could do was to stay hidden and alive and that the bunker was their only lifeboat in the raging tempest of this brutal war.

November flowed into December. The weather was getting colder, and life in the bunker ground on. The women generally worked well together, although nerves were occasionally frayed over seemingly inconsequential events. Little Dolek was well behaved, and Zofia received help from the other women in caring for him. Housekeeping consisted of emptying the nightly bucket that served as a toilet, keeping clothes as clean as possible, and fighting lice and fleas. Food was divided and distributed. Life went on, and everyone told each other that it could be worse. But how, they all wondered to themselves.

One day in late December, a new member was unexpectedly added to the bunker. Zylko Janowic was a tall, handsome man of thirty years old. Anna introduced him, and it was assumed, but never confirmed, that he would take the place of Mendel Ruder, who had been gone for several months. With Mendel gone, the space was not being paid for, and Anna wanted to fill the spot. Janowic was very friendly but never revealed much of his background. Some in the group suspected he was a Polish army deserter. A Jew, yes, as Zofia had later accidentally found out at the waste bucket the next morning. The older Regina Wurm expressed little interest in the handsome Pole, but young Blima flirted with him constantly. With no word from Mendel, Zofia began to look in Janowic's direction.

Life in the Lackie Wielkie forced labor camp was brutal. At first, the *Judenrat* in Zloczow tried to help by sending food, but that effort soon failed.

Many prisoners, including Mendel Ruder, were put to work building or repairing roads. Adding insult to injury, the prisoners were forced to break up Jewish headstones in nearby cemeteries for material to build the roads. It was backbreaking work, and many prisoners quickly succumbed to the sheer physical exertion, sickness, and lack of food. In spite of his small stature, or maybe because of it, Mendel somehow managed to persevere. He had seen many prisoners die, some from exhaustion where the body simply gave out, others from beatings, and still too many from brutal executions. At first, Mendel kept to himself, not wanting to connect with any of the other prisoners. He had not gotten over the sense of blame for foolishly putting himself in the position to be captured. He hoped the bunker wasn't discovered and that his wife and son had successfully fled to this sanctuary.

Soon, however, as the reality of his situation began to take root, he started making a few friends. Two such friends were thirty-year-old Dawid Neiss from Hrushowice and forty-one-year-old Jakob Gruenbaum, a merchant from Tarnopol.

In quiet moments after a brutal day of trying to dig dirt in the partially frozen ground, the men conversed in hushed tones. Gruenbaum was the first to reach out to his fellow prisoner.

"Mendel, what's your story? How did this fine place find you?"

"Stupidity," replied Mendel after a short pause. He would say no more, afraid he would reveal hints about the existence and location of the bunker—if indeed it still existed.

Gruenbaum nodded, understanding his fellow prisoner's reticence. "I was a merchant in Tarnopol, or at least I was until the Russians came. I had a big store, a successful one. The Russians took it away and filled it with all their crap. I was allowed to work in a warehouse. Most of the good things were available through the black market, and I made a good living at it, especially watches. Those crazy Russians loved watches; they couldn't get enough of them."

Mendel laughed at the thought. He, too, had seen Russian soldiers, even officers, with multiple watches on their arms. He knew he would remember that as long as he lived, though he didn't know how much longer that would be.

Neiss spoke up next. He was a dark-haired man of medium height and build. He was a lawyer from Zloczow and was picked up at random during the same sweep that caught Mendel and Jakob.

"I was minding my own business in Zloczow when I was captured. There was no warning. They just beat me and brought me here. I think things are going to get worse. I am worried about my mother Feiga and my father Mailech."

As new arrivals soon filled the camp, they brought word that additional work camps had been established in the area. Jews were being seized and put to work in these camps.

MÜHLDORF, GERMANY, 1942

Ludwig Häusl had joined the Deutsche Reichseisenbahnen, the German Reich Railways, shortly after it was established in 1920 after his discharge from the army. Several state railways had been merged into this single, large organization, which now had national responsibility for all railroads because of the new Weimar Republic constitution. In 1924, it was reorganized again under the control of the Deutsche Reichsbahn-Gesellschaft (DRG), a private railway company, which was wholly owned by the German state. In 1937, again, during the Nazi regime, the railroads were reorganized as the Deutsche Reichsbahn. Swastikas were applied to railcars, along with the traditional eagle symbol, the *Hoheitsadler*, as were the letters "DR."

Ludwig had survived the various railroad reorganizations. He was a hard worker and progressed through the ranks up to the position of train driver, an engineer who drove locomotives pulling both freight and passenger trains, mostly in Bavaria. Ludwig was proud of his railroad, which, at the beginning of the war, boasted sixty-eight thousand kilometers of track. Stations and depots for freight and passenger service numbered 12,317 with another 1,708 on private lines. Rolling stock consisted of some twenty-three thousand locomotives, 1,892 miscellaneous engines, sixty-nine thousand passenger cars, twenty-one thousand baggage cars, and 605,000 freight cars. Interestingly, the railroad system was not considered critical to the coming war effort because Hitler confidently assumed his motorized army and newly constructed autobahn system would effectively handle the transportation needs of his war machine.

"Good-bye, Maria," Ludwig called to his wife. It was early, and the four children were still asleep.

"Did you pack a little extra food for my lunch?" he asked.

"Yes, Ludwig," she answered, handing her husband his black lunch box. "I don't know why you are eating so much lately. You're still skinny as a rail. Food doesn't grow on trees, and we are using up our ration cards."

Ludwig laughed. "It must be all that bicycling I do to the rail yard," he said. "I will probably be late today; maybe I won't be back until tomorrow sometime. I don't know where I'll be going until I get to the rail yard." Ludwig kissed his short wife on the forehead and left their small whitewashed house, mounted his bicycle, and with a push, made off for the rail yard just outside of town.

Mühldorf was a railroad marshalling yard where trains were made up and broken down, coming in and going out in all directions. In late 1939, guns, tanks, ammunition, oil, and other war-related freight was headed eastward to support the Russian invasion. Soon, however, a new commodity was also headed east into what had just a few years ago been Poland, and this particular traffic would increase steadily.

Lately, Ludwig had begun to dread going to work. After years of delivering troops, tanks, ammunition, and other supplies to the front, he now had responsibility for moving human cargo on the *Sonderzuge* (Special Trains) eastward to what everyone knew were not resettlement camps. Well, almost everyone. The passengers waiting to get on the trains thought they were headed for resettlement or labor camps. They were confused, shocked, and stunned to find up to fifty-five cattle cars sitting ready on the tracks waiting for them. Ludwig usually sat in the steam locomotive cab while the SS guards loaded the human cargo aboard. He knew the real destination and what fate most likely awaited the human cargo. Sometimes he made the short run to Dachau. Often, he delivered freight and supplies for the camp. At Dachau, the tracks came into the camp on the side that housed the SS Training Camp and Garrison on one side of the Wurm River. Occasionally, the cargo was made up of Jews. Ludwig could see them being herded into the smaller camp on the other side of the river, which was really a concrete-sided canal.

Dachau was the first concentration camp established in Germany in 1933. Originally incarcerated were "enemies of the regime," trade unionists, and political opponents. The Nazis also used Dachau as a site for the execution of the SA Storm Troopers captured in the 1934 purge. Gypsies, Germans, and then, after 1938, Austrian male homosexuals and Jehovah's Witnesses were also imprisoned there. Dachau was the model camp after which the others like Auschwitz, Treblinka, Gross-Rosen, Plazsow, Bergen-Belsen, Buchenwald, and the other man-made hellholes were modeled.

The railroad was paid by the track kilometer, one half pfennig for each Jew transported, regardless of the final destination. Children were half price. As long as they were paid, the railroad felt they had a duty to move the cargo, no matter what or who it was or where it went. During the war years, it is estimated the Deutsche Reichsbahn earned 240 million Reichsmarks for their transportation of the Jews to the concentration camps.

Ludwig Häusl and his family were devout, church-going Catholics. Ludwig and Maria understood that there existed a Concordat that the Holy See and the Third Reich had signed in July 1933 outlining and protecting the division of church and state and spelling out the rights of Catholics. However, Maria, in particular, distrusted the Nazis and often complained about real or imagined breaches of the Concordat. She had good reason to be distrustful. Hitler understood quite clearly that National Socialism and the church could not coexist. He wanted a secular country, and there was no room for religion. For now, however, he had other priorities, and this problem would be addressed after the war. In any case, the Häusl children attended Catholic school in Mühldorf. For young Marile, in particular, reconciling the Catholic teachings with those of the Hitler Youth was not too difficult, especially toward the Jews. They were, after all, not really humans.

Still, as a religious man, Ludwig felt uneasy as he witnessed the pathetic walking skeletons in tattered striped uniforms beyond the barbed-wire fences he passed on the way into and out of the camps. But these were not really people, were they? Not according to Himmler, and as a member of the Nazi Party, Ludwig reluctantly accepted this doctrine. Yet his unease persisted as he performed his duty and delivered trainloads of poor, wretched souls to various parts of this Nazi-conceived hell.

Perhaps, in an attempt to push the unease back into a dark corner of his mind, Ludwig sometimes tossed his lunch over the barbed-wire fence when no one else was looking, a bold move considering the times. In the overall scheme of things, it was a little thing, but Ludwig hoped God was watching.

In spite of the war, or perhaps in part because of the war, it was a good year for Ludwig Häusl's oldest daughter Marile. She had graduated from her primary-school class near the top of her class. The nuns teaching at her school were proud of Marile and were not surprised when she scored high marks and exceptional typing skills at her interview and was subsequently hired as an intern of sorts by the Landratsamt Ernahrungsamt Abteilung B (District Nutritional Department Office B) in Mühldorf. She had just turned fourteen. While Marile's job tasks were of a low-level support role, she learned that her department was involved in the management, tracking, and distribution of food to the German people and others, which included workers and prisoners in camps. Monthly food ration cards were distributed, controlling amounts of various foodstuffs each person could procure for a one-month period. She typed and made duplicates of many reports showing food production, allocation, and distribution throughout the Mühldorf district of Bavaria. The reports were sent to Munich and then to Berlin. The food allocation system was carefully controlled by the Third Reich. It was used as a tool to feed the German masses, much of the food coming from captured territories. Ominously, it also proved an effective tool of starvation in Germany's occupied territories, including the General Government in what was Poland. While Marile was a smart girl, she didn't understand the meaning or implications of the reports she helped prepare and distribute. She did note that shortly after she was hired, the rations for Jews still in Germany were drastically cut on September 18, but that meant little to her. Much more ominously, she was unaware of the Nazi targeting of the so-called "subhuman" (*Untermensch*) for extermination and work at slave labor camps. The Nazi plans called for the deliberate starvation of the "subhumans." By mid-1941, the German minority in Poland received 2,613 calories per day, while Poles received 699, and Jews in the ghetto only 184. This meant that the Jewish ration fulfilled a scant 7.5 percent of their daily needs, and the Polish rations, while significantly increased, only provided 26 percent. Only the ration allocated to Germans provided the full needs of their daily caloric intake, at least on paper. That was to change too as the war ground on.

As an adult, Marile would have been shocked at these facts, but as a four-teen-year-old schoolgirl working in the German government, the details buried in the reports were beyond her ability to objectively analyze or to comprehend the outright immorality and cruelty they represented.

THE LVOV/LEMBERG GHETTO, AUGUST 1942

Rifka Goldblatt had not given up on her husband Izak. Back on June 24, he and Julius Kaplan had gone out with half of what valuables the group had pooled to buy some food on the black market. They had not returned in almost six weeks. The remaining group of six had managed to survive on what food was left, sharply cutting rations. Bela and Samuel Goldblatt, Rifka's two young sons, were both sick with fevers. Jakob Lansky, his wife Sarah, and his seven-year-old daughter Chaja were not much better off. Life in the ghetto was getting worse by the day. The food situation had become disastrous. There were just too many people to feed. Starvation was rampant, with hundreds of people dying in the streets. Typhus and other diseases took their toll. To the Germans, all was going according to plan.

On August 10, the population overcrowding problem in the ghetto would improve, but not for many of the residents. The SS, Ukrainians, and the Jewish police began what would be called *The Great Action*. Jews were told to gather on Teodor Square, at Sobieski School, and on the square in front of the Janowska camp. There, they were told, they would be transported to resettlement or work camps. Many Jews believed this. Anything was better than life in the ghetto, despite the fact that about one thousand Jews had been shot in the ghetto, including Jewish orphans and patients at hospitals. The ghetto population would soon drop by almost fifty thousand during this action. The Janowska work camp population was to increase by some sixteen hundred inmates.

Rifka Goldblatt and her two sons dutifully arrived at the gathering point, suitcases in hand. The suitcases contained the remainder of their possessions that they had been able to bring into the ghetto. The crowd continued to grow. Soon there were about four thousand people milling around the square, desperate souls betting that life at the other end of the tracks would be better than the one they were leaving in the ghetto.

Many in the crowd were speculating on where they would be relocated and what kinds of work would be available. One man could be heard saying, "I'm an engineer. Certainly there would be work for me." Another said, "Well, I'm a banker. Surely people would need a place to put their money and take out loans." People all through the crowd were expressing hope at what was awaiting them farther down the tracks.

The SS and Jewish police were estimating the size of the crowd. Down at the Kleparow railway station, fifty-five cattle cars stood ready to receive the human cargo, eighty or so to a car. Maybe even one hundred or so if necessary, they calculated. That would fill all the cars. That would be efficient. The Deutsche Reichsbahn would be pleased with the half pfennig per kilometer mile for each Jew transported that day.

"Put your name on your belongings," said the Jewish policeman. "They will be put on the train and will arrive with you where you can pick them up." This was a lie, of course, but one that was well practiced and repeated throughout Central Europe.

As the Jews were being readied for loading, a selection was taking place. An SS guard scanned the lines going toward the train. Jakob Lansky and his family shuffled up to the guard.

"Halt," the SS man said. "What is your name, age, and occupation?" he asked Lansky. Lansky related his name and age. "I am an architect. This is my wife and daughter."

The guard scrutinized Lansky a bit more intently. "Go over there to the right, over to that group. Do not go on the train." Pointing to Sarah and her daughter, he said, "You two, keep moving."

"Jakob!" cried Sarah. "What's happening? Where are you going?" The mother and daughter were pushed along toward the waiting train cars. They looked back toward Jakob, but soon their cries were lost in the crowd. Sarah and her daughter would never see Jakob again.

A shrill whistle blew. Several Jewish policemen began to shepherd the crowd toward the Kleparow railway station. As the Jews from the ghetto approached the station, they couldn't help but notice the line of cattle cars. A palpable unease spread over the crowd like a heavy blanket. Some people were on the verge of panic. The Jewish police were there to ensure the trains were filled and to allay fears of the deportees. The process was the same as before. The suitcases were either put in a pile to be loaded on the train or actually put on a train car at the end of the train. Either way, the suitcases never made it to the destination. After all, the Jews wouldn't need them when they arrived at their final destination.

It was hot that August day. The cattle cars were filled to capacity with up to eighty individuals crammed into each one. There was only one small window high up on the outside. It was too small to provide much ventilation. It took over an hour to fill the train with its human cargo. Those loaded earlier began to feel the effects of the cramped cattle cars. People were tightly bunched together, unable to sit or move. The heat was stifling, and many were on the verge of suffocation. All were gasping for air. Those closer to the small window had a chance at a passing breeze, but not much air penetrated the car. Finally, the door on the last car was slammed shut and locked. The whistle blew again, and the train slowly left the station, picking up speed. It reached a switch and then veered off to the left. One of the Jewish policemen checked a clipboard, wrote something on it, and then walked away. They were getting accustomed to it.

Several people on the train wondered why the train had taken the track to the left. Normally, the passenger trains would navigate onto the track to the right and loop back toward the middle of town. They could do nothing about it except wonder, but after all, this was not a passenger train. Today, it contained human cargo.

Back at the station platform, a group of Jews quickly emerged from the station and fell upon the pile of suitcases. Like the scavengers they had been forced to become, they sorted through the suitcases in a highly efficient, well-practiced process, and soon piles of various valuables, clothes, books, blankets, and miscellaneous items were left neatly on the ground. These would be added to the piles accumulating all over Central Europe for distribution back to Germany.

Twenty-two men did not catch the train that day. Instead, they were marched across the tracks to the Janowska labor camp.

Every few days for the next twenty days, much the same process was repeated. Jews gathered at Teodor Square, at Sobieski School, and in front of the Janowska camp waiting for a train ride that would take them out of the confines of the ghetto and Lemberg. The Jewish policemen did their jobs well, and somewhere around forty thousand to fifty thousand Jews took their last train ride into a nightmare called Belzec. In all, there were about 750 Jewish policemen scattered throughout the ghetto conducting enforcement and control activities, including the loading of the deportation trains. They worked for the *Judenrat*, but in reality, they did the bidding of the SS. At the end of the twenty days, on September 1, eleven of them were hanged by the Gestapo, along with Dr. Henryk Landesberg, chairman of the *Judenrat* at their headquarters building in the ghetto. By August 30, the so-called "Great Action" had been completed.

In the Janowska camp, the twenty-two new inmates were given the usual welcome and assigned to various barracks. None of the barracks were at full strength for very long. Starvation, beatings, shootings, and suicides rapidly reduced their numbers. Replacements were frequent and in demand. Jakob Lansky was one of them, along with Aaron Adler, a former machinist in Lvov. Adler, who was twenty-nine years old, had left an expecting wife on the platform. He would never see his newborn child. He was assigned to Barrack number five, which housed the *Ostbahn-Brigade*, the Jews working at the railway station cleaning locomotives. For some reason, this brigade was blessed with intense SS brutality and supplied a large quota for the frequent executions in the camp. Replacements were particularly in high demand for this barrack, and Aaron Adler was unfortunate enough to be such a replacement. Jakob Lansky was assigned to a general work barracks located two buildings over from where Julius Kaplan and Izak Goldblatt were slowly getting accustomed to work camp life and death.

On September 1, 1942, immediately following the *Great Action* roundup, the Lemberg/Lvov ghetto population was reduced to around sixty-five thousand people. Of these, fifteen thousand or so were considered "illegal" by the SS because they failed to report to the deportation center or had no work permits. While the population was significantly reduced, conditions were still primitive with no water, insufficient food, no electricity, and no effective medical facilities. Winter was not far off, and there would be no heat. The ghetto was still enclosed in barbed-wire fencing and heavily guarded.

Meyer Rosenthal was living with his family in a small apartment with another family, the Sangers. Max Sanger was convinced he and his family should obey the SS order to report to the deportation centers, so on August 15, the Sangers said good-bye and left the ghetto to face their fate.

Meyer Rosenthal, the lawyer, with no clients and no laws to argue and, most importantly, no work permit was now considered an "illegal" resident of the ghetto, as were his wife Dreisia and his fourteen-year-old son Falik. Meyer, always the optimist of the group of friends that had played cards just a few years ago, had believed the Germans would be fair and civilized when they overran the Russian-occupied part of Poland in 1941. Events of the last year had made him realize how wrong he was and had convinced him not to report to the deportation centers. Few knew what happened to those who were crammed into the trains going north, but piles of luggage left at the train station and the inhuman mode of transport did little to inspire confidence in the SS promises of resettlement camps.

"It looks like it's quiet," said Dreisia Rosenthal. "They say there are no cattle cars at the station today."

"They will come again," said Meyer. "We need those work permits to stay in the ghetto. Only the *Judenrat* can issue them. I think in order to survive, we need to obtain such permits. I've decided to go to the *Judenrat* to see what can be done. How much money do we have left?"

"Not much, but I hope it's enough," said Dreisia. "Meyer, I'm afraid. All of our friends are gone. First, Simon is in that horrible prison. Who knows if he's alive. And Lola and the children—we haven't heard a thing about them. Julius

Kaplan and Jakob Lansky, same thing, and Dr. Deutsche and his family. Such nice people, such good friends. Will we ever see them again?"

"I know, Dreisia. Maybe they are in work camps like the one up on Janowska Street." In his heart, Meyer Rosenthal doubted that, especially regarding the women and children. He had heard about the March deportation of women and children. He knew Simon had been captured in August of 1941 and taken away to Loncki Prison. He doubted Lola and the children could have survived without him.

Unknown to Meyer Rosenthal, Dr. Deutsche and his family had been deported from the Lvov ghetto in June 1942. After a short stay at the Janowska camp, they were sent to the Belzec extermination camp, where they perished.

The new head of the *Judenrat* in the Lvov ghetto was Dr. Eduard Eberson, and he proved to be just as ineffective as his recently hanged predecessor. During his tenure, he would see the ghetto devolve into more of a work camp, because all the occupants were now required to have work permits. Everyone else was considered unnecessary and, therefore, "illegal" and was to be eliminated.

Meyer Rosenthal made his way to the *Judenrat* office building. The bodies of the hanged former *Judenrat* head, Henryk Landesberg, other *Judenrat* members, and a number of Jewish policemen had recently been removed from the front of the building. Rosenthal entered the building and asked for Dr. Eberson. He was told to wait, as the new chairman was very busy. Busy, indeed, trying to keep his neck out of a noose, thought Rosenthal. He waited for several hours before he was able to see the new chairman.

Rosenthal was led into the chairman's office and was bidden to sit down. The fifty-six-year-old Eduard Eberson looked tired. "How can we help you?" asked Eberson.

"Sir, my family and I are seeking work permits. I understand this documentation is required to stay in the ghetto."

"That is true," said Eberson. "But there is no work. The factory is full. No work, no permits. I'm sorry, there is nothing we can do for you. I have thousands of requests for work permits on my desk at this moment."

"Is there any way to obtain a permit? Any way at all?"

Eberson made a show of pensiveness on his face. "Well," he began. "Under certain circumstances, we can accept contributions to the fund for the general welfare of the community. For food and medicine and such things. This is to help the ghetto residents, provide some relief from their suffering, you understand. Perhaps a suitable contribution could expedite the issuing of work permits. How many did you say you needed?"

"We are looking for three permits. One for myself, my wife Dreisia, and my son Falik."

"How old is your son?" asked Eberson. "Does he look his age, or older perhaps?"

"Falik is a tall boy. He is fourteen, but could easily pass for sixteen or seventeen."

"How much of a contribution were you considering?"

Rosenthal reached for a piece of paper and wrote down a number and slid it over to the chairman. Eberson glanced down at the number. "That may be sufficient for two permits. You will have to choose which two. Unless of course...."

Meyer Rosenthal knew full well there was no general fund, but still, he might be able to save himself and his family. He retrieved the paper and crossed out the original number and wrote down another. With a sigh, because he knew the new number would leave his family with nothing but perhaps their lives, he again slid the paper toward the chairman.

Eberson picked up the paper and smiled. "Yes, I am confident the *Arbeitsant*, the Jewish employment office, will look favorably upon this generous contribution. Leave the names you want on the permits with Rebecca outside. Come back in two days, and we shall have your work permits. Oh, and bring the contribution with you."

Rosenthal wrote down his full name and those of his wife and son and left the note with Rebecca at the desk.

Satisfied with himself, Rosenthal made his way back to the apartment to rejoin his wife and son. On the way, he noticed a less-crowded ghetto. It seemed like half as many people walked the streets these days. To be sure, people still starved and begged in the streets, but clearly not as many as a week ago.

Rosenthal rejoined his family in their small apartment. They were living alone now. "I wonder where the Sangers are," asked Dreisia.

The whereabouts of the family that had lived with them wasn't such a mystery to Rosenthal, but he didn't say a word. After all, in two days, he and his family would be safe.

Two days later, Rosenthal returned to the *Judenrat* office with the money for what he knew to be a thinly disguised bribe masquerading as a so-called contribution. The payment left him almost without any money, but he was more worried about surviving in the short term than an uncertain future.

He made his way up the stairs to Dr. Eduard Eberson's office. This time he didn't have to wait. "Come in, Meyer," said the chairman. "How are you? We have been waiting. The items you requested are ready. Did you bring the contribution?"

"Yes," said Rosenthal, pulling out the small bag hidden in his trousers containing the money to which the parties had agreed and placing it on Eberson's desk.

Eberson opened a desk drawer and pulled out three cards. He showed them to Rosenthal. "Here they are," he said. "They are very well done and should fool anyone."

Rosenthal looked at the three work permits. He checked the names for spelling. Perfect, he thought. He was listed as a chemist at the DAW plant, his wife Dreisia was an assembler of artillery shells, and son Falik was listed as a seventeen-year-old general laborer.

Eberson opened the bag and took out the bills and started counting. Satisfied, he shook hands with Rosenthal.

"Thank you," he began. "The community thanks you. Good luck with your new jobs."

Rosenthal carefully slid the precious documents down his trousers, making sure they were secure. As he made his way back to his apartment, he thought that at least the thieves had honor.

OBERTIN, POLAND, SUMMER 1942

Things were relatively quiet in the small town of Obertin, Poland, after the Nazi occupation began in 1941 and the Russians had been driven out of Poland. At first, the town was under control of the Hungarians, but soon the Germans took over and, as elsewhere in the former Polish state, the systematic extermination of the Jews began.

For the parents of Simon, Izak, and Mendel Ruder, the ordeal would be over soon. Seventy-five-year-old Mordko Fischel and his seventy-one-year-old wife Chija Frima were among approximately six thousand Jews rounded up during June and September of 1942 and sent to a ghetto set up in nearby Kolomyja. After a short stay, they were transported to the Belzec extermination camp. Sadly, because of their advanced age and their inability to work, their tragic fate was sealed.

Had the pair been able to look out of the crowded cattle car, they might have been able to identify the Kleparow train station in Lvov where they had made a brief stop to change locomotives. Had they known, they might have wondered about the fate of their son Simon who they knew lived in Lvov with his wife and children. They would not have known that Simon was, at that moment, only a kilometer away, imprisoned in Loncki Prison by the Gestapo, and that Lola and the children had been murdered by the SS at that very spot while attempting to escape from being herded onto just such a train going to the same final destination.

The train, with fifty or so cattle cars packed tightly with Jews, left the Kleparow station and continued to the left toward the Belzec camp, where Mordko Fischel and Chija Frima Ruder would perish in the gas chambers of the Third Reich before they would see another day.

ZLOCZOW, POLAND, 1942

It seemed that the SS, both German and their Ukrainian clones, had an insatiable and obsessive need to hunt and kill Jews. Diverting manpower and serving no strategic military value, they nonetheless spent scarce resources playing this deadly cat-and-mouse game.

For the five Jews hiding in a bunker below a stable on a farm outside Zloczow, the game was getting more serious. The SS would make frequent sweeps of the area looking for Jews. On several occasions, SS officers searched the farmhouse and the nearby stable. Jew-hunting had become a science. The SS had learned many tricks employed by the clever Jews in the ghettos around Poland and had developed equally clever tools to help them ferret out the Jews that had been eluding them. The easiest solution was to just burn them out and shoot them as they emerged from the burning buildings. However, in the pastoral environs surrounding the bunker, these methods were inappropriate. The Ukrainians were brutal but sometimes lazy. During previous visits to the stable, they had conducted the obligatory stabbing and shooting into the piles of hay. That done, they made a cursory inspection of the stable, looking for concealed trap doors or other signs of possible hiding places. They had found nothing and left.

This visit, however, had proved to be unusually heart stopping for the five Jews hiding under the stable. They could see the bottom of an SS officer's black boots as he walked back and forth across the stable floor. He was a German, that much they could tell. The others were most likely Ukrainians. No one breathed, hiding less than one meter below the wooden, straw-covered floor. A light shone dimly through the tight gaps between the floor planks but did not penetrate enough to reveal the sanctuary below. One Ukrainian had a hammer and was striking the floor at different locations throughout the stable. It all sounded the same no matter where he struck.

At that moment, Anna Sawicki entered the stable with a tray of refreshments and food. The Ukrainians looked at the German, and he nodded. They quickly surrounded Anna, and the refreshments and food were soon gone. The German officer turned his head toward Anna and checked his watch. He only had one, and it worked.

"Thank you, Frau Sawicki," he said. "Let us know if you see anything out of the ordinary. We heard there are Jews hiding in the area. Be careful."

Anna noticed the insignia on the German officer's tunic. "Thank you, *Obersturmfuhrer*. I feel safer already. I certainly don't want any filthy Jews wandering around here."

The German officer smiled and bowed slightly, surprised that this Polish farmwoman had the ability to correctly identify his rank. He didn't wonder why, though. The group of SS soldiers finished the refreshments as the SS first lieutenant motioned to his team, and they left the stable, climbed into their gray Kubelwagen, and drove off. Anna watched them disappear over the low hills until they were out of sight.

The quintet of Jews under the stable floor began to breathe again. Even little four-year-old Dolek had understood the need for absolute silence. Zylko Janowic had been ready, however, in case the toddler forgot.

For the remaining Jews of Zloczow, the nightmare was far from over. As planned, the second major *Aktion* took place on November 2 and 3, resulting in another twenty-five hundred Jews from Zloczow and many brought in from the vicinity being loaded into cattle cars and taken to Belzec. On

December 1, a ghetto was established in a small area of Zloczow. The remaining Jews from Zloczow and nearby communities such as Olesko, Sasow, and Bialy Kamien were crammed into the small area, where many died from disease and starvation.

1943

LVOV/LEMBERG GHETTO, POLAND, JANUARY 1943

As it turned out, the money that Meyer Rosenthal had paid for the work permits was no bargain, buying only a four-month reprieve. During the first week of January 1943, between fifteen thousand to twenty thousand Jews were taken to the "Sands" and shot, including the remaining members of the *Judenrat* and their JOL police force. The Germans dissolved the *Judenrat*, and the Lvov ghetto was officially designated a work camp renamed *Judenlager Lemberg*. Around twelve thousand Jews were still officially eligible to work in the SS war industry. Meyer Rosenthal and his family were not among their numbers because of the discovery of their forged work permits, and they subsequently met their fate at the Sands.

Annoyingly, at least to the SS, there were a few thousand "illegal" Jews still hiding in the newly renamed work camp. A constant thorn in their side, in June of 1943, the Germans finally took action to destroy the Jewish quarter. They entered the ghetto to flush out any remaining Jews. They met with limited resistance, as most of the Jews, women, children, and the elderly, had gone into hiding into so-called bunkers they had prepared earlier. The Germans burned down most of the buildings in order to flush out these remaining Jews hiding in their bunkers. The Jewish hospital in the ghetto faced a brutal and tragic end as patients were thrown out of the windows and buried while some were still alive.

A few Jews managed to escape, and a small number were able to successfully hide in the sewers, but the former Lvov/Lemberg ghetto and the *Judenlager Lemberg* work camp, along with approximately two hundred thousand Jews were no more. History would show fewer than one thousand Jews would survive.

Simon Ruder's group of Jewish tailors held in Loncki Prison worked hard to meet the increasing demands of their Gestapo captors. As the war on the Eastern Front raged on, more uniforms were ordered for the various SS units, so the group of tailors remained extremely busy. Work quality was good, and the quantity of uniforms, hats, and other items barely managed to keep pace with the orders.

ZLOCZOW GHETTO, POLAND, APRIL 1943

The end of the small ghetto in Zloczow, Poland, came on April 2, 1943. The German and Ukrainian SS surrounded the ghetto, and the inhabitants were concentrated in the market square. In a blatant ruse, the Germans ordered the head of the *Judenrat*, Zigmunt Mayblum, to sign a document claiming the liquidation was necessary to stem a typhoid epidemic. Mayblum refused and was murdered on the spot. Other members of the *Judenrat*, Schwartz and Yakir, met the same fate when they too refused to sign the bogus document.

The Jews were taken by truck four kilometers east to a spot near the village of Yelhovista, where they were shot and buried, many while they were still alive. About six thousand were executed, and later reports indicated that only two Jews had escaped the massacre.

THE BUNKER NEAR ZLOCZOW, MAY 1943

In the bunker under the stable on the farm of Anna Sawicki, things were becoming tense. While the bunker continued to provide a safe, though tenuous, haven for the five inhabitants, nerves were constantly being frayed. Food was becoming an issue, but worse, the Germans were scouring the countryside and were frequent, unwanted visitors to the farm, and they showed a particular interest in the stable. Thankfully, once again, they found nothing.

Zofia Ruder was having difficulty coping with the stifled environment she had been enduring for over a year. Her husband Mendel had not returned, and she had assumed the worst. News from the outside was not encouraging. One morning she said something about her sister, a sister no one had heard about until now. She said she was worried about her and wanted to go look for her. Regina Wurm and her daughter Blima tried to talk Zofia out of this foolhardy idea. It was far too dangerous, they pleaded. Everyone went to bed on edge.

The next morning Zofia Ruder was gone. No one saw or heard her leave. Little Dolek was still there, asleep. Zylko Janowic was gone as well.

Not satisfied with the massacres, the Germans and their Ukrainian henchmen continued to hunt for any Jews still in hiding in the Zloczow area. For the next two days, they managed to root out a number of Jews who were taken to the same site near Yelhovista and shot. Thereafter, any Jews caught were taken to the city cemetery and shot.

Zofia Ruder met her end at the city cemetery, as did the handsome Pole, Zylko Janowic. The circumstances of their exodus from the safety of the bunker remains a mystery and can only be the topic of speculation.

WIELKIE LUCKI FORCED LABOR CAMP, AUGUST 1943

For Mendel Ruder, his two friends Jakob Gruenbaum and Dawid Neiss, and the other prisoners at the Wielkie Lucki forced labor camp, living had become akin to being on automaton. The brain retreated into the background and watched what was going on but didn't deign to participate. It was summer, hot and dusty in the camp. Day after day of brutality from the SS guards, the backbreaking work, and the relentlessness summer heat combined to overwhelm the prisoners, and many died of starvation, exhaustion, and disease. They were, however, easily replaced.

Soon, though, as news began to filter in from replacement inmates, several informal leaders began to emerge among the motley ranks of prisoners. News of the liquidation of the Zloczow ghetto proved particularly disheartening, and everyone now understood that chances of their spouses, parents, children, grandparents, and friends having survived had most likely died with them. They had nothing to lose now, and the few leaders, mostly hotheads with revenge driving them, were determined to fight back.

The nearby woods were frequent targets of sweeps by the Ukrainians, not only because Jews were hiding there, but partisans were also known to operate from that well-camouflaged area. Most of the partisans were Polish and had no real love for the Jews, but they hated the Ukrainians more, and this sometimes resulted in some level of cooperation with the Jews. Some Jews were even allowed to join their ranks. In this case, however, cooperation took the form of small arms, ammunition, explosives, and other small weapons smuggled into the work camp.

Gruenbaum and Neiss, who had befriended Mendel, were collaborators in the planned uprising. Mendel was not by nature a violent man. He still held out hope that his wife and young son were still alive, safe in the bunker he had procured for them. While he agreed that some sort of uprising was justified, he doubted that the few weapons would make much of a difference against the Ukrainians and especially the Germans. He was sure any armed resistance would immediately provoke a brutal and merciless response, so he held back. He thought there was still a chance to reunite with his family once the war ended, and he wanted to be there when it did.

On a hot August day, many of the inmates of the Wielkie Lucki forced labor camp outside of Zloczow, now called Zolochiv, attacked their Ukrainian and German guards with pistols, clubs, and other makeshift weapons. The attacks managed to kill and injure several guards, but the revolt was soon put down by the overwhelming numbers and superior weapons of the Nazi SS captors. Many inmates were killed during the revolt. Gruenbaum and Neiss survived the revolt but were immediately executed by the Germans for their roles in the revolt. While Mendel and about thirty other inmates were spared, a decision had been made to liquidate the camp.

The next day dawned sunny and hot. The bodies of the dead Ukrainians and the few Germans killed in the revolt were removed for a proper burial. The dead Jews had been left where they fell. After taking a final roll call, the remaining prisoners prepared to leave the camp. Two never made it. A German guard quickly dispatched two unfortunates with his Luger. History would not record the reason for their deaths.

Soon, two trucks arrived, and the prisoners were quickly loaded. By early afternoon, the two trucks carrying twenty-eight Jews and ten Ukrainian guards began their westward journey to some unknown destination, unknown at least to the Jews. None of the Jews knew why they were not just shot, so they assumed they would live to work another day at another camp. Mendel was riding in the second truck and was able to see the passing landscape. He knew they were traveling west, past what was left of Zloczow toward Lvov, possibly to the notorious Janowska camp on the northwest side of town.

As the two trucks slowed to shift gears on the approach to a steep hill, Mendel and several others decided this was their chance to escape from the truck and flee into the dense woods on the right side of the road. The Ukrainian guards were half asleep, their bodies bouncing up and down in rhythm with the truck's passage on the uneven road. Feigning sleep, seven of the prisoners were alert, waiting for the precise moment when the conditions of the speed of the truck, the advantageous terrain, and the dozing guards came together to provide a window of opportunity for an escape.

The moment came as the trucks had to negotiate a deep rut in the road while they were going uphill at a steep angle. The truck slowed abruptly, noisily shifting to a lower gear. The guards were jolted awake but were forced to hold on to something to avoid being thrown from the truck. At that instant, Mendel and six other prisoners leaped over the tailgate of the truck onto the road and made for the woods to the right. The guards, struggling for balance shouted, "Halt or we will shoot!"

No one halted. Seven guards quickly exited the truck and gave chase. Shots rang out. Two prisoners fell, their thirty seconds of freedom ended. Five others made it as far as the thick woods. Mendel ran as fast as his short legs would allow, occasionally stumbling or tripping on a half-buried root or rock. He heard more shots and screams of pain as more of the remaining escapees fell. He heard shrieks and more screams. The seven guards now gave chase to the remaining escapee.

Mendel ran faster. Running too fast, he suddenly tripped on a half-buried rock and went tumbling down an embankment and landed in a large flowing creek or small river. It didn't matter to him, though, as he was up to his neck in cold, fast-flowing water. He looked up, shaking the water from his head and eyes. He realized he had fallen about thirty feet down the side of the steep riverbank. He could hear the guards approaching from above.

"Come out, little Jew," they called out tauntingly in Polish. "We are going to kill you." Mendel frantically looked around and spotted a nearby deep undercut in the embankment toward which he quickly made his way, squeezing himself as close to the wall as he could. Though the water was deep, he realized he was hidden from his pursuers above who were looking over the edge trying to find him. He could just hear a guard who was peering over the edge, loose dirt and leaves falling to within a foot of where he hid.

Shivering in the neck-deep water, Mendel stoically endured the cold. Gradually, the shouts from above faded away as the pursuers gave up, assuming the small Jew had been swept away by the cold current, or so that is what they would report. Mendel could hear more shots in the distance and soon the groan of the trucks as they continued their uphill journey westward.

After several hours, Mendel thought it would be safe to leave his watery hideout, dry out, and get warm. In spite of the August heat, he felt cold in the shade of the canopied forest. He continued to shiver and experienced difficulty walking or even standing. He couldn't think straight. After a few more steps, he fell down and didn't want to get up. Hypothermia did that to a person, and Mendel was in grave danger.

Sometime later, Mendel found himself wrapped in a blanket surrounded by a group of people he couldn't identify. He looked at them, bewilderment obvious on his face. A large bearded man with a rifle looked at him and in Polish said, "Hello, little Jew. We saw you escape from the Germans and those damned Ukrainians. We saw you almost drown in the river. We felt sorry for you and decided maybe you might be of use to us. Get some rest for now. We will talk later and decide your fate."

MÜHLDORF, GERMANY, DECEMBER 1943

As the war raged on, fifteen-year-old Marile Häusl and her childhood friend Anton Becker, now eighteen, continued their training activities in their respective Hitler Youth organizations. Marile was particularly delighted to knit socks for the soldiers. She was proud to be doing her part. She was also involved in collecting coats and other items of clothing that were destined for the front. Both Marile and Anton wondered why the government didn't provide these items but had faith in the Fuhrer and assumed this was a show of patriotic support for the troops, a chance for the German people to participate in the war. Anton had almost completed his Hitler Youth training, and all the marching and other paramilitary activities in which he had participated were designed to facilitate his effective transition into the regular army. He was well accustomed to marching, wearing a uniform, practicing with firearms, and especially following orders without question.

His transition came quickly. He was called up for duty later that month. The two friends met the day before Anton was scheduled to leave with a number of other Hitler Youth boys. "Are you excited to go, Donei?" asked Marile. "Are you scared?"

"No, I'm very anxious to go, to fight for the Fatherland," said the young man, his voice not nearly matching his brave words. "Word is we are going east to fight the Russians. Don't worry, my little Marile. I will be fine. The war has lasted longer than the Fuhrer planned, but I know we will win in the end."

Anton Becker, nicknamed Donei, hugged his friend, as a brother would a sister, and as he turned to leave, he said, "Remember, one day when this is over, we will get married."

Tears in her eyes, Marile smiled and waved as he walked away. With her step-brother Alois and her uncles Max and Leonhard already fighting, she hoped for the best but wondered when she would see him again.

1944

BUNKER OUTSIDE ZLOCZOW, JANUARY 1944

For the remaining Jews hiding in the bunker under the stable on Anna Sawicki's farm outside Zloczow, life continued to go on. News from the outside seemed encouraging as the Russians continued their westward push toward the heart of Germany. First, however, they needed to come through Galicia, and their arrival was greatly anticipated. Regina Wurm and her daughter Blima, along with young Dolek Ruder and the Birnbaums, endured the January cold, the hunger, and the wild emotional swings between the sheer boredom of daily life and the heart-stopping searches by the Nazis and their Ukrainian henchmen. The group had been hiding since November 1941 and knew that, if found, they would meet a quick but brutal death. The group had heard that a ghetto had been established to warehouse the Jews from the vicinity but that it had since been liquidated. Over six thousand Jews had met their deaths as part of the liquidation. Word was that there were few, if any, survivors.

It was a cold, cloudy day in January that witnessed a remarkable reunion. A small figure, dressed in what could only be described as rags, cautiously emerged from the nearby woods and made its way to the farmhouse. As the figure came closer, Anna, looking through a window, could see that a long black beard graced his face. He looked around, scanning the area, before coming up to the door and knocking.

"What do you want?" asked Anna through the door.

"It's Mendel, Mendel Ruder. Please let me in. Quickly."

Anna was stunned by the vision of Mendel standing by her door. She hesitated, trying to make sure it was really him. The beard, almost five inches long, made for a good disguise, but she finally recognized him and quickly opened the door. Mendel stepped in just as quickly.

"Where have you been, Mr. Ruder? We all thought the worst."

"I'll explain later. Are my wife and son safe? Are they in the bunker?"

Anna hesitated before answering. "Herr Ruder, I think you should go down to the bunker. They will tell you what has happened."

In spite of being gone for over a year, Mendel knew where the entrance to the bunker was hidden and hurried out to the stable. He opened the trap door leading down to the bunker and entered. He heard gasps as he came into view. He looked around for Zofia, and when he failed to locate her, he felt a moment of panic. Then he saw little Dolek with Regina Wurm, and understanding began to dawn on him.

"Where is my wife?" he asked to no one in particular. Regina and Blima looked at each other. The Birnbaums looked at their feet. Dolek began to cry and was immediately shushed by Regina.

"What has happened to my Zofia?"

"Herr Ruder," began Regina. "We are very surprised to see you. What happened to you? Where have you been for over a year?"

Mendel, having surmised the situation, was overcome with emotion and sat down on a makeshift stool. He put up his arms and said, "Not now, please, I need to rest for a while."

He heard Blima say, "Dolek, it's your father. Go to him."

Dolek looked at the small man who was his father. He hadn't seen Mendel for over a year and was confused, especially by the beard.

Mendel looked up toward his son. Tears on his cheeks, he said, "Come here, my little Dolek. Come to your father."

Hearing Mendel's voice finally convinced Dolek, and he ran to his father. Mendel kissed his son and then looked up at the four other Jews in the bunker. They had sad looks on their faces.

"What happened to Zofia?" he finally repeated.

Regina spoke up first. "Herr Ruder, Mendel. Zofia was with us until about the middle of last year. She was having a hard time coping with the situation, the stress and the constant fear of the SS and the Ukrainians hunting for us. With no word from you, she thought, as we all did, that you were dead. One day she announced she was concerned about her sister. We didn't know about any sister, but she insisted on going out to look for her. We pleaded with her, but the next morning she was gone."

The group looked at Regina. She discreetly shook her head. The motion indicated "Not now."

"We heard the Ukrainians murdered any Jews they caught. We believe she was caught. We are not sure, but we fear the Ukrainians killed her at the cemetery."

Mendel thought about Zofia. As was common, theirs had been an arranged marriage. The couple had argued from time to time, but overall, theirs was considered a good marriage. He drew Dolek closer and hugged his son.

"Maybe she escaped. Maybe she is safe with her sister," Mendel said softly to no one in particular.

Regina looked at the other women. They nodded almost imperceptively. "Mendel," Regina began. "We think a Pole named Zylko Janowic left the bunker at the same time Zofia left." Mendel thought about that for a silent moment. He had never met Zylko Janowic but hoped the Pole had managed to save the two of them. He never asked about why the two apparently left together, perhaps because he didn't want to know.

LEMBERG/LVOV, APRIL 1944

The war continued to go badly for the Germans. The Red Army continued making broad advances westward, and it was clear they would soon be approaching Lvov. The Gestapo, which still ran the prisons in Lvov, made a decision to evacuate and send their prisoners westward in advance of the rapidly approaching Russians. Only history would know why these prisoners, especially those in Loncki Prison, were not executed but instead were sent westward toward Auschwitz. Perhaps they could be used as labor elsewhere or used as hostages in possible negotiations with the Allies.

"*Raus! Schnell, schnell!*" barked the SS guard. "Everyone out." With only a few minutes' notice, the prisoners were allowed to take a small suitcase with them. Simon quickly packed some extra clothes, sewing thread, needles, a watch, some money he had managed to hide, and other personal items accumulated during his almost three years in the prison.

The Gestapo staff cars were gone. It appeared the prison's higher-ranking personnel had already left, and only the guards and lower ranks were still there. Once out in the prison courtyard, the group of about thirty or so was loaded onto a waiting truck. They were unsure about what was happening or where they were going. One of the guards had a clipboard in his hands. It appeared to be holding a list of some sort. Simon inched his way near the guard. While he couldn't see the entire list, he did see the words "KZ Auschwitz" on the top of the form.

So Simon Ruder and a group of other prisoners were taken by truck to the Kleparow railway station, the starting point for so many deportation trains. This time there were no selections at the station. The train was shorter than usual, consisting of only twenty or so cars instead of the usual fifty-five. Several other trucks arrived with more prisoners, probably from the other two prisons in Lvov or maybe the nearby Janowska labor camp.

This time the cattle cars were not so crowded. After the prisoners and their meager suitcases were loaded onto the cars and the doors were locked, a whistle blew and the train slowly moved forward and switched onto the track leading back around town, where it looped around and headed west.

Unknown to the prisoners, the Belzec extermination camp, the final destination of so many deported Lvov Jews, had been shut down and dismantled the previous year, so instead, they were being transferred to a concentration camp called Auschwitz.

In spite of his isolation during his imprisonment at Loncki Prison, Simon had a good idea about Auschwitz and what it meant. Prisoners coming into Loncki Prison talked about things they heard went on there, the exterminations and horrendous conditions there. There were even rumors of horrific experiments by a German Dr. Mengele. As these thoughts ran through Simon's mind, he made a quick decision. While he couldn't really see exactly where the train was, he had a general idea. If he were right, they would soon come into an open rural area of farms worked mostly by the hated Ukrainians. Simon was a gambler, and he decided to take his chances. Using his suitcase as a weapon, he began to work on the door, repeatedly hitting the area where the locking mechanism was located. After a number of solid blows, it gave way, and the door partially opened. The train was moving slowly, perhaps twenty-five kilometers per hour. Simon looked through the door, which was slightly ajar. He saw a good spot coming up, and, timing his jump just right, he sprang from the train. He landed hard, the wind knocked out of him, but he managed to hold on to the little suitcase. He quickly recovered and looked around the area. He spotted a barn nearby and, making sure no one was watching, made his way across a plowed field toward the barn not too far way.

Back on the train, none of the other prisoners were willing to take their chances, and they all stayed on the train. If anyone jumped, Simon did not see him.

Simon stealthily approached the barn, opened the door slightly, quickly entered, and closed the door. It was not too dark inside. He could see no animals, so he made his way toward a pile of hay in the back of the barn. He sat down in the pile of hay and partially covered himself with it. He needed to rest and soon fell into a pathetic sleep.

Suddenly, the barn door swung open, and the Ukrainian farmer, rifle in hand, slowly entered the barn. In Ukrainian, the farmer said, "Come out, Jew. I have a weapon. Come out now." The farmer spotted Simon partially exposed under the pile of hay. "I see you, Jew. Stand up."

Simon raised his hands and slowly got to his feet. He spoke several languages, but Ukrainian wasn't one of them. He answered the farmer in Polish. "Please, I don't want any trouble. Just let me be on my way. Here, take my watch. I have a little money. You can have that too. Just allow me to stay here tonight."

Simon held out his watch for the farmer to see. Then he showed the man the money. The farmer looked at Simon and examined the items. After a moment of indecision, the Ukrainian, in broken Polish, said, "Yes, is good, but you must be gone by the morning." With that, the man stepped over to Simon and took the watch and money. "You can sleep over there. Hide in the hay if you want, but be on your way by sunrise."

"Thank you. I'll be no trouble for you," said Simon. The Ukrainian nodded, walked toward the door, and closed it behind him. It wasn't too long before the Ukrainian started to have second thoughts about what had just happened. He remembered punishment for helping a Jew escape was death. He looked at the watch and money in his hand and decided the risk was too great. Making up his mind, he went to the edge of town where he knew some Ukrainian SS soldiers often congregated, and told them about the Jew hiding in his barn. He forgot to mention the watch and money.

Simon was asleep when the SS guards burst into the barn. He had completely covered himself in hay and was not easily discovered. One of the SS guards began to shoot into the hay. One shot, two, a third, all missed their mark. Simon quickly decided he had probably used all his luck and was not willing to risk a fourth shot.

"Wait," he shouted. "I surrender. Don't shoot." The guards laughed as the little Jew stood up, straw cascading from him, but much still clinging to him. The guards, three of them, grabbed Simon and hit him with the butts of their rifles.

"Get up, Jew!" the leader shouted. The blows stopped, and he was taken outside to a vehicle some distance away. He was roughly tossed into the back of the truck and driven eastward, back toward the town. The Ukrainian SS guards took him back to Loncki Prison. The SS guards still at the prison were packing up records and supplies and were surprised to see Simon. They were at a loss as to what to do with the former inmate. Normally, he would just be shot.

The Ukrainians led Simon into the main building and outside to the courtyard. He was lined up against a wall, expecting to be shot. The three Ukrainians were about to shoot when they heard someone yell out, "Halt!" It was the SS guard *Oberschutze* Johann Lichtner still at the prison making final preparations for the last phase of the hasty evacuation. He laughed when he saw Simon. "Did you fall off the train?" he asked. "I have no time for you now. I could shoot you now, but I think I'll send you back to the station. Be on the train tomorrow morning. There won't be another one for you. Good-bye, Simon." He motioned to the three Ukrainians guards. "Put our guest in a cell. Be sure to wake him in the morning. And make sure he gets on the train."

"Thank you, SS *Oberschutze* Lichtner," said a very relieved Simon. "I won't forget your kindness." SS Guard Johann Lichtner grunted and waved his arm as if to dismiss them. "Don't thank me yet. Take him away before I change my mind," he said to the three guards. They looked at each other, confused. They were unaccustomed to an SS guard showing the slightest concern for a Jewish prisoner but didn't object as they led Simon down the long hall and hustled him into a small cell. He thought it might be the same cell he had been locked in when he was first captured in August of 1941. He saw and felt the five marks he made on the wall to keep track of the days.

After a night of sleeping on a cold stone floor, he and several other prisoners were taken to Kleparow railway station, where they joined a group of other Jews waiting to be loaded on the waiting train. Simon didn't know these Jews or where they had come from. The SS guards loaded the group into the dreaded cattle cars and locked the doors, and with a whistle from the locomotive, the train began its journey westward. *At least I'm still alive*, Simon thought.

The train traveled through the German-occupied General Government and passed through, Przemysl, Tarnow, and several other small villages until it finally stopped in a southern suburb of Krakow at what appeared to be a large camp. Simon wasn't sure why they stopped here. He remembered his geography and thought this place was on the way to Auschwitz but didn't think this actually was Auschwitz. The camp had been officially known as *Zwangsarbeitslager Plaszow des SS-und Polizeifuhrers im Distrikt Krakau*, more commonly referred to as Plaszow, a notorious forced labor camp run by the sadistic SS *Untersturmfuhrer* Amon Goeth from Vienna. However, as of January 10 of that year, the camp had been elevated to a full concentration camp status. Goeth had run the work camp with brutal impunity, murdering and torturing inmates at will, satisfying his sadistic impulses. It was said that Goeth wouldn't have breakfast until he shot someone and that he enjoyed killing many Jews himself. With the new status of the camp came a more structured chain of command, making it somewhat more inconvenient for Goeth to do his murdering, but he was also very clever, and the new procedures for punishing and killing inmates did little to stop the atrocities. This monster was responsible for thousands of deaths, and the war would conclude for him at the end of a hangman's rope.

Having escaped from the earlier train leaving Lemberg, Simon had become separated from his Loncki Prison inmate group, a situation the waiting SS soon corrected. After unloading the human cargo, much of them having perished in transit, Simon heard a guard call out his name.

"Here," he said weakly, expecting to be summarily executed as he stumbled toward the front of the line. The guard marked something on a sheet of paper on a clipboard and led Simon away toward one of the barracks and shoved him inside. Soon a group of inmates returned from some sort of work duty. In the group were young William Weiss, his father David, and several other tailors from Loncki Prison.

In war, there invariably occur ironic and often astonishing twists of fate, and Simon was to unknowingly participate in one such peculiar phenomenon. When he arrived at the Plaszow concentration camp, he was unaware that his older brother Izak had been saved from the worst of this atrocious labor camp and was, at that very moment, working literally next door at 4 Lipowa Street in Oskar Schindler's DEF factory (Deutsche Emaillewaren-Fabrik), also known as Emalia.

Life at the camp was brutal. Simon was assigned to work in a nearby stone quarry. Conditions were inhuman, made more so by the sadistic depredation by the guards. Simon learned of prisoners being taken outside the camp to a large hill called *Hujowa Górka* and executed. Thousands lost their lives in this fashion. More prisoners arrived every day, most by truck. Simon persevered through sheer willpower as he absorbed beatings, abuse, and starvation diets. He knew what it meant to be sick and unable to work. Goeth was an unusually large man, a full two meters tall. Simon once caught a glimpse of Goeth pompously riding through the camp on his horse.

One morning Simon was at work pushing a load of dirt in a wheelbarrow when he heard a shot ring out. A worker just a few meters away from him fell over, dead. Simon stopped momentarily, trying to make sense of what had happened. He quickly realized he could be next and hurried off as another shot rang out. The bullet hit the dirt just behind where he had been standing. Simon ran for the cover of a barracks before another shot could find him. Goeth merely laughed. He really didn't know at whom he was shooting, nor did he care. These were simply targets, objects at which to shoot. These were not people, after all; these were rodents, vermin. These were *untermenschen*, not worthy of sympathy or kindness. Goeth might as well have been at a carnival shooting targets to win a prize, except in this case, the prize fed his own sadism.

PLASZOW CONCENTRATION CAMP NEAR KRAKOW, MAY 1944

Surprisingly, after less than three weeks, Simon and a group of other prisoners were sent over to the railroad tracks and were told to wait there for a train. On this day in May 1944, a train was headed the sixty-five kilometers to Auschwitz. Simon could not imagine a worse camp than the one he had just left. Reality, however, would soon prove him wrong.

The train was similar to the hundreds of others run by the Deutsche Reichsbahn for this purpose. As it approached the camp, Simon could see that while it came in with a full complement of cattle cars, it now only brought in ten cars to be unloaded. The train screeched to a halt, belching steam. Guards immediately rushed to the cars and opened the doors. Simon and the group were ordered to stand back as the human cargo was being unloaded. Over eight hundred Jews were crammed into the first ten cars. About six hundred were able to exit the cars on their own. Two hundred needed help but were still alive. The rest were carried out of the cars and stacked like firewood next to the tracks. Many were taken immediately to *Hujowa Górka* and shot. The process was repeated five times, ten cars, one at a time. Each time, more than half were able to exit the cars on their own, some others still needed help, and the rest didn't care. Simon noticed that it seemed the farther back in the train, the more Jews survived, but just marginally.

It took about three hours for the train to be unloaded, reassembled, and turned around. More prisoners were approaching the tracks from the camp, including some women. Soon the prisoners were being herded to the cars and loaded. Simon held back, waiting as long as he could before getting into the cars. This time there were two tracks. More prisoners were coming from the camp. Simon continued to stall until finally, after three hours of loading, it was his turn, and he was pushed up into a car. The two lines of cattle cars were joined, and soon the train was ready to leave. In a few minutes, the familiar whistle blew, and the train slowly picked up speed and left the Plaszow labor camp with over four thousand Jewish prisoners headed for the decidedly unfriendly confines of Auschwitz.

The destination was only about sixty-five kilometers away, and it should have taken a few hours to get there. Unfortunately, the human cargo trains were assigned the lowest priority on the railroad, so anything else on the tracks took priority. Freight trains carrying war materials and troops took top priority. The trains no longer went nearly as far to the east as they had two years earlier as the eastern war front had begun to inexorably move westward. As a result, the prisoner train sat on various rail sidings for several hours at a time while a succession of higher-priority trains sped past. Every hour, less of the human cargo survived, especially in the early-summer heat. The railroad didn't care because they had already been paid. The Auschwitz camp didn't care because this saved them the cost and trouble of gassing those who didn't survive the trip. Only the overcrowded, cramped, thirsty, starving, and otherwise miserable occupants of the cattle cars cared.

On May 17, the train finally completed the journey to what was to become the very symbol of Nazi atrocities during the war years: Auschwitz. Its name would forever conjure images of unspeakable human depravity and brutality.

As the train trundled to a squealing halt, the debarkation process began as the cramped Jews spilled out of the cattle cars. Those who died en route were suddenly left unsupported by the mass of people around them in the cars and just collapsed, so much dead weight. Those still in the cars stepped over them.

Once on the platform, the Jews who had survived milled about, not sure what to do next. The camp was immense, with many buildings dotting the grounds. A tall chimney belching dark, acrid smoke was visible not too far away. The smell was new to most people, but one no one there would ever forget it as long as they lived. Most wouldn't have to remember it for too long. The cacophony of noises assaulted Simon's ears—people wailing, children screaming, and the ubiquitous barking of guard dogs. SS guards and officers soon made an appearance, their voices adding to the mix. "Achtung! Your attention!" came through a loudspeaker. The families were split up, men on one side, women on the other. "You will all move toward the officers waiting for you. They will tell you where to go. You will be fed, cleaned, and instructed on what to do. Do not worry. We will take care of you."

The throng moved slowly toward two waiting SS officers. They gave each person a cursory glance and pointed to the left or right. One SS officer in particular seemed to be looking very intently at the passing prisoners. Simon noticed him because he was wearing a white coat over his SS uniform. There were several sets of twins, mostly children nearby, apparently selected by the officer. They were always sent to the right. Most women, the elderly, and the sick were almost always sent to the left.

While he waited in the mass of prisoners, Simon had a chance to observe the camp. He noted the double barbed-wire fences enclosing the complex. He also heard music and finally noticed an orchestra playing uplifting music as people walked toward the officers. He didn't recognize the tune. Very strange, he thought. He looked at the growing crowd on the left. Instinctively, he looked at the billowing black smoke coming from the tall chimney and wondered if there was a connection.

Soon it was Simon's turn. One of the SS officers examined him for a brief moment. He saw only a small Jew with intense eyes standing in front of him. The officer motioned him to the left. As Simon started in that direction, he heard another other officer yell, "Halt!" It was the older of the two SS men, the one wearing the white coat. He motioned Simon over to him. "What is your profession?" he asked.

"I am a tailor and was working in the Loncki Prison in Lemberg making uniforms for the SS, sir." Simon made sure he used the German name Lemberg instead of Lvov. The SS officer looked Simon over with a practiced eye, and Simon later remembered the man quickly glanced at his own uniform, partially visible under the white coat. Dr. Josef Mengele thought for a brief instant and then barked, "You, go over to the right."

Dr. Josef Rudolf Mengele was known at the camp as "der weiße Engel" (the "White Angel") because his outstretched arms and white coat evoked in image of a white angel. He had come to Auschwitz in May 1943, having replaced another doctor who had fallen ill. On May 24, 1943, he became the medical officer of Auschwitz-Birkenau's *Zigeunerfamilienlager* ("Gypsy Family Camp"). In August 1944, this camp was liquidated, and all its inmates were gassed, and Mengele subsequently became chief medical officer of the main infirmary camp at Birkenau. Interestingly, Dr. Josef Mengele was not the chief medical officer of Auschwitz; that role was filled by his superior, SS *Standortarzt* Eduard Wirths. After the war, the good doctor would find his way to South America, where he reportedly died in 1979.

Simon did as he was told and joined the group that would live to survive another day. The far larger group on the left would not last the day. In an hour or less, they would be gassed, using the very effective Zyklon-B poison, and sometime later, stripped of everything of value, they would be part of the smoke now billowing into the air.

After the life-and-death selection process was completed, a group of prisoners gathered up the belongings left on the train and sorted them into large piles, which were then stored in special "Kanada" warehouses, so named because of the impression that Canada was a wealthy country. These items included clothing, eyeglasses, medicine, shoes, books, pictures, jewelry, and prayer shawls. These would be bundled up and periodically shipped back to Germany. Similar activities had been in place for years at various deportation sites.

Simon's group went through a process of institutionalized dehumanization. They were relieved of all of their clothes and valuables they may have brought with them. Their hair, all over their bodies, was shorn, like sheep.

Each prisoner received a striped prison uniform and a pair of fabric-covered wooden shoes that didn't fit. Completing the induction process, a tattoo was applied to their upper-left forearm. Simon's number was B-6867, and it was part of a new numbering system just recently initiated. The B series had begun a few days ago on May 13. The prisoners were then assigned to various work camps within the sprawling Auschwitz complex.

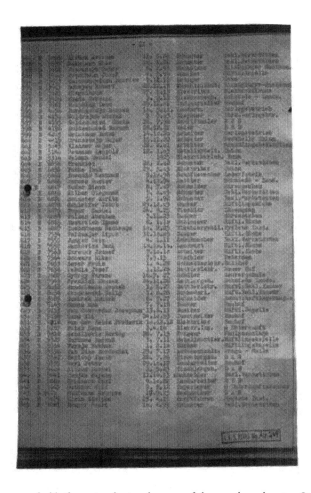

A document, probably from Auschwitz, because of the numbers showing Simon Ruder, number B-6867 as a "schneider," a tailor, and a streetbuilder.
Courtesy International Tracing Service.

Not that it mattered at the time, but Simon and his fellow prisoners were housed in what was officially called Auschwitz II-Birkenau, the largest of the three main camps and where the majority of exterminations took place. Also unknown to Simon was the reassignment of the entire Auschwitz camp to Rudolf Hoss, who had been replaced late last year by Arthur Liebehenschel, who was soon deemed to be too soft on the inmates. Hoss, whose alleged infractions were forgotten by the SS command, was put in place to prepare the camp for the major influx of Hungarian Jews. The railway spur from the main line was completed, enabling delivery of the human cargo directly into the camp, where a new ramp awaited the deboarding prisoners. The reign of Auschwitz as the major killing center of the Third Reich was to begin in earnest under Rudolf Hoss's leadership.

Simon was assigned to work in an arms factory producing artillery shells for the *Wehrmacht*, the German army. The pace was furious, and if you failed to keep up with the flow of parts, you were beaten severely. If you were no longer able to work, you were either shot or sent to a special barracks where your food rations were drastically cut and you slowly starved to death. Life expectancy was measured in weeks, if not days.

At night, it got worse. The prisoners were crammed together in wooden bunks, crude large shelves with wooden planks serving as sleeping surfaces. Three prisoners were crowded in one bunk. A bucket would have to suffice as a toilet, and by morning it was usually overflowing onto the floor. Interestingly, but not to the prisoners, the barracks were originally prefabricated horse stables meant for the Eastern Front. They were designed to hold 250 prisoners, but now some held up to one thousand.

Prisoners would assemble for roll calls called *Appel* early each morning. They were made to stand for hours regardless of the weather conditions, be it intense heat or freezing cold.

From there the prisoners would be marched to the factory or other work locations. The workday was twelve hours long with no breaks or rest periods. After work the prisoners were marched back to the camp and were made to endure another roll call. The guards particularly enjoyed the roll calls, as they provided them a chance to showcase their brutality.

Food, or more precisely, the lack of food, was a major challenge for the prisoners. Food was scarce. A substitute coffee called *Ersatzkaffee* was provided in the morning. Simon was familiar with this concoction. After work and the roll call, the evening meal consisted of a bowl of watery soup and a small amount of bread that contained sawdust. The life expectancy of a forced labor prisoner at Auschwitz was about three months, a goal that was consistently achieved by the limited food availability and overworking. Usually, prisoners died of being worked to death or by starvation. But that was by design, because while work had to be done, the Jews were also to be exterminated, so the absolute maximum work output from each prisoner had to be extracted before the prisoner invariably died.

One night, after the roll call and after the meager food rations had been distributed, Simon was talking to some of the other prisoners. They talked in hushed tones. Guards called Capos were everywhere. These individuals were most often common criminals working for the SS. They proved to be extremely brutal, mostly because they felt they had to show their masters that they possessed the brutal skills necessary to terrorize and control the prisoners.

"Simon, where are you from? How did you arrive here?" asked David Sachs, a prisoner who had survived for three months. Sachs looked emaciated and was showing the ill effects of the camp. Simon worried about how he was going to look in three months. Not like that, he hoped.

Simon replied, "I'm from Poland, from Lemberg. I was a tailor. I had a shop on Legionow Street. I was captured by the Gestapo and held in a prison for almost three years. I was sent to the Plaszow camp outside Krakow and then here. I arrived on a train two days ago."

"Do you have a family, Simon?" asked Sachs. Simon paused as he thought about Lola, Hanna, and Artur. "Yes," he started, "I had a wife and two children. Very nice children, a girl named Hanna and a little boy, Artur. A policeman told me that they were shot in Lemberg. That's all I know. God bless them, and damn those Nazis who killed them."

"I'm sorry, Simon. My wife and children were with me when we arrived here from Lublin three months ago. We were separated. I was taken for work.

They were killed, gassed over there. I think they burn the bodies over there too. See that chimney? That's where they go. That's what the black smoke is."

The others, those who still had the will to speak, had similar stories. They had come from all over Europe from ghettos in Warsaw, Lublin, Bialystok, Krakow, Radom, Minsk, Brest, and many others. The Auschwitz complex was receiving transports of Jews daily. Few were made to work.

The days dragged on into weeks, then months. Some days were better than others. Occasionally, Simon escaped the beatings in the mornings only to make up for it later that evening. The dreaded Capos enjoyed tormenting Simon, partially because he was small in stature and partially because they could not break his spirit. He was a constant target of their abuse. He continued to do his job at the factory. He was occasionally transferred to do outside heavy labor. He had outlived his stay, and they wanted him dead. But he refused to die.

Simon was frugal with his food, meager as it was. He tried to save a small piece of bread from each day. Every calorie counted here. Every potato peel was religiously saved, hidden until it could be consumed or traded. Every scrap, every crumb was saved. The bowls were licked to ensure that not a molecule of food was left behind. After four months, Simon had amassed a collection of stale bread crusts. Potato peels would turn black and rot quickly, so they were consumed or traded, but bread would last for some time. He had surpassed the average life expectancy of an Auschwitz inmate, but his survival was far from assured.

NEAR ORCHA, BELARUSSIA, JUNE 1944

Freshly promoted *Obersoldat* Anton Becker, whose unit had been hastily trained and rapidly transferred to the East to stand against an expected Red Army offensive, was anxious to see some real action, and though just a year out of the Hitler Youth, the nineteen-year-old was confident he could make a difference in the struggle to save the Fatherland. His chance would come quickly.

Operation *Bagration*, the codename for a major Soviet strategic offensive operation, began on June 22, 1944. The operation was named after Georgian Prince Pytor Bagration, a general of the Imperial Russian Army, who had been killed at the Battle of Borodino in September 1812. The objective of the fighting was to drive German forces from Belarussian SSR and Eastern Poland. The main offensive began in the early morning of June 23 with an artillery bombardment of unprecedented scale against the defensive emplacements set up by the Germans. The attack was extremely successful, and within hours, parts of the German defenses were starting to crumble.

Obergefrieter Max Kiermeier was one of the casualties of the first day of the massive Soviet offensive that would cost an estimated three hundred thousand or more German soldiers. *Obersoldat* Anton Becker, though a relatively raw recruit, was one of the fortunate German soldiers who was captured, bringing the total German prisoners of war held by the Russians to over two million. The war was over for *Obersoldat* Anton Becker, but his suffering was about to begin.

The massive Soviet offensive would soon accomplish its objective of pushing the Germans ever westward.

Two of the author's great uncles, Leonhard, Max, and uncle Alois. All were in the Wehrmacht and fought in the war. Max and Leonhard were killed somewhere in Russia in 1944. Alois wears the Black Wound Badge, indicating at least two wounds in battle. He returned to Germany after the war but succumbed to his injuries in 1947.

BUNKER OUTSIDE ZLOCZOW, JULY 1944

Mendel Ruder had been back at the bunker outside Zloczow for almost five months. He had accepted the disappearance of his wife and had acclimated himself to the daily routine of hiding. He spent much of his time with his son Dolek. News from the outside suggested the Russians were close by, and occasional bombs and artillery were heard not too far off. It grew louder day-by-day, and the occupants of the bunker were certain liberation was close at hand.

It was hot on July 18 when the Red Army captured Zloczow, and the few hiding Jews in the area cautiously made their way out of the bunkers that had been their sanctuaries for so long. The six Jews hidden under the stable on Anna Sawicki's farm, too, wasted no time making their way out into daylight. Little Dolek cautiously followed his father out of the bunker, into the stable, and finally, out into the sunlit open landscape. Unaccustomed to being outside, the young boy gazed at the endless blue sky and suddenly panicked and ran back into the bunker. The five other Jews chuckled as Mendel went back for him and led him out, softly reassuring the boy.

"It's all right, my little Dolek. We are saved. Do you hear the cannons? That's the Russians driving out the Germans. Soon we can go back home."

But Mendel knew that would never happen. He suspected that Zloczow was finished as a Jewish community but decided to explore what was left of his hometown. He also knew the war was not over, not until Berlin was captured, and he didn't care whether the Americans or the Russians got there first. He should have.

The war was still raging as Mendel and Dolek started making their way west toward Zloczow. They could hear the Russian Katyusha rockets launched from their ZIS-6 trucks. The rockets delivered a devastating quantity of explosives, and the actual launch made a hellish sound that was hard to forget. The retreating Germans answered with their own artillery barrages, but with little effect on the advancing Red Army. It was under this furious exchange of artillery and rockets that Mendel and his son followed the Russians westward. While not the main thrust of the Russian assault, the infantry was supported by a number of T-34 tanks and were utilizing them to good effect. Overhead, aerial dogfights between the remnants of the German air force, the *Luftwaffe*, and the Russians played out as the Germans retreated westward.

After a few kilometers, Mendel, intent on watching the fighting ahead and above of him, lost sight of Dolek. He has assumed the child had been following behind him, but suddenly, he was nowhere to be found. Mendel called out to his son. There was no answer. They had crossed a clearing, which had been surrounded on both sides by dense woods. He heard a loud noise, and suddenly, a T-34 tank came up behind Mendel. The tank slowed and stopped. A Russian officer hopped down off the tank and addressed Mendel.

"Where are you going? Don't you know it's dangerous?"

"Comrade, I'm looking for my son. We were just liberated yesterday by your glorious army. I'm worried about him. He is only six years old."

The Russian officer laughed and motioned Mendel over to the tank.

"We will find him, comrade. Follow us. We will go slowly, and you can watch for him the woods. But be very careful. I think we have chased the Germans away, but you can never tell."

A few hundred yards later, a crying Dolek, hiding in the woods, was watching as the Russian tank was coming slowly in his direction. He spotted a small figure, not in uniform, walking alongside the tank. He heard the figure calling out something but could not make it out over the roar of the tank. He squinted to see better and suddenly realized the small figure was his father walking beside the monstrous Russian tank.

Relieved to find his father again, Dolek ran from the woods and joined him beside the tank. The tank lurched to a halt, and the officer motioned the two to climb aboard. Both reluctantly did so, finding purchase on various appliances on the tank. The ride was slow, bumpy, and noisy, but it was better than walking. The tank finally came out of the clearing and came to a dirt road on the side of which was a farmhouse. The tank stopped, and the officer motioned the two down.

"Are you hungry, my friends?" he asked.

Mendel answered, "Yes, we could use a little food. It's been a long time since we last had something to eat." Dolek nodded his head in agreement.

"Follow me," said the officer as he made his way to the farmhouse.

A woman came out of the door and, shielding her eyes, took in the scene. The Russian officer called to her. "We need some food. Bring out what you have."

The Polish woman tried to wave them away. "I have nothing. Go away."

The officer laughed again. He looked back at his tank and made a twirling motion with his hand and pointed to the farmhouse. A few seconds later, the turret on the tank began a slow arc, and the big 76.2 mm gun and two machine guns were soon trained on the farmhouse. The woman screamed, a sound that could be heard over the idling tank, waved her arms, and, in obvious panic, ran into the house. Within minutes, she returned with a large plate piled high with a mountain of pierogies.

The fighting raged on, though there were lulls from time to time, and during one such lull, Mendel and Dolek bid farewell to their liberators.

"Zloczow has been liberated and soon Lvov," said the Russian officer as he climbed back onto his tank. "Then we will chase these bastards back to Berlin." Finally, with a good-natured laugh, he said, "Good luck to you, my friends. Be careful."

They were. The road to Zloczow was badly cratered, destroyed military equipment littering the countryside, often still ablaze or smouldering. Occasionally, the pair came across dead horses strewn on the roadside. Some had been recently carved up, the meat a bonanza for the war-starved population. They slowly navigated the appalling obstacle course, and a day later,

Mendel and Dolek arrived in the liberated town of Zloczow. They cautiously entered the town and began to search for any remnant of their former lives. The Russians were there in force and had started to settle in. Civilians were also busy trying to reclaim their lives, but Jews were either still in hiding or gone. Not surprisingly, the town was extensively damaged, but still some parts were reasonably intact. Mendel sought out his old apartment building. It was only slightly damaged, but his apartment was occupied. He remembered the missing suitcase and the unfortunate events that had followed. Better to avoid a confrontation, he thought. The pair continued through the town. No eyes met theirs as he and little Dolek walked quietly toward his old tailor shop. It, too, stood but had a new owner. Dejectedly, Mendel and Dolek moved on to search for friends but found none. At least the Germans were gone, fleeing westward. The pair continued their exploration. They passed a number of civilians, all Gentiles. Mendel could sense the thoughts behind the furtive glances ranging from "So you made it" to "Which hole did you climb out of?" No joy, no happiness, no reunion with old friends and acquaintances. They moved on, passing rubble-strewn remnants of the town Mendel had called home and the birthplace of Dolek. They crossed the street, barely avoiding a wagon pulled by a horse that would soon be lying in a ditch on the side of some dirt road. They passed more people who, after a quick glance at the pair, turned their heads and looked down, as if searching for something on the ground.

Suddenly, a woman yelled, "Mendel!" Surprised, Mendel turned around and slowly recognized his old landlady. The look in her eyes reflected surprise that he had survived, yet it betrayed a glimmer of pity.

Not knowing what to say, she nonetheless managed to continue. "I'm so glad to see you," she lied. "I see little Dolek has grown. How is Zofia?"

A sad look played across the small tailor's face. The landlady understood. "I'm so sorry."

"Thank you. I appreciate your words." He looked around. "What has happened since I was gone?"

"Those damn Germans. They came and rounded up most of the Jews in town and sent them off somewhere." She didn't mention the outright murders that had taken place. "I think there may be a few left, but not many."

Mendel struggled to hear what the woman was saying, his hearing limited at best, but he managed to follow the conversation.

He looked at her, and as the words sunk in, she asked, "What are you planning to do, Mendel? This is not a good place. The Russians are here and are taking over again. This time for good. Our world has changed, I'm afraid."

Mendel slowly looked around again. "I think you are right. Dolek and I will be moving on, maybe to Lemberg. Maybe things will be better there. Is there a place we can stay for a day or so?"

"Yes, I have a small room you can use. Maybe we can find some food. The cherry crop is good this summer."

It quickly became obvious to Mendel that few Jews were left in Zloczow and that they were not wanted. A few days later, after a short and tension-filled stay, the pair thanked their old landlady and began the next step of a journey whose end they could not have imaged. Literally on the heels of the Russian offensive, the diminutive father and young son began the almost seventy-kilometer trip to what was once called Lemberg, then Lvov.

LVOV/LVIV, POLAND/UKRAINE, JULY 1944

It had taken the Russians another week to fight their way to Lvov, but on July 26, the city was liberated. Mendel and Dolek arrived there a day after the Russians. With no concrete plans, Mendel decided to stay there, at least temporarily. He had visited the city many times before the Germans had captured it in 1941 and was familiar with the layout. The liquidated Jewish ghetto and remains of the Janowska work camp marred the surroundings, though much of the city still reflected the aftermath of fighting. The three prisons, however, were still in operation, although the jailers had changed once again. It was obvious to Mendel that the Russians would once again impose their ideology and the system that embodied it. He had already experienced both several years earlier and was not sure about his prospects a second time around.

He did find work quickly as a tailor at a government factory making clothing. This was similar to the work he had done in Zloczow before the Germans had retaken the city in 1941. He and Dolek found a place to stay in a small, unheated two-room apartment. Dolek was enrolled in a Russian-speaking school with many Poles and a few Russian children. Life was difficult for the growing child, but he had food and was allowed to play games. Being one of less than a handful of Jews in school ensured he caught the attention of the Ukrainian and Polish pupils. Having endured two years in hiding had affected his social development, but he had learned to fight, a skill that would prove to be useful in the coming years.

AUSCHWITZ CONCENTRATION CAMP, SEPTEMBER 1944

Simon Ruder had survived four months in Auschwitz, but in spite of the saved food, he began to slowly succumb to hunger, hard outside labor, and constant beatings. He was unable to appear at the roll calls and was sent to the hospital barracks, abandoned to die. He was emaciated, and hunger was rapidly draining what strength he still had. Life was leaving Simon, and he welcomed it. He thought of how it would feel to be black smoke rising up and out of the chimney. Death was the price of freedom for him and he was ready to receive it. He hoped to see Lola and the children soon.

Then a voice, distant yet familiar, said, "Here, drink this. Slowly." A bowl was lifted to his lips, and he instinctively drank the warm broth. The voice continued. "And some bread." He devoured the bread like the starving creature he had become. He didn't notice, but it was good bread, not the sawdust shit he had had in the barracks. Simon tried but he couldn't identify the voice or the figure that stood over him. In fact, he wasn't sure the figure was real. Only the drops of broth on his lips convinced him that the episode had really happened. He licked his lips until the tiny drops were gone.

"I'll be back when I can," said the voice.

The visitor came back two days later with more soup and bread. Simon began to regain his strength, slowly but steadily. He didn't die, not then. Again, he wondered who his savior was. He still had no idea.

He surprised everyone when he emerged from the hospital barracks on his own two feet a week later. Few ever had. He was led away by two SS guards and taken to the factory.

He was led to an office where several officials were working behind desks. An SS guard approached him. Simon shook his head to try to clear his thoughts.

"You are a tailor?" asked the guard.

"Yes," answered Simon. "I made SS uniforms in Lemberg. For almost three years, I made uniforms."

"Good," said the guard. "You have been assigned to sewing duty here in the factory starting tomorrow. You will report here. And you have been reassigned to another barracks. Now go."

As Simon prepared to leave the office, another SS guard was walking toward him. Simon tried to focus, tried to identify the face. Then recognition set in. It was the face of *Oberschutze* Johann Lichtner, one of the SS guards from Loncki Prison. As they passed each other, Lichtner whispered, "Now you can thank me."

It was October, and the weather was beginning to get colder. More trains came in, and more black smoke belched from the chimney. More workers were being selected. The new arrivals brought news that the Allies had landed on the coast of France at a place called Normandy and were working their way toward Germany. The Russians, too, were making swift progress from the east.

The barracks to which Simon was assigned had the same layout as the one he had left. Some of the prisoners were in much the same condition as Simon, hungry, emaciated, but still able to function. Others were walking skeletons, sunken eyes with no trace of life in them. Soon they would be taken to the hospital barracks and left to die. There would be no savior for them.

The brick stove that ran the length of the barracks did little to provide adequate heat on really cold days. Prisoners continued to die due to the usual mistreatment, hunger, and cold and were replaced, and life went on. Simon's new job in the factory eased his suffering to some extent. The guards still practiced their beatings and other tortures, but Simon was able to persevere. Because of the snow and freezing temperatures, roll calls became brutal. Standing at attention for extended periods of time was the norm, and many prisoners could not bear it and were shot.

Simon continued in his role of sewing uniforms and mostly making repairs to old ones. The old ones were torn, full of holes, and had just recently been cleaned of blood and other fluids. He also completed some carpentry at the factory. He was weak but surviving. He had not seen *Oberschutze* Johann Lichtner since his encounter with him in the factory office hallway. He made a promise to thank him after the war, should he survive that long. Unknown to Simon, however, *Oberschutze* Johann Lichtner had been transferred to the Stutthof concentration camp.

LVIV, UKRAINE, DECEMBER 1944

Life in what was now Lviv, Ukraine, dragged on for Mendel. While it provided needed refuge for him immediately after liberation, he had no intention of continuing to live under its restrictive yoke. In the last five months, the Soviet economic system had taken hold, and he wanted no part of it again, so he started making plans to move, to start anew in another, perhaps more liberal, city with more Jews.

It was the end of December, and little Dolek was delighted to meet Old Man Frost, or *Ded Moroz* as he was called. He resembled Santa Claus, with his coat, boots, and long white beard. He wore a heel-length fur coat, a semiround fur hat, and *valenki* or jackboots on his feet. He walked into the classroom with a long magical staff and passed out small toys and treats to the children. For young Dolek, it was a wonderful time, but that was soon to change.

1945

AUSCHWITZ CONCENTRATION CAMP,
JANUARY 1945

As 1945 dawned, it was becoming more apparent to the Germans that the war was lost. The Nazis were taking desperate actions to try to forestall the inevitable. The Nazi regime was being squeezed from the east by the Russians and from the west by the British and the Americans. The Russians were closing in on Auschwitz. It was time to leave. Work had already been started on dismantling the crematoria in a vain attempt to hide the atrocities that had been committed there.

The prisoners were lined up for roll call on the frigid morning of January 17. It would be the final roll call at the Auschwitz complex. Just over sixty-seven thousand inmates were accounted for. The next day a general evacuation began, and inmates were sent out in a series of "death marches" to camps further west.

Simon Ruder was among the approximately fifty-eight thousand inmates who left the Auschwitz complex on January 18, 1945. They were forced to march in knee-deep snow fifty kilometers through Mikolow to Gleiwitz near the German border. Ironically, that was where the war had started in September of 1939. The prisoners were given a loaf of bread and a blanket. Many were barefoot; others wrapped rags around their feet. Simon, with rags covering most of his wooden shoes, trudged along in the snow, trying to focus on surviving. He was sure the war would be over soon, and he was determined to see it, to outlast these Nazi bastards and see justice done. One foot in front of the other, he kept thinking. Keep moving; it will keep you warmer. Many prisoners were just too weak to continue. They were shot immediately. It was often a toss-up between dying of pure exhaustion or hunger or being shot by the guards for failing to keep up. Perhaps it was a choice for some. A rapidly faltering David Weiss, perhaps sensing the end, whispered hoarsely to Simon, "Take care of my son." Simon grunted a promise to the forty-two-year-old who had shared the Loncki Prison work detail in Lwow along with his son, William. A trail of corpses, blood soaking into the snow like little red flags marking where they had fallen, lined the road to Gleiwitz, and at some point, David Weiss joined them. The guards made sure those who fell stayed that way. Simon kept moving, his limbs freezing and aching, his strength being sapped with every step. His feet and legs felt like blocks of unfeeling ice. He heard a shot ring out but was too weak to turn around. *Just a little farther*, he told himself. *I must do this. I must somehow survive to avenge my wife and children, to tell the horrific story of suffering and murder. Focus on the striped uniform in front of you until it falls, and then search for another to follow.*

Simon realized he was near the middle of the group and slowly falling farther behind. The farther the group struggled on, the fewer prisoners were still marching. He looked ahead of and behind him. The cluster of prisoners behind him was strung out, and every few minutes or so, a gunshot rang out. The rear continued to dwindle as the marchers gave up, either succumbing to the suicide by not keeping up or simply dying of exhaustion, starvation, and exposure. In either case, the always vigilant guards were there to finish the job.

Simon became alarmed as he became aware that he was falling back and was no longer near the middle of the group, a result of the stragglers being dispatched. He did not want to appear weak or unable to continue; that would get him shot. He knew he didn't have the strength to move up in the line and was sure that expending the effort to do so would quickly exhaust any energy reserves he might still have.

The group approached a barn, and one of the SS guards yelled, "Into the barn, you dirty Jews. We will rest here." Simon thanked God, the same God he feared had abandoned him earlier. He had heard a saying once. "There are no atheists in the trenches." *The same could be said about death marches*, he thought sarcastically.

The pitiful group from Auschwitz II-Birkenau was grateful for the chance to rest. They had been marching through the cold and deep snow all day. Inside the barn, they felt better and warmer. At least they were out of the wind and snow. The guards didn't bother with roll call. Neither did they keep track of how many prisoners were shot or had died along the way. It was obvious, however, that many more had started this march than were now in the barn.

The next morning they continued the march, and about half of the prisoners in this group finally reached Gleiwitz. Not among the group was young William Weiss's forty-two-year-old father David, who, weakened by starvation and exposure, had died somewhere on the march. William had survived, and he and the other members of the group were forced to stay at the Gleiwitz camp for a few days while the SS arranged transportation further west into Germany. It was getting more difficult to schedule trains because of the requirements of the *Wehrmacht* to move personnel and materials across Central Europe. Once transportation was available, the prisoners were divided into transport groups and taken to the ramp to be loaded into freight cars.

The prisoners were dispatched to several camps, including Buchenwald, Gross-Rosen, Sachsenhausen, and Mauthausen. Simon Ruder was part of the group that was sent on to Gross-Rosen. William Weiss was not with the group. In the cars, no one knew where they were being sent or why. There were no selections. The prisoners traveled in open cars this time, and while it was still unbearably cold and they were exposed to the elements, it was better than struggling on foot through the deep snow. As they traveled through various towns, people seemed to have learned a new sport. For amusement, they would throw bread at the moving cars and then watch the ensuing mad scramble. It was like throwing seeds to a flock of pigeons and watching them greedily go after the food. Many more prisoners would freeze to death or die of hunger on the way. The dead were often thrown out of the open cars.

The train arrived at Gross-Rosen on January 21. The Gross-Rosen complex consisted of some sixty sub-camps, including Brunnlitz, which was made famous after the war because it was there that Oskar Schindler took his "Schindler's Jews" after the evacuation from the Plaszow forced labor and later concentration camp in Krakow. By now, however, the main camp served as a transit point. After a short stay at Gross-Rosen, Simon and a group of other prisoners were once again loaded into open cars and sent to Dachau, near Munich in Bavaria. Simon recognized some of the survivors from his original group from Gleiwitz, but others were unfamiliar. The Nazis were frantically evacuating camps in the east as the Red Army kept up its westward march. It would reach Gross-Rosen in three weeks.

The trip to Dachau took almost a week. More prisoners died in transit, and again, starvation, hunger, exposure to the elements, and disease ravaged the human cargo as the train made its way to Bavaria. More corpses marked the passage of the train. In all, of the twenty-two thousand or so prisoners sent to Bavaria, around eight thousand died or were murdered before they reached Dachau.

The train arrived at the Dachau main camp on January 28. The prisoners were unloaded, and the bodies of those who had died in transit and had not previously been thrown out of the cars on the way were disposed of. During the induction process, the surviving prisoners all received new identification numbers. In Simon Ruder's case, he was assigned prisoner number 140258.

The following two documents show the transportation of inmates from the Gross-Rosen concentration camp to the Dachau main camp and their prisoner number assignments. Simon Ruder's name is on the second page. (Documents courtesy of the International Tracing Service.)

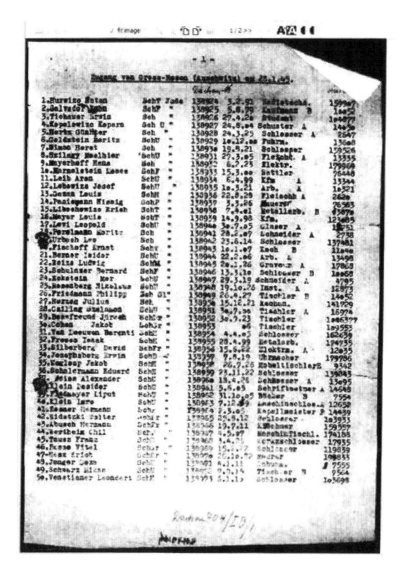

The following three documents are prisoner cards and a questionnaire from various Dachau camps.

B 6867 / v. Aw

Konzentrationslager ~~Neulau~~ *Art der Haft:* Sch. Juden-Pole *Gef.-Nr.:* 140.858

Name und Vorname: RUDER Simon
geb.: 8.7.07 *zu:* Oberleszn Polen
Wohnort: Lemberg
Beruf: Schneider — Tischler *Rel.:* ist
Staatsangehörigkeit: Polen *Stand.* verh
Name der Eltern: *Rasse:* jud
Wohnort:
Name der Ehefrau: Sternberg Lola *Rasse:* "
Wohnort: Lemberg
Kinder: 1 *Alleiniger Ernährer der Familie oder der Eltern:*
Vorbildung:
Militärdienstzeit: von — bis
Kriegsdienstzeit: von — bis
Größe: *Nase:* *Haare:* *Gestalt:*
Mund: *Bart:* *Gesicht:* *Ohren:*
Sprache: *Augen:* *Zähne:*
Ansteckende Krankheit oder Gebrechen:
Besondere Kennzeichen:
Rentenempfänger:
Verhaftet am: *wo:*
1. Mal eingeliefert: 28.1.45 *2. Mal eingeliefert:*
Einweisende Dienststelle: v Auschwitz
Grund:
Parteiangehörigkeit: von — bis
Welche Funktionen:
Mitglied v. Unterorganisationen:
Kriminelle Vorstrafen:

Politische Vorstrafen:

Ich bin darauf hingewiesen worden, dass meine Bestrafung wegen intellektueller Urkundenfälschung erfolgt, wenn sich die obigen Angaben als falsch erweisen sollten.

v.&.u. Ruder Simon **Der Lagerkommandant**

XL/635.64 200.000

Besides the main camp in its namesake town northwest of Munich, Dachau itself had 123 sub-camps. In Bavaria, the Mühldorf concentration camp was named for the nearby city of Mühldorf. The complex was also known by two other names, MI Lager and Mettenheim. The Mühldorf concentration camp was composed of four sub-camps, including Waldlager IV and Waldlager V, which, because of their location in the woods, were referred to as the Forest Camp, Mittergars Lager, which was also known as Cone Lager, Thalheim Lager, and Gendorf Lager. The inmate population of the Mühldorf camps numbered between twenty-five hundred and three thousand. Waldlager IV and V had between fifteen hundred and two thousand, and Mittergars had between two hundred and three hundred. Thalheim had only about one hundred civilian inmates and a few prisoners of war. Another sub-camp of Dachau was also located in Ampfing, which provided prisoners for labor in a nearby munitions factory. Simon Ruder was to become familiar with most of them.

Having had most of their major war factories in Germany destroyed by incessant Allied bombing, the regime hoped to build new production facilities underground and thus were immune to the constant pounding the B-24s, B-25s, and B-17s had inflicted on the Fatherland. To accomplish this, they needed a massive amount of labor for construction.

To that end, in 1944, the Third Reich began work on the construction of a partially underground bunker factory codenamed Weingut I (Vineyard I) in the forest known as the Mühldorfer Hart, slightly to the west of Mühldorf am Inn. The bunker was designed around a massive reinforced concrete barrel vault supported by twelve arch sections under which Messerschmitt Me262 jet engines would be manufactured in a nine-story factory. A similar installation in the area of Landsberg am Lech, Weingut II was where the final assembly of the planes was to take place. These facilities were to ensure the production of the Me262s when the Allies had already gained air superiority over German airspace.

MÜHLDORF CONCENTRATION CAMP, FEBRUARY 1945

SS *Hauptscharfuhrer* (SS Technical/Master Sergeant) Franz Auer prepared a requisition for another group of eight hundred concentration camp workers for the Waldlager V camp. Auer had the responsibility of supplying slave laborers for this huge worksite. These eight hundred represented a significant percentage of the twenty-five hundred to three thousand inmates at the worksite and were drawn from survivors of concentration camps such as Auschwitz, Gross-Rosen, Flossenburg, and other Dachau sub-camps. They included a large number of Hungarian and Polish Jews who would be subjected to beatings, overwork, exposure to the elements, a starvation diet, inhumanely unsanitary living conditions, and a patent disregard for medical needs. In short, they were expected to die within weeks after expending their final energies in the futile attempt by the Third Reich to build an underground aircraft factory.

On February 23, the eight hundred slave laborers arrived at the site accompanied by a neatly printed record summarizing their totals by occupation and additional records itemizing each person, his prisoner number, and his specific occupation. Among the occupations listed were electricians, engineers, carpenters, tailors, mechanics, workers, cooks, locksmiths, metalworkers, and others required to operate and maintain the worksite. Simon Ruder's name appeared toward the end of the list as a *tischler*, a carpenter, though he would perform a number of other tasks during his time at the camp, as would Jeno Weissbluth, his son Tomas, and William Weiss.

The following pages are a set of documents reflecting the assignment of eight hundred prisoners from the Dachau main camp to the Waldlager V camp outside Mühldorf. The prisoners worked on the massive construction site for an underground Me262 jet engine factory. The last of the three pages shows Simon Ruder, line number 768 of the eight hundred, categorized as a tischler, *a carpenter. Courtesy of the International Tracing Service.*

```
A.L.Waldlager V
Fp.Nr.27451 N

    L i s t e   der  800  Zugänge von  K. L. D a c h a u
    ==================================================================

   1. Fellner          Jakob        79164    Kutscher
   2. Brisak           Otto         89915    Elektriker
   3. Stern            Zoltan       90690    Tischler
   4. Jakubowicz       Miklos         692    Arbeiter
   5. Lubochinski      Samuel      109841    Koch
   6. Granek           Jakob          918    Sattler
   7. Fischer-Kramer   Heinz          980    Schauspieler
   8. Margolius        Rolf        110002    Optiker
   9. Smietanski       Felix          034    Maler
  10. Friedmann        Abraham        042    Schüler
  11. Spiewak          Simon          067    Schüler
  12. Kaplan           Siegmund       118    Schüler
  13. König            Moses          125    Schüler
  14. Herzberg         Chaim          155    Schmied
  15. Mittenberg       Fissel         165    Schüler
  16. Freund           Mosek          198    Ingenieur-Chemie
  17. Grünberg         Israel         283    Friseur
  18. Grünberg         Chiel          284    Schüler
  19. Grünberg         Hersch         285    Schüler
  20. Lauberstein      Moses          309    Schüler
  21. Silberfenig      Chaim          344    Schüler
  22. Grünspan         Isek           364    Schuster
  23. Grünspan         Josek          366    Schuster
  24. Kessner          Samuel      112049    Schüler
  25. Glaser           Menachem       053    Schuster
  26. Kohn             Adolf          091    Sattler
  27. Kessner          Tibor          102    Schüler
  28. Rosner           Lajos          219    Schüler
  29. Bolder           Samuel         226    Schüler
  30. Stein            Peter          243    Schüler
  31. Weinberger       Herrmann    118112    Elektriker
  32. Günger           Samuel         467    Landwirt
  33. Gardos           Ladislaus   137399    Kraftfahrer
  34. Tyrnauer         Adalbert       411    Beamter
  35. Pollak           Ernst          423    Koch
  36. Adler            Eugen          425    Buchhalter
  37. Schlüsser        Mor            566    Tischler
  38. Tennenblatt      Jakob          567    Tischler
  39. Pinkasz          Desider        610    Glaser
  40. Kormos           Lajos          621    Bäcker
  41. Benko            Paul           703    Musiker
  42. Steuermann       Georg          707    Bäcker
  43. Speiser          Miklos         709    Koch
  44. Feldmann         Julius         710    Weber
  45. Hurwicz          Nathan      138924    Radiotechniker
  46. Tichauer         Erwin          926    Med. Student
  47. Kopolowicz       Kopern         927    Schuster
  48. Hertz            Günther        928    Schlosser
  49. Goldstein        Moritz         929    Kutscher
  50. Simon            Horst          930    Autoschlosser

                          - 1 -
```

751. Freudmann	Erich	140238	Sprachlehrer
752. Goldberg	Schmerl	239	Schlächter
753. Besnicki	Nahim	250	Friseur
754. Beirnbaum	Martin	232	Uhrmacher
755. Biernbaum	Leopold	233	Koch
756. Rubinstein	Jakob	234	Kutscher
757. Badryner	Jekob	235	Maler
758. Brostowski	Moses	238	Zimmermann
759. Erlich	Gerhard	241	Lederarbeiter
760. Spruscher	Max	243	Maler
761. Klein	Andor	246	Schneider
762. Eisenberg	Nuta	248	Tapezierer
763. Elnbaum	Salamon	249	Gastwirt
764. Kern	Ernst	251	Kürschner
765. Wachmann	Karl	253	Arbeiter
766. Luxberg	Josef	254	Automechaniker
767. Friedmann	Otto	256	Drogist
768. Ruder	Simon	258	Tischler
769. Birnbaum	Beni	259	Fleischer
770. Nirnbeum	Emanuel	260	Stellmacher
771. Altus	Abraham	262	Kutscher
772. Skiersobolaki	Michel	263	Arbeiter
773. Badoszinski	Mema	265	Schneider
774. Holzmann	Wolf	266	Schneider
775. Feinsilber	Josef	267	Friseur
776. Bau	Markus	268	Tischler
777. Schwartz	Miklis	269	Tischler
778. Roth	Josef	270	Kasserl.-Mont.
779. Kaufmann	Emil	272	Tischler
780. Sobol	Paul	273	Mechaniker
781. Lipak	Noah	274	Elektriker
782. Katz	Robert	278	Kutscher
783. Sobol	David	279	Tischler
784. Polsay	Herbert	280	Beamter
785. Raas	Benedikt	281	Elekrtiker
786. Lypaki	Model	283	Tischler
787. Keller	Imre	284	Installateur
788. Bak	Majer	285	Elektriker
789. Klein	Karoly	286	Tischler
790. Fliegenspan	Bernard	287	Autoschlosser
791. Ducsinner	Schmul	288	Mechaniker
792. Koppto	Zylko	289	Sänger
793. Herskowits	Majer	291	Schuster
794. Kohn	Jol	293	Klempner
795. Pinkens	Josef	295	Tischler
796. Kain	Tivadar	296	Gärtner
797. Rosenfeld	Barna	297	Landwirt
798. Weinberger	Armin	298	Tapezierer
799. Kutlsarakl	Max	303	Schneider
800. Adler	Imre	304	Uhrmacher

This and the following lists show prisoners from Dachau assigned to one of the four Mühldorf camps. Courtesy of the International Tracing Service.

Konzentrationslager Dachau
Arbeitseinsatz

Dachau, 3 4.dez

Dem Aussenkommando **M ü h l d o r f** zugedacht:

1. Jacques(An)Norman .... SchUJude 133646 ... 14. 9.13 Arbeiter
2. Abelsky Ignats .... SchP " 139291 ... 1. 1.94 "
3. Abend Bernard .... SchP " 139263 ... 3. 2.05 "
4. Abraham Hans .... Schupt" 30722 ... 24. 7.13 Arzt
5. Abrahmowicz Eugen .... SchU " 139333 ... 6. 7.21 Arbeiter
6. Abramowicz Mieczyslaw ... SchU " 110014 ... 14. 8.07 "
7. Abusch Hermann .... SchUP" 139566 ... 19. 7.11 "
8. Adler David .... SchU " 139109 ... 14. 7.01 "
9. Adler Eugen .... Schindumd 137449 ... 4. 1.17 Buchhalter
10. Adler Felix .... SchUJude 139321 ... 10. 6.86 Arbeiter
11. Adler Hendrik .... SchU " 140084 ... 7.12.04 "
12. Adler Ivre .... SchU " 140504 ... 02. 8.18 "
13. Adler Marion .... SchU " 139343 ... 23.10.13 "
14. Adler Elhoyin .... SchUkr" 139645 ... 2. 4.02 "
15. Alcaben Bernard .... SchP " 139378 ... 27.11.06 "
16. Alton Abram .... SchUSA" 140082 ... 13. 3.02 "
17. Alper Bela .... SchP " 140080 ... 6. 4.24 "
18. Altman Marcel .... SchP " 139299 ... 2. 5.23 "
19. Althaus Emel .... SchP " 139345 ... 28.10.24 "
20. Altman Israel .... SchP " 139422 ... 19. 5.10 "
21. Altman Simon .... SchP " 140170 ... 14. 1.15 "
22. Aniolowicz Isach ..... SchP " 139946 ... 22. 3.95 "
23. Apel Benjamin .... SchP " 139764 ... 27. 5.00 "
24. Apfel Erich .... Schusm " 140000 ... 15. 7.04 "
25. Aptalon Ulrich ...... SchP " 140092 ... 27. 1.02 "
26. Attali Robert .... SchP " 139462 ... 11. 2.00 "
27. Auerbach Fischel .... SchP " 139776 ... 1. 9.24 "
28. Auerbach Jakel ...... SchP " 139777 ... 10.11.05 "
29. Avikor Jack .... SchP " 139204 ... 23. 3.24 "
30. Axol Hain .... SchP " 139092 ... 23.12.05 "
31. Bachner Fredi ..... SchP " 139769 ... 22. 3.05 "
32. Baisor Majer ..... SchP " 139642 ... 10.11.01 "
33. Bakonyi Lajos .... SchUJude 109299 ... 4. 9.89 "
34. Balitsky Chaim ... SchUJude 139799 ... 28. 7.20 "
35. Bargarde Abraham . SchUJude 139700 ... 1. 1.21 "
36. Buni Chaim .... Sch " 110199 ... 20. 6.26 "
37. Buchwar Zakob .... SchP " 140235 ... 14. 8.97 "
38. Bartel Jakob ..... SchP " 137732 ... 10.11.03 "
39. Bard Paul .... SchU " 140285 ... 19.12.21 "
40. Bartenka Sandor .. SchU " 139114 ... 27. 11.12 "
41. Baruch Silvio .... SchU" " 139900 ... 11. 1.17 "
42. Baufreund Jürgen . SchU " 137024 ... 30. 1.18 "
43. Beck Adolf .... SchU " 137607 ... 20.11.89 "
44. Brauni Stefan .... SchU " 139598 ... 1. 3.04 "
45. Biber Leon .... SchP " 139535 ... 1.10.08 "
46. Bellali Abram .... SchUr" 139217 ... 11. 1.15 "
47. Bellali Schloumi . SchUr" 139215 ... 5. 7.25 "
48. Bellali Isaak .... SchUr" 139214 ... 11. 2.18 "
49. Belvani Abraham .. SchP " 140282 ... 19. 3.14 "
50. Deux Henen .... SchP " 139309 ... 17. 6.03 "

Simon Ruder, prisoner number 140258, is on line 865 listed as Arbeiter, *or a worker. This probably relegated him to carrying the 110-pound cement sacks.*
Courtesy of the International Tracing Service.

This list shows Simon Ruder being transferred from the Thalheim camp probably to Ampfing along with another prisoner. This handwritten report was most likely prepared by another prisoner. Courtesy of the International Tracing Service.

Another example of a register containing the names of prisoners. Simon Ruder's name
appears on this meticulously prepared handwritten document.
Courtesy of the International Tracing Service.

The conditions at Dachau were similar to what Simon had already experienced at the other camps for almost four years. He spent a few weeks doing carpentry work at the Thalheim camp and was then was transferred to the Waldlager V camp as part of a group of eight hundred prisoners assigned to work on the massive Weingut I underground factory.

From an engineering and construction perspective, the Mühldorf location was excellent, as it possessed all of the critical resource requirements. For example, there was a solid gravel bed beneath the River Inn, and the water table was sufficiently deep. These natural resources would be used to produce the tremendous amount of concrete required for the bunker. The strategically important railway junction of Mühldorf provided logistical advantages for delivering labor and materials for the construction. Finally, the forest of the Mühldorfer Hart would offer camouflage for the completed bunker.

The worksite was immense. At times, it boasted around ten thousand workers. Of those, about eighty-five hundred workers were forced laborers, while the rest were made up of personnel from the construction firm of Polensky and Zollner (PZ). Overall, responsibility for the project rested with Organization Todt (OT), a Nazi government construction and engineering agency. As usual, the SS was responsible for providing the forced labor.

Simon was assigned a number of backbreaking jobs associated with the construction of the massive underground bunker. He and hundreds of other prisoners were assigned to carry 110-pound bags of cement up a ramp to a machine that mixed the cement powder with gravel and water to produce a concrete mixture. This concrete mixture was then carried by a narrow-gauge railway system to the spot where the concrete was poured.

Many of the prisoners were Hungarian Jews, though the Capos didn't care. They harassed all of the prisoners with clubs, whips, or other weapons. Those moving too slowly bore the brunt of the punishment. As the late-winter weather turned cold and wet, those already weakened by starvation or illness got worse, and many died. Special sick bay barracks were set up to house them. Food rations were cut, and few, if any, ever emerged alive.

Simon found some inner strength he did not know he possessed, and somehow he was able to haul the heavy sacks day after day. At night he was able to talk to some of his fellow prisoners. Some spoke Polish, and Simon learned they were from Hungary. Among the prisoners were fourteen-year-old Tomas Weissbluth and his father Jeno from Mezocsat, Hungary, who had recently arrived from Auschwitz-Birkenau and the Munchen-Allach labor camp.

Life, if one could call it that, continued, cement bag after cement bag. After several months, young Tomas and his father were moved to the Mittergars labor camp.

MÜHLDORF, GERMANY, MARCH 19, 1945

Marile Häusl was at her job in the Landratsamt Ernahrungsamt Abteilung B building in Mühldorf, Germany, on the morning of March 19, 1945. She had not missed a day of work since she started in 1942 at the age of fourteen after graduating from elementary school and entering vocational school. It was a crisp, sunny Bavarian morning. Marile and several friends who worked with her decided to go home for lunch. The girls were anxious to enjoy the nice weather. While the war was swirling around them and they all had brothers and uncles who had been killed or were missing in action, for them, the war was something far away. They had all been in the *Bund Deutscher Mädel (BDM)*, the women's component of the Hitler Youth and had made various clothing and other items for the soldiers and visited the woods to collect chamomile and nettle for ointments. Perhaps more importantly, they were taught how to be good German wives and mothers and how to select a proper husband. All that ceased to matter now. Germans were beginning to understand the full dimensions of the war and that it was rapidly catching up with them. Yet they went on. Major German cities, Munich, Hamburg, Dresden, were bombed into ruins. The war was surely lost, so why go on? But they did, waiting for the end. Soon the war would be brought to the little town of Mühldorf.

Mühldorf was a strategic railroad marshalling yard through which significant freight traffic flowed in all directions. That morning, as usual, Ludwig

Häusl arrived at the yard office on his bicycle. He signed in at the counter and received his orders for the day. He scanned the orders and left the office and met his fireman, Heinrich Bauer. "We need to hurry today," said Ludwig to his fireman. "This is shipment very high priority and must to be delivered as quickly as possible."

Today the orders indicated he was to move a number of cars loaded with cement bags destined to a worksite in the woods just outside of the town. This was one of many such deliveries he had made to the same site. The huge, partially completed structure was impressive, but he was not sure of its purpose when it was completed but heard it was some sort of underground factory having to do with the construction of aircraft.

Looking at his copy of the orders, Heinrich said, "I think we have to shunt about thirty cars to make up the train. Then we have a few other cars to add. It shouldn't take more than two or three hours. Then we can have lunch on the train once we get moving."

"Very good, Heinrich," said Ludwig to his fireman. "I'm just glad we aren't moving Jews today." The two Deutsche Reichsbahn employees looked around, then at each other, let out a sardonic laugh, and began their workday in earnest. At around 11:10 a.m., the Mühldorf area air raid sirens wailed.

Earlier that morning final preparations for a bombing mission had been completed and put into motion. At around 9:48 a.m., thirty-five B-24 Liberator bombers had taken off from the Bovino Aerodrome in Italy. The bombers were from the 451st, 461st, and the 484th Bomb Group, all part of the Fifteenth Air Force. The target was the Mühldorf marshalling yard. As described in the mission-classified document, the yard consisted of extensive facilities enabling the rapid switching of railroad cars, taking them off incoming trains and making up new outgoing trains. Recent intelligence revealed the yard contained 1,360 cars carrying a variety of freight, mostly military related. It was thought by the US Army that bombing this facility would not only disrupt the movement of critical freight but also put a significant strain on the Germans' overtaxed equipment and repair forces.

Supporting the bombing mission were fifty-three P-51 fighter aircraft from the 317th, 318th, 319th, and the 325th fighter squadrons providing fighter escort to and from the target. Three P-51s experienced mechanical problems before takeoff, so the force was reduced to fifty operational aircraft.

Captain Robert L. Boone, commanding one of the B-24s, checked the fighter escort assignments and was slightly disappointed that none of the P-51s were from the 332nd fighter squadron, the now famous Tuskegee Airmen who were readily identified by their signature red-tailed aircraft. The German Air Force, the *Luftwaffe*, called them the *Schwartze Vogelmenschen* (Black Birdmen). The fighters took off at 10:40 a.m. from the Rimini Aerodrome in Italy, rendezvoused with the bombers, then headed toward their target in Bavaria.

Marile and her three friends were on the road heading out of town. They heard the air raid sirens and froze dead in their tracks, not knowing what to do. They were approaching a church on the left away from the River Inn. The girls knew there was a shelter of sorts in the church and quickly decided that was the best course of action. Marile's farmhouse on Xaver-Rambold Strasse was not too far away, and she instinctively decided to run home. In unison, the other three girls turned and ran toward the church. All four girls could hear the bombers approaching from the south. Marile watched her friends disappear toward the church while she turned in the other direction and ran toward her home.

Ludwig Häusl and his fireman Heinrich Bauer heard the sirens and quickly realized they would be sitting ducks for the American bombers. Ludwig was a patient man not given to panic. He calmly stepped down from the cab and made his way under the heavy locomotive, determining that would be the safest place to be given the circumstances. He motioned Bauer to do likewise, but his fireman, apparently too frightened to leave the cab, stayed there and waited for the bombs to fall.

Twenty-four-year-old Technical Sargent Bill Neutzling was a radio operator and waist gunner on Captain Boone's crew, one of the 484th Bomber

Group's B-24s. He was lying on his stomach in the waist, or middle section of the plane, peering through the camera hatch. The bombing run started, and bombs were beginning to drop. He watched as the first bomb fell harmlessly into the River Inn. Then he saw the next bomb hit in front of a church. The bulk of the bombs then hit their intended target, the marshalling yard. He didn't know that the second bomb had killed the three young women seeking refuge in the church, and it would be another forty-five years before he discovered this fact.

Over the next ten minutes, the bombs from the thirty-five B-24s rained down on or near the target. The bulk of the rail cars were destroyed. Many cars contained fuel for tanks or aircraft and went up in flames. The rail yard turned into a raging inferno. The train station was destroyed. Tracks were torn up, twisted into grotesquely curved shapes. A bomb hit near the locomotive Ludwig and Heinrich had been driving just minutes before. The cab of the locomotive was demolished, instantly killing fireman Heinrich Bauer.

While the bombing raid would be considered successful, the bomb pattern was scattered over a comparatively large area, and many of the bombs missed their targets and hit or destroyed houses and other nonmilitary-related facilities. Witnesses would later report that 114 houses were totally destroyed, 309 were damaged, water and sanitation pipes were damaged, and twelve hundred people were left homeless. One hundred and thirty people were reportedly killed on that day, including Marile Häusl's three friends and Heinrich Bauer, the railroad fireman.

Once the bombing ceased, Ludwig Häusl crawled out from under his damaged steam locomotive. The cab was gone and with it most of Heinrich Bauer. Ludwig suffered minor injuries to his head and arms and was taken to a makeshift infirmary where his injuries were treated. The yard office was heavily damaged, though still standing, but his bicycle was a mangled mess. Deep craters dotted the yard. It was obvious the rail yard would be out of action for at least a few days.

omb damage caused by the 15th A.F. bombers to the Marshalling
ards in Muldorf, Germany.

Above and next two pages: US Army Air Forces reconnaissance photographs of the bombing mission targeting the Mühldorf Germany railroad marshalling yard on March 19, 1945. Ludwig Häusl was an engineer on one of the locomotives involved in the bombing. He survived by taking refuge under his locomotive. (Courtesy of Bill Neutzling's B24 Liberator website from "Anatomy of a Mission: Mühldorf, Germany 19 March 1945")

INDEXED 58620 A.C.

mb damage caused by the 15th A.F. bombers to the Marshalling rds in Muldorf, Germany.

A22 038

Marile Häusl hurried home. She heard the bomb blast and then felt the shock wave just before it knocked her down. Getting up, she looked back toward the church and was horrified to see a large cloud of smoke where she and her friends had been just moments ago. She said a prayer for her friends but feared the worst. She thanked God that something had made her run home instead of staying at the church with her friends.

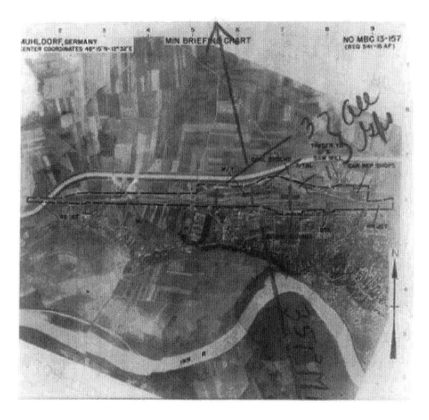

US Army Air Forces briefing chart for bombing mission on Mühldorf.
Rail marshalling yard is located in the center of the photo marked by the "+" signs.
The River Inn is at the bottom of the photo.

Actual bombing photograph taken from one of the B-24 Liberators taking part in the raid. Marile was walking home as the bombs began to fall. One bomb hit the church where three of her friends sought refuge. They died when the church took a direct hit. Marile decided to run home instead, probably saving her life.

*One of the B-24 Liberator bombers on the way to the Mühldorf,
Germany, marshalling yard on March 19, 1945.*

Marile found that her home on Xaver-Rambold Strasse was undamaged,
although some bomb craters dotted the field just north of the small farmhouse.
Her mother, two sisters, and her brother Wiggi were all at home. They had
hidden in the cellar of the house. The electricity had been knocked out, but
they had a manual pump on the well, so they could get fresh water. The farm
animals were panicked but survived. The geese had scattered but were slowly
coming back.

Marile walked into the house. Her mother and siblings were relieved to
see her and grateful she had not been injured or worse. Marile looked around.
"Where is Papa?" she asked.

US Army Air Forces reconnaissance photo after the March 19, 1945, mission. The rail marshalling yard was the target, but the photo shows a widely scattered bomb pattern outlined by the craters north and south of the yard. Marile barely escaped death when a bomb hit a church near the River Inn south of the target.

Her mother answered, "We haven't seen your father since he left for work this morning, and we don't know what has happened to him. The station and rail yard were hit very hard. We saw the smoke coming from that direction. We can only pray to God he is safe."

Sometime later, Ludwig Häusl came home, bandages on his head and left arm. He entered the house and was greatly relieved to see his family safe and sound. He hugged his wife and four children and wept.

"What happened to you, Ludwig?" asked the elder Maria. "Are you badly injured?"

"I'm going to be fine. A little bump on the head and some scratches on my arm from flying debris. The rail yard is being repaired. I heard we will be bringing in several thousand prisoners to do the heavy work. I will be going back tomorrow to help supervise and inspect the locomotives. We must get the trains moving as quickly as possible."

"Was anyone else hurt?" his wife asked.

Nodding his bandaged head, he responded, "Yes, Bauer, my fireman. He was in the locomotive cab when a bomb hit very closely and he was killed. I don't know about anyone else, but I did see some injured being cared for."

Ludwig looked at his oldest daughter. "Marile, why are you home? Shouldn't you be at work?"

"Yes, Papa, but my friends and I decided to go home for lunch. It was such a nice, sunny day. Then the sirens sounded, and a few minutes later, the bombers came over the river. We were in front of the church. We didn't know what to do. My friends, they ran to the church. I ran home. I don't know why I did that. I think a bomb hit in front of the church. I was knocked down but was not hurt. Oh, Papa, I don't know what happened to them, but I'm afraid they were hurt or killed."

Marile started to cry and ran to her father. Ludwig hugged his daughter. "It's all right, Marile, it's all right. I'm so glad you're safe. I'm afraid this will all be over soon. We are finished. Then we will see what will become of us." Ludwig had good reason to be afraid.

DACHAU CONCENTRATION SUB-CAMPS AROUND AMPFING, MARCH 1945

The prisoners at the Waldlager V camp heard the bombers approach and saw and felt the bombs detonating in Mühldorf, not very far away. They were excited because it was obvious the Allies were closing in. Liberation, if they could survive a little longer, seemed close at hand.

Several hours after the bombs stopped falling, the camp Capos came around and demanded volunteers to help repair the damaged rail yard. For the Germans, it was critical to repair the tracks in order to move materials, especially cement, to the construction site. Simon, although considerably weakened, sensed a potential benefit and volunteered immediately. Shortly afterward, some three thousand prisoners from the Mühldorf concentration camp complex were marched to the severely damaged rail marshalling yard to begin repair activities.

It was obvious to Simon that there was a sense of urgency in the air. The *Wehrmacht*, managers and workers from the Deutsche Reichsbahn, were giving orders. The ever-present SS guards watched over the prisoners. The Capos were shouting at the prisoners to work faster. Simon and a group of Hungarian Jews were assigned the task of filling the bomb craters. Dirt and rubble were slowly shoveled into the deep holes. The bomb-damaged, twisted rails were removed and set aside to be scrapped or reused later. New rails were brought up, many having been stored nearby for just such an emergency. Ties, the lengths of wood to which the rails were attached, were also stored nearby or reused. The rails, new or salvaged old straight rails, were fastened to the wooden ties. Temporary tracks were laid to get around very deep craters.

Ludwig Häusl was back at the yard office. He watched the Jewish prisoners working to restore his railroad to some semblance of operation. They were all over the yard, some three thousand of them, filling holes, removing damaged rail, moving damaged cars, and cleaning up the mess. He was secretly glad they were still alive. At least the Nazis hadn't managed to kill them all. He wondered how many of these prisoners he had taken to the camp on these very rails. He tried hard not to notice the extreme emaciation these prisoners suffered. Most were no more than walking skeletons wrapped in skin. Their uniforms, or what was left of them, hung loosely on their bodies. They were all struggling with their shovels and other tools, barely able to stay upright. Most of these unfortunates were so fragile it seemed a sudden gust of wind would blow them over. Ludwig thought that the work these three thousand prisoners did could have easily been done by a few hundred healthy workers.

As he helped manhandle a new section of rail into place, Simon noticed a tall, slim man with an engineer's dark-blue uniform inspecting a locomotive that had sustained minor damage. The man looked at Simon, and their eyes met for a moment. The man nodded ever so slightly to Simon, an acknowledgement of the help, or perhaps something more. This was surely not an SS man thought Simon as he looked away and continued with his work.

Within a day, the rail yard was marginally back in operation. Trains began moving again.

With the major, though mostly temporary, repairs to the rail yard completed, the prisoners were taken back to their respective labor camps. In Simon's case, it was the Waldlager V camp, the construction site for the ill-fated Weingut I underground Me262 jet engine factory complex.

Work quickly resumed on the huge bunker. The Capos were eager to get the prisoners back to work to make up for the lost time at the rail yard. Five of the planned twelve arches rose high into the Bavarian sky looking like the sun-bleached ribs of a huge beached sea monster. Simon was put back to work carrying the heavy bags of cement up to the worksite. The work was brutal, especially for an already severely weakened thirty-eight-year-old prisoner. Younger men faltered and died. Work continued at a frenzied pace. Simon labored for the next two weeks under extremely harsh conditions. The weather turned colder and wetter. The Capos continually harassed the workers. Many died of being overworked or by starvation. The Capos had their orders from the SS, who received daily work schedules from the Organisation Todt. As motivation, the Capos ruthlessly meted out beatings and whippings on the workers, and Simon stoically endured his share. He could feel his strength eroding and knew he couldn't continue for much longer, yet the knowledge that if he faltered, he would probably be killed on the spot proved to be the tiny difference that kept him going. The SS didn't care; they would just obtain a marginally fresher prisoner from a surrounding camp and work him for a week or so until he dropped.

DACHAU CONCENTRATION SUB-CAMPS AROUND AMPFING, APRIL 1945

By sheer force of will, Simon survived this latest ordeal at the construction site, and on April 12, he and several other prisoners were transferred to another nearby Dachau sub-camp in Ampfing. The camp supplied slave labor to a nearby munitions factory. The living conditions in the camp were horrific. A fifteen-foot, triple barbed-wire fence enclosed the camp, and guardhouses with spotlights stood at each corner. A few wooden barracks and several green silo-like buildings were scattered under the trees. More ominous were several bunkers set in trenches about eight feet underground at the bottom of a set of wooden steps. The bunkers were about ten feet deep and wide and about six to eight feet in height. Triple shelves, used as beds, lined both sides of the bunkers.

The work in the munitions factory was slightly less physically strenuous than Simon's job at the construction site. This allowed Simon to regain a modicum of strength, which enabled him to perform some measure of work at the munitions factory, enough at least not to draw too much attention from the Capos. Each day Simon stubbornly held on, kept going by the conviction that the war would be over soon, within days or weeks at most. Food was virtually nonexistent. The thin broth with something floating in it did little to sustain a human body. The bread was fit for termites, comprised mostly of sawdust.

The work was still hard and dangerous, and having only marginally recovered from the tortuous work at the construction site, Simon began to weaken. He was struggling to keep up. The Capos were quick to notice and harassed and beat him. They were like a pack of wolves singling out a weakened member of a herd. At the end of two weeks, he had reached the very limits of his endurance and collapsed at his worktable. The ever-alert Capos viciously fell upon Simon with clubs and sabers, intending to put an end to his ordeal. They never finished the job, however, and suddenly ran off into the surrounding woods like the cowards they were.

Simon found himself in a subterranean bunker lying on one of the shelves. He didn't remember how or when he got there. The stench of human waste, decay, and sweat was overpowering. The shelves held what had once been men. Their bodies were wasted to skin stretched over protruding bones, their knees now the thickest part of their legs. Dozens of them, all alike now, their shaven heads hanging limply, their eyes staring out of deep sockets, their mouths open. Most had given up, hoping for a death that was waiting patiently only hours away. Simon, too, waited, but not for death. He had seen too much death, mountains of corpses, and others neatly stacked like firewood. Corpses strewn on the concentration camp grounds like so much garbage. Corpses half burned in the crematorium at Auschwitz and other camps. And now, some unnamed corpses occupying the shelves, silent comrades in his hellish bunker. He drifted in and out of consciousness. He dreamed of his childhood in Obertin, then part of the Austria-Hungary Empire. He thought of the 1918 flu pandemic and imagined he was back there lying in bed, fevered and near death. He thought of selling bricks as a twelve-year-old, bricks from bombed-out buildings after World War I. He imagined talking to the corpses around him as they were before the war. This one talked about the books he had written, this one about the patients he had treated as a doctor. Another told of his teaching duties at the gymnasium. Simon's thoughts shifted to Lola and his children. Where were they? Where did they go? Something about a train station, he thought. Yes, that was it. Suddenly he remembered the policeman, Salzmann, telling him his family had been shot trying to escape boarding the train to Belzec. Sadness at the thought shocked him back to the present. In a moment of lucidity, he swore he was not going to become one of the Nazi victims, and though he realized he was well on that path, as long as he breathed, he would continue to hold on, one precious breath at a time.

LVIV, UKRAINE, APRIL 1945

Having lived and worked under the Russian-imposed order in the city of Lviv, formerly called Lemberg, Mendel Ruder decided that it was once again time to leave. He had tried to locate his older brother Simon or his family without success. He now worked in a large, state-run clothing factory, making use of his tailoring skills to produce a line of uninspiring, utilitarian clothing for the millions of other workers in this so-called workers' paradise. Before the war, he had had his own tailor shop in Zloczow, now called Zolochiv. He longed for the freedom that life once reflected. He had been an excellent tailor with a large clientele and was well known and respected for the quality of his clothing. Now he was also disillusioned with the conditions imposed by the Russian economic system. While he had experienced the system during the 1939–1941 Russian occupation prior to the Germans taking over in mid-1941, he was disappointed that the same measures were once again being implemented. He decided that his best course of action was to head west, maybe immigrate to the United States. First, however, he had to leave Lviv and the unfriendly confines of the Soviet Ukraine. There were hardly any Jews there, and he felt alone and alienated from the Jewish community, which had all but disappeared, most Jews having been outright murdered, sent to the nearby Belzec extermination camp, or having died in the Janowska slave labor camp formerly standing on the northwest edge of town. In fact, there were fewer than one thousand Jews in Lviv, survivors of the original 120,000 Jewish population prior to the war.

He planned to move first to the larger city of Lodz in Poland to the northwest, a long trip of some 457 kilometers.

As Jews, Mendel and his eight-year-old son Dolek experienced much the same treatment they would have received before and during the war. Anti-Semitism took root in the region and never went away. The journey by train was reminiscent of the countless trips to a plethora of death camps. Neither the Ukrainians nor the Poles had any concerns about their Jewish passengers, especially those without money, so Mendel and young Dolek found themselves in the confines of freight cars, cattle cars to be more specific. Though less crowded than their recent predecessors, it made for a very uncomfortable ride. Neither food nor water was provided.

The journey would take the two refugees from the Ukrainian city of Lviv into the newly reconstituted Poland, which would emerge from the war some-what smaller. Not unexpectedly, the pair found the ethnic Poles and Ukrainians unsympathetic toward them, offering them no comforts along the way to Lodz. Food was in short supply, so at one stop, in Kielce, Poland, Mendel was determined to take action. He took the jacket young Dolek had been wearing for several years and used it to trade for a loaf of bread. The jacket, made to fit a three-year-old, had sleeves that now came up to Dolek's elbows. Mendel grabbed the jacket and quickly left the train car looking to make a trade near the platform of the Herbskie railway station. A few moments later, the whistle blew, and the train slowly left the station. Young Dolek anxiously awaited the return of his father, but as the train picked up speed, hope faded that Mendel would be able to return to the car. All the young boy could do now was wait until the next stop to see if his father had caught the train.

Had the pair traveled this same route a year later in early July, they would have witnessed what history would call the *Kielce Pogrom*, where forty-two Jews were murdered based on a fabricated story of abduction by a nine-year-old Polish boy.

At the next stop, Mendel, who had barely been able to climb aboard the last car on the train with his loaf of bread safely hidden in his clothing, was reunited with his son.

A few days later the father and son completed their 457-kilometer trip and arrived in the Polish city of Lodz. The pair noticed flags flying at half-mast. They later learned that the US president, Franklin Roosevelt, had died on April 12.

Lodz was the second largest city in Poland, and with Warsaw destroyed, many remaining Jews had made their way there after the war. Like other cities in Poland, it too had endured the ghettos, murders, deportations, and pogroms. Following the end of the war, the Provisional Jewish Committee (PJC) was formed in February 1945, and it quickly established organizations to create manufacturing and services cooperatives aimed at providing jobs for the Jews. The Jewish Health Organization and vocational training societies resumed operations as many Jews repatriated from Russia increased the Jewish population.

It was into this seemingly hospitable and Jewish-tolerant environment that Mendel and Dolek had managed to transport themselves. With his skills always in demand, Mendel had no problem finding employment, and Dolek was enrolled in a school with Jews and Polish students. It was the middle of the year, and things looked better for Mendel Ruder and his young son.

DACHAU CONCENTRATION SUB-CAMPS AROUND AMPFING, MAY 1945[II]

As the Fourteenth Armored Division of the US Seventh Army advanced into southern Germany, it uncovered several sub-camps of the Dachau concentration camp system. Near the towns of Ampfing and Mühldorf, they discovered four large underground munitions plants, some fifteen thousand tons of high explosives, and three large forced labor camps containing thousands of prisoners. On May 3, 1945, the Fourteenth Armored Division liberated the Ampfing forced labor camp.

Simon thought he heard voices. People, live ones. He wasn't sure, but he thought he could tell the difference. Then he heard shouting coming from somewhere, not in his bunker, but nearby.

"Americans, Americans!" someone shouted.

The Americans were shocked by what they saw. Concentration camps all over Western Europe were being discovered and liberated. Liberation was the easy part; most of the SS had fled, and there was little resistance. Sometimes they tried to murder any remaining prisoners. Many times they planned to but ran out of time, fleeing instead to save their necks. Other times they just melted into the night. At Ampfing, the guards managed to kill about twenty prisoners before they fled into the forest.

The US Army was not prepared to deal with a humanitarian crisis of this magnitude. In major camps like Buchenwald, evacuation hospital facilities could be set up to deal with the large number of freed prisoners, but dealing with many of the smaller, scattered camps proved problematic.

The group of US Army personnel that entered the town of Ampfing this day included Omar C. Hopkins, senior sanitary engineer, whom everyone called "Hop," and Michael Shimkin, a medical officer with a rank of major, both from the Public Health Service. Shimkin was in charge. A driver named Mike rounded out the trio.

As they drove through the streets, Shimkin stopped the first civilian they encountered and, drawing on his hundred-word arsenal of German words, shouted, "You, come here!" The German turned and came up to the car. If the German was apprehensive, he certainly managed to hide it well. Shimkin then asked, "Where is the Militärregierung, and is there a Bürgermeister?" The German apparently did not know anything about the military government but did manage to convey that the mayor was also the baker and waved his arms in the direction of the bakery. Shimkin then asked him where the camps were, the labor camps, the concentration camps. "In the woods," answered the German, "by the factories, all around." Shimkin tried to get more information but had apparently exhausted his German vocabulary. Frustrated, he looked over to Mike, his driver. "Okay, Mike, let's go find the bakery."

Following the general directions, the group soon found the bakery. Outside of the small building, they spotted a man in a dirty striped uniform, the familiar symbol of the concentration camps. Another man similarly dressed came out of the bakery, his arms loaded with large loaves of bread. He walked over to a horse-drawn wagon into which he dumped the loaves.

"Hello," shouted the American. By force of habit, both men immediately turned and quickly removed the caps from their shaven heads. Shimkin motioned them to come forward. Neither man moved, apprehension obvious on their faces. After a moment, they finally dared to look at each other.

The smaller of the two, having summoned the courage, spoke up. In a French accent, the man said, "I speak English, sir. May I help you?"

Quickly, Shimkin asked, "Can you show us where the camp is?" The man stared at the American, unsure what to believe.

"Just tell the driver how to get there." Shimkin, not wanting to waste time, continued with the questioning. "How many people were there at the camp?"

"About six hundred, but many of them have fled," the man answered.

The American continued, "What were the conditions?"

"Bad, very bad."

"Were there any Americans at the camp?"

"No, but an American officer had been there a few days ago and said there would be help."

The man produced a dirty slip of paper that read "*This authorizes the bearer to draw all necessary supplies for his camp.*" As a normal precaution for these kinds of vouchers, the signature and serial number were illegible. The man was getting bread for the camp.

"Was there any water or electricity at the camp?" asked Hop.

"No, nothing; electricity failed three days ago. Many people are dying."

Shimkin asked the man his name. "Andre Israel, sir," he said. He pulled up his sleeve to reveal a tattooed number on his left forearm, a sign he had been to Auschwitz, the only camp where the Germans had used tattoos to identify the prisoners.

Andre continued, "I have been here six months and was appointed a clerk because I spoke German."

"Was this an extermination camp with gas and incinerator chambers in it?" asked Shimkin.

Andre shook his head. "No, it is a work camp for the factories. One makes explosives and the other cement."

"Are there any other camps around here?"

"Yes," said Andre. "About ten. Most of them were labor camps of the Organisation Todt that was responsible for the building projects."

"OK, Andre, show us the way to the camp," said Shimkin.

Andre and his partner were finally convinced to climb aboard the car, and with Andre as their guide, they headed to the camp. When they arrived, Andre left the car and ran to the gate and shouted some names. Two men emerged from the nearest wooden barracks and quickly ran to open the gate.

"Who is in charge here?" asked Shimkin as the group entered the largest barrack. They walked into a dispensary containing a wooden examination table, a few rusty instruments, and a row of ointment jars on a shelf.

"Who is in charge?" Shimkin asked again. Andre translated, and soon a tall, hunched-over man with wire spectacles came into the room.

"This is one of the doctors," said Andre.

"Doctor," said Shimkin, "how many sick people do you have here? Do you have a list? How many of them need immediate hospitalization?"

"They are all sick," said the doctor. Andre translated. "One hundred, two hundred. They should all be hospitalized."

"What about food?" asked Shimkin.

"The cook told me he had a few supplies left, mostly potatoes, and more were on the way. Bread, too, from the bakery. There is enough food for maybe two or three meals for the surgical cases in here."

The doctor opened the door to the large room, taking up the remainder of the barrack. Shimkin saw double-deck beds made of wooden planks covered with filthy straw where men with shaved heads, ulcerated legs, and unhealed whiplashes on their backs were kept. As a doctor, Shimkin recognized the signs of protein-deficient flesh that was unable to recuperate from even minor wounds. Numbers were tattooed on their forearms or across their chests.

"Show us the worst," said Shimkin.

Liberated inmates at the Ampfing sub-camp. Simon Ruder was among them but lying near death at the hands of the fleeing Capos.

"Come," said the doctor. "I will show you the bunkers."

The group ran out to the car, and with several on the running boards, the doctor directed them through tree stumps and mud holes to a small rise with what looked like a stovepipe sticking out of the ground.

"This is where we keep the ones in the worst shape," the doctor began. "Most die. There is little we can do for them," Andre translated.

Shimkin looked around. The smell was overpowering. How could people be treated this way? He looked around and knew these poor souls needed immediate attention.

Looking at the doctor, Shimkin asked, "Are there any large buildings in town?"

The doctor thought for a moment. "Yes, the Organisation Todt Bureau has a building here in Ampfing. I believe the school in Mühldorf was converted into barracks and has plenty of good beds; at least it did when I was there last. There is a school also in Mühldorf."

After dropping off the doctor, Shimkin and his group returned to Ampfing and were able to find the Organisation Todt Bureau. It was a one-story building with two sections leading from a central reception hall. The sections were divided into numerous rooms filled with office furniture. For sanitation, there was only one flush toilet, but there were several hand sinks, but only a weak trickle of water could be coaxed from the faucets. The electricity was off. An adjacent building housed a large kitchen with wood-burning stoves with large German six hundred-liter soup kettles.

Shimkin walked through the building, accessing the layout and mentally placing the patients, beds, and medical equipment. He decided the Organisation Todt building was suitable and could house 150 people with some crowding.

A German in the mustard-yellow uniform of the Todt labor corps attached himself to the group, following Shimkin and Andre, opening doors ahead of them. Shimkin turned to the German and asked, "Are you in charge here?" Andre relayed the question. "Yes" came the answer from the German.

"Good," said Shimkin. "In two hours, I want every piece of furniture out of this building. All of the rooms must be swept and cleaned. I want you to leave only the beds, if you have any, and I want one chair in each room. I will order the mayor to provide help for you, but it is your responsibility."

By habit, the German snapped to attention and began to speak rapidly to Andre.

"He wants to know if he can stay here. He has one small room," said Andre.

"Tell him we are bringing typhus patients in here, and he has two hours to get out, but not before the work is done."

Shimkin noticed the German's face reacted to the word *Fleksfeber* (typhus), and the man turned and quickly walked away.

Mike, the group's driver, took Shimkin back to the mayor's bakery. Inside, a woman met Shimkin, wiping her hands on an apron. Shimkin demanded to see the mayor, and he soon emerged from a back room.

Approaching the mayor, the American officer said, "I want you to get fifty strong people to start work immediately. You know the O.T. Bureau, clean it up, and I want all of the furniture out. We are bringing concentration camp people in there, typhus, starved, very sick people. Find fifty women, and have each one bring a pail of hot water, soap, washcloths, and towels. These women are to wash the prisoners. I want you to get food, chicken or meat broth, mashed potatoes, bread, enough for one hundred fifty people. And from the kitchen, have them bring cups, plates, knives, forks, and spoons. All this must be done by two o'clock, three hours from now."

The mayor, looking dazed and confused, tried to repeat the instructions. "Fifty people, food for one hundred fifty, soap, pails, hot water, towels, ah, and what are we to do with the furniture?" he asked.

"Throw it out of the windows. I want it all out of the building. There is a court in back, just stack it up there. But I want it neat."

For emphasis, Shimkin added, "You know the penalty if all this is not done?"

The mayor/baker gulped. "It will be difficult, very hard," he said.

Shimkin, looking as mean and ferocious as a medical officer could, snapped his souvenir riding crop against his shoe. "Go, now!"

The frightened mayor moved away from the wall and ran out of the door. Shimkin and Andre could hear his voice summoning someone.

"Andre, I want you to stay here and keep the mayor on his toes, you understand? See that he does everything that I ordered."

"I will," said Andre with a smile. "What are you going to do?"

"I'm going to get some ambulances and trucks to get those beds. I'll be back in about two hours."

Shimkin drove back to Dorfen to give his boss, Lieutenant Colonel Edward J. Vanderear, chief of the preventive medical section, a report on their findings.

"So what do you think you need?" asked the lieutenant colonel.

"We need a medical unit in there, ambulances, and hospital rations," Shimkin began.

Vanderear thought for a moment and said, "Yah, and blood plasma too."

"Yes, and vitamins, food, and care," said the medical officer. "Every hour means another life, and I mean literally."

As Vanderear picked up the telephone, he turned to Shimkin. "How many ambulances can you use, Major?" he asked.

"About a half dozen and a couple of trucks." Vanderear reached the 187th Medical Battalion and, in less than twenty minutes, arranged for a platoon of the 662nd Clearing Company to take over the treatment of the concentration camp patients. They could provide seven ambulances and two trucks, rations, and medical supplies.

In less than an hour, Shimkin and Mike were out on the highway to where the medical battalion was bivouacked. When they arrived, they were happy to see that the ambulances and trucks were lined up ready to go. Shimkin met with the officer in charge and outlined his plan.

Shimkin said, "I'll go to Mühldorf with the trucks to pick up the beds. In the meantime, the ambulances and a guide will start for the camp a half hour later. I think several trips will be required to evacuate all the people. The medical platoon will arrange reception at Ampfing."

When Mike and Shimkin returned to Ampfing, they found the O.T. Bureau buzzing with activity. As ordered, most of the furniture had been stacked up in the court. Numerous papers, forms, and books were lying around in the halls. Women were scrubbing floors, and some German children were running around. A number of American soldiers had arrived, adding to the confusion, so Shimkin ordered everyone out but the actual workers.

"Let's go get those beds," Shimkin said to Mike and Andre. "And Andre, get your friend to show the ambulances the way to the camp."

The trio drove off with the two trucks following them. On a bluff to the right, they could see a cathedral and some large buildings overlooking the river.

"Ecksberg convent," volunteered Andre when he saw the American look in that direction. Shimkin filed the information in his head. He knew they were not supposed to disturb religions installations, but the Germans had already converted many of them for other, much less religious purposes. After that, the troops assumed the prohibition was no longer in effect. They drove on, and Mühldorf suddenly appeared as they crossed a bridge. It was obvious the north section of the town had borne the brunt of last month's bombing raid on the railroad marshalling yard. The streets were mostly empty, but as they drove along, people began to come out, and suddenly the streets were filled. Shimkin told Mike to stop, and Andre called out to the Germans to assemble. Hesitatingly, they came forward. Andre translated that they wanted ten men to climb up on the trucks to help them load things for about a half hour. Not surprisingly, there were no volunteers, so Shimkin picked out the strongest-looking men and ordered them on the trucks. Because the German towns were devoid of younger manpower, none of those selected was under forty years of age, and most considerably older.

The Mühldorf School was a few blocks to the right and consisted of two stone buildings, one of which had been converted into barracks. It had a gaping hole in the roof where a bomb had apparently penetrated three stories of the building, but the walls were still standing, probably due to faulty explosives. Plaster was all over the floor or ready to fall off the walls due to rain damage. The barracks contained a number of double-decker wooden beds with gunnysacks stuffed with straw as bedding. Shimkin knew that not many of the waiting patients would be able to climb to the upper decks. The straw-filled bags, however, could serve as mattresses. He ordered 160 of them to be loaded and told the drivers to see that only those that were clean and not torn were to be taken.

While the Germans were working, Shimkin decided to explore the other building. The door was unlocked, and he and Andre entered a number of schoolrooms. They each had desks, blackboards, and other items for education. Behind the teachers' desks were Nazi flags and pictures of Adolf Hitler. The second floor contained an office and a small apartment. The bed appeared to have been recently occupied, the butts of American cigarettes scattered on the floor. Some of the butts were stained with lipstick. Nearby, a civilian suit was hanging on a hook.

Shimkin looked at the suit. "Why don't you change your clothes and throw away your uniform?" he asked Andre.

Andre looked at the suit and tried on the coat. "If you don't mind, Major," he said, "I'd like to keep my clothes."

Shimkin looked at the man. He began to understand that the concentration camp uniform had become a badge of honor, a symbol of survival, and was usually kept by the liberated inmates as they wandered over the roads of Germany.

The trucks were finally loaded with the straw mattresses and what beds could be carried. Shimkin dismissed the sweating Germans. They headed back to Ampfing. When they arrived, they found the ambulances had already left. "Mike," said Shimkin, "find some Germans and get these mattresses into the hospital. You'll have to put five or six in each room—and see that the rooms are clean."

"Yes, sir," said Mike as he hurried off. Trucks and jeeps began to arrive at the gate. The personnel of the medical platoon had already picked one room for treatment and dressings and another one for an office. They began to unload their medical supplies. Shimkin looked around. It was not quite what he would have wanted, but it was the best they could do under these extreme circumstances.

The ambulances soon arrived at the makeshift hospital. Shimkin noted the grim look on the drivers' faces, men that had seen it all on the battlefield.

The stretchers were unloaded first, and they were taken directly to the emergency room. Simon Ruder was among the first patients to be carried in.

He was barely conscious but appeared to understand that he had been rescued. "Danke, danke," he said, his voice, waveringly weak.

As the stretcher-bound patients were being unloaded, a group of American soldiers and Germans watched from a distance. Even from their vantage point, they could tell the men on the stretchers were in terrible shape.

Once the patients on stretchers had been unloaded, the rest of the patients began to emerge from the ambulances. They had been packed eight to each truck. They were mere skeletons wrapped in pale skin, some without clothing, filthy blankets wrapped around their groins, sores visible all over their bodies with little or no hair. The pitiful figures were having obvious difficulty, making slow, painful, halting progress, stumbling and falling as they made their way to the hospital. Most needed help. They shuffled a few steps, quickly became exhausted, and had to stop and rest.

As the line of patients slowly and painfully made their way to the hospital, the onlookers gasped, soldiers and German civilians alike. The Americans swore. The German women wrung their hands. *"Mein Gott, mein Gott!"* they cried. Shimkin watched and thought the anguish was genuine. Two of the women who had been cleaning up the hall stood, their jaws dropped. "How can it be!" they cried. They threw down their brooms as a Jew stumbled and rushed over to help him.

Mike, too, rushed forward to help. "This is Hitler's work. You should be proud!" he yelled at the women in English.

Shimkin intervened. "Mike, why don't you help get these patients settled." It was not a question.

"Yes, sir," said Mike, scowling back over his shoulder at the German women as he left. Later, as the rest of the patients finally made their way to the hospital, the German women somberly went about the task of washing them.

As it turned out, the makeshift hospital could only accommodate 150 patients. Shimkin learned that, due to a miscommunication, several other barracks with liberated prisoners had not been counted. They would be treated and left at the camp until new facilities could be brought online.

Once he was situated, the medics and nurses began tending to Simon. In a creaking, weak voice, he managed to let them know his name. They had already noticed the tattoo on Simon's left forearm. His general condition was one of the worst they had encountered, and their prognosis was grim, though they tried to put the best face on it. Simon had suffered grievous wounds at the hands of his captors, wounds inflicted at several SS prisons and camps including Loncki Prison, Plaszow, Auschwitz-Birkenau II, the main Dachau camp, and the Waldlager V sub-camp there at the Ampfing complex. He was extremely dehydrated and covered in lice, sores covering much of his body, and he was starved and inflicted with typhus. He weighed a scant sixty-nine pounds. Injuries to his head were severe with several lacerations across his neck, as though he had been sliced with a saber.

He was given intravenous glucose infusions to stabilize him, and his wounds were cleaned, treated, and bandaged. That night Simon slept on a clean mattress, even though it was just a gunnysack filled with fresh, clean straw. Had he been able to, he could have actually stretched out without rolling over another prisoner.

Simon awoke the next morning, surprised he was still alive. He felt slightly better, though still very weak. He looked around, unsure of where he was. He felt the bandages on his head and neck. He saw the little tubes ending in his arm. The room was clean, something he hadn't seen in years. He vaguely remembered being placed gently on a stretcher and being carried out of that hellhole bunker. The fresh, cool air felt good. He remembered being sprayed with a powder. It was DDT to kill the lice that caused the typhus, but he wasn't aware of that. He remembered people speaking in what he assumed was English. He didn't understand the words, but the caring demeanor was apparent. He remembered "Danke, danke" and then realized that it had come from him.

After a few days, Simon began to regain some of his strength. He was fed a nourishing hot broth and then moved on to some solid food.

That day Simon had two visitors. One, a Jew from France named Andre who served as a translator, and an American, a medical officer, Michael Shimkin. Shimkin spoke in English, and Andre translated.

"Hello, Simon," began Shimkin. "My name is Michael Shimkin, of the Public Health Team Number Two of the United States Public Health Service attached to the Third US Army. I'm a doctor. We were worried about you. How are you feeling today?"

Simon looked at his benefactor. "I think I'm feeling better today. Maybe a little bit stronger too. Soon I think I will be playing soccer again."

Andre translated, and he and Shimkin both laughed.

"I'm afraid that's going to be a little while longer. We have controlled the typhus, and you are gaining some weight and getting a little stronger. I think, in time, you will make a complete recovery. But it will take time." A lie to be sure, but intended to provide hope to Simon.

Shimkin examined the obvious wounds. He realized the neck wound was probably a result of a saber slash intended as a killing stroke. It also inflicted a deep cut to the scalp that would require a number of stitches to close. To be sure, Shimkin realized that this poor man had endured many beatings, many blows to the head, and a myriad of other injuries, but those physical injuries could eventually heal. On the chance Simon could survive the physical torture, Shimkin was more worried about the emotional and psychological effects.

"Right now I'm concerned about your head and neck wounds, especially the neck. Can you tell me what happened?"

Simon tried to remember. He barely remembered the vicious attack, but then the memories flooded back.

"Yes, that last day when the Americans came. The Capos rampaged through the camp. They had sabers and were slashing the sick prisoners, those too weak to escape. I think they were trying to kill everyone. The guards, they attacked me with clubs and swords. They hit me with clubs then used the swords on my neck. Before they could finish the job, they ran away."

"Well, Simon, I think you were lucky to survive. I don't think you would have lived too much longer. I'm glad we found you and were able to help you. I think it will take a few more months for you to recover enough to start moving around again. Your neck should heal, the wounds were not too deep, but they will leave a large scar. Your head wounds should heal without any lasting effects. You have a broken finger that didn't heal properly. Your legs are very weak, and your feet are infected. You will need crutches to get around once you are strong enough."

"Thank you, thank you, Doctor."

"I also have news for you. The Fuhrer committed suicide. The Germans will not last much longer. The war in Europe should be over soon."

Surprisingly, Simon reacted angrily to the news. Not because the Germans were about to surrender, he was sure that would happen, though not so sure he would be around to see it. Not because the Fuhrer was dead. He was angry because of the price he had to pay, his wife and children, his possessions, his tailor shop, the pain, and the four lost years of his life, all because of the Germans.

Shimkin observed Simon's reaction to the news and nodded understandingly. "Simon, I have to go now. The Medical Corps will take over and will be responsible for your care. You will stay here until you are strong enough to move. Then you will be transferred to another hospital we set up in the Ecksberg convent. After that, we should have a better hospital established in Mühldorf where I hope you will complete your recovery. Best of luck to you, Simon."

Simon watched as his savior walked away, never dreaming that he would one day outlive this fine American doctor by some twenty-two years.

A few days later, Simon and a few other liberated prisoners were taken to the makeshift hospital at the Ecksberg convent situated on a bluff overlooking the town of Mühldorf. Having been extremely fortunate to be rescued and saved by the Americans, he now began yet another journey to heal, physically and emotionally.

The unconditional surrender of Germany was signed at Reims on May 7 and ratified in Berlin on May 8. Sporadic fighting continued in a few pockets, and the Russians were busy fighting resistance in some of their captured territories, but Germany was finished.

Two months earlier, after the bombing of Mühldorf, Ludwig Häusl, like so many Germans, wondered what would become of his Germany. Ominously, the answer soon began to unfold. Suddenly, hundreds of thousands, if not a million, forced labor prisoners, many from countries and towns that no longer existed, roamed the German countryside, competing with the Germans for food, shelter, and survival. Food was scarce, much of the habitable shelter destroyed, with chaos and lawlessness rampant. Murders of Germans for revenge occurred with authorities helpless to impose law and order. In Bavaria, the Americans were struggling to achieve some measure of control of their partition of Germany.

Unfortunate ethnic Germans outside of Germany were to feel the full force of retribution, hatred, and revenge. Many were murdered or suffered similar fates of the concentration camp victims, albeit on an infinitely small scale.

Yet the bigger picture of what would become of Germany was still being discussed, argued really, by the Allies. Proposals included a complete deindustrialization of Germany, effectively removing or destroying all remaining production capability and returning the once mighty country to a nineteenth-century agrarian economy. More pragmatic proposals emerged in the realization that future reparations were better paid in hard currency rather than potatoes and the chance that eventual population discontent would lead to yet another war. Those were seeds no one wanted to sow.

The planning for a postwar Germany had actually begun several years earlier as the Allies debated issues ranging from punishment, denazification, various forms of government, school reform, and other policies.

Germany was divided into four zones, with Bavaria and parts of Austria being administered by the Americans through an organization called the Military Government. The Americans were starting to understand the staggering dimensions of the human disaster and the challenges that confronted them. Emergency hospital facilities had been set up at numerous liberated camps throughout Germany, some elaborate, others makeshift at best. These facilities proved effective in saving the lives of thousands of prisoners whose lives were literally hanging by a thread.

One issue most agreed on was the complete removal of Nazi influence of or participation in any future government. Called denazification, the process began quickly. The Nazi lice had to be painstakingly combed out of the German hair with a very fine comb. They were, unfortunately, deeply entrenched in both the fabric and minds of many Germans, and the task was undertaken by the four Allied powers, albeit with a significant difference in the sense of urgency.

The Americans, in particular, pursued this program zealously. They purposed to identify former Nazi Party members, remove them from office, and, as appropriate, mete out punishment. The program also sought to remove Nazi symbols like the swastika from Germany. At first, Germans were required to fill out a 133-question, twelve-page questionnaire called *Fragebogen* to document their activities and memberships during the Third Reich. Based on these questionnaires, Germans were classified into five categories, including Major Offenders, Offenders, Lesser Offenders, Followers, and Exonerated Persons. The Americans applied these categories to all Germans over the age of eighteen in their zone. Completed in German, the questionnaires soon began piling up, and processing them in a timely manner became impossible.

US Army Captain Jerome Greene made his rounds through the various administration buildings in Bavaria. As part of the American Military Government, he was responsible for various governmental functions, including the distribution of food ration cards. The ration cards authorized a specific number of calories per person depending on status, the average amount being around 1,550 calories. The total calories would be further reduced the next year. Germany was facing severe food and fuel shortages, and these ration cards became a critical lifeline to survival for most Germans. Marile Häusl was one of the staff distributing these cards. Captain Greene, whom many speculated was Jewish, was nonetheless tolerated, if not respected, by the Germans. He spoke some German but relied on a translator to assist with more complex matters. Outside the office, however, he was forbidden to "fraternize" with the Germans. Unfortunately, that didn't stop some of the American soldiers in their relationships with young German girls.

MÜHLDORF AREA, GERMANY, MAY 1945

As the Allies continued their march into a now defeated Germany, they discovered a number of indescribably horrific concentration camps. At Dachau, Buchenwald, Dora, Mauthausen, and numerous forced labor work and detention camps, shocked US infantrymen encountered thousands of dead and dying prisoners, emaciated and horribly diseased. As word of these findings reached General Eisenhower, he began to fully understand and appreciate the magnitude of the crimes against humanity carried out by the Nazis. He also understood that the utter brutality of the crimes could lead to attempts by certain groups to dismiss the evidence as propaganda. He personally visited many of the camps to view the evidence. He ordered that all the civilian news media and military combat camera units be required to visit the camps and record their observations in print, pictures, and film. Some local US Army commanders went even farther.

Marile Häusl, after her close call on March 19, paid more attention to her surroundings. She missed her three friends who had died that day, unintended victims of an American bombing mission. Now, three months later, she was at her job in the government building where she had been working since 1942. The war was over, and Germany, for the second time in less than fifty years, felt the bitter sting of defeat. This time, though, it was much worse because it was a defeat without honor. It was the defeat of a brutal regime that crossed the moral line of inhumanity to such an extent that it would forever stain the reputation and honor of the German people. They didn't just approach that line or step on it. The regime had willingly plowed across it like one of their Panzers smashing through a hedgerow.

At around noon on a bright day in May, the citizens of Mühldorf were about to experience an event, the memory of which would stay with them for the rest of their lives. For some, it would forever alter the path of their lives in unimaginable ways. Marile Häusl would be one of them.

Anxiety spread through the government building when the Americans suddenly arrived with a number of trucks. In German, they announced that everyone must leave the building. The voice on the loudspeaker said, "By order of the captain, everyone must board a truck waiting outside. You will be taken to a place to contemplate the actions of your Third Reich and Nazi Party."

The Germans looked at each other questioningly. They shouted and complained, but no one resisted. The soldiers herded the workers outside. Everyone at work that day was forced to come along. The soldiers checked each office, closet, and bathroom looking for anyone who had managed not to hear the announcement. Several stragglers were found and were made to join the crowd leaving the building. Once everyone was loaded, the trucks departed the city center and drove for a distance on the main street to a dirt road leading to a forest. The caravan turned right onto a bumpy road, and people were being jostled about in the back of the trucks. A few kilometers into the woods the trucks slowed. As they screeched to a halt, another truck full of people was leaving. The sight relieved many of the people in Marile's truck. At least people were presumably going back to town alive.

Again, in German, the crowd was ordered off the trucks and told to gather at a spot designated by a soldier. The crowd became hushed and did as they were told. The soldiers began to move the crowd forward in ones and twos. They walked for a short distance to a clearing in the woods. The soldier pointed to the right, and the crowd looked in that direction. Their reactions were momentarily delayed as their brains tried desperately to make sense of what they were seeing. One soldier, a captain, stepped forward, waiting for the realization to sink in. It did, slowly at first. Gasps then punctuated the silence as a hundred Germans came face-to-face with the truth about their fallen regime.

In the clearing, the bodies of several hundred people had been dug up from a shallow mass grave. The captain, through a translator, announced that these bodies were prisoners who had been shot or garroted by the SS just days before the US troops had arrived in the area. They were made to look at the emaciated condition of the corpses.

Picture of German civilians forced to go through concentration camps such as this scene at the Flossenburg camp. Marile Häusl was one of the countless Germans who had to witness these gruesome scenes.

They were told that these bodies were from Dachau and from the four Mühldorf sub-camps that had just been liberated. They were told of the conditions at the camps and the fate of the inmates.

As the crowd took in the gruesome scene, many began to weep, groan, and wail at the sight. Anguished cries of "*Mein Gott, mein Gott*" were heard. Others were heard saying, "No one told us. We were deceived." Like hell, thought the captain. Most, however, were silent, lost in their thoughts. Flies were everywhere, and the stench was overpowering. Several women in the crowd fainted, and many others vomited. The American captain had seen these reactions before and, in fact, was expecting them. After a few minutes, he was satisfied that the lesson had been successfully administered, at least to some of them here in a clearing in the bucolic woods just outside of Mühldorf, Germany.

Marile Häusl took in the grisly scene in stunned silence. She had been a member of the *Bund Deutscher Mädel (BDM)*, the women's component of the Hitler Youth since she was ten. She had been taught, indoctrinated, into the philosophy that Jews were the cause of all strife in the world. They were dirty and no better than vermin. They were carriers of epidemics and were to be exterminated for the good of Germany. She had been taught about the racial purity and superiority of the master race to which she belonged. Yet here she stood, looking at the grotesque line of corpses of those she was taught to hate, and yet she felt only pity, sadness, and the overwhelming moral wrongness of it. In an instant, the meticulously crafted belief system, so insidiously delivered day after day by a dying Reich, crumbled away, laying bare a horrific truth. Suddenly, she didn't feel like a member of a master race. She felt shame for her people and for herself. It had been difficult enough for her to reconcile the Hitler Youth teachings with those of the Catholic Church, and something that she was never quite able to accomplish, but now, coming face-to-face with the brutal results of the Nazi doctrine, she made up her mind. No one should do these things. They were simply unacceptable and unforgivable. She thought back eight years when she had been chosen to present the Fuhrer a bouquet of flowers as a naïve ten-year-old. She remembered the gentle pat on the head administered by the Fuhrer himself and shuddered uncontrollably. A vision of a monster, far worse than any caricature of the Jews, flashed through her mind. Though only seventeen, she knew she was at a pivotal crossroads in her young life, and no matter which road she took, her life would be forever changed.

The desired effect achieved, the captain and his men dispersed the crowd, and they were loaded back onto the waiting trucks. The ride back was filled with silence. There were a few sniffles as handkerchiefs came out and noses were blown and eyes were wiped. Heads were hung as the trucks made its way back on the bumpy dirt road and then onto the main road back to town.

When the trucks reached the town, the occupants were unloaded in front of their government building. It was only 2:30 p.m., but the Americans told them to go home—go home and think about what they had seen. Tomorrow they would take a small step to begin to make things right.

Marile walked home, images of the corpses lying in the clearing burned in her mind. Her immediate reaction had been abject horror, and she knew the guilt she felt would gnaw at her forever.

When she arrived at home later that afternoon, her father was already there. No trains were running to the forced labor camps scattered around Mühldorf. Her sisters and brother were home because school had been canceled when their schoolhouse had been converted to a German army barracks, and more recently, part of it had been bombed during a March 19 air raid. Now it had been taken over by the Americans. It was somber at the Häusl home. Only Marile and her parents had been subjected to the grisly tour of the massacre site; the younger siblings had been spared the nightmare. They knew, or at least sensed, the grave atmosphere pervading the small farmhouse.

The older Maria, a devout Catholic with long-standing reservations about the Nazis, quietly broached the subject no one wanted to discuss.

"I knew it," she began. "Those damn Nazis have brought shame and infamy on Germany's people. This war was folly. That maniac Hitler and his crazy staff have destroyed our country."

As a Catholic, the elder Maria had no great love for the Jews. After all, they had killed her God, hadn't they? Now that the truth was openly disclosed, she began to have feelings of guilt and sorrow, but was it for what her Third Reich had done or that they were caught? After all, the Jews really weren't humans, were they? She had never met a Jew, at least a live one, and she also knew that she never wanted to. At the moment, however, she was more concerned about what would happen to her Germany and to her family.

Ludwig, on the other hand, had glimpsed the horror of the camps and in his small way tried to atone for himself, and perhaps for his country, by throwing his lunch over the barbed-wire fence at Dachau or other camps to which he delivered cargo, human or otherwise. He recalled the image. As his train slowly rumbled past, he saw inmates shuffle over to the caloric windfall to gather up the food. Though he didn't see, many of them stuffed the food into their dirty uniforms, food to be carefully saved for later, food that would often be enough for later to actually happen.

No one at the dinner table asked questions about who knew about these atrocities. They all knew but were now in denial. The signs were all there, but in a state where children turned in their parents, where people who complained were never seen again, collective denial had become a way of life. After all, Adolf Hitler was their savior. He had lifted Germany out of a worldwide depression. He had provided jobs for everyone. He had propelled Germany onto the global stage. The Germans had forgotten the humiliation of the Treaty of Versailles. They had hosted the Olympics in 1936. They had showcased the new, ultra-modern Autobahns. They even had their version of the Model T, the Volkswagen, the people's car. Germany's future had seemed bright. The period from 1933 to the beginning of the war was hailed as wonderfully prosperous. In the end, however, the cost turned out to be staggering in terms of human lives, human dignity, and a forever-disgraced national image.

Marile, who had gone through the Hitler Youth indoctrination and had invested her faith in and loyalty to the program, was devastated. Like so many others in Muüldorf, she had also never met a Jew. This afternoon had changed her life in ways that were just beginning to unfold. Her education would continue as the aftermath of the war began to take shape.

The Americans were starting to understand the staggering dimensions of the human disaster and challenges that confronted them. Emergency hospital facilities had been set up at numerous liberated camps throughout Germany, some elaborate, others makeshift at best. These facilities proved effective in saving the lives of thousands of prisoners whose lives were literally hanging by a thread. Now stabilized and with greatly improved chances for survival, the liberated death camp survivors needed facilities for housing and their general welfare. Displaced Person (DP) camps were established near former concentration camps to fulfill this requirement. The first, and probably the most famous, was Feldafing, established by the Americans on May 1, 1945, to house Hungarian Jews rescued from a railroad siding near the Tutzing railroad station. These Jews had been saved from certain death by a sympathetic, or at least a pragmatic, *Wehrmacht* transport commander who had kept delaying the train until it could be liberated by advance units of the US Army. The train had originated from the Mühldorf-Mettenheim concentration camp and was transporting only Jewish prisoners gathered from Mittergars and Wald Lager IV and V concentration camps to be massacred in the Tyrolian Mountains by a waiting SS contingent. Ironically, because the train had an anti-aircraft gun on one of the cars, it was mistaken for a military transport and was strafed by Americans fighter planes, killing and injuring several prisoners. Sadly, fear of the planes was greater than the guards, many of whom were planning their own escapes. The train never arrived, and the Americans eventually liberated the prisoners, many of whom were the first to be housed at newly established Feldafing DP camp. Among them were fourteen-year-old Tomas Weissbluth and his father Jeno.

Ironically, the DP camp was set up on the former grounds of a major Hitler Youth facility on land partially confiscated from Jewish owners. In charge of the camp was First Lieutenant Irving J. Smith, a Jewish soldier who was a peacetime attorney serving in the army's Civil Affairs Command.

The camp itself was made up of stone and wooden barracks and several individual homes on the grounds of the Reichsschule Feldafing. In all, there were seven large two-story buildings, at least a dozen temporary buildings, and six or seven associated large villas and an elite school for *Hitlerjugend* (Hitler Youth). Though the US Army originally opened the camp to house three thousand Hungarian Jews, the camp also housed many non-Jewish concentration camp survivors. In July 1945, an American chaplain, a rabbi named Abraham Klausner, helped convince the commandants of Dachau and Feldafing to empty the DP camp of its non-Jewish Polish and Hungarian DPs and replace them with the remaining Jewish survivors from the Dachau sub-camps. In autumn 1945, the first all-Jewish hospital in the German DP camps was founded at Feldafing, containing one thousand beds.

BRUNNLITZ, MORAVIA, MAY 8, 1945

Izak Ruder, the older brother of both Mendel and Simon, was elated at the news. Oskar Schindler had just announced the unconditional surrender of Germany followed by a masterful speech.

The nonconditional surrender of the German armed forces has just been announced.

As hundreds of thousands of privates of a broken army flood back along country roads into their homeland, after millions of victims have died in six years of mass murder, and as Europe attempts to return to peace and order, I would like to turn to all of you, those of you who have been with me throughout these many difficult years and have feared that this day would never come, to all of you, who in a few days will return to your destroyed, plundered homesteads, searching for survivors from your families—I appeal to all of you to strictly maintain order and discipline. This will minimize panic, the consequences of which would be unpredictable.

In his proclamation today, Montgomery has declared that we must deal with the defeated in a humane manner. We must differentiate between guilt and duty. The soldier on the front, like the common man, who does his duty everywhere, should not be held responsible for the actions of a few who also called themselves Germans. The fact that millions of you, your parents, children, and brothers, have been murdered, was not acceptable to thousands of Germans, and even today, there are millions of Germans who do not know the extent of these atrocities. The documents and records found in Dachau, Buchenwald, and the other camps are the first pieces of evidence pointing to this monstrous destruction. Nevertheless, I ask you to behave in a humane and just manner. Leave the prosecutions and revenge to those who have been assigned to these matters. If you have accusations to levy at anyone, do so with the proper authorities, because in the new Europe, there will be judges—incorruptible judges—who will hear your pleas.

Many of you know the persecutions, harassment, and obstacles that I had to overcome in order to keep my workers during these terrible years. Although it was already difficult to protect the limited rights of a Polish worker, to help him keep his business, protect him from being deported into the Reich, protect his property, and preserve his modest belongings and assets—the difficulties of protecting Jewish laborers often seemed insurmountable. Those of you who have worked with me from the beginning, through all these years, know how I made innumerable personal interventions after the closure of the ghetto, how I worked with the camp administration on your behalf in order to save you from deportation and liquidation, or how I managed to reverse orders that had already been given. How many worries it caused me, how threatening the danger was, to think that I might lose my Jewish laborers, when you were kept away from the factory under various pretenses for days, in some cases even for weeks. Very few of the workers who were sent to me actually had experience as skilled laborers before the war, the kind of workers that I was looking for to do this work, and it is a miracle that we were able, thanks to your positive attitude, to overcome the greatest difficulties.

I have demanded some productive output from you, which must have seemed rather senseless to most of you, since you were shielded from seeing the overall situation, but it was always my will to demonstrate and defend humanity, to conduct my affairs humanely, the principle that guided all of my decisions. Continue to maintain your discipline and order. When, after a few days spent here, the gates of freedom are opened to you, think about what many of the people who live around this factory have done for you in terms of providing additional food and clothing.

I have tried and risked everything to acquire additional food for you in the past, and I pledge to continue putting everything on the line to protect you and provide you with your daily bread. I will continue to work around the clock to do everything for you that is within my power. Do not go into the houses around here to forage and steal. Show yourselves to be worthy of the sacrifice of millions from your ranks, avoid every act of revenge and terrorism. The Schindler Jews were off-limits in Brünnlitz. I charge all of the Capos and overseers to continue to uphold order and enforce good conduct. Tell this to all of your people, because it is in the interest of their security. Thank the Daubek Mill, whose energetic support improved your nutrition, often beyond the realm of the possible. I wish to express sincere thanks to Director Drabek on your behalf, who personally did everything I requested in order to get food for you.

Do not thank me for your survival, thank your own people, who worked day and night to save you from annihilation. Thank the dauntless Stern, Pemper, and those others who, in the course of their duty, above all in Krakow, looked death in the eye at every moment, thought of everyone and cared for everyone.

This solemn hour reminds us of our obligation to remain alert and maintain order; as long as we remain here together, I ask you all, among yourselves, to decide upon courses of action that are humane and just. I thank my personal staff for their restless sacrifice for my work. To the SS guards and the marines who are assembled here, who were assigned to this duty without their consent, I thank you also; as heads of families themselves, they have long realized the capricious and senseless nature of their orders. They have behaved in an extraordinarily humane and proper manner.

In conclusion, I ask all of you for three minutes of silence, to remember the innumerable victims who have fallen from your ranks in these terrible times.

Izak had survived the war in large part due to the intervention of Oskar Schindler. He had been spared the worst of the horrors of Amon Goeth and the Plaszow forced labor camp by working in Schindler's DEF factory (Deutsche

Emaillewaren-Fabrik). When that factory was closed, Schindler made arrangements, mostly through bribes and gifts to high-ranking SS and local officials, to open an armament factory in Brunnlitz, Moravia. The plant was said to have never produced a good artillery shell. Izak was one of the fortunate Jews who found his name on what history called "Schindler's List." Shortly before the Russians arrived on May 9, 1945, Oskar Schindler and his wife Emilie left Brunnitz. When the Russians arrived, the inmates were free to leave. But to where?

MÜHLDORF, GERMANY AREA, MAY 1945

Marile Häusl was on her way to work. In town, she encountered a group of American soldiers. One of them was black. This was something she had never seen, at least not in person. She had seen pictures of natives in Africa, but this was different. As the group approached her, she tried not to stare at the black GI. He smiled at her, and she wasn't sure how to react. The GI laughed when he saw her reaction. He started talking, but she did not understand the words. The group seemed friendly, though. One of them reached out and waved a dark-brown object at her. She could read "HERSHEY'S."

"Chocolate," said the American. "Fraulein, please, ah bitte, this is for you. From America." Marile eyed the chocolate bar and, after a moment or two, hesitatingly took it from the outstretched hand. "Danke," she said and smiled at the GIs who were laughing and whistling as they continued their march through the town. She put the chocolate bar in her pocket and quickly made her way to her office building. It was starting out to be an interesting day. She thought about the Americans she had just encountered and wondered what America was like. Sadly, she thought about her own devastated country. The "Thousand-Year Reich" had lasted but twelve years, taking with it an estimated sixty to seventy million lives, including an estimated twelve million in concentration and forced labor camps. Six million of those were Jews, and soon, she would see her share.

Not too far away, in Ampfing, Simon Ruder barely clung to life in the makeshift hospital facility at the Organisation Todt building. The doctors didn't hold out much hope for his recovery but continued to care for him. After a few weeks, he began to show signs of wanting to live. Slowly, he gained back some of the weight that had dwindled down to the sixty-nine pounds he carried when he was liberated. He was unable to walk because of the injuries to his legs, and large white bandages covered his head and the left side of his neck, the result of the brutal attacks by the camp Capos as the Americans had approached the notorious work camp at Ampfing.

In the meantime, the Americans had set up a more substantial hospital facility in the Ecksberg convent situated on a bluff overlooking the town of Mühldorf and were transferring patients from Ampfing to that new facility. One of the last to be evacuated, Simon was taken by stretcher to a waiting ambulance and transported the few kilometers to the Ecksberg facility, now considered a small DP camp. He was taken to a room with several other patients, mostly camp survivors, at least in his room. Many had suffered similar injuries and sickness and would later tell stories about the horrific treatment they had endured at the hands of the now vanquished Nazis. The injuries were not like those in an army hospital where limbs were blown off or flying shrapnel had shattered bodies. These were injuries resulting from torture, disease, malnutrition, and abuse, not conditions normally confronting army or civilian doctors. One of the major issues facing the doctors was the psychological damage that had manifested itself in the survivors. Initially, there was the guilt of having survived when so many millions of their people had perished. Why me? Why did I survive? Then came the grief, the realization, that those they loved, the wives, husbands, children, aunts, uncles, brothers and sisters, and parents were all gone because of the maniacs that had run the very country in which they now found themselves.

The room in which Simon now rested was freshly painted a pastel shade of light green. Even now, beds were being set up, having recently been moved back from the Ampfing facility. The Americans were in charge, but many of the doctors were German. Simon was trying to rest as one of them came by to check on him.

"Herr Ruder," said the doctor, a man of perhaps fifty or so years old. "I am Dr. Wiesermann. How are you doing today?"

Simon thought about how to answer. Goddamn Nazi, he thought, but held his tongue. He thought he could sense remorse in the doctor's demeanor. Surely the doctor understood that his own countrymen, the civilized Germans, had inflicted these wounds on Simon and the other patients in the ward. This doctor himself could have committed atrocities.

Evil thoughts receding, Simon turned to the doctor. "I have some pain in my head and neck. It comes and goes. And my legs hurt as well."

"You need rest, Herr Ruder. You will be here for quite a while, but I think you will make a good recovery in due time." Not particularly convincing, thought Simon. "I will have someone give you a shot for your pain."

"Thank you, Herr Doctor," said Simon as he tried to get comfortable in the new bed. He looked around but didn't recognize any of the other patients. As promised, presently someone arrived and administered a shot of morphine, and Simon was soon drifting off into a troubled sleep.

The nightmares came again. Piles of corpses, mouths open, sticklike limbs twisted in bizarre shapes and angles, of horrific train journeys in cattle cars so crowded the dead were unable to fall to the floor. He dreamed of the stench in the camps, of the mud, the cold, and the dogs. The damn dogs, always barking. He dreamed of the fights for moldy breadcrumbs and stale potato peels, of eating dirt and sawdust bread. He relived the beatings, the clubs and whips. He whimpered as he dreamed of the executions of friends and unknown prisoners, some by bullets, others by hanging. He remembered their faces, contorted in pain and agony. Then came the sickly stench of black ash raining down on him at Auschwitz, followed by visions of the brutal march in the dead of winter in knee-deep snow. Simon involuntarily shivered in his sleep. He remembered the bastards like SS *Oberscharführer* Oskar Waltke at Loncki Prison, Amon Gothe at the Plaszow concentration camp, the vicious Capos at all the camps. He thought of his poor wife Lola and his children, Hanna and Artur. He tried to scream but managed only stifled, agonized grunts. Thankfully, he finally fell into a more peaceful sleep.

CZECH REPUBLIC, JUNE 1945

Izak Ruder, like thousands of camp survivors, had to decide where to go and what to do after freedom finally came. For him, the decision was not difficult. He would travel eastward, back to Krakow, to find what, if anything, remained of his former life. A number of the Brunnlitz factory Jews thought likewise and formed a group determined to return to Krakow. It would be a slow journey as they were limited to the speed of the slowest of them, so the 339-kilometer distance took them three weeks to negotiate using whatever transportation means were available, including many days on foot. More returning Jews joined them on the way, hoping a larger group would provide a margin of safety from ever-present dangers on the road. In all, a total of some forty-three hundred Jews returned to Krakow after the war. The number would soon rise to around ten thousand with an influx of Jews returning from the Soviet Union. However, rather than finding answers, most of the Jews quickly found disappointment, their former shops and homes gone, and no word of relatives or loved ones. Almost as bad was the reception that greeted them. Not surprisingly, they were simply not wanted, a pervasive attitude common throughout much of Poland. The group stayed together and did the best they could in this hostile environment. They found other Jews to help them but all the while looked over their shoulders, and with good reason.

ECKSBERG CONVENT DP HOSPITAL, MÜHLDORF, GERMANY, JULY 1945

Dr. Wiesermann made his rounds, checking on his patients' progress. He was efficient but showed little emotion, yet he seemed to care about the poor souls under his watchful eye. "Herr Ruder," he began. "There is someone to see you."

The man, wearing an American army soldier's uniform, looked at Simon with a genuine look of sympathy on his face and introduced himself. "I am Rabbi Abraham Klausner. I am here to find as many of the concentration camp survivors in Bavaria and make a list. I am going to add your name to the list. In Hebrew, it's called the *Sharit Ha-Platah*. Can you tell me your name and where you originally came from?"

Simon looked at the man. a rabbi, an American. "Yes, Rabbi. My name is Simon Ruder. I was at Auschwitz, Dachau, Ampfing, Thalhiem, and now I'm here in this, this convent. That's all I remember now. I came from Lvov in Poland."

The rabbi wrote down the information. "Simon, Lvov is now in the Ukraine, not Poland. It is called Lviv now. I'm afraid very few Jews survived in Lvov. We are doing the best we can to locate the survivors. We have set up Displaced Person camps in Feldafing and Deggendorf, and some others will be set up soon. There is a hospital in Mühldorf, and I hear you will be moved there soon."

"Danke, Rabbi," said Simon. "I'm still hoping to go back to Lvov to find my family one day."

"Good luck to you, Simon," said Rabbi Klausner, shaking his head as he left the convent hospital.

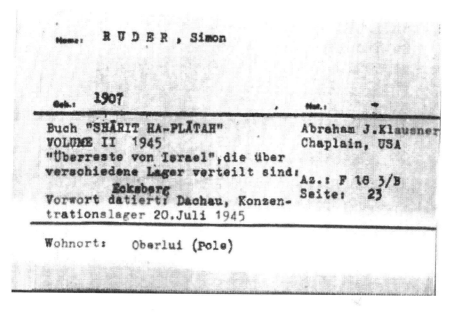

The record of Rabbi Abraham Klausner, a US Army chaplain documenting Simon Ruder at the Ecksberg convent hospital in Mühldorf.

As Rabbi Klausner had predicted, Simon was moved a day later to the Mühldorf hospital and was taken to a room, somewhat bigger and brighter than the one he had left behind at the convent. He was tired and soon drifted into a fitful sleep.

Sometime later, a young woman nurse's aid was making her rounds. She picked up the clipboard that contained patient information. She noted the man had just been transferred from the now closed Ecksberg facility. She looked down at the pitiful figure sleeping on the bed. She hated to wake him, but the orders were to bring breakfast.

Checking the clipboard to make sure, she said, "Herr Ruder. I have brought breakfast for you."

Simon heard the pleasant voice but thought it was part of his dream. He ignored it but wondered what it had to do with the dreams.

Then again, the voice. "Herr Ruder, please wake up."

This time he realized he was not dreaming. He tried unsuccessfully to open his eyes. The room was filled with light, and he thought it might be morning. He tried again, this time blinking as his eyes tried to adjust to the light.

Finally, he was mostly awake, and with effort, he raised his head, opened his eyes, and gazed into a face that made him think he was in heaven.

Marile Häusl, now seventeen, had volunteered for patient care duties at the hospital. Her school had provided her with the necessary patient care knowledge, and she wanted to help however she could. Besides, the Americans were encouraging the German civilians to assist wherever possible, and when the call came for volunteers, she quickly accepted.

She looked at the frail figure staring back at her. She noticed the bandages on his head and neck; they were hard to miss. A pair of crutches leaned against the wall next to the bed, a testament to further injuries.

Marile's heart went out to the man. Ever since the Americans had forced her to view the corpses outside the town, her attitude toward the Third Reich had changed dramatically. Being a good Catholic engendered a deep sense of shame for the crimes and atrocities that had been uncovered.

Simon had difficulty sitting up. Marile rushed over to the bedside and repositioned his pillow and helped him into a sitting position. She placed the tray of food on his lap. The tray contained bread, coffee, and a sausage. Simon was finally able to eat more solid food while he recovered from the various life-threatening conditions, including typhus, severe neck and head wounds, leg injuries, severe dehydration, and intestinal problems due to the starvation rations over the last four years.

He was hungry and slowly began eating the bread and sausage. The coffee was hot, too hot in fact, and he had to blow on it to cool it down. He looked at the young woman. She certainly was pretty, he thought. He tried to drink the coffee and managed to sip about half of the cup.

Soon, however, he became fatigued and asked the young woman to help him with his pillow. Marile again repositioned his pillow and helped him into a comfortable sleeping position.

"Thank you, Fraulein," he said. "Thank you very much." Soon Simon began to doze off, but not before images of Marile's face filled his mind, and soon he was fast asleep.

Sometime later the doctor returned to check on his patient. "Herr Ruder. Time to wake up. I must check your bandages and vital signs."

Simon awakened and peered at the doctor through silted eyes. Yes, he thought. A real German doctor. He could tell by the ultra-professional demeanor, almost as if he was doing his duty but not happy about it. *Get used to it, you Nazi bastard*, Simon thought but again remained silent.

As the doctor examined the bandages and made notes on the clipboard, Simon asked, "Doctor, who was that nice young Fraulein that brought me breakfast this morning?"

The doctor looked puzzled, as if in thought. "Herr Ruder, you have been sleeping for over twelve hours. Maybe you were dreaming, but I think perhaps it might have been Maria, one of the volunteers. She works only one or two days each week. Pretty thing, and smart too. I understand she has another job working for the government. I don't know when she will be back."

"Thank you, Doctor. Yes, for a time, I thought I was dreaming."

The doctor smiled, but the smile did not reach his eyes. "Herr Ruder, you are doing well. Soon, when you regain enough strength, you will be able to get around the hospital. We have an area we call the sanatorium where you may rest and convalesce. I think maybe next week we will assign you there. You must still come back to this room every day, but the change should be good for you."

From that point forward, Simon's recovery was progressed. He still wore the bandages on his neck and head and required the use of crutches to get around, though he adamantly refused to be pushed around in a wheelchair. He started to spend time in the hospital sanatorium where he could rest comfortably while convalescing and talk to some of the other patients, many of them liberated survivors like him. But most of all, he was hoping to catch a glimpse of Maria Häusl, one of the young women volunteers at the hospital. He remembered seeing her when he had first arrived a few days ago when he thought he was dreaming.

One morning he was dozing off in a chair in the sanatorium when one of his fellow patients nudged him awake. "What?" a startled Simon exclaimed, looking at the other man. The man nodded his head toward the long hallway to the left. Simon turned in that direction, and there she was, the young Maria Häusl pushing a cart. Simon thought she was even prettier than when he had first seen her and wasted no time trying to get up out of the chair. Needing the crutches didn't make the action any easier, but he managed and intercepted her as she walked past his chair.

"Fraulein," he started. "I want to thank you for bringing my breakfast the other day and your kindness."

The young woman regarded the bandaged man leaning on a pair of crutches, barely able to stand. He smiled at her. She recognized him from the other morning. He was in terrible condition, and as she was staring at him, an image of Jesus just off the cross formed in her mind. She blushed at the thought. A good Catholic shouldn't think like that. Ironically, she was frighteningly close to reality, for this man was Jewish and had literally come back from the dead.

"Thank you," she replied sweetly. My name is Maria Häusl, but I'm called Marile."

"I am Simon Ruder. I remember you from the other morning. Again, I thank you for your kindness, Fraulein."

Marile blushed, not knowing exactly how to respond. "Yes, I remember you. It's good to see you up and around."

"I'm very glad to see you again. How often are you here at the hospital?"

"I come here twice a week, but only when they call me. It's not the same every day. I work at the Landratsamt Ernahrungsamt Abteilung B here in Mühldorf. I am helping with the issuing of the food ration cards. When you are released from the hospital, you must come see me to get your cards. But I must go now. I have other patients to visit."

"Wait!" said Simon. "Please wait. Fraulein, do you have any free time, a break or lunch perhaps? I would love to talk to you sometime."

Marile looked hesitant. "Herr Ruder. I don't know if that is such a good idea." She looked at the poor man for a moment, and her heart went out to him. She could imagine the horrors he had lived through. "Well, maybe for a little while during my lunch break. Perhaps if the weather is nice I could push your wheelchair outside."

Simon smiled, a genuine smile for the first time in years. "That would make me very happy, Fraulein. I think it would help me get better too. I look forward to it."

"Today is Tuesday. I will be back on Thursday. I will meet you here in the sanatorium. Good-bye, Herr Ruder."

That Thursday Simon and Marile Häusl spent almost an hour talking just outside the hospital building. It was a perfect fall day in Bavaria, not too cold, just right for sitting in the sun and talking.

"Tell me about your family," said Simon, trying to keep the conversation on a lighter note.

Marile looked around as if unsure to answer. No one was near. "I have two sisters, Bette and Rosie, a younger brother Ludwig, and a half brother Alois. We live on a small farm just outside town."

Marile knew enough not to ask about Simon's family and steered clear of the topic.

"What about your parents?" asked Simon.

Marile hesitated, not knowing what to say. Her mother, the elder Maria, had no love for the Jews and made the point many times, especially now that the Third Reich was finished. She wasn't sure about her father, with whom she was much closer. He showed some sympathy for the Jews, but never spoke openly about his feelings, especially in front of his wife. He told Marile about how he had often thrown his lunch over a barbed-wire fence at a camp to which he took his train, but at the time, she wasn't sure exactly where or what that meant. As news of the Nazi horrors emerged and with the memories of her trip to the corpse-filled camp still fresh in her mind, Marile began to understand the guilt and horrific images that her father must now be enduring. She now also understood the small gesture his actions had represented. She also suspected her mother never knew.

"My father works for the railroad," she began. "He is an engineer." Marile paused as she noticed that Simon suddenly had a far-off look on his face.

Behind the far-off look, Simon's mind went back to last March following the American air raid on Mühldorf's rail marshalling yard. He and several thousand prisoners, slave laborers really, had been forced to clean up the yard so that trains could run again. He remembered a tall German giving orders to the Capos, brutally ordering the prisoners around. He had looked directly at the man who had looked back at him and nodded slightly. Could that have been Marile's father? Simon hoped so, for this man seemed to have had compassion.

"What about your mother?" he asked.

"My mother works at the post office, at night. She also works on the farm."

Simon noticed Marile's reluctance to continue talking about her mother and decided not to press further.

The lunch break was quickly drawing to a close, and Marile had to get back to work. She wheeled Simon's chair back to the sanatorium.

"Thank you for your time, Fraulein. It was very pleasant, and I hope we can continue in the near future."

Marile smiled as she started to turn and walk away. Over her shoulder, she said, "Perhaps. I'll be back next Tuesday."

Simon watched the young woman walk away. He felt a sense of elation, an emotion he had thought incapable of ever experiencing again. He didn't really understand why, though right now it didn't matter. He only knew that next Tuesday could not arrive soon enough. He also understood that this developing friendship with a young German girl could go no further, especially because of her age. She was young enough to be his daughter, and she was German and a Catholic. Yet he was drawn to her, and contact with her seemed to draw him out of the deep abyss of depression in which he often found himself. At least temporarily, and that was a start as her visits gave him something to look forward to. The nightmares of the camps continued; they would never go away, but Simon was slowly learning to cope with them. He still woke up in the middle of the night screaming, as did all of the survivors, but the images were marginally more bearable because when he realized where he was, he immediately had thoughts of Marile, and that was often enough to ground him in the new reality of postliberation and safety.

The following weeks saw Simon's condition improve rapidly. He spent more time in the sanatorium and began developing friendships with other survivors. Most of them were from nearby camps from around the Mühldorf area. Several of them were from Hungary and were anxious to get back to their homeland. For the Polish Jewish survivors, however, there was no homeland to which to return. Stories of returning Jews being driven out or murdered began to circulate. The group also learned of special camps for so-called displaced persons established to house the survivors until arrangements could be made to repatriate them or, as would be the case for the vast majority, allow them to immigrate to Israel, Canada, Great Britain, or the United States.

Many of the recovering survivors in the hospital began to share their stories. Some related stories about death trains sent into the nearby mountains, the prisoners to be executed by waiting SS troops. Most of these prisoners survived because of the actions of the *Wehrmacht* and some civilian workers, who, realizing the war was lost, delayed the train until the American army had arrived to liberate them. In an act of particular savagery, the SS had installed an artillery piece on the last car of a prisoner train to deceive the American fighter pilots into thinking the train was a military target, resulting in inadvertent deaths of scores of Jewish prisoners. Simon was unaware that two of the Hungarian Jews, young Tomas Weissbluth and his father Jeno, fellow Waldlager V inmates who had survived their death-train ordeal, were now at the newly established Feldafing DP camp.

The small group of pathetic, liberated, and recuperating Jews began to pass time playing cards. More stories were exchanged, details of families, wives, children, and parents. The full extent of the Nazis' murderous atrocities was still coming to light, and no one was sure of the fates of their loved ones, though most feared the worst. One of the card players, Josef Goldburg from Krakow, embittered by the loss of his wife and children, was unreserved in voicing his opinion of the Germans.

"They are all evil," said Goldburg. "May they all rot in hell. They all knew what was going on. They knew about the camps. Their hands are stained with our blood. The world will never forget, and we shall never forgive."

Others at the card table murmured and nodded in agreement but were not so quick to paint all Germans with the same broad brush of hate.

Simon spoke up first. "Josef, I understand your feelings about this. We all lost loved ones, lost everything we had. I, for one, cannot forgive. But I met some good, decent Germans. An SS guard even saved my life twice. I wouldn't be here without his help. A German doctor is caring for us. He no doubt fought in the war, but now he is helping us recover. To be sure, the Americans may have convinced him, but still, he takes care of me, and in the end, that's all that matters."

Goldburg dropped his cards and looked directly at Simon. Wagging a finger in Simon's face, Goldburg said, "I would expect that from you, Simon. We all see how you fawn over that young German girl. Can't you see what you are doing? She's the enemy. She was probably in the Hitler Youth; her parents were Nazis. How can you even talk to her? You are a traitor to your own people!"

Taken aback, Simon was suddenly speechless. The words stung, and he searched for a response. None came. He looked to his two card-playing colleagues for support. They shook their heads in unison but said nothing.

KRAKOW, POLAND, AUGUST 1945

The pogrom in August of 1945 was merely a harbinger of more to come throughout the following year. Murders of Jews were frequent. Krakow proved to be a chimera of safety, a dangerous place for the returning Jews.

Izak found sporadic work using metalworking skills from the Brunnlitz ammunition factory, and his tailoring skills enabled him to work in a clothing shop. The bolt of cloth he had received from Oskar Schindler was carefully hidden, to be used only in an emergency.

The small group of Jews met frequently to discuss their situation. They were appalled at the news. The death camps, the labor camps, the sheer numbers of Jews killed, the attempted annihilation of the Jewish culture in Europe. Now, the Soviet Union was tightening its stranglehold on Poland. It became obvious that Krakow was not the answer for them.

Izak knew that two of his brothers, Simon and Mendel, had lived in the Lvov area farther east before the war and that the area was now within the borders of the Ukraine. *Too far east*, he thought. *Too close to Russia.* The group decided to stay in Poland. Lodz, they reasoned, was not too far away, almost due north of Krakow. Maybe life would be better there. Several members of the group, including Izak, agreed that was their best option, and after several more weeks of preparing, they struck out for Lodz. Their destination was around 262 kilometers in distance, and again, travel proved problematic at best. Yet the small group persevered and, after a grueling two-week trek, arrived in the second-largest city in Poland.

Unknown to Izak Ruder, his younger brother Mendel and his son Dolek had arrived in Lodz four months earlier and had settled in. Like Mendel, Izak was surprised to find various Jewish health and vocational training organizations in full operation. He also found that many repatriated Jews were returning from Russia. To Izak and the small group of Jews just arrived from Krakow, they hoped some small salvation was at hand.

MÜHLDORF HOSPITAL, SEPTEMBER 1945

Life at the Mühldorf hospital continued for Simon. He had just finished providing information to a young man who filled out a DP registration form. Now he was official. He still planned on going back to Lvov to find his family, and that was the destination he indicated on his DP registration form. Yet he still found himself looking forward to conversations with young Marile Häusl, a German volunteer at the hospital. His health had continued to improve, and while he hoped to be released soon, he realized he had nowhere to go. He remembered Josef Salzmann, the Jewish ghetto policeman who had told him that his wife and children had been murdered by the Gestapo in what was Lemberg in 1942, but he thought maybe someone had survived, and he would make the trip to make sure.

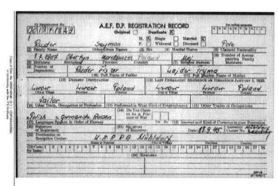

Simon Ruder's DP registration record. His desired destination was recorded as Lwow in what used to be Poland. It would be a journey he never took.

LODZ, POLAND, SEPTEMBER 1945

Working through the Jewish organizations, Izak soon found work and a place to stay. He was put in charge of a small group of workers in a factory producing metal products. Just like Brunnlitz, he thought, but without the SS. It would do for now, but he knew it was merely a short stop on the way to the West. It would take time, but eventually, the immigration doors would open.

One day Izak decided he might need a better suit, especially for his manager role at the metal factory. He had always been a snappy dresser, but the last four years had put a stop to that. He noticed a clothing store that was actually the front of a larger building that housed a clothing factory. Peering through the window, he saw a few rows of racks containing suits. He assumed these were for customers who had ordered them and that the suits were awaiting pickup. Curious, he stepped into the store to examine the suits. Maybe he would order one. A bell on the door loudly announced his arrival. After a minute or so, a small man emerged from the back room and approached Izak. Without looking up, he asked, "May I help you?"

Izak was about to answer when he got a good look at the man. A look of recognition tried to form on his face, but he wasn't quite sure. The small man looked up, wondering why his customer hadn't answered. Recognition sputtered for several heartbeats but suddenly took hold. Both men shouted out each other's name in unison.

"Mendel! Mendel. Is that really you?"

"Yes, Izak! It's me."

The two men hugged each other. They hadn't seen each other for over five years. Both men had aged and were both thinner than they had remembered. They just stood there, looking like they were going to cry. The men remained speechless. Besides Mendel still having young Dolek, neither man had seen or received word from any of their other family members. Perhaps this was a positive sign, they thought. Maybe the others had survived. Izak spoke up, resuming his role as the older brother. "Mendel, I'm so glad to see you. We have much to catch up on. Let's meet this evening. Is there a place around here?"

Mendel turned his head, favoring his good ear. "Yes, we can meet in my apartment. Dolek is in school now, but he will be there. He's seven now."

"Wonderful. I look forward to seeing him. How is Zofia?"

Mendel just paused and slowly shook his head.

Later that evening Izak and Mendel Ruder met for the first time in over five years. As the host, Mendel served some schnapps as the two men sat in Mendel's small apartment. Izak had brought a few cigarettes. Young Dolek had been banished to a bedroom to study.

Izak lit up a cigarette. "So where do we start? Zofia?"

Mendel just shook his head again. Izak understood and moved on. "Our parents. What do you know of their fate?"

Mendel responded slowly. "I know nothing, Izak. I was in Lvov for eight months. It was a terrible time. Almost all of the Jews were gone. I heard most were killed at a place called Belzec. Zloczow, too, was devoid of Jews, and Obertin has no Jews left from what was said."

"And our brother and sisters?"

"Again, nothing. I searched for Simon and Lola in Lvov and found no trace of them. I know nothing of our sisters. About Dobrysza and her husband the carpenter and two children, I have heard nothing. The same for Frieda Ryfka, Miriam, and her barber husband, and little Fani and her children. Sadly, I'm afraid they are all gone."

Their oldest brother Abraham was not mentioned. He had fought in World War I, during which time he had suffered a serious head wound. He later left for Cuba and had married there. Unknown to both brothers, he had died in Cuba in 1941, leaving a son, Max.

"So, Mendel, what are your plans?"

Mendel looked at his older brother, some nine years his senior. "I'm waiting to see what happens. I've been here several months. I have a small job, as you saw. I'm trying to make extra money making suits, but cloth is hard to come by."

Izak smiled. Mendel was the youngest of the four brothers. The three older boys had taken it upon themselves to protect him, at least while they were growing up in Obertin.

Izak put down his cigarette, got up, and walked over to the door where he had placed a package upon entering. "I may have something that could help you." He picked up the package and handed it to his younger brother.

"What's this?" asked Mendel, a puzzled look on his face.

"Something I have been saving. Maybe you can use it."

Mendel gently opened the package, being careful not to tear the paper. The paper could be reused. He finished removing the wrapping, revealing the bolt of cloth. Surprised, Mendel ran his fingers across the cloth, feeling its texture with the practiced fingers of a tailor.

"This is wonderful," he said. "Where did you get such a treasure?"

"It's indeed a long story. Maybe I will tell you about it some time."

As the evening wore on, both men became pensive, lost in their own thoughts. So many lives lost, so much of their family destroyed. Both men were reticent about the details of their experience during the war years. Suffice to say, they had survived and were eager to move on.

Breaking the silence, Mendel asked, "Have you been back to Krakow?"

Izak laughed, blowing out a puff of smoke. He sighed and looked at his brother. "Yes, I was there a few weeks ago. There is nothing left for the Jews, just like in Lvov."

Mendel looked down at the fine bolt of cloth. "So where did you find this?"

"Maybe another time, Mendel. It's getting late, and I must be going. I will meet Dolek some other time. I have much to think about."

"Izak…I cannot thank you enough for the cloth. It will be a great help. Don't be a stranger. We must see each other often, maybe play cards."

"Yes, Mendel, we will. You are very welcome. The cloth has an interesting story. I look forward to the day I can tell you about it, but I'm not ready."

Mendel understood. He was not yet ready to tell his story of being captured by the SS, taken to a slave labor work camp, escaping, hiding in the woods, and then finally cowering in a bunker for the rest of the war.

As Izak got up to leave, he asked, "Mendel," a little louder in deference to his younger brother's hearing impairment. "Are you going to stay here in Poland?"

Knowing the answer, he paused just the same. "I'm not sure, but I think not. I will see what happens with the Soviet system taking more control. I think, though, I want to go to England or the United States if they let us in. We hear the Americans have set up camps for what they call 'displaced persons.' I think that means us. We really have no place to go. Maybe I'll take Dolek and travel west toward Germany to find a camp. Dolek doesn't care as long as he has a place to sleep and food."

Izak nodded to himself. "Yes. I'm thinking England or America too. Either one is fine with me. Whoever takes me first, that's where I'll go."

Izak turned and kissed the Mezuzah on the doorframe as he left. "Good-bye, little brother. If you need some help or a little money, let me know." With that, Izak left to rejoin his small group of Jews. They needed to make decisions and plans.

MÜHLDORF, GERMANY, NOVEMBER 1945

With his continued improvement, Simon was finally released from the Mühldorf hospital. He still needed the aid of crutches and took them with him most of the time. He also wore a small bandage on his neck and head covering the wounds he had received at the hands of the Capos at the Ampfing camp.

The authorities at the hospital told Simon he needed to make a decision about where he would go after he was released. They told him again about the new camp established for displaced persons that was set up near Munich in Feldafing. He could go there for as long as it took for him to get settled. He could also stay in Mühldorf temporarily at a small apartment. The rent would be paid by a Jewish assistance organization until he could find work.

Simon thought about his options. Since he had only seen very limited parts of Mühldorf consisting only of the hospital, the DP camp at the Ecksberg convent, and the bombed rail marshalling yard he had been forced to help repair, he decided it would be a good time to do some exploring. It was a cloudy day in late November as he slowly made his way through the arch that led through the centuries-old clock tower leading into the main downtown section. He was amazed that much of the bomb damage he had heard about had been repaired, and the streets and buildings appeared in good condition. There was an impressive fountain in the square, and a neat row of buildings lined both sides of the main street. In the distance, he could see the spires of three distinct churches. He thought the town was not as cosmopolitan or as large as the Lemberg he remembered, but it seemed nice nonetheless. He walked past butcher shops, apothecaries, and a variety of merchant shops selling a very limited array of goods. He noticed a lack of the fashionable coffee houses that had dotted the main Lemberg streets. He saw a tailor shop and wondered if the town could support another one. Over the next half hour, he decided that he liked the town and thought that maybe he would remain here until his emigration application was approved. It shouldn't take too long, he thought. Besides, thoughts of returning to his Polish homeland had started to evaporate as news of the treatment of the few returning Jews had surfaced. Many were murdered outright.

Simon realized he was fortunate that a family in Mühldorf had agreed to temporarily take him in, an arrangement made through some Jewish relief organization and Simon's agreement to do some tailoring. This would start next month. He was sure this would be a short stay until he could find permanent work and move out on his own. The second-floor apartment was located at 6 Luddendorfstrasse just off the Stadtplaz main street.

The next day Simon notified the hospital staff he had made the decision to stay in Mühldorf, and the final arrangements were completed for him to move the next day.

That night Simon thought about the young German girl, Marile. He would miss her. She was more than someone kind he had met at the hospital. For Simon, her spirit and compassion were an oasis of hope in the aftermath of the brutal Nazi desert he had just barely survived. Yes, he would miss her in ways he was just beginning to understand.

The next morning Simon was discharged from the hospital. He was disappointed that Marile was not at the hospital. In fact, he had not seen her in a week. Sadly, he wrote her a long note thanking her for the kindness she had showed him and how much he had enjoyed talking to her. He said good-bye to some of the remaining patients, wishing them luck, even Josef Goldburg, who had now forgiven Simon for his association with the young German girl, whom Goldburg now grudgingly accepted as a "good German."

Simon was moved to a temporary room in a small hostel arranged by and associated with the hospital for the next few weeks and then to the Luddendorfstrasse address. While somewhat apprehensive, he was nonetheless confident about his future and was sure that Israel, Great Britain, or even America was waiting for him in the future. Yet somewhere in the back of his mind, he experienced a nagging feeling he was leaving something behind.

MÜHLDORF, GERMANY, DECEMBER 1945

The postwar chaos in Germany dragged on as Ludwig Häusl sat quietly at the small table in the kitchen of the Häusl farmhouse on Xaver-Rambold Strasse 7 and lovingly puffed on a very rare cigarette, one somehow acquired from the Americans. He thought about the situation and what it meant for his family. The Third Reich, touted by Hitler to last one thousand years, had run its sadistic course in but twelve, taking with it upward of sixty million people. The country had survived, but just barely. The cost was horrendous.

Christmas was being celebrated, albeit in an austere fashion. The Häusl family had managed to cobble together a tree of sorts, decorated with whatever was available. Candles, nubs really, left over from better times, were lighted on the branches, held in place by metal clips that had managed to survive being melted down. Meager gifts were exchanged, mostly knitted gloves or socks. Oranges, a luxury in prior years, were almost nonexistent, available only through the black market at exorbitant prices.

Having taken the few last puffs of the cigarette, he snuffed it out and gingerly put away what was left of it. His family had slowly gathered around the table. Ludwig's wife Maria tried to look happy, a state in which she rarely found herself, and so the attempt failed miserably. She still found it difficult to cope with the catastrophic end of the regime and couldn't quite understand how her husband seemed to fare much better. Marile, Bette, and little Rosie entered the room with Wiggi, the youngest, in tow. Ludwig looked at his family, and his thoughts went back almost seven years ago when two of his brothers-in-law, Leonhard and Max Kiermeier, dressed in their crisp *Wehrmacht* uniforms, had sat at this very table, anxious to fight for the Fatherland, talking about quick victories and glory. How had it all gone so wrong?

Ludwig sighed, cleared his throat, and faced his family.

"Tonight we celebrate Christmas, though this night is far from holy. Leonhard and Max are gone. Alois is back with us but spends most of his time in the hospital. Uncle Sepp has returned, and we are thankful for that. Our dear friend Donei has not returned, and we have no idea where he is. Perhaps he was captured by the Americans."

He looked over to his wife, and she gestured him to continue. Ludwig then looked over to Marile and continued. "We must pray for his safe return. Marile, you are still engaged to him, and we hope the marriage will still take place someday. We are looking forward to that day, but all we can do now is wait and pray."

Unspoken, the warning passed between Marile and her father. He hoped this nonsense with the Jew had been put to rest and that his daughter was now focused on moving forward.

As if acknowledging the message, Marile smiled at her father and communicated to him with an almost imperceptible nod. For Ludwig, it was enough to allay his worry, at least for now. It shouldn't have.

1946

Nineteen forty-six began as the previous year had finally ended, with much of Germany still rumble strewn, millions of people starving and homeless, and an economy that barely functioned, except for the black market. Food was scarce and was tightly controlled through rationing. The new face of Eastern Europe was quickly crystallizing into its postwar configuration, with the Russians consolidating their newly acquired territories. Large numbers of German prisoners of war were still unaccounted for, held in special prisoner camps in Siberia. Unknown to his family and friends, Anton Becker was one of them. Most would never see the Fatherland again.

For Simon Ruder, the last few weeks passed quickly into the new year, as he eagerly prepared to leave the small room in the hostel. He had few possessions, so the move went quickly and smoothly. Fortunately, the weather, while cold, cooperated, and there was no additional snowfall.

The family with whom Simon was staying, the Weidermeyers, owned a small house near the hospital on Luddendorfstrasse and consisted of Wilhelm, the fifty-two-year-old father of two sons who were both in the *Wehrmacht*, and his wife Lotte. Neither son had survived the Russian front, and the

Weidermeyers were embittered by the outcome of the war and what they felt was the senseless carnage and destruction of their beloved Germany. Perhaps in part for atonement, they had agreed to help Simon on his path to a new start.

The Weidermeyers avoided questioning Simon about his experiences in the camps, and he likewise eschewed any conversation that led in that direction. They all understood that his physical condition and scars silently attested to a brutal, harsh past and left it at that.

A few days after settling in, Lotte politely reminded Simon that he was no longer in a DP camp and needed to register for food rationing cards. Food was still scarce, and one needed the rationing cards to obtain the allotted quantity of daily foodstuffs.

"Thank you for the reminder," said Simon. "I was planning on going to the administration building today."

"Very good, Herr Ruder. That will help a great deal. Thank you."

Simon noticed that the Weidermeyers always addressed him in a formal manner, almost as though he were someone important, and he suspected it was out of remorse for what the Germans had done to him. Though they never openly discussed it, Simon sensed their apologetic demeanor. In fact, though, he actually hoped they wouldn't apologize because he knew it would be empty, hollow, totally useless, and altogether inappropriate. They had no moral right to apologize any more than he had to accept it. How could there be forgiveness for the unforgivable? And so there developed a balance, a truce of sorts, where both sides respected the other and symbiotic equilibrium developed.

Simon knew about the Weidermeyers' two sons and privately mourned for Wilhelm and Lotte, but that was as far as he could go for now. Maybe in time, he could go farther, but not now. He needed time to reflect on the real target of his anger. Was it the whole of the German people? Certainly the Nazis, but how can you distinguish the good from the evil? Can or should one paint an entire population with a broad brush of hatred? He suddenly realized that to do so would make him one of them. Were there any good Germans, he wondered.

With these thoughts in mind, he made his way to the government offices to register for his food ration cards. Ironically, that last question that had lingered in his mind was soon to be answered.

Riding his bicycle to the rail yard in the cold January air, Ludwig Häusl thought about what was happening to his beloved Germany. He, like millions of other Germans, had gone through the "denazification" process. Though a member of the Nazi Party, he had been exonerated and hoped the ordeal was now over. While work was slow, he felt fortunate to have a job with the railroad. Little freight moved these days. Passenger traffic was light as well, though some returning soldiers came trickling back. Most would not. Ludwig thought about the Americans. Strange people, he thought. First they vanquish us, and now they seem truly determined to help us rebuild our country. However, he had doubts the Americans could actually purge all of the Nazis from the government, industry, and the universities. Many Germans resented the process, especially one imposed by the victors. Yet the packages of food arrived more regularly now. They were called CARE packages from the Cooperative for American Remittances to Europe organization. Some packages had the words GIFT on them. Ironically, in German, that meant poison. Regardless, he appreciated the food and the American generosity toward its former enemy. He wondered about his daughter Marile. She seemed to be getting along well with the Americans, and they seemed to like her work. He was thankful her schoolgirl silliness with the Jew was over. His thoughts then drifted to his dead *Wehrmacht* brothers-in-law, Leonhard and Max, killed somewhere on the Eastern Front. He would miss them. His wife Maria was still grieving the loss of her brothers. Alois was still in the hospital suffering from a stomach wound inflicted by the Russian army, and the whole family was hoping for the best.

Ludwig arrived at the rail yard, parked his bicycle, and looked out over the myriad of tracks, repaired once again after the bombing almost a year ago. Sadly, he thought of his fireman, Heinrich Bauer, who had been killed during the Allied air raid. He remembered the legions of emaciated prisoners forced to clear the yard of debris and twisted track. Their gaunt faces and deathly gait still haunted him. Most of all, though, he hoped Germany would never again find itself in a situation where he would have to deliver human beings to hell.

Ludwig sighed as he entered the cold office and began his workday.

Seventeen-year-old Marile Häusl had been working at the Landratsamt Ernahrungsamt Abteilung B since graduating from primary school in 1942. She had started working in the office while still attending vocational school. Her job performance had been recognized as exceptional, and she had been assigned to work with the American relief effort. She and her thirty-five-year-old colleague named Kuni worked with Captain Jerome Greene of the US Army Military Government. Kuni was a pretty blond woman with a nice smile. Marile had long outgrown her pigtails and now had long brown hair. Both young women were very pretty, the very image of the ideal Aryan female.

For Kuni and Marile, many of their job duties had not changed, even after the war had ended. The pair continued distributing the all-important food ration cards to the German population, but now new faces began appearing in the lines. There were several DP camps in Bavaria that housed thousands of displaced persons. Many were native Poles, Ukrainians, Hungarians, and many of those who had a homeland to which to return. Unless they were Jews. Over time, many of the non-Jews would return to their homes, now under different flags, but still "repatriable." Many, however, feared persecution under the new rulers and had decided to stay. For the Jews, however, the choices were few. The British were not allowing significant immigration into Israel, nor were Western countries like the United States eager to accept a population they envisioned as a drain on their postwar economies. So now displaced persons who left the camps waited in line for the ration cards. Simon Ruder was one of them.

Kuni was surprised at the condition of some of the new people in line. Many still showed signs of the years of abuse they had endured. Marile, however, had firsthand experience from her volunteer work at the Mühldorf hospital. Not surprisingly, many of the Germans were resentful of the newcomers, and the two women often encountered thinly disguised hostility, as though the plight of the Jews was solely their fault. However, a smile from a pretty girl was often all it took to ameliorate the situation.

Simon Ruder made his way to the government building to register for his food ration cards. These cards, he learned, gave him the ability to purchase limited quantities of foodstuffs such as butter, eggs, and meat. The cards did not necessarily guarantee availability of the items, but supplies were getting better.

Simon had always had an eye for pretty women, and as he recovered from his injuries, that trait had begun to resurface.

Waiting his turn in line, Simon noticed the two women. They were obviously not Jewish. He hobbled up to one line, at the end of which sat the pretty Kuni. When his turn came, he addressed her in German. "Good morning, Fraulein, my name is Simon Ruder, and I have come to register for food ration cards. Can you help me?" Kuni regarded the short Jew, noting that he had obviously been mistreated during the war. Though significantly recovered, she noted signs of earlier injuries.

"Yes, *mein* Herr. First you must fill out some forms. I will get them for you. When you have completed them, please return them to us."

She was efficient, professional, but it seemed to Simon, without a trace of remorse for the situation that had resulted in her having to distribute these cards to him in the first place. Not like the Weidermeyers. As he turned, he noticed the other, younger woman, a girl really, who looked over at Simon. He squinted to get a better look at her and thought he recognized her. It was Marile Häusl from the Mühldorf hospital with whom he had had many conversations. She smiled at Simon; her gaze lingered for a brief moment and then vanished as she turned back to another person waiting in line.

Kuni returned with the necessary forms and slid them over to Simon. "Thank you," he said as he gathered up the forms and made his way out of the building. He had a smile on his face. But he had other priorities.

Before heading back to the apartment, he stopped at the Mühldorf hospital for his weekly appointment. He had no idea who was paying for his care but assumed it was some sort of Jewish assistance program. Anyway, he didn't care.

"Herr Ruder," said Dr. Weisermann. "Maybe today we can remove the rest of these bandages for good. Let us take a look." The doctor slowly began to remove the bandages that had covered the grievous wounds inflicted by the fleeing Capos at Ampfing as the Americans approached. That had been over eight months ago.

As the last of the underlying gauze was unwrapped, the doctor smiled and said, "This is coming along very nicely, Herr Ruder. The scars have healed over, though I'm afraid you will always carry them as a reminder of the camps. I believe, however, we can now dispense with most of the bandages. You will have to be careful because the area will be sensitive, but I think it's time. Congratulations."

Using his left hand, Simon felt the area around his neck where the Capos had slashed him. This was the first time he had been able to accomplish this since May when he was liberated. The skin on his neck felt rough but tender, but it was finally out in the open. He walked over to a mirror on the wall and tried to turn his head to see the scars. The doctor came over with another smaller mirror in his hand. "Here, this will help."

As the doctor held up the mirror, Simon could finally see the results of the Capos's attack on him. The scars were ugly, red.

The doctor saw Simon's reaction. "The redness will go away, Herr Ruder. Soon it will not be so noticeable. Now, let's check your scalp wound. The last time we looked at it, it was healing nicely.

"I think we can get by with a small bandage on the scalp wound. Maybe for another few days. How are your legs? Do you still need the crutches?"

"I think they are getting better. I can move around much easier now, but I don't think I can do it without the crutches yet."

"You need to continue to strengthen the muscles in your legs. Carrying all that cement damaged your legs, but I think soon you will be able to walk and run again. It just takes time. I will see you again in a week."

Simon had completed the forms required for the food ration cards and made his way back to the administration building. He found himself whistling as he remembered the young woman at the counter, the one from the Mühldorf hospital. He made sure his completed application was still in the small leather case he had been given by the Weidermeyers. Old, but still serviceable. Ostrich, he thought, but he didn't want to know where it came from. He made his way to the food ration card counter. It was 11:43 a.m. He entered the office and looked around. He was disappointed when he did not see the young Marile. However, Kuni was there, and she noticed Simon. She waited for him to come over to the counter. Simon acknowledged her but did not approach her counter. He looked at his leather case, made a gesture of frustration, turned, and left the office.

The poor dummy forgot his application, thought Kuni. She smiled to herself as Simon left. Poor Jew, she thought.

Simon waited outside near the office. Though it was cold, he found a bench that was intact and sat down. He sat there thinking about his future and where it would take place. His family was gone; he knew that. He also knew he would recover and, at some point, start a new life. But where? Germany, perhaps. No, not long term. They still hated the Jews, and nothing would change that. Israel then, or Canada? What about America? They do not like Communists, he had heard. Would they let him in if they knew about his political leanings? He doubted it. He wondered about his two brothers, Izak and Mendel, and Mendel's small son Dolek who was Artur's age. Then his thoughts shifted to the young woman he was so anxious to see. Why, he wondered. Certainly a pretty German Fraulein would have nothing to do with a penniless, pitiful-looking Jew, and while she seemed sympathetic, he knew there could be nothing beyond that. Then he thought about his own religion. Was even thinking about a Gentile woman a sin, something to be condemned? He wondered if the rabbis would chastise him if they found out. He thought of Lola. It had been an arranged marriage, something over which he had had little control or say-so. He realized he still felt a profound sadness over the loss of Lola and especially Hanna with whom he had had a special relationship. He had had plans for little Artur to carry on the tailor shop. But now he would be on his own. There were various Jewish organizations that provided assistance. Now that the world was forced to recognize the atrocities committed by the Third Reich, help was finally being provided from a number of sources. He knew there would be many decisions to be made in the coming months and maybe years. But he had survived, and no one could take that away from him.

Simon's reverie was suddenly interrupted when Marile Häusl arrived at the office. She did not see Simon as she walked briskly into the building with several other women.

Simon took a deep breath. He decided to wait a little while before going back into the office. He wondered if she would remember him. He wondered what he would say to her. Then he realized how improbable this was; the thought of a pretty young German woman befriending a middle-aged Jew fresh from the camps.

After what Simon judged a suitable amount of time, he struggled to his feet and slowly made his way from the bench outside into the building. This time he saw Marile Häusl at the service counter and hobbled toward her line. Kuni was there at the end of the other line. She saw Simon and looked as though she was about to say something. Her mouth opened and closed quickly, like a fish. Simon waited in Marile's line and soon came face-to-face with the young woman.

"Good day, Fraulein. My name is Simon Ruder. I have my application for food ration cards. Can you help me, please?"

Marile looked up at the man. A glimmer of recognition crossed her face. "Certainly, Herr Ruder," she said. "I remember you from the hospital. You look much better now. She examined him more closely. I see the bandages are almost gone."

Simon smiled at her. "Yes, thank you for noticing. Maybe the next time the crutches will be gone too. Here is my application."

Marile took the form and started to review it. She unconsciously recoiled as she read the list of camps this man had endured. Quickly regaining her composure, she stamped the application form and said, "I will be right back." She went to a small metal cabinet and returned a few moments later with the ration cards. "Here you are, Herr Ruder," she said, handing the cards to Simon. "We will see you next month. Maybe without the crutches."

"Thank you, Fraulein. Maybe next time we could sit and talk for a little while. There is a nice bench outside. It's been a long time since I have had the privilege of speaking with a pretty young woman."

Marile blushed. She remembered the strict rule from her not-so-distant Hitler Youth days severely admonishing Germans, especially women, to avoid contact with Jews. Unbidden, the image of the grisly scene of the corpses at the pit in the woods outside of town came rushing back and with it the profound sense of guilt she felt. Well, she thought, the war is over, the Third Reich is gone. "Perhaps," she said hesitatingly and without really knowing why. "Yes, perhaps next time."

Simon carefully placed the cards in his leather case and left the building with a rare a smile on his face.

Simon had always been driven by a need to do something, to work at a craft, to be successful again. The time he spent recuperating in various hospitals since his May liberation had given him ample time to think about what had happened to him, his family, and his people. Up to now, he had focused on surviving, on merely living longer than the Nazi bastards who had done this to him. Now, with his physical condition finally improving and having secured a place to live, Simon had begun to accept the reality of it all. He realized that he had taken the first tentative, fragile steps on the long road to healing, the end of which he might never reach. But it was a start.

He thought about the pretty Fraulein, first from the hospital and now at the counter, and wondered what role she might play in his future. A silly thought? Perhaps, but the mere thought gave him hope, and that was enough to help him take a few more steps down that difficult road.

Simon realized that, in order to move forward, he needed to get some kind of closure, and to accomplish this, he had to find answers. The past could not just be buried, forgotten, or ignored. He could not just walk away. He thought some of the answers he sought might be at the recently established Feldafing displaced persons camp near Munich. He heard there were lists of survivors posted there and was anxious to see if any of his family or friends had survived.

He learned the camp was set up, in large part, to house the Hungarian Jews liberated from the Dachau sub-camp near Mühldorf, some of whom he had briefly encountered. Many had died, but some might have survived. He hoped he might find them there. He was also interested in determining what relief assistance was available and how he could qualify. He had lost everything during the war and had no money and no real possessions. He needed to start over, and now it was time to begin.

FELDAFING DISPLACED PERSONS CAMP, JANUARY 1946

The next day Simon decided to visit the DP camp at Feldafing. He discovered that train travel was sporadic and through the help of a sympathetic train station worker, managed to get a ride from an American convoy headed in that direction. The ride was bumpy and took some three hours to cover the 123-kilometer distance. Several soldiers helped him get off the truck. Simon thanked them, and he slowly made his way to the camp. He was amazed at the living conditions at the camp. Since opening a mere five months ago, the Feldafing camp's educational and religious life flourished. The camp included both secular elementary and high school systems as well as religious schools, including a Talmud Torah, a yeshiva, and several seminaries, including Beth Medrash Lita and Beth Medrash Ungarn. In addition, a rabbinical council supported its religious offices. The council soon gained considerable respect and influence within the camp. The camp also published several newspapers and magazines as well as organizing several theater troupes and an orchestra. One survivor in particular, Jeno Weissbluth, became director of a boarding school called the Kindercasino and later organized a Hungarian newspaper as well as becoming the president of the Hungarian Jewish Federation for the US Zone. He and his son Tomas would play a role in Simon's future.

Unknown to Simon, big changes had occurred at the camp. Originally, the US military had no idea how to set up and run a camp for displaced populations, so they had relied on military discipline and organization. Unfortunately, they were ignorant about or insensitive to the ethnic or religious composition of the inmates. Thus, Polish Jews and non-Jews were herded together along with some Ukrainians, therefore recreating the precise mix of centuries-long hatreds and prejudices and wrapping it all in barbed wire. Fortunately, General Eisenhower and others recognized the absurdity of this and ordered changes to make this and other camps exclusively Jewish.

Unlike much of the population at the Feldafing camp, Simon had already started to build his new life and was not sure he wanted to stay at the camp for too long. He would check the survivor lists first, and then, depending on what he found, he could chart his path based on what he discovered. He was fairly certain that his wife and two children had perished but was eager to learn about the fate his friends.

Simon asked a passerby where he could find out about possible survivors and was directed to a large administration building. He entered the office building and quickly found the lists of survivors as well as the inquiries from camp inhabitants for information on their loved ones and friends. He checked various lists. Not unexpectedly, he found nothing on his family. He then searched for the family of Dr. Deutsche, the Goldblatts, the Lanskys, and others but found nothing. He searched for his brothers, Izak and Mendel. They were not at the DP camp, nor were their names on the lists. So far he had heard nothing about their fates. Mendel's young son Dolek would be eight years old now. He hoped they had survived the horrible ordeal and that he would someday be reunited with them.

Dejected, he sighed and walked slowly out of the building. He was unsure of how to get back to Mühldorf. He wondered if the trains were running but decided to stay the night. He slowly made his way around the facility until he came to a spot overlooking the west shore of Lake Starnberg. Tired, he sat down on a bench and laid his crutches on the ground beside him, when a familiar voice interrupted his thoughts.

"So you survived too," said the voice. "It's good to see you, my old friend."

Simon slowly, painfully turned around to see a man leaning on a single crutch. It took Simon a moment to identify the man. As recognition set in, he said, "Julius Kaplan! How are you?"

"I'm well, but as you can see, I'm better than you. I have only one crutch."

As with all of the liberated prisoners, Kaplan, too, wore the scars of his mistreatment. Though not as emaciated as he was several months ago, Simon noticed his friend's stooped-over posture, his sluggish gait, and his noticeable limp as he made his way to the bench and slowly sat down.

"Nice view," said Kaplan, looking out over the snow-covered landscape surrounding the lake and the Alps in the distance. "So peaceful, so tranquil, it's almost as if none of this horror ever really happened. Almost." A pause and deep sigh. "So, what happened to you, my friend?"

Simon thought about how he should respond, wondered how one could possibly describe his time in hell.

Stalling for time, he said, "Tell me about you first, Julius. What happened to you?"

Kaplan looked at his friend. The smile fled his face, replaced by a far-away look. "They came through the ghetto in June of 1942. I think it was the twenty-fourth. I was out with Izak Goldblatt. You remember Goldblatt, the bookseller. We were trying to find some food for our families. The Ukrainians and SS came through the ghetto and rounded up maybe two thousand of us. Goldblatt and I and about a hundred others were taken to the work camp on Janowska Street. The damn bastards shot all of the rest of those who were rounded up. I know this because I was on the burial detail behind the camp at Piaski the next day."

Kaplan paused, another memory coming back. "In 1943, I think, something changed at the camp. They started killing Jews, not just for sport, but seriously, in great numbers. We could tell the difference. Then that asshole Wilhelm Rokita, a high-ranking SS officer, decided we needed music to accompany the selections and executions. The music was called the 'Tango fun Toyt' (Tango of Death), and it was composed and played by the prisoner orchestra."

Simon shook his head understandingly. He had had his share of Nazi and SS bizarre practices and rituals. It seemed each camp had its own idiosyncrasies based on the often psychotic and perverted personalities of the commandants. "What about our friends? Any word?"

"I don't know for sure, but I heard Dr. Deutsche and his family were taken to Belzec and perished there. I know nothing of Lansky, but I think Sarah and young Chaja were also sent to Belzec. Goldblatt and I were separated, and I lost track of him. His wife Rifka and her two boys likely were rounded up and also sent to Belzec."

"I'm sorry to hear that, Julius. May God bless them all. So how is it you are here?"

"I was just lucky, Simon. They were going to liquidate the Janowska camp. They transferred me to Plaszow, then I was sent to Auschwitz."

Simon instinctively glanced over to his friend's left forearm, but it was obscured by the sleeve of his worn coat. Kaplan continued. "I saw that maniac Mengele at the train platform. Most of the people were sent directly to the gas chamber. I worked in a dispensary of sorts, probably because I was a pharmacist. Then in January, they evacuated Auschwitz and sent us on a march in the snow. We went to Gleiwitz for a week, then we were sent to the Dachau camp. From there, I was sent to Mühldorf, to Mittergars, I think. We worked on some giant building. Later, they loaded us on a train that sat for days until the Americans rescued us. Then we were sent here. I have been here since the middle of May."

Simon listened with great care. He realized his friend had followed a similar path to get to this place, but he seemed in better condition.

"So tell me, Simon, how did it go with you?"

Slowly, painfully Simon began. "You mentioned the ghetto. I only saw it one time. I was captured by the Gestapo in August of 1941. I think they were looking for me. They took me to Loncki Prison, you remember that gloomy place at the end of Sapiehy Street near the Technical High School where no Jews dared to go near? I was questioned, interrogated, and beaten. I do not remember the order. Apparently, they did not like Communists. I was locked up for several days. I think I was saved because I was a tailor and they needed to make uniforms."

"So how did you see the ghetto? It's clear on the other side of town."

"They sent me out to find some cloth for a goddamned dress for the commandant's wife. Can you imagine that? A dress."

Simon paused and looked away, as if in deep thought. A brief smile crossed his lips. "Actually, it was a very nice dress. They sent a Ukrainian guard with me. The idiot waited outside the ghetto for me to return. I went to my old shop on Legionow Street to retrieve some old bolts of cloth I remembered stashing away. The real reason I went to the ghetto was to try to find Lola and the children. Then I was going to make my escape. I met a Jewish policeman who was a former apprentice of mine, Josef Salzmann, who told me that Lola, Hanna, and little Artur had been shot by the SS when they tried to run away while Jews were being put on the train going to Belzec. You can imagine how I felt. I was despondent. When I saw the condition of the ghetto and the people inside, I made up my mind that the best thing for me to do was go back to the prison."

"Simon, it's a good thing you did that. The ghetto was liquidated and torn down in 1943. Not many survived. We heard about a family that hid in the sewers and were saved. You probably didn't think so at the time, but it may have saved your life. I think you were fortunate. Most Jews were deported or murdered. What happened then?"

"The Russians were getting closer to taking back Lvov, and the Germans were making preparations to evacuate. I was sent on a train to Auschwitz, I think. I was able to escape from the cattle car and made my way to a barn where I hid. The Ukrainian farmer found me there, hiding in the hay. I gave him a watch and what money I had hidden to let me stay until morning, but I think he turned me in anyway. Damn Ukrainians, you can never trust them. I was captured and beaten. They took me back to Loncki Prison. An SS guard there saved my life, at least until the next day when they put me on another train. This train went to Plaszow, and I stayed there for maybe two or three weeks. I might have been there at the same time you were. Then they sent me to Auschwitz-Birkenau. I think it was in May of 1944."

Simon showed his friend the number tattooed on his left forearm, B-6867.

"You know, Julius, I think that demented Mengele actually saved my life during selection. When we got off the train, the SS officer sent me to the line on the left. I found out later that line led directly to the gas chambers. The good doctor called me back and asked me my profession. I told him I was a tailor from Lvov and I that was in Loncki Prison making SS uniforms. I swear I saw a very small smile on his face, and he looked down at his own uniform. He looked at me, very intensely, and then he sent me to the other line. I have no idea why he did that, but I was not gassed that day."

"Amazing. So when did you leave Auschwitz?"

"In the middle or late January. They made us march through the deep snow. Same as you, I think, though the way we looked, we probably wouldn't have recognized each other. I wasn't sure I would survive. I really don't know how I managed to survive. Many died on the way, and the bastards shot many more who couldn't keep up. We made it to Gleiwitz and stayed there for a few days. Then they sent us to Dachau. After a day or two, I was one of maybe eight hundred prisoners they took to Mühldorf at a camp called Waldlager V, where I was forced to carry heavy cement bags. I think it was for the same giant structure you mentioned. I remember there were many Hungarian Jews. Finally, I was transferred to Ampfing to make explosives. I got sick and couldn't work. I was taken to the 'sick bay' where they left me to die. Then, just before the Americans arrived, the camp Capos tried to kill me, and as you can see, they almost succeeded. The cowards ran away, and I was lucky they did. I found myself in a temporary hospital at Ampfing and stayed there for several weeks, if I remember correctly. The Americans saved me. Then I was moved to another hospital the Americans had set up at the Ecksberg convent. There was an American army rabbi there, Abraham Klausner. He told me he was sure God will understand about the convent. He was preparing a book of survivors. I think it was to be called *Sharit Ha-Platah*. He took my name and told me about the camp at Feldafing and suggested I go there after I recovered and check on the status of loved ones and friends and maybe apply for assistance to get me back on my feet. I thanked him and he left. When I was released from Ecksberg, they took me to another hospital in Mühldorf. I was there for five or six months. My neck and head wounds have healed, and I feel much better and stronger. I was finally released from the hospital last month, and I have been in Mühldorf for a few weeks getting settled. So I'm taking Rabbi Klausner's advice, and here I am."

Kaplan sighed. "I'm glad you came, Simon. I can help you with all that. Maybe we can play cards again, you know, like the old days. But we need two more players. I don't know what happened to Rosenthal or Lansky. No sign of them on the lists."

Simon sighed. "Have you seen anyone else from Lemberg?"

"Only one, a young man. I think he mentioned his father who was a tailor like you. Unfortunately, he said his father died on a death march from Auschwitz."

Simon perked up. "What was his name?"

"I think the young man's name was Weiss, yes, William Weiss."

Simon's face betrayed a smile. *So the young man had survived.*

"In fact, he has been friends with another survivor, a fine woman named Regina, and it is rumored they are planning to be married."

"Are they here right now?"

"I'm not sure, Simon. I haven't seen either of them today. Sometimes they go to Munich."

"I would like to see William. Can you tell him I was here and let him know I'm in Mühldorf?"

"Certainly. I think it would be a good idea to post your name and address on the wall inside before you leave."

"That's a good idea, Julius."

The two men sat there looking at the pristine lake as the sun was high in the cold, blue Bavarian sky. Silently, they each reflected upon the events that had so cruelly short-circuited their lives, stripped them of almost everything, and had left them here in Bavaria like bits of driftwood washed ashore by the waves of war. It had been a tumultuous journey, one that was far from over, but at least both men had survived this far.

"Simon, what do you think you want to do now that the war is over?"

Simon turned and looked at his friend. "Ah, Julius. I'd like to get rid of these damn crutches. They tell me it will take a little while longer. Then I would like to find the SS guard that helped me and thank him. He had a heart; he was a *mensch* in spite of the uniform. After that, I don't know. There is nothing for me in Lvov. I think there are no more Jews left there. My tailor shop is gone. My family is gone."

Kaplan thought about that. "I think you may be right, but I may want to return just to see what is left. I didn't see any names of anyone I recognized on the survivor lists, but you never know. We will have to wait and see what the Americans and Russians do this time. Lvov may be part of Poland or Russia or the Ukraine. God only knows."

Simon continued. "I would like to immigrate, Julius, maybe Israel, the United States, or even to Canada," said Simon. "But for now, I will stay in Mühldorf. I am living temporarily with a nice family, the Wiedermeyers. They told me I could apply for assistance and then apply for an emigration permit. It may take longer than I hoped. I heard that the United States still has very tight quotas for now and very few immigrants are being accepted. I hear Palestine is also difficult."

"As I said, I think I can help you, Simon. We can go back to Mühldorf to apply for the assistance with the Jewish agencies. How are you supporting yourself now?"

"I'm doing odd jobs, mostly tailoring work and a little carpentry. I'd like to get a job as a driver for a hauling company, but I have no license. Maybe that won't matter. I will be making a little money, and that's all that is important right now. I think I want to open an auto chauffer business later on. I'm looking for a chance to buy an automobile. I think I can get some assistance to buy the car. But first I must get rid of these crutches. And, Julius, I know someone who works for the German government but is working for Americans who run things. She distributes food ration cards."

Kaplan looked at his friend. "You mean a Jew is working for the Germans already? Are you sure? How can this be?"

"Julius, she is not a Jew. She is a young Gentile German woman. I met her at the hospital in Mühldorf where she was volunteer and then again at the office for food ration cards. I went there a few days ago after I was released from the hospital. The family I'm living with insisted I get the ration cards because I was eating into their food rations. She helped me with my application. She is very kind and is sympathetic to the Jews. Very pretty too."

"I see," said Kaplan, a little look of suspicion on his face. He let it pass, though, and the question in his mind remained unspoken.

When the two men returned to the main area of the camp, they found it abuzz with activity. The Allied commander, General Dwight D. Eisenhower, had arrived for a tour of the camp. He was walking around inspecting the living conditions. Cheering throngs followed him as he made his rounds. The survivors knew he was responsible, at least in part, for the establishment of the camp, and they showed their gratitude.

Simon stayed at the Feldafing DP camp until the next morning. While he was still there, Kaplan introduced him to a number of survivors, many from as far away as Norway, Lithuania, and France. A few were from Lvov, and the stories they told were heartwrenching. Simon did not know any of them from before the war. He asked about his friends Jakob Lansky, Dr. Deutsche, Meyer Rosenthal, and Izak Goldblatt, or their families, but no one had any information. Simon took it all in. He looked around and made a decision.

"Julius, it is wonderful to see you again. I'm very glad you survived. This is a fine place, and we should be grateful to the Americans, but honestly, I am getting depressed by it. It reminds me of everything and everyone I lost. I think after I see about the assistance application tomorrow, I'll go back to Mühldorf. I must move on and try to forget the past, and this place reeks of it."

Kaplan nodded in agreement. He had similar feelings, but since he had lost no immediate family, he felt his situation was different from that of his friend's.

"I understand, Simon. I know how you feel and understand your desire to start a new life as quickly as possible. I know you can't go back to Lvov, especially with those crazy Ukrainians in charge. I'm almost afraid to go back there myself. Tomorrow I will introduce you to the people at the assistance office."

"Thank you, my friend. Thank you for understanding. It's just hard for me to spend time around so many people."

After a dinner the likes of which Simon hadn't experienced in many years, followed by wine and schnapps, he fell into an easy sleep. The dreams came again, but this time they were not filled with mountains of skeletal corpses or dark ashes raining down from the sky. Instead, he dreamed of the young German woman in the government building in Mühldorf, and he was suddenly looking forward to seeing her again.

Simon and Julius had a quick breakfast the next morning, with real coffee, not that brown shit they were given at the camps. Simon checked the lists of survivors one more time and came up empty with the exception of William Weiss and, remembering to post a note with his name and address on the board, followed Kaplan, who took him to the office to introduce him and see what assistance could be obtained from the Jewish organizations. Simon carefully filled out a form requesting information about his background, where he had spent the duration of the war, what he had lost, and whom he had lost. He gave them his Mühldorf address, Luddendorfstrasse 6, and turned in the completed form. He was assured they would evaluate the application and some form of aid would be possible. Simon thanked the clerk and rejoined his friend.

As the two walked out of the administration building, Kaplan said, "Simon, I think I would like to see Mühldorf, I mean the city, not the former camps. I would like to go with you and look around if you have no objection."

Simon was somewhat taken by surprise by his friend's request but said nothing. After all, he had known this man for many years, and although he was skeptical about the real reason for the unexpected request, he found he had no real objections.

"Certainly, my friend. You are most welcome. I will show you around."

With that, the two friends slowly made their way to the nearby train station and waited for the Mühldorf-bound train to arrive. While not actually saying so, both men still experienced a touch of anxiety when traveling on a train, and although they knew there were no more cattle cars, the sights, the shrill sound of the whistle, and the smell of the smoke conjured images from a very painful recent past. Soon the train arrived, almost exactly on time as was expected of the Deutsche Reichsbahn in spite of the war-torn times. The train squealed to a halt, and the two men boarded. The car was less than half full, and the pair had no problem finding empty seats. The passenger cars were shabby, the seats well-worn, obviously a reconverted troop carrier from the war. There were a few Germans on the train, and they looked the other way as the two Jews sat down. Whatever thoughts the Germans had, they were keeping them to themselves. The engineer looked out of his locomotive cab, waiting for the signal from the conductor to proceed. When the signal finally came, Ludwig Häusl pulled the cord for the whistle, released the brake, and engaged the throttle to start the train moving again toward his hometown of Mühldorf.

As the train raced eastward through the Bavarian countryside, much of the war damage was still evident. The rural areas were mostly untouched, but occasionally, a barn or farmhouse was burned down. As the train traveled through some of the larger towns, the American army became more visible, as did the damage from the fighting. The train finally reached the three-storied, eleven-arched *bahnhof* in Mühldorf. As the pair disembarked, it was obvious that major repairs had been made to the impressive edifice since the March 19 air raid last year.

The two men left the train station and headed toward town. They passed under the impressive, centuries-old clock tower that had miraculously survived the bombing and walked out into the town center. They passed by the fountain, when Kaplan suddenly said, "You know, Simon, I would like a coffee. Let's find a place to sit for a while."

Simon sighed. "I haven't found any coffee houses here, but let's ask around."

Coffee was difficult to obtain but was available if one knew the right black market contacts. After asking around, they were told that a certain establishment around the corner might be able to accommodate them. The two followed the directions and soon found themselves in front of a small restaurant that served a very limited menu, but coffee was not on it. Undeterred, the pair went inside. It was warm inside, and the two men removed their coats. The proprietor motioned them over to a corner table, and they sat down. There were several other patrons in the small space. They looked over at the two newcomers and turned away, ignoring them. The proprietor obviously knew the two men were Jews, but after the horrors of the Third Reich had been finally exposed to the world, many Germans tended to treat them with a small measure of respect and deference, though anti-Semitism certainly remained in practice throughout the reality of the emerging postwar Europe.

"What can I get you gentlemen?" asked the proprietor. He was elderly, perhaps in his sixties. He had probably been part of the Nazi last-ditch and futile attempt to defend the Fatherland by a rag-tag militia called the *Volkssturm*. Near the end of the war, the recruits, most of them forced, consisted of any male between the ages of thirteen and sixty not fighting at the time.

"My friend and I would like a cup of coffee. The real thing. We heard you might be able to provide some."

The proprietor looked around. "I may be able to come up with some for you. It's hard to get and will be expensive."

Kaplan smiled. "Thank you. Please bring us two cups."

The proprietor was about to say something but apparently thought better of it. "Yes, sir, give me a few minutes."

The two men relaxed around the small table, waiting for their coffee. "Well, Julius, tell me, why are you here? Why did you really want to come to Mühldorf?" asked Simon.

Julius Kaplan smiled as the coffee came. "Here you are, gentlemen," said the proprietor, carefully placing the two cups in front of his Jewish customers. Both men blew on their coffee without testing it first. They assumed it would be hot and were not disappointed. Simultaneously, they sipped the brown liquid. "Ah," they both said in unison.

"Not bad," said Kaplan. "Almost as good as the stuff we get at Feldafing. I think that comes from the Americans. I have no idea where this comes from, probably from the black market through those Ukrainian gangsters."

Taking another sip, Simon agreed, "Not bad. But, Julius, my friend, I believe you are stalling."

"Simon, I have known you for many years. In fact, from the time you moved to Lvov from Obertin. I knew Lola and your children, God bless them."

Simon looked at his friend, not quite sure where this was leading.

Kaplan continued. "Three things worry me, Simon. First, you are assuming your family is dead. You are probably right, but how can you be sure? Don't you think you should go back to Lemberg or Lvov or whatever it's called now to make sure? How will you ever know otherwise?"

Simon thought about what Josef Salzmann, the now dead JOL policeman in the Lvov ghetto, had told him about the fate of his family.

"Julius, I'm sure about what happened to them. I think it would be a waste of time to go back to Lvov. There are no Jews left, and the Ukrainians don't want us there. I hear the Poles are shooting Jews that try to come back. I think it's as simple as that."

"Well, my friend, if your conscience can live with that, I can accept it as well."

"Thank you, Julius. You said there were three things."

"Yes, Simon. I must ask you. Are you still involved with the Communist Movement?"

Simon closed his eyes before he responded, as if in deep thought. "Yes, Julius. I think now more than ever. You saw what happened to the Jews. We Jews and the rest of world must make sure this can never happen again. I'm convinced Communism is the best solution for us."

Kaplan shook his head in frustration. "Simon, I strongly disagree with you. This is nonsense. How can you possibly think this will be best for our people? That monster Stalin has killed millions of his people, and many of them were Jews. What's good about that, Simon?"

Simon calmly sipped his coffee. "As I have always said, Communism does not threaten the Jewish way of life, and I think it holds great promise of power and influence for us. Most importantly, I'm sure it ends state-sponsored anti-Semitism. Why can't you understand that?"

"Simon, I think you are wrong. You should look to America. That's where I'm going as soon as I can. I have some relatives there. They are doing well and will help me get established there. There you will have real freedom."

"But how can you have freedom if the workers are under the yoke of the rich? Who will protect the workers? Who will make sure we have jobs?"

"Well then, why don't you just go to Russia?"

"No, no, no, Kaplan. I don't care about Russia. If I never see another Russian I'll be happy. It's the system I admire. The government controls, plans, and executes everything. It makes sense. We each see our place in it and do our job. Besides, I think the system will bring stability and security."

"Simon, can you not see the fallacy of what you are saying?"

Simon finished his coffee and put the empty cup down. "Julius, I know what I'm doing."

Kaplan recognized the look on his friend's face and knew better than to argue with him once his mind was made up.

"All right, Simon, I wish you well. Good luck to you. I think I should be getting back to Feldafing. The train will arrive soon."

The proprietor came by the table as the two Jews prepared to leave. "Gentleman," he started. "The coffee is, as they say, on the house."

"Thank you very much," said Kaplan.

"Come back again," said the proprietor, genuine conviction obviously lacking in his voice.

Simon and Julius made their way back to the Mühldorf train station. "You said there were three things, Julius."

"Yes. This German girl you mentioned. I'm curious. Well, maybe more than curious. What's going on?"

"Nothing, my friend. Nothing. I first met her here in the Mühldorf hospital. They moved me there from the Ecksberg hospital in the convent. She was a volunteer there, and we had several nice conversations. She works for the government and the Americans distributing food ration cards. I would like to get to know her better. She is very pretty."

"Are you meshuga, Simon?" said Kaplan with a suddenly raised voice. Embarrassed, he lowered his voice and continued. "Has that injury to your head affected your common sense?"

Simon merely shrugged, a gesture of defeat. He understood the protestation of his friend, and in fact, he had little in the way of answers for him. After all, he was an Orthodox Jew, and now he was chasing a German Gentile girl, a Hitler Youth graduate, one that was half his age.

"What were you thinking, Simon?" continued Kaplan. "Or were you only thinking with your *shmeckle*?"

Simon laughed cynically and looked at his friend. "Julius, I understand what you are saying. I know how it sounds. But I swear, this girl is different. I think she has genuine remorse for what was done to our people. Look, we are in Germany. The war is over. I am going to stay here, at least until my emigration can be approved. My family in Poland is gone. All my Jewish friends there are probably gone too. I think Lola would understand."

"But this girl's not Jewish. Do you know what that means? Her parents were Nazis. How can you make peace with that?"

Both men remained silent while waiting for Kaplan's train back to Feldafing. As the train arrived, both men said their good-byes, realizing they would take different paths and would probably never see each other again.

MUNICH, GERMANY, FEBRUARY 1946

If Simon Ruder was a survivor, he was also every bit an entrepreneur. At the age of eleven, in Obertin, Poland, he and his brothers collected and sold bricks from bombed-out buildings and even built houses at the end of World War I. Now, having survived the death camps of the Nazi regime and liberated in Bavaria, he sought to support himself, to become the self-made man he had once been, and to start his life anew. His stalled relationship with Marile Häusl merely added a sense of urgency to his plans because without a means of support, he feared the relationship would be permanently doomed. The economic conditions in the immediate postwar Germany were bleak. Food and other commodities were rationed and not always available. At least not through legal channels, and as a result, there developed alternative channels through which certain goods could be bought, sold, and traded. Prices for these goods significantly exceeded the so-called legal prices, but with those goods in such short supply, the so-called "black market" thrived. The black market provided mainly higher-end, luxury items that would include fruits, meat, medicines, bicycles, and coffee, and it was through the latter that Simon thought to make his fortune.

Operating out of a nondescript building in the Bogenhauser district of Munich on Mohlstrasse, Simon and several other Jewish concentration camp survivors had set up their new enterprise. Black market transactions were often conducted in the open or in taverns or other establishments.

Many times the actual commodities were stored nearby and exchanged after the deals were struck. The German police sometimes conducted raids on various such operations, often infuriating the operators of these illegal businesses, and many Jews viewed the German police as nothing more than Nazis in new uniforms. Yet, in spite of the challenges, the black market managed to acquire and distribute goods not otherwise readily available. Many black market operations were rooted in the various DP, or displaced person, camps spread around Germany, such as the nearby Feldafing and Deggendorf camps, where food was becoming an issue. Surplus army rations were often provided to the DP camp inhabitants instead of meat and other fresh foodstuffs, circumstances generating considerable complaints and tension. It was natural, therefore, for these conditions to develop a robust black market culture.

One day in late February 1946, Simon and his colleague were expecting a shipment of coffee beans to be delivered in the usual large burlap sacks. Business had been good with coffee in short supply and a market eager to consume the product. Izak Goldblatt, a fellow survivor from what was now called Lviv in the Ukraine, was a partner in this enterprise. Goldblatt was a friend of Jacob Lansky from Lvov. He was a former bookseller who had managed to survive a round of 1942 selections in the Lemberg/Lvov ghetto by convincing the SS he was a carpenter. He went instead to the Janowska concentration camp just outside the town. Goldblatt's wife, Rifka, and children, Bela and Samuel, were thought to have perished in Belzec, though, like so many survivors, he had no real confirmation of their fate. After the war, he had looked for them and checked the various lists of survivors, but to no avail, though he had not given up. He planned one day to open a bookstore in Munich, but the country had other priorities, so the rebirth of his beloved profession would have to wait. Besides, he remembered, many of the books he had once sold and cherished had ended up in many large bonfires.

Simon had agreed to accept Goldblatt as a partner based on the recommendation from his long-time friend, Jacob Lansky, who was still at the Feldafing DP camp. Lansky was the contact at the camp responsible for the coffee transactions. During the last few months, Simon had developed a good business and friendly relationship with the former bookseller. They shared stories about their times in Lvov/Lemberg, the classic beauty of the city, and especially the numerous coffee houses spread throughout the city. In a dark way, they joked about the *Ersatz* coffee they had endured at the concentration camps and somehow felt that supplying real coffee to the Germans was somehow poetic justice. Beyond that, however, neither man shared details of his particular ordeals. Goldblatt had been fortunate, though at the time, it was not obvious to him. He had been transferred out of the Janowska camp shortly before it was eliminated in November of 1943, during which time six thousand prisoners had been murdered. Simon neither shared nor asked for information, though he was curious how his partner had survived and what path he had taken to end up here in Bavaria. He did notice a lack of the infamous Auschwitz tattoo on Goldblatt's left forearm.

While nervously waiting for the shipment to arrive, the two men smoked black market cigarettes from America, something called Lucky Strikes. Exhaling a plume of gray smoke, Goldblatt looked at his partner. He looked nervous.

"Simon," he began. "Why do you go to Mühldorf so often? Do you have business there too?"

Simon smiled to himself, a pleasant thought having formed in his mind.

"Just business, Izak, just business," Simon lied.

Slowly exhaling another impressive plume, a look of obvious skepticism formed on Goldblatt's face. "A woman, perhaps?"

"Why do you say that?" Simon asked, a little too quickly.

Goldblatt coughed and cleared his throat as if stalling for time. "The last time I talked to Lansky, he told me the story of you and a Gentile woman. A girl, really, much younger than you. Can this be true, Simon?"

Taken aback, Simon felt trapped. Here it comes, he thought. He tried to keep his relationship with the young German girl secret. In his mind, the reasons were obvious and necessary, at least for now, even if it meant lying to his Jewish friends.

After a long pause, Simon regained his composure. "I know what I'm doing, Izak. This is my decision. I have only known her for a few months now. I don't know where it will lead, but she is a fine woman, and I enjoy her company very much."

"People have been talking, Simon. They call her the *Shiksa*."

Simon's temper flared at the word. *Shiksa*. It referred to an attractive Gentile woman who might be a temptation to Jewish men. Rabbis perceived them as an intermarital threat to Judaism because they might steer her sons away from the faith.

To Simon, however, it was an offensive term, certainly not applicable to his dear Marile. It was, of course, but he often found himself defending her. As a leader in the Jewish community in nearby Ampfing, he understood the thinking and rationale. Were it someone else, he would agree, but this was somehow different, though he hadn't quite convinced himself how, and a pang of guilt sometimes worked its way into his conscious.

Goldblatt continued. "So it's true? What are you thinking, Simon? Are you completely *meshuga*?"

Simon let out a sardonic laugh. He remembered those were the same words spoken by Jacob Lansky at the Feldafing camp just a few months ago. He was tired of the criticism by his own friends.

"Izak, please, let's not talk about this right now. We have a shipment coming in any minute now. Let's prepare."

Goldblatt nodded his head. "We will continue this later," he said ominously.

Soon a knock came on the wooden door in the back of the building. The shipment had arrived. Both men quickly made their way to the door. They looked at each other, nodded, and unlock and opened the door. The middlemen in the transaction were a group of Ukrainians who had delivered two large sacks as agreed. Simon hated Ukrainians, but after the war ended, business was business, and though he didn't trust them, they were a source of a scarce commodity, so he tolerated the relationship. The Ukrainians carried the two sacks into the building and deposited them in front of Simon, who picked one of the sacks at random and opened it. He found what he expected and scooped up a handful of the green coffee beans. Carefully examining them, he concluded they were the real thing and carefully returned the handful to the bag, careful not to drop any of the small coffee beans. The two Ukrainians looked at each other but said nothing. The exchange of money concluded the transaction, and the Ukrainian thugs left the building and quickly disappeared down Mohlstrasse, perhaps to conduct other business.

The coffee beans were destined to be sold to the highest bidder, sometimes a restaurant, café, or even one of the DP camps at nearby Feldafing or Deggendorf. No one questioned the source of the merchandise, and the black market was tolerated, even at the exorbitant prices being charged. To Simon, the risk was small and the potential gain well worth the effort.

A short time later, Simon went over to the second bag and again opened it and carefully scooped out a handful of the beans. As before, he carefully examined them cupped in his hand. He noticed one of the beans seemed to be different. Curious, he dug deeper into the bag and found more of the round, green, misshapen beans. They looked like dried peas. He tried to make sense of what he was seeing, and as the reality of the situation slowly began to dawn on him, he felt sick, his face ashen. Goldblatt noticed and quickly came over to Simon and the open burlap bag.

"What is the matter?" asked Goldblatt, a sense of panic in his voice. Simon held out his hand full of peas. Goldblatt looked stunned but said nothing.

"Bastards!" shouted Simon as he ran to the door and scanned the alleyway for the thugs who had swindled him. They were gone. An expensive lesson learned.

Yet, in spite of this unfortunate episode, business was good and growing. The black market continued to act as a lifeline to many people, Germans and Jews alike, whose rations were simply insufficient to survive. Though his future was still far from secure, Simon was optimistic and thought another year or so would find him in Israel or the United States—anywhere but in this land of Jew-haters.

His black market dealings generated some money but hardly made him rich, yet he was grateful for the opportunity in a land where many were left on their own without viable options. His plan for starting an automobile taxi business would have to wait until he accumulated enough money to purchase an automobile—not an easy task in the postwar chaos. Then there was also the matter of obtaining a driver's license. So Simon continued his black market activities, resolved to become successful, to start with nothing and build a business, one that would be enough to start a new life. With Izak Goldblatt as his partner, the pair had established a varied clientele, from the DP camp at Feldafing to numerous small enterprises, such as restaurants and shops in Munich, Mühldorf, and nearby Ampfing. Coffee continued to be a staple, as well as cigarettes, and from time to time, whatever fruits were available. Business was good and slowly growing. Simon was beginning to learn how to operate in the black market. He swore that after the recent debacle with the Ukrainians, he would never be swindled again.

Throughout that cold and barren Bavarian winter, Simon looked forward to the coming spring. He was thankful for the space the Wiedermeyers rented him but made plans to one day move to a larger apartment. He eyed the buildings on the Stadtplaz, a main street of Mühldorf, looking for a suitable location. For now, however, he resigned himself to stay with the Weidermeyers, to whom he now occasionally provided coffee or other items from his black market dealings. They gladly accepted these items and asked no questions.

Simon was also busy in the small Jewish communities in the area. Small pockets of Jews, really, for many of the old communities would never recover or be rebuilt. Many Jewish survivors stayed in the various DP camps such as Feldafing, though eventually, some tried to return home only to find they were unwelcome, very unwelcome. Some were murdered as they sought out lost relatives or property. Emigration was an option many sought, but the red tape and politics were a real nightmare, and those plans too would have to wait. Some survivors left the DP camps and tried to settle, at least temporarily, in the nation that had tried to annihilate them. The armbands and stars were gone but not the anti-Semitism. Now it was popular to blame the Jews not only for the war but for losing it as well. Yet small pockets of Jews sprang up and tried to rebuild their culture.

Simon kept busy with his black market activities but was also involved with an effort to rebuild a small temple in Ampfing. He began to become more involved in the Jewish affairs in the area and was soon considered a leader in the small community. He gave speeches and attended various memorial services for Mühldorf-area concentration camp victims. A new life was emerging for Simon, yet he sensed something was missing. It was not difficult for him to identify exactly what that was.

Simon Ruder speaking at the Mühldorf Concentration Camp Memorial, possibly at the dedication or at a later service.

A few days later, it was time to pick up the monthly food ration cards again. Frau Weidermeyer had dropped hints to that effect, but in reality, Simon had been counting the days, anxious to see the young woman Marile again at the government office. He was determined to make a good impression. His bandages had been removed except for a small one on the left side of his neck, and he decided to leave the crutches at home. This time he would ask her to join him outside on the bench to talk.

Simon arrived at the government office early in the morning when he thought the line would be shortest. His hunch proved correct, and there was only one person ahead of him in line. Soon he was face-to-face with the pretty Marile Häusl.

"Good morning, Fraulein," he said as he locked gazes with her.

"Good morning, Herr Ruder," she answered. "Back for your ration cards, I assume."

"Yes, Fraulein. Another month has gone by."

"I see you are much better today. The bandages are gone, and I see you are getting around without your crutches."

Marile excused herself and went to get the cards. She soon returned and, with a smile, handed the cards to Simon.

"Thank you, Fraulein." He took the cards, and, screwing up his courage, he said, "Fraulein, I was hoping to spend some time with you, perhaps to talk during your lunch break. I noticed there is a bench outside, and it is a nice sunny day."

Marile had anticipated the invitation based on their last conversation and worried about how she would respond. Her inclination was to take the logical choice of politely declining the offer. However, this man was charming and polite, and the fact that he had endured hardships she couldn't imagine at the hands of her own people compelled her to accept. What could it hurt, she wondered.

"Herr Ruder. I would normally not accept such an invitation, but maybe I could make an exception this one time. I take my lunch break at eleven thirty. I will be sitting on the bench outside. If you would like, you can join me there, but you must bring your own lunch."

Simon tried not to show his elation. "Thank you, Fraulein, I look forward to it."

As Simon left, Marile said to herself, "*Gott im himmel*. What have I done?" Soon, however, a smile formed on her face, and suddenly, she was hoping the morning would go by much faster.

Simon looked at the cheap watch he had been given at Feldafing. It was 8:35 a.m. He still had almost three hours until his lunch meeting with Fraulein Häusl, so he decided to return to his temporary apartment on Luddendorfstrasse to turn over his food ration cards to Frau Weidermeyer and to freshen up.

As he made his way to the apartment, he noticed a dark-blue automobile parked in front of his building. He approached the vehicle and closely examined it. Automobiles were not common following the war, and it was difficult to obtain one. Simon had been petitioning the Jewish assistance organizations to obtain a used vehicle for use in a taxi and rental business he wanted to establish. His current job as a truck driver for a hauling company was difficult for him given his still-mending physical condition. The car was an Opel Olympia L38, probably produced in 1937 or 1938. Not fancy, by any means, but more than adequate for his business. He would visit the aid organization to find out how to go about acquiring a car. He knew it would be a challenge but was confident he would be successful.

In his room at the apartment, Simon shaved, combed his hair, and put on his best suit and tie. He put on his only coat, a castoff from Mr. Weidermeyer. He wanted to make a good impression on the young Marile. He left the apartment and stopped at a bakery to purchase a few rolls and then, using a ration coupon, bought a sausage for his lunch with Marile. Extravagant, he thought, but worth it.

At precisely 11:15 a.m., Simon sat down on the bench outside the offices of the Landratsamt Ernahrungsamt. It was a sunny day in Bavaria, and he was anxiously waiting for seventeen-year-old Marile Häusl to join him.

At 11:30 a.m., Marile Häusl left her office building and walked to the bench occupied by a waiting Simon Ruder. His heart almost missed a beat as he watched her approach. She wore a heavy gray coat that had seen better days under which she had on a blue dress with a flowered pattern. Her shiny dark-brown hair was combed back. She wore no makeup or lipstick; that was considered forward, and people assumed you were a loose woman or worse if you did. Marile brought her lunch in a small satchel.

Simon moved over on the bench, making more space for the young woman. Marile sat down, not too close.

"Good day, Fraulein Häusl," said Simon, trying to hide his nervousness. "How are you this beautiful morning?"

"I'm fine, Herr Ruder."

"Please call me Simon."

"So, Simon, how are the ration cards working out?"

"Just fine, Fraulein. I turn most of them over to my landlady, Frau Weidermeyer. I live close by at Luddendorfstrasse 6, in the middle of town."

Simon remembered some of the conversations he had with the pretty girl while in the hospital but realized that now was his chance to get to know her in a much better setting. Besides, he knew how bad he must have looked, bandaged and crippled, lying in his hospital bed or being pushed around in a wheelchair.

"How are your parents?" asked Simon. He already knew their names but wanted to be polite.

"They are fine." Marile was hesitant to explain further. She knew her father Ludwig had transported many Jews to several camps, and, in fact, this very one could have been among those numbers. He was also a member of the Nazi Party, and so were millions of other Germans. At least for now, she would stick to prewar conversation.

Sensing her reluctance, Simon changed the direction of the conversation. He was sure this young woman had been thoroughly indoctrinated into the Nazi ideology, as had her parents, so he, too, surmised that the last six years were off-limits, at least for now. Besides, he thought, to talk about the horrors he had endured would only engender sympathy, something he wanted to avoid with this young woman. So, prewar it was.

"Simon, I was wondering why you spoke such fine German. Are you from Germany?"

"No, Fraulein. I was originally from Obertin, which was then part of the old Austro-Hungarian Empire until 1919. Many of us learned German and Polish. I have used German as my main language ever since."

"Ah, so Simon, you are Austrian then?"

"In a sense," he said, suddenly forgetting he was Polish.

"What did you do before the war?"

Simon thought about how to answer the question. *Before the war* seemed to be a good boundary. It was safe and did not tread on dangerous ground. Both knew what it meant, and so some ground rules slowly developed between the two individuals, two people from almost inconceivably opposite backgrounds.

"I was a tailor in Lemberg. I was also an actor in a number of plays. I also used sing and play musical instruments."

The statement was not an exaggeration because Simon had played the violin and harmonica before the war and had high hopes for a musical future for his daughter Hanna, whom, he presumed, had perished.

"I played soccer too," he continued. And for emphasis, he said, "I was even paid for it." An exaggeration, perhaps, though the token payment helped with the uniform.

Marile was impressed. Most of the eligible German men had gone off to war, many never returning, and more returning with horrific injuries. She and her family were awaiting news of Anton Becker, Marile's childhood friend whom she was to marry. He had joined the *Wehrmacht* in early 1944 and had not yet returned from the Russian front. The German spirit had been broken, and a collective shame pervaded the Fatherland. Marile had endured her share of the shame after being forced to view the consequences of an SS massacre just six months ago. But she was young, and perhaps meeting this survivor served as kind of a catharsis for her. Besides, she was enjoying the conversation with this interesting and charming man.

"Herr Ruder, I think we should eat our lunch. I have to get back soon. The Americans are running things now, and I want to make a good impression."

"Of course, of course, I understand," said Simon. "What did you bring?"

Opening her sack, she said, "My usual: dark bread, a piece of cheese, and an apple."

Marile removed the contents of her lunch sack and waited for Simon.

He took out the sausage, which was still wrapped in the coarse brown paper from the butcher shop. He offered it to Marile, which she declined. Simon took out the roll he had purchased and began to eat. Extravagant, to be sure, but he wanted to impress the young woman. Marile followed suit. They were both quiet as the lunch break was quickly drawing to a close.

Looking at her watch, Marile hurriedly finished the last of the bread and cheese and said, "I must get back. It has been nice talking to you."

"We should do it again," said Simon. "Maybe tomorrow."

Marile thought about the question and the wisdom of whatever she decided. "Yes, maybe." A pause. "I think so. Then you can tell me about your acting."

Simon finished his sausage. "Thank you for a very entertaining time. I look forward to seeing you tomorrow. Good-bye for now."

Marile folded the wrapping paper and placed it in her sack. She then stood up and went back into the building. She looked back at Simon and smiled.

As Marile returned to work, her supervisor quizzed her about her lunch break. Frau Bilstein was a thirty-year employee of the department and was under the impression that she needed to know everything that went on, both inside and outside the building.

"That was just one of the people who receives food ration cards. He asked me some questions, that's all."

"Someone told me he looks Jewish. You better be careful, young lady. People are watching. Soon they will be talking. The department doesn't need any gossip."

Feeling chastised and confused, Marile went back to her desk. She wondered what she should do. Surely this was an innocent encounter. The charming man was much older than her, and there certainly was no romantic attraction, but she found she was nonetheless strangely drawn to him and tried to understand the attraction. Perhaps it was because he was Jewish. She had never met a Jew, and he was not what she was taught to expect. While she was concerned about the warning from Frau Bilstein, she made up her mind to continue the conversation with this interesting man. Besides, she thought, maybe we owe him that much.

The next day Simon was looking forward to meeting Marile Häusl to join him for lunch. He was waiting for her in front of her building on the same bench as the day before. At precisely eleven thirty, the young woman left the building and quickly made her way to the nearby bench. Simon did not fail to notice the lack of a smile on her face.

"Herr Ruder, do you mind if we take a walk instead of sitting here on the bench today? Are you cold? Are you well enough to walk?"

"Yes, if you wish, that would be fine. How are you today?"

"I'm fine, Herr Ruder," said Marile, but the tenor of her voice said otherwise. She quickly hustled Simon off the bench and away from the building.

Simon guessed why but let it pass, not wanting to disrupt the short time they would have. "So what shall we talk about today?"

Marile looked around, as if worried about being seen. Satisfied, she looked at Simon. "Well, I have been thinking, and I'm curious about your acting. Did you act in any plays? What was your favorite role?"

A smile formed on Simon's face as he remembered some acting role seemingly from another lifetime.

"Fraulein, since you asked, I will tell you. My favorite role was that of Tevye. The play was called *Tevye the Milkman*. I don't know if I can explain it to you. Our cultures may be too different for you to fully understand."

"Please try, Herr Ruder. I want to know what it was about."

"In that case, I will. The play has been performed in many places in Eastern Europe, and it has gone by several names. It takes place in Tsarist Russia before the revolution. It is about a Jewish family. The father is Tevye, a milkman with several daughters."

Marile listened intently. She assumed Jews had families like everyone else but had never thought about it. Her Hitler Youth indoctrination somehow failed to mention the close-knit Jewish families and the cohesiveness of the communities.

Simon continued. "Tevye was poor, but pious. I played that role, and though the character was older than me, I had makeup that made me look more his age."

Simon continued the story about life in the Jewish community in prerevolutionary Russia. He related the stories of Tevye's daughters, who and how they each married. He related Tevye's love for each of them and his reaction to the choices his daughters made, the poor tailor, the revolutionary, and especially the Gentile Russian soldier.

Marile could imagine Tevye, and she quickly developed a liking for the character because he reminded her so much of her own father. She wondered how Ludwig would have reacted in the same situation. Ironically, she would find out in the course of events.

Simon paused for a moment as he noticed Marile's far-off gaze.

"What are you thinking?"

"I was just thinking of my own father and how much he sounds like the character in the play."

Simon wondered about that as he finished his narrative of the play. Finally, he mentioned the figure of the fiddler. Marile was confused about the role of this figure.

"Why a fiddler? What does that mean? How does he fit into the play?"

"Fraulein," he began. "I think the Fiddler is actually a metaphor for survival, for survival through our traditions and joyfulness. I know that may be hard for you to understand. There is a painting by a Russian Jew named Marc Chagall called *The Fiddler*."

Pensively, she answered. "No, I think I understand. Thank you for sharing your story with me."

"My pleasure, Fraulein."

The lunch break was quickly drawing to a close as Marile and Simon hurriedly finished their food.

"I must get back," said Marile.

MÜHLDORF, GERMANY, MARCH 1946

The elder Maria Häusl was furious. Frau Erma Bilstein from the Landratsamt Ernahrungsamt Abteilung B had made a special trip to the Häusl farmhouse to report that the young Maria had been seen with a Jew, one much older than her, on several occasions and that she feared a scandal would ensue. She complained that this could affect the entire department and reflect badly on the family.

As a Catholic, Maria Häusl had no illusions about the Jews. The church certainly viewed them with contempt for what they believed the Jews had done to their Messiah. The church stood by and tacitly approved the brutal measures taken by the Nazi regime to annihilate them. There was no real or effective outcry, and this attitude filtered down to the common church-going Germans. Combined with the constant onslaught by the Nazi propaganda machine, the German perception of the Jews changed little after the war, even after the all the hand-wringing and anguished cries of "Oh my God, we were deceived."

A staunch supporter of this unyielding mindset, Maria Häusl determined to resolve this situation quickly and decisively.

Barely keeping her anger in check, she managed to say, "Thank you for bringing this to my attention. I will most certainly take care of this immediately."

"I'm sure you will, Frau Häusl. We can never be too careful with our children, especially now. Your daughter is a fine worker, and I would hate to see anything damage her reputation. She is doing such a good job, and the Americans like her too."

"Do not worry, Frau Bilstein. I assure you that I will take care of this. Marile is sometimes a headstrong girl. Her father sometimes allows her too much freedom. Thank you again. I'm sure this behavior will not be repeated by my daughter."

The elder Maria bid Frau Bilstein good-bye and watched the woman ride her bicycle back toward the town. It was only one o'clock, but Maria was already practicing the conversation she knew she must have with her husband later this afternoon. Her anger built throughout the afternoon, and she was having difficulty focusing on her chores. She wondered how Ludwig would react to the news.

Several hours later Ludwig Häusl came home from his job as a train engineer. Much of the war damage to the rail marshalling yard and the train station had been repaired and trains were moving again, but the postwar economy was still in shambles.

Ludwig entered the small farmhouse totally unprepared for the onslaught that was to follow. Before he had a chance to greet his wife, she immediately started her well-rehearsed tirade.

"Do you know what your precious daughter has been doing? I had a visit today with her supervisor who came out to tell me little Marile has been seen with an older Jewish man several times. It's becoming quite a scandal. What are we going to do? I think it is shameful and embarrassing for our family."

Ludwig sighed. You should talk, he thought to himself, but wisely decided to hold his tongue. Ludwig had his own opinion on the Jews, shaped perhaps because he had delivered so many to their deaths at the camps. He had seen firsthand the brutality endured by those not immediately murdered upon arrival. He had experienced his own recurring nightmares.

"Do they know who he is? What are they doing? Are they just talking? What do we really know about this person?"

"Does it really matter? My God, he's Jewish. A Polish Jew yet, and I'm told he is old enough to be her father. He is barely out of the hospital and cannot support himself. That's all we need to know. Our daughter cannot be seen with a Jew. She cannot spend time with a Jew except when required for her job. That's all there is to it. I absolutely forbid it! I want you to talk to her. We must put an end to this nonsense. After all our Germany has gone through these last six years because of them, this is what our daughter does. No, Ludwig, this must stop."

Ludwig shook his head, not because he didn't agree with his wife, because she was probably right, but in sadness for the conversation he knew was coming with his beloved daughter. He left the small kitchen and went to the bathroom to clean up after a busy day at the train yard.

A short time later, Marile came home to a strangely quiet farmhouse. "Hello, Mama," she said. "How was your day?" Her comment was met with stony silence. Sensing something was not right, she said, "Where is Papa? I saw his bicycle outside."

"Your father wants to talk to you, Marile." The young woman instantly knew that something bad was in the air. Perhaps another uncle had been confirmed dead in the war or had been sent to a Russian prisoner-of-war camp. She was not prepared for what came next.

Ludwig Häusl quietly entered the kitchen and smiled at his beloved daughter. The smile faded, too quickly for Marile's liking, and she sensed the tension in the small room.

"Sit down, Marile," began her now serious father. Marile looked around for support from her mother, support that was obviously not going to materialize.

"Marile, you know your mother and I love you very dearly, but sometimes we just don't understand your behavior. Maybe I allow you too much freedom. Now we hear that you have been behaving inappropriately at work."

Shocked, Marile quickly thought about what behavior could have possibly resulted in the accusation. She didn't have to think too long or hard to realize it probably had something to do with her supervisor, Frau Bilstein, and the chastisement she had received a few days ago.

Waiting for what she knew was coming, she tried to organize her thoughts.

Ludwig continued. "Marile, I understand you have been talking to an older man, a Jew no less. Your supervisor is very worried about the matter and how it looks. She thinks it could become a scandal, one we certainly don't need." He looked at his wife, who glared back at him.

"Papa," began the young woman, somewhat flustered under the weight or implications of the accusation.

"No!" said Ludwig with more emphasis and emotion in his voice, more than Marile had ever heard. "You are not to be seen with this Jew. I know you must help him with food ration cards, that's your job, but that's all, that's as far as it goes." He looked at his daughter, and with a softer tone, he continued. "You must understand the situation. Germany has been defeated, humiliated. We are reviled by the world for what we have done. I'm ashamed to say I have contributed to what happened, but we all played our part."

Ludwig suddenly became quiet as memories of walking skeletons in striped rags raced through his mind. Their gaunt faces peered accusingly back at him. He remembered the thousands of prisoners forced to repair the bombed marshalling yard in March of 1945. He clearly remembered the pathetic figure, barely able to stand, with whom he had made eye contact. For some reason, he wondered if the man had somehow survived but doubted it.

Just as quickly, Ludwig snapped out of his thoughts and remembered the conversation with his daughter. "We now have a terrible burden to bear, but I swear that burden does not include my daughter befriending a Jew and creating a scandal. Do you hear me? You are not to talk to this Jew again."

"But Papa, he is a good man. I learn things from him and enjoy talking to him. He tells me stories. What's wrong with that, Papa?"

"No, my dear daughter. It's just not right. Don't ask me why. I said you are not to see him again. Please, my little Marile, do this for me. Besides, Donei should be coming home any day, and we are expecting you to marry him."

Holding back tears, Marile looked at her father. She knew better than to try to reach out to her mother. "Yes, Papa," she began. "I understand and will do what you ask."

"That's my good daughter," said Ludwig, sneaking a quick glance at his still fuming wife. "Now get ready for dinner."

"Yes, Papa," she said as she went to the small bedroom she shared with her younger sisters. She was tired and plopped down on the bed and began to think about what had just happened. Though a precocious child, Marile now found herself in a confused and troubling dilemma. Her experience at the site of the camp outside of town had forced her to come face-to-face with the atrocities of her beloved Third Reich. The sights and smells and the realization of what they represented had shaken her to the core. She realized she no longer harbored an allegiance to that failed and disgraced regime and wondered how that affected her attitudes toward the Jews, attitudes that, until recently, had been unquestioningly part of her psyche.

Now that she had actually met a Jew, a survivor of the horrific actions of her government, she was amazed that a bond had developed with him. She wondered why. She realized that Simon embodied all that she was taught to loathe, to hate, since she was ten years old. She wondered about her feelings toward the man. To be sure, there was nothing romantic or sexual; after all, he was very much older than her. He had charm and charisma, though, and she admired the fact that he had survived the horrific ordeal, but what was it that really attracted her to him? Perhaps it was because he was a window to a broader world, a world unknown to her. He'd lived in other countries and large cities while she was just a farm girl. He was an actor and a soccer player. He was a big shot in the Jewish community. He could tell exciting stories. To a seventeen-year-old, it was new and exciting. And now it was forbidden.

Yet there was another dimension that she began to explore. It was called guilt, a feeling of shame for what her people had done, and in a way she did not yet fully understand what her religion had and hadn't done, though the full implications of the latter were not yet clear. She wondered if, in her own way, she was attempting to achieve redemption for her people. Could she really do that, and was it even appropriate or possible to try? For a seventeen-year-old farm girl, these were indeed complicated issues with which to deal, and she wondered how and why she was suddenly thrown into the turmoil in which she found herself. Try as she might, her God provided no answers, no signs, to the path she should take, but her conscience began to drop hints. She wasn't sure, however, that she liked the direction the hints were pointing.

Mülhdorf was a small town, and virtually every family had been touched by the war. By now the remaining six thousand or so inhabitants had been forced to accept the deeds of their leaders, and in hushed tones, they shared their excuses for not knowing what was going on under their very noses. They also shared gossip, and a juicy tidbit concerned Ludwig Häusl's oldest daughter Marile and her reported Jewish friend.

A few days later, Marile's childhood friend Lisle tried to talk to her. It was hard to believe that it was only eight years earlier that Marile had presented the Fuhrer a bouquet of flowers. Lisle remembered the Fuhrer hugging her. She tried to smile at the thought but could not. Now he was dead and so was Germany. She dismissed the thought and turned to her friend. "Marile, what's this I'm hearing? What are you doing? I hope it's not true."

Marile looked at her long-time friend and shook her head. "I don't know why everyone is so against this. I told my parents I would not associate with him, and that's the end of it."

"Good," said Lisle, not believing a word of it.

Over the next few days, Marile began to wonder if her parents were right, that any friendship with this Jew was pure folly and out of the question. While she still harbored a feeling of guilt for the crimes of the regime and a profound sympathy for Simon, she realized the relationship would continue to upset her parents and friends and impact her work life. She was not prepared to swim upstream in those dangerous, anti-Semitic currents.

This decision having been made, she tried to gently break off further friendly conversations with Simon. Certainly she was polite to him when he picked up his ration cards, but she gave him no hint of anything beyond that. She was efficient, cold, and distant. Even Frau Bilstein noticed and reported the greatly improved, more proper behavior to Marile's mother, and the potential scandal seemed to be averted, much to everyone's relief.

Everyone but Simon, who became confused and dejected over the seeming rejection he was experiencing from his new friend. He felt rejected and realized it was strange after what he had endured during his hellish last five years. He wasn't sure why he felt rejected; after all, the relationship was doomed from the start. Everyone had told him so. His heart was broken, but his head told him the reason for her behavior. He was, after all, a Jew, and even after the war, after the true nature of the Nazi atrocities were irrefutably disclosed, old prejudices still held fast.

While Marile felt saddened by her treatment of Simon, she was happy to be working for the Americans, especially Captain Greene. For the past nine months, the Americans had been administering the government offices and functions through what they called the Military Government. She blushed as the captain walked by, said good morning, and asked her how things were going. So different from her former supervisor, Frau Bilstein, who had suddenly disappeared. Marile's view of the world was evolving. First, her beloved Germany had been defeated, still in chaos and ruins. Her faith had been shattered as she walked through the horrors of the concentration camp. Then, as if predetermined by fate, she had met a Jew straight from the horrors of the concentration camps and had befriended him, albeit to the vehement disapproval of her parents. Now she found herself working for a presumably Jewish American army captain. She thought back to her Hitler Youth indoctrination and could no longer reconcile it with her experience with these two individuals, especially after her denazification interview, the results of which exonerated her.

As she prepared for another busy workday distributing food ration cards, a young woman clerk approached her. "Fraulien Häusl," said the clerk, a young woman she didn't know. "A letter came for you. It was dropped off at the front door."

Surprised, Marile took the small envelope from the girl. "Thank you," she said as she apprehensively put the letter away. She would open it later, perhaps at lunch.

She put the letter out of her mind as the townspeople began to line up for their valuable food ration cards. Food was still problematic for the general population with caloric limitations carefully controlled. Many people survived only with the additional food the CARE packages afforded them. The Americans were viewed as liberators rather than occupiers, at least for now, the darkest days after the defeat. This view would slowly change over the next year as the "denazification" process became, at best, cumbersome and, at worst, a failure, with many former Nazis retaining influential positions throughout Germany and many being hired by the Americans to participate in the very process designed to purge them.

At around noon Marile remembered the letter. She slowly took it out of her desk drawer and looked at the envelope as if it were a snake. It was small, beige, and had her name handwritten in blue ink. She noted the absence of a postmark, so she assumed it had been hand delivered. In the room that served as a lunchroom, Marile stared at the letter. Her workmate Kuni came by. "Are you well, Marile?" she asked. "You look pale."

"I'm fine, Kuni. It's just that I received this letter, and I don't know who it's from. I'm afraid to open it. I don't know why."

Kuni laughed. "What can it be? It's not an official letter, so you're not going to prison."

Marile gave her friend a disgusted look. "Don't make fun. I think I'll open it at home."

A short distance away at the repaired *bahnhof,* or railroad station, Simon Ruder was hoping the train to Munich would arrive. He hoped his letter had reached the young Marile Häusl, and though he doubted she would even read it, much less respond, he nonetheless felt a sense of urgency to maintain some sort of connection with her. He had written the letter in longhand using his best German with some Polish variations and a smattering of Yiddish. It was, he hoped, enough to reestablish some sort of communication with the young woman, tenuous as it might be.

The workday was drawing to a close as Captain Greene made his rounds again. Marile was totaling up the food ration cards distributed that day and handed the tally to the captain. "Thank you, Fraulien Häusl. You are doing a fine job." Marile thanked the American officer and smiled, pleased with the compliment.

Before leaving the office, Marile tucked the letter under her coat. The coat was a bit too small but still serviceable, and it would be months until a better one would be available. Though still light, the evening was fast approaching. She walked briskly toward her home on Rambold-Xaver Strasse, a kilometer or so away. She kept an eye out for American soldiers but had not experienced any problems.

She arrived at home and greeted her mother and sisters Bette and Rosie. Hiding the letter, she went to the room she shared with her sisters and put the letter in a drawer under some clothes. Somehow she thought if she didn't open it, it did not exist. She came back and tried to act naturally. Bette looked at her older sister but said nothing.

Later that evening curiosity began to intrude into her thoughts, and she finally decided she would open the letter. She thought it would be best to open it at work, where at least there was a modicum of privacy. Besides, it was dark in the small farmhouse and reading by candlelight would draw unwanted attention from her family.

The next day Marile left for work as usual, the letter safely tucked in her coat. She arrived at her building and began preparing for the day's work. The captain was not yet in, probably in a meeting. The Americans held a lot of meetings, she noticed. She thought about the unopened letter and had second thoughts, but soon realized how silly she was being. It was only a letter, and she resolutely determined to open it during a break.

An hour or so later she had an opportunity to excuse herself and made her way toward the bathroom at the other end of the office area, the letter hidden under her blouse. Her friend Kuni watched her leave and looked over at her. Marile gave her a "Leave me alone" look and continued down the hall. She entered the small room and, taking a deep breath, removed the envelope. She held it up to the light but could not make out the contents. Finally, after a moment or two of procrastination, she found the resolve to open it.

As she had both feared and anticipated, the letter was from Simon. She thought she had successfully avoided him for the last month or two, or had at least put him off to the extent he understood the relationship was not going to grow, and while it saddened her, she knew she had done the right thing. Her parents had told her so in no uncertain terms. Yet, in spite of her misgivings, she carefully unfolded the letter and began to read it. The handwriting was neat, but she found it difficult to make out all of the words, and while it was mostly in German, some of the words were in Yiddish and what may have been Polish, and it took her several times through to understand it. Simon wrote about how much he enjoyed talking to her and how he was sad that she no longer seemed to want to be his friend. She thought his writing style reflected a real sense of honesty and feeling that, as a seventeen-year-old, she had not experienced. She had read books, but this was different. This was a grown man writing to a seventeen-year-old as if she were an adult, something to which she was totally unaccustomed. It made her feel important, and she read the letter several times. At the end of the letter, Simon asked her to meet or at least talk to him. Panic! She had no idea what to do or how to respond, so she decided to ignore the letter, at least for now. She carefully folded it and put it back in the envelope. It was time to return to work, and she quickly rejoined her coworkers in the office. Kuni looked up at her friend, who simply smiled as she sat down.

Later that evening Marile hid the letter under some knitting she was working on at home and tried to put it out of her mind. She had a vague understanding of the consequences of following through with a response, yet she experienced a feeling of excitement, a feeling she knew was wrong. She patted the letter and made sure it was well hidden. She would think about it for a time, but Pandora's box had been opened.

A week later another letter arrived. This time she opened it at her first opportunity. As she expected, it was from Simon. He wrote how much he missed her and would love to see her, even if just briefly. He pleaded with her to meet with him. He let her know about how successful his business had become, though omitting the actual nature of the endeavor. He said he would be waiting at the *bahnhof* two days hence and hoped she would be there at noon. She reread the letter several times. Finally, she smiled as she replaced the letter in the small envelope and went back to work. Two days from now would be Thursday, and she found herself looking forward to the rendezvous.

Simon returned to Mühldorf Wednesday evening and headed to his small room on Luddendorff Strasse. He was tired from a day of making deals with various purveyors of goods for his business, yet was preoccupied with his meeting the next day with Marile Häusl—a meeting he hoped would take place. He hadn't seen the young woman for over a month, so he wasn't at all sure she would show up.

The next morning Simon prepared for the meeting as though it would actually happen. He shaved and donned his best suit, one he had tailored himself. Simon looked in the mirror and thought that he looked much better now, indeed, very dapper. He imagined how horrible he had looked several months ago, just out of the hospital, deathly thin, limping badly, and still wearing a number of bandages. He was different now, not that creature that had endured unspeakable horrors. Thus bolstered, he put on an overcoat and made his way to the *bahnhof*, hoping for the best.

At her job, Marile was nervous as well. So much so that even Captain Greene asked her if she was well. She had thought about this meeting for two days. Sometimes it was a good idea, other times not so. It was eleven thirty, and she needed to make a decision. She realized that not making a decision was itself a decision. Finally, as the noon hour approached, she decided that there was no harm in meeting Simon, so she picked up her lunch bag, left the building, and made her way to the *bahnhof*.

Simon was waiting outside the *bahnhof*, looking at his watch. He tried to look calm without success. He scanned the street, turned around, and paced a few yards, then turned back. He almost ran into Marile as she approached. They both laughed nervously.

"Fraulein Häusl, you look wonderful," began Simon, repeating a speech he had practiced for two days. "How have you been?"

Marile noticed that Simon appeared much healthier and very distinguished in his new coat. "I'm very well, Herr Ruder."

"Please, call me Simon."

"Herr…Simon. You are looking much better. Much better than the last time I saw you. How are you? What have you been doing?"

"It's cold out here. Let's go inside the *bahnhof* building. I brought something to eat. I see you did too."

The pair found a bench to sit on and unwrapped their food and talked between bites.

"I have started a business in Munich," began Simon. "Business has picked up. Maybe there are some business opportunities here in Mühldorf."

Marile had some idea of the business and wanted to ask about it but thought better of it. "What are your plans?"

"Fraulein Häusl, to tell you the truth, I don't really know. For now I think I'll stay in the area. I would like to get a driver's license and start an auto taxi company sometime. I'm also starting to do some tailoring work, but people don't seem to have money to spend on new clothes right now. I would also like to move into my own apartment, maybe something in town. However, at some point, I would like to immigrate, maybe to the United States. Germany, well, it's a very beautiful country, and I'm sure it will rebuild itself, but it's not for us Jews, not in the long run."

Marile nodded to herself as images of corpses of the Jewish camp victims she had been forced to view materialized once again in her mind. She shook her head as if to rid herself of the memory, but was unable to do so.

"I understand, Herr…Simon. Those were bad times. The Americans, they tell us how evil we Germans are and how we must pay for the sins of our leaders. I don't know how Germany will survive, but I hope we will. I don't know how long the Americans will stay, but I think it may be a long time."

Simon took a bite of his sausage as Marile worked on her piece of bread. The lunch hour was rapidly winding down, and Simon tried to remember the speech he had so carefully crafted in his mind. "How is your family?" he asked.

By the look on the young woman's face, he realized this could be a sore subject. "They are fine," she lied. "Papa is back at work on the railroad. My half brother Alois is still in the hospital. My friend Anton is still missing. We have heard nothing."

Taking a breath, Simon then asked, "How is your mother?"

Marile's eyes flashed for just a second. Simon noticed and regretted the question. Yet he had to know.

"She is still devastated over what has happened to Germany. Her Germany. All because of…Can you blame her?" Marile wanted to say more but didn't want to hurt Simon, so she kept her silence.

Simon guessed at her unspoken words but didn't press the issue.

It was time for Marile to get back to work. "Herr Ruder, it was nice to see you again. I'm glad you are doing well. I wish you the best, and maybe you will go to America soon. I have to go back to work now."

Simon stood up and walked Marile to the door. "Thank you for meeting with me. It was a pleasure to see you again. Maybe we can do this again sometime. Can I walk you back to your office?"

Marile turned to Simon. "Thank you, no. It would be very awkward." After a pause she said, "I'm afraid my parents have forbidden me to see you. I am taking a big risk right now. I hope you understand. I'm sorry, but I can do nothing about that." Another pause. "Good-bye, Herr Ruder."

Simon watched the young woman leave the building and make her way back to her office. Though the conversation didn't go according to his plan, he nonetheless felt satisfied with the results. This was going to be a challenge, but one he was eager to undertake.

All eyes were on Marile as she returned to her office. Kuni was especially interested. She slowly approached Marile. "Where have you been? I saw you walking toward the *bahnhof*. Were you meeting someone? It wasn't that old Jew, was it? For your sake, I hope it wasn't."

Marile just smiled. "Don't be silly," she said and sat down at her desk. People had already lined up at the counter for their ration cards, and it was time to get back to work.

LODZ, POLAND, MARCH 1946

As the Russians continued to implement their economic and political system with increased speed and vigor, Mendel Ruder was becoming more disillusioned with his future. Having endured the Soviet system for almost a year in the Polish city of Lodz, he had decided it was time to move on while it was still possible to escape. His young son Dolek, now eight years old, was enrolled in school and had been indoctrinated in the fine points of the Soviet system and had learned the Russian language. He had also learned to fight, a skill that he was forced to utilize much too frequently. Being a Jew was still risky, and the future began to look significantly less bright.

Word circulated through the small Jewish community that displaced persons camps had been established in Germany and that liberated Jews had found reasonable living conditions in several such large camps, some near former concentration camp sites. The Polish/German border was about a 363-kilometer distance from Lodz, a precarious journey, especially crossing the now heavily guarded border, but one Mendel was nonetheless determined to undertake.

On a chilly day in March, Mendel and Dolek left yet another city. Mendel had quietly sold as much of his cloth and inventory as he could without arousing suspicion and packed other items as best he could. Sadly, some of his possessions had to be left behind in his small apartment, but that wasn't the first time such actions had been necessary. The first part of the journey took them by train to the city of Poznan, almost halfway to the German border. From there, they traveled westward utilizing a variety of transportation modes, including automobiles, trucks, and finally, within a few kilometers of the border, a hay wagon. The wagon was pulled by a single, worn-out horse, and hidden in the belly of the wagon, under an immense stack of hay, five Jews held on the best they could as the wagon slowly traversed the bumpy road. Hidden with Mendel and Dolek were a couple and their infant child no more than a year old. They had all paid for their passage to be smuggled into Germany. As they slowly made their way toward the border, Mendel began to worry about the infant, who had been quiet so far, but one could never tell.

"Quiet!" hissed the wagon driver, urgency in his voice. "The border is near. Do not make any noises."

Everyone understood. Everyone except the infant, who suddenly began to wail. The mother frantically tried to quiet the infant to no avail. The border was quickly approaching, and the line was short. To stop now would arouse unwanted suspicion. Suddenly, the infant's cries stopped. The border crossing went smoothly after a cursory search by the Polish guards. Four of the five Jews hiding in the belly of the hay wagon had successfully made it across the border into Germany.

Once in Germany, the next goal was the still free city of Berlin, some two hundred kilometers away. It was in April 1946 that the pair finally reached Berlin and made contact with the Americans, who, after a short investigation, took them to the Jewish aid organization. They were soon on their way to the displaced persons camp in Deggendorf in the American sector in Bavaria. Mendel and Dolek were loaded onto a military truck, part of a convoy headed south. In addition to the several other Jews riding in the back of the truck, a shipment of supplies shared the space, including a large shipment of Passover matzos destined for the camp. The Jews soon took advantage of the matzo bonanza and began opening the boxes and helping themselves. As the convoy made its way through the streets of a still partially destroyed and starving city, the Jews, seeing firsthand the starving Germans begging for food, in a scene at once ironic and tragic, began throwing out matzos to the starving Germans, who, like pigeons, scrambled to get their share. It didn't matter that the food came from Jews and was part of a Jewish tradition. The Jews simply shook their heads, not oblivious to the irony playing out before them.

The pair was eventually brought to the Deggendorf DP camp around the time of Passover. They were surprised to find the camp exceptionally active with many political groups, several newspapers, a theater group, a kosher kitchen, a sizable library, and even a *mikve*, a Jewish ritual bath. The camp administration even issued its own currency, dubbed the "Deggendorf dollars." Mendel learned that many of the camp inhabitants were former inmates of the Theresienstadt concentration camp. Mendel and Dolek settled in without too many complications. Soon, however, it became obvious to Mendel that a number of political factions operated within the camp, each with its own vision of how the Jews should fit into the evolving postwar period and beyond. While Mendel was wary of joining any particular group, young Dolek was approached by and joined the Betar Movement, a Revisionist Zionist youth movement founded in 1923 in Riga.

Dolek Ruder in the Deggendorf Displaced Person Camp in 1946.
He is wearing the uniform of the Betar organization,
a Revisionist Zionist youth movement.

MUNICH/MÜHLDORF/AMPFING AREA, APRIL 1946

More letters arrived for Marile Häusl at her office. Simon Ruder was persistent, and the pair met surreptitiously several times during the spring. These meetings often took place at the *bahnhof*, sometimes at various restaurants in town, or at parks. It was a difficult time for young Marile. To be seen in public with Simon was risky for her, especially if word got back to her mother. Marile's older friend Kuni had her suspicions and one day confronted her.

"I know you've been seeing that Jewish man. What is going on? Tell me the truth."

Marile wasn't sure how to answer. In a way, she felt relieved. "Yes, I've met with Herr Ruder a few times. We just talk about things. He is very interesting, not like anyone I have ever met. He opened my eyes about the Jews."

"So why are you sneaking around? The war is over. Germany lost and things will get back to normal again."

"But what is normal? My parents still hate the Jews, especially my mother. She would be very unhappy with me if she knew." Marile paused, a pensive look on her face. "Are you going to tell her?"

Kuni smiled at her young friend. "Marile, remember when the J-...Herr Ruder first came into the office for his ration cards? Remember how badly he looked? I will never forget that sight. Yet, in spite of him being a Jew, I felt sorry for him. Now he has recovered and looks much better. At the very least, I have to admire the man for what he went through and how far he has come."

Kuni paused. "To answer your question, no, I will not tell anyone. As long as it comes to nothing, I can keep quiet. When your friend Donei comes back, well, then you must do what is right."

Much relieved, Marile thanked her friend and went back to work.

Marile and Simon continued to meet throughout the spring and summer. Kuni became a convenient excuse for some of the longer meetings, and the pair occasionally traveled by train to Munich to attend a soccer match or play. At one soccer match, Simon brought lunch, a salami and schmaltz sandwich, which he offered to Marile. The young woman recoiled at the sight and smell, a horrified look on her face, and with her arms frantically waving said, "No, no, take it away!"

Simon laughed at her reaction and handed her a more traditional German sausage and a piece of bread instead.

Over the next few months, the relationship evolved into a genuine friendship. Marile realized this man bore no resemblance to the large-nosed, smarmy-complexioned Jewish caricature so familiar on the Nazi propaganda posters for so long. Simon was always clean-shaven and immaculately attired. She found him unusually generous. He was intelligent and funny. She found him to be the antithesis of all she had learned was Jewish. Yet, in spite of this, the specter of anti-Semitism hung over the relationship like an ominous black cloud. Neither knew where it was going or how it would end.

While the pair met a few times a month, Simon knew that the elder Maria's unyielding anti-Semitism continued to be a major obstacle, and he feared the relationship was beginning to stall. Marile could give no assurances that her mother would ever change her mindset. They both knew something would have to change. Marile still thought of Simon as a good friend, someone whose company she enjoyed. For Simon, however, the depth of the relationship went beyond that, but he wasn't sure why. For now, though, the pair would meet whenever it was possible without arousing suspicion, a situation he would have to accept, at least for now.

Simon's circle of Jewish friends and business associates also expressed their uncomfortableness with the relationship that he professed as being "nothing." While not outright condemning it, comments were made with an obvious implied disapproval.

Izak Goldblatt, his black market business partner, was particularly troubled. "You are a Jew, Simon. You are part of the Jewish leadership. Did the camps not convince you of anything? How can you do this?" Simon stopped listening, and the constant haranguing began to take its toll on the partnership.

Others were less direct but shared similar sentiments. Surrounded by this constant disapproval, Simon often had second thoughts, yet try as he might, he could not shake his feelings for the young woman.

There were other signs. On a particular train trip to Munich, the conductor looked at Marile and complimented Simon on his pretty daughter. Simon merely thanked the well-meaning conductor and let it go. Marile was embarrassed, and she, too, did not correct the man, but seeds of doubts began to take root in her mind.

Over the summer, Simon continued to successfully expand his business activities in Munich, Mühldorf, and Ampfing. He received his driver's license in September. Soon after, he started his auto chauffer business with the acquisition of a vehicle, a 1938 Opel Olympia L38, in late 1946. This proved to be a difficult process with several legal challenges and trips to Munich, but Simon had prevailed.

Simon's first acquisition, a well-used 1938 Opel Olympia L38.

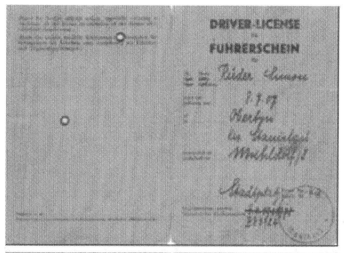

Simon Ruder's driver's license issued in both English and German languages.

By August, he had saved enough money to finally move from the Ludenndorf Strasse address to a more spacious apartment at Stadtplatz 44, where he set up a tailoring shop. With his black market business in Munich still generating some income and the tailoring business growing, things looked promising for him. Except for his relationship with the young Marile Häusl. Her mother still strenuously objected to her relationship with Simon. He was tired of sneaking around with Marile but was afraid to bring the situation to a head, most likely precipitating an outcome he was not yet prepared to face.

Over time, and influenced by his miraculous survival, Simon's love affair with Communism had burned itself out after his liberation from the Ampfing concentration camp, and ironically, his black market dealings had transformed him into a bona fide capitalist. While he had done well in this strange land, after several years, he had become frustrated with the way the Americans were running the Bavarian government and especially the slow or nonexistent progress toward immigration. Simon possessed many skills, but among them knowing when to stay silent about certain issues often escaped him. To that end, he regularly made public speeches, mostly to Jewish audiences, voicing his opinions. The Jews listened. And so did the Americans, and Simon's name was added to yet another list, one that could potentially block his goal of moving to America.

Simon Ruder delivering a speech in 1946.

LODZ, POLAND, JULY 1946

Like his younger brother Mendel, Izak Ruder realized that while decep-
tively comfortable in Lodz, Poland, the end was coming. Not the cataclysmic
end endured by the Jews of Poland seven years earlier, to be sure, but the signs
of major changes to come were unmistakable. Izak's job at the metal factory
was rumored to be eliminated as the Soviet economic system once again took
hold in earnest. How the Jews would fare under this system was not something
Izak wanted to experience firsthand. He understood that friendship with the
Poles was, at best, veneer deep, their laughter disingenuous and their smiles
never quite reaching the eyes. It was time to leave. He had not heard of the fate
of Mendel other than he had left two months earlier headed toward Berlin. He
hoped Mendel and Dolek had reached safety.

Several of the original Brunnlitz group and new members met regularly to
play cards, talk politics, and make plans. All still harbored dreams of emigrat-
ing, but politics and prejudices still barred the way. Frustratingly, England,
Israel, and the United States may just as well have been on the moon. So the
group discussed their strategies. Izak's idea was to somehow get into Germany
and then out at the first opportunity. They looked at a map, albeit an old
one much out of date. It showed countries that no longer existed and the
names of cities that, too, had changed, especially Polish ones reverting back to
German. The group discussed potential destinations. Izak reasoned that a large
city could offer more opportunity, even to Jews. Nothing permanent. They

understood that, but wanted somewhere to keep their heads down, survive, until they could emigrate. Anything was better than what the group feared awaited postwar Poland under the Soviet yoke. They sensed the window of opportunity to escape quickly closing, so they hastily finalized a plan, sold off as many of their possessions without arousing suspicion, and on a warm, sunny day in early July put their plan in motion.

Their plan was simple, naively so. They would make their way westward through Wroclaw across the German border toward Dresden, which they reasoned was the closest major city. They had no idea Dresden was still a bombed-out moonscape of rubble. Singly and in pairs, they made their way to Wroclaw without major problems. Crossing out of Poland and into Germany was another matter altogether, but one that bribery could still overcome. The border-crossing challenge behind them, Izak's group was dismayed to learn that they were now in the Russian Occupation Zone of the partitioned area Germany. This was certainly not where they wanted to be, so they hurriedly moved on toward Dresden. Russian soldiers were everywhere but paid the group little attention. German civilians, many as bad off as the passing Jews, merely shrugged, accepting that the Jews were a burden they would have to endure. Besides, they had their own problems.

The group moved on, and on a warm, late-July day, they finally reached the outskirts of the once beautiful city of Dresden. They were shocked at what they encountered as they traveled through the city. The incongruity of the sunny blue skies and the black, white, and gray of the rubble made a profound impression on the group, as war-dulled eyes set in gaunt faces peered out of gaps and holes in the ruins. Izak realized these ruins were their homes and they had nowhere else to go. He wondered if total destruction on this level was really necessary, even against such a hated enemy.

The group moved on as more refugees began to crowd the roads. Surprisingly, the Jews noticed many groups of Germans moving along the same roads, fleeing westward. Izak marveled at the irony of these panicked and frantic master race ethnic Germans and his group of *Untermenschen* sharing the same road to freedom. The Germans kept to themselves, though, pushing wagons piled with whatever they could carry. After the fall of the Third Reich, they had been violently expelled from the conquered territories. These were the lucky ones. Many others had been murdered, imprisoned in work camps, or drowned as the ships they boarded in escape attempts were sunk by the Russians.

Izak's group, now totaling one hundred or so, stopped outside of Dresden. By firelight, several of the leaders examined the old map. Directly to the south lay what the map indicated was Czechoslovakia, but no one was sure if it still was. News of Germany's conquest of the country and the establishment of a puppet Slovakia state clouded the issue, and the actual political status was unclear. All agreed that to try to cross multiple unknown borders would be too dangerous, so they decided to move to the southwest into what they hoped was the American sector. They moved on. The journey took them past Freiburg and Chemnitz, soon to be renamed Karl Marx Stadt. The fleeing Germans stayed back a considerable distance, but eventually, a tacit peace developed as both groups understood they had the same destination. But for the Germans, it was home, and they would be repatriated. For most of the Jews, it was merely a way station on the road to an uncertain future. Still, in spite of the fact the groups made no contact, it seemed the Germans begrudgingly recognized the Jews as fellow humans.

Izak's group finally reached the border of the American Occupation Zone, which encompassed Bavaria and Austria. The Russians guarding the border did not hinder the Jews. The Germans, however, encountered exhaustive questioning, delays, and confiscation of property. Izak and his group did not look back.

The Americans were better organized, and revised refugee policies had been implemented. The group was taken to a temporary location for the night. A German-speaking GI, sympathetic to the Jews, talked to members of the group. Obviously, he had done this before. Izak explained he would like to go to Munich. The GI laughed and said, "You and your group will be taken to a displaced persons camp that has been set up to accommodate refugees who have no place to go after the war. I think you certainly fit the description. It is a large camp for Jews. The camp is outside Munich and called Feldafing. You will leave tomorrow morning."

Early the next morning, the group was awakened, given a small breakfast, and loaded onto waiting army trucks. They drove for a while to the town of Nuremberg where the so-called Tribunals were wrapping up in the nearby Palace of Justice. The group stopped for the night. They met several other groups of refugees, mostly Jews, who shared stories of survival. Several Jews told of hiding in bunkers, in attics, and beneath stables. Others had been liberated by the Russians and had tried to return to their former lives only to find entire towns and Jewish communities destroyed. Synagogues were demolished or turned into warehouses or, worse, stables. They realized that because of the still rampant anti-Semitism and Soviet domination, escaping to the West was the only alternative left to them, so they, like Izak Ruder and his group, found themselves on the way to a displaced persons camp. The refugees were treated fairly and efficiently and were provided with food and shelter for the night as the Americans prepared for the trip farther south toward the Feldafing camp located just southwest of Munich.

The next day the group, now consisting of all Jews, was loaded onto several military trucks and began their 207-kilometer journey deeper into Bavaria. The countryside was beautiful, but echoes of the war still reverberated. The convoy passed by Ingolstadt and continued south, skirting Munich and coming within a few kilometers of Dachau. They saw the road sign pointing west toward the town that had held the infamous concentration camp. Several Jews made crude gestures and told of how they had been liberated near here by the Americans last May and had made their way back to Poland only to find heartbreaking disappointment. Bitterly ironic, they were now returning. Soon the convoy arrived at the DP camp, a former Hitler Youth retreat on the west shore of Lake Starnberg.

The refugees found the camp in full operation, having been established in May of the previous year. Izak Ruder and his group soon blended in with the Hungarian and other Jews and tried to make the best of a bad situation. At least there was food, shelter, and a sense of Jewish community. Izak determined he would bide his time until he could plot his future. He was near Munich, the next stop on his way to the West.

Izak did well at the camp. Like his brothers, he had been a tailor in Krakow before his unexpected career change to a metalworker at Plaszow and Brunnlitz. He made friends and found useful work, but more importantly, he soon made contacts in the black market, dealing in coffee, sugar, cigarettes, and American dollars.

DEGGENDORF DISPLACED PERSONS CAMP, SUMMER 1946

Mendel Ruder and his eight-year-old son Dolek had settled into the Jewish community at the Deggendorf DP camp. They enjoyed the social and political environment. Mendel worked as a tailor and carpenter as the camp became more and more self-sufficient. Everyone understood that the situation was temporary and that one day they would have to leave, but as the international policies toward the Jews were still being hotly debated, they made do with what was available. Many Western countries such as the United States and Great Britain still resisted the influx of these Jews. In the United States, President Harry Truman was opposed by both his Departments of State and Defense when it came to the subject of the Jews and the future status of an independent Israel. The British greatly limited the immigration into Palestine as well as to England. So the Jews at camps like Deggendorf, Feldafing, and many others spread across Germany and Austria waited.

MÜHLDORF, GERMANY,
SEPTEMBER–DECEMBER 1946

Simon continued to prosper in the land of his former tormentors. Through skill and luck, he had managed to acquire another vehicle, an Adler for his auto chauffer business, while his tailoring business grew as his small clientele began to expand. His trips to Munich took up some of his time, overseeing the black market activities, and he often traveled to Ampfing to help rebuild the small temple there. Every once in a while, he marveled at his situation and thanked God for his good fortune. A far cry from the horrors of the Dachau camps where he had lain near death some sixteen months ago. Thinking back to Poland, he wondered how he had come to be here, when had he taken that very first step on the path that had brought him here. In reality, the path had been laid out many years ago when a nondescript Austrian corporal stumbled out of a mustard gas–filled trench in World War I.

On this day Simon was in nearby Ampfing with a group of Jewish elders discussing various issues affecting the small community. They discussed politics, especially the future of emigration from Germany. Most wanted to go to Israel, but as of now, very few had managed to leave. So, in the meantime, they discussed what steps to take to revive the Jewish community. It was never very big and was decimated, as most of the Jews had been sent to the "East," which meant exterminated. Some thought rebuilding would be an act of defiance;

others thought it would be an act of insanity. In the end, work began on rebuilding the small temple, and Simon would play a role.

The rabbi, originally from Krakow and a survivor of Dachau, asked Simon about his experience during the Holocaust. Though reluctant at first, Simon shared his journey with the old man. After listening intently to Simon's story, the rabbi asked, "Have you gone back to Lemberg to find any survivors, your wife and children?"

Too quickly annoyed by the question, Simon wondered at his reaction but was able to effect a perception of calmness.

In answer to the too-often-asked question, Simon repeated the story told by the long-dead Jewish Lwow ghetto policeman, Josef Salzmann. "No, Rabbi, I learned of the death of my beloved wife Lola and my two children from an eye witness. They perished in Lemberg. I was thinking of returning, but the situation in the Ukraine is very bad for the Jews, so I think maybe it is unnecessary or unwise at this point. I think it's better to let them rest in peace."

"Maybe so," said the rabbi, looking directly at Simon. "Maybe so," he repeated, but somehow his voice lacked conviction.

Simon and Marile continued to meet throughout the summer and fall, albeit not on a consistent basis. The logistics of meeting had proved to be frustratingly complex. Mühldorf was a small town with many eyes and loose tongues. So far Kuni had served as a logical excuse, but their meeting had started to attract unwanted questions. Marile was happy with the status of their relationship, but Simon wanted more. His letters told of love, of how she was the center of his life, of how he wanted to take her away. He wanted a commitment from Marile, and that meant a confrontation with her parents, a step she was still not prepared to take.

"Please, give me time, Simon. I have strong feelings for you, but I can't commit to you right now. I enjoy our time together and our conversations, and I hope we can continue, but anything more is impossible."

Simon sighed as he looked at his young friend. "My Marile, my sunshine. I'm disappointed, but I will try to be patient. A better life awaits us. I'm sure of it. We were destined to be together, you and I, and I promise we will be one day."

At work Kuni just shrugged. "Eleven letters and two birthday letters in July. What's going on? How serious is this getting?"

"Kuni, I don't know. Maybe I shouldn't have started meeting with him last December. But honestly, I really have feelings for him, but I don't know what to do. My parents will be very upset and hurt if they find out. I'm stuck in the middle and can't seem to decide."

"Do you love him?"

"I don't know. I think I loved Donei, but he is gone. I don't know what I'll do if he ever comes back. We were promised to each other, but I think that is now impossible. It's different with Simon. He's so much older and mature. And he's Jewish. I think I can accept that, but no one else seems to be able to. Simon and I talked about this, and I think he understands. We just have to be careful about being seen together."

The pair continued to meet, though much less often than Simon would have liked. Kuni religiously kept her friend's secret, but they all knew something had to change. The present course of the relationship could not be maintained. Then, during a rendezvous in December, propinquity led to the inevitable, and the relationship took on a new whole dimension.

1947

MÜHLDORF, GERMANY, MARCH 1947

The early March morning dawned grayly as a cloud cover foretold a bleak, dreary day ahead. Marile Häusl awoke in a mood that seemed to match the weather. For several days now she had felt queasy but had passed it off as something minor, nothing more than a temporary inconvenience, and certainly nothing to affect her perfect attendance record at work.

Her mother was preparing breakfast for Ludwig, and as he looked up from the table, he smiled as his oldest daughter entered the small kitchen area. "Good morning, Marile," he said. "How are you feeling today?"

"I'm fine, Papa," she said, but the look on her face said otherwise. "I'm not hungry this morning."

"You must eat something," protested Maria. "It's a cold and rainy day. You must have your strength, Marile. Here, at least have some bread."

"Yes, Mama," said Marile, and she reluctantly took a slice of dark bread with butter and began to eat it slowly. She felt better and was able to keep it down that day.

"That's a good girl," said Ludwig as he looked over at his wife. Maria just shook her head and then picked up a small brown parcel.

"Here's your lunch, Marile, just a small sausage, bread, and a plum."

"Thank you, Mama." Marile gave her father a quick hug, smiled at her mother, and then left the small farmhouse. She decided to ride her bicycle the few kilometers to work today despite the gloom and threatening rain.

Later that morning Marile decided she should see a doctor, just as a precaution. She knew Dr. Weisermann from her volunteer work at the main Mühldorf hospital and remembered that he had an office in town not far from her workplace. She decided to visit the doctor during her lunch break. No one needed to know, and she hoped to be back to work quickly.

At precisely noon, Marile left work and walked quickly through the town archway, past the fountain, to 46 Stadtplatz, where the office of Dr. Weisermann was located. She walked up two flights of stairs to the doctor's office and entered.

"Well, good afternoon, Fraulein Häusl," said Regina Weisermann. "I don't see you on the appointment list today. Is there something I can do for you?"

Suddenly flushed, the young woman answered, "I would like to see the doctor, if possible. It's probably nothing, but I would like to make sure. Does he have a little time?"

Regina smiled and checked the appointment book. "He is taking his lunch right now, but let me see if he has a bit of time for you. Please, have a seat."

Regina left and returned after a minute or so. "Fraulein, the doctor will see you now. This way please."

Marile followed the older woman into the doctor's office where he was just finishing his lunch. He looked up and smiled at Marile and walked to the sink to wash his hands.

"Hello, Fraulein," he said. "How have you been? It's been, what, over a year since you last worked at the hospital? I'm sorry about your brother. Now, what can I do for you?"

Marile looked around the small office. She remembered the doctor from the time immediately after the war when she was a volunteer at the Mühldorf hospital and he was treating Jewish camp survivors. They were no longer called

Jews. The new name was Israelish. Marile thought back to when she had first met Simon.

"Fraulein!"

"Oh, sorry, Doctor. I was hoping I could see you. I'm having some symptoms I don't understand and would like your opinion."

"Of course. What sort of symptoms?"

"I feel sick in the morning. Sometimes I throw up. It usually goes away."

"Hmm."

"What does that mean, Doctor?"

"Nothing yet. Let's do some quick tests. I will need to take a blood and urine sample."

"Urine?" she asked, somewhat apprehensively.

"Please, trust me, Fraulein."

The doctor conducted a series of checks on the young woman, including the blood and urine samples. He went over to his desk and made some notes on a piece of paper. He looked over to Marile and said, "Nothing to worry about, Fraulein. You are in perfect health. I'll be back in a moment."

With that, the doctor left the small room and gave instructions to Regina. Marile could not make out the words but did not sense anything unusual in the exchange. She saw the note the doctor had left on his desk. Always curious, she quickly walked to the desk and glanced at the notes the doctor had scribbled. The scribbles were hard to decipher, but one word stood out: *schwangerschaftstest.*

Shocked, Marile barely made it back across the room before the doctor returned. Entering the office, Dr. Weisermann noted the look on his young patient's face. He knew shock and disbelief when he saw it. He looked across the room to the note he had left on the desk. He turned back to look at his young patient and said, "We will know in a few days."

A week later a note arrived at the Häusl farmhouse on Xaver-Rambold Strasse 7 that would dramatically change the course of a number of lives.

Maria Häusl apprehensively took the note from the young messenger at the door. She dreaded any message these days. Even after the war, news of those brothers, uncles, and friends still missing in action was usually bad. Taking a deep breath and saying a quick prayer, she unfolded the note and read it. A look of horror formed on her face, and she dropped the note and hit the floor before the note did. It took her a few moments to regain consciousness, and she was not happy about it. Panicked and angry, she waited for her husband to come home, all the while thinking of what to do to avoid the disgrace that would surely follow. After all, she knew firsthand about disgrace and knew that this was going to be worse, much worse.

Ludwig Häusl arrived home after another busy day at the rail marshalling yard. He was tired, and the last thing he wanted was another confrontation with his wife. Coming through the door and hanging up his engineer's hat, he immediately sensed something was brewing. Maria's demeanor was different, subdued yet tense, as if something was about to explode. He looked at his wife in anxious anticipation. He sensed something bad was in the air. Suddenly, moving like a banshee, she approached her husband with a piece of paper in her hand and waved it in front of his face.

"What's this?" he asked, a perplexed look on his face. "Did someone die?"

"Might as well have," she said, finally handing him the note. "See what your precious daughter has done this time."

Ludwig took the piece of paper, carefully put on his reading glasses, and took his time reading the note from Dr. Weisermann. Maria became more frustrated as he read and reread the note, making sure he understood what it said. He was a patient man and considered the implications and possible rami- fications. After a few moments, he sat down at the small table, put down the note, and with a heavy sigh, said, "What's for dinner?" He realized it was the wrong thing to say, and he immediately regretted it.

"How can you think of dinner?" Maria shouted. "You know what this means. She must go away, Ludwig. I can't bear this disgrace, not to our family. Maybe we can send her to Bad Reichenhall to live with Frau Gruenburger. You remember Paula Gruenburger. Maybe Marile can stay at the convent there un- til the baby is born. My God, we don't even know who the father is, but I pray it's not that damn Jew she was sneaking around with. How could your precious Marile disgrace us like this?"

Unspoken was the Nazi stricture against Aryans having sex with Jews, and while no longer on the books, it was still ingrained on the minds of many Germans. What would people think if that turned out to be the case?

Ludwig listened intently, his face reflecting the pain he felt, both for his daughter and himself. He started to say something but realized anything he said now would only exacerbate the issue. While his sympathies were with his daughter, even he had to admit she had strayed too far for him to support her. It seemed she had turned her back on everything she was, everything she had learned. Even worse would be the talk around town that the father was a Jew, a man much older than the eighteen-year-old Marile. No, he thought, Maria is right. It would be best to spirit her away to Bad Reichenhall, a small resort town eighty-seven kilometers away, tucked in the Alps across from Salzburg, Austria. Perhaps time in the convent would straighten her out. He thought about the child. Ironically, he had already raised a stepson, Alois, whom he had never formally adopted. Sadly, Alois had survived the war but was grievously wounded and was even now in and out of the hospital. Ludwig was not looking forward to raising another child, not at his age.

Across town Marile Häusl was at her job at the Landratsamt Ernahrungsamt Abteilung B. Lately people had begun to notice a difference in her behavior. She had become more introverted. Privately, she knew the strain of keeping her secret was beginning to affect her work and her health. More urgently, though, she had been anxious about the results of her *schwangerschaftstest*, her pregnancy test. She prayed it would be negative.

Captain Greene made his usual rounds after the morning staff meeting, the purpose of which Marile still didn't comprehend. His German was improving, and he could manage a decent conversation beyond the basics.

Seemingly preoccupied, he walked past Marile without a word. He shook his head slightly. Kuni, too, noticed and looked over to Marile, who just shrugged. How unlike the captain, she thought, and a sense of foreboding suddenly overcame the young woman.

Later that day, as Marile prepared to leave, Kuni stopped her. "Did you notice the captain? I wonder what is bothering him."

"You noticed it too? Well, it's probably nothing, just some army thing. You know how the Americans are."

"You are probably right, but I've never seen him so preoccupied. Good night, Marile. See you tomorrow."

The late afternoon began to cool off as Marile rode her bicycle home. She could not shake the feeling that something was wrong, and it gnawed at her all the way until she reached her house. As she arrived, she noticed her father's bicycle was stored in its spot next to the house. That's good, she thought, for no particular reason. Then she noticed the absence of the other bicycles that should have been there. Her sisters should be home from school by now. Something was not right. She stored her bicycle next to her father's and entered the house.

"Where are Bette and Rosie?" she shouted as she walked through the door. Her parents were sitting at the kitchen table with a piece of paper between them and very solemn looks on their faces. Even her father. Marile realized this was serious.

The elder Maria looked at her husband and nodded. Ludwig cleared his throat. "Marile, sit down. We have something very urgent we must discuss. We sent your sisters away so we could talk."

Marile looked down at the paper in front of her parents and could guess what message it held.

"Sit down, Marile," her father said. Her mother just glared at her daughter as if barely able to hold back some angry words. Apparently, it was decided that her father would speak for both of her parents.

"Marile, you have disappointed us. We are very upset with you." Uncharacteristically, he pounded the piece of paper on the table. "Do you know what this is?"

"No, Papa" she lied. He picked it up and waved it in front of her. "This is from Dr. Weisermann, and it says you are pregnant. My God, Marile." Ludwig bent over the table, rubbed his temples, and sighed. He looked over to his wife, who sat there with her hands folded in front of her as if restraining herself. She nodded. "Your mother and I have several questions. But we must ask the most important one first, but before you answer, think carefully. There will be no good answers, but some will be much worse than others." The specter of one in particular hung like a dark cloud above the small table.

Marile sat there like a trapped animal realizing there was no escape. "Yes, Papa," she said quietly, accepting her fate.

The inquisition began. "Who is the father, Marile?" asked Ludwig, afraid of the answer.

Marile knew the answer but stalled for time, something Ludwig incorrectly took for a good sign. Many thoughts ran through Marile's mind. If she said she didn't know, what message would that send to her parents about their beloved daughter? Conversely, if she revealed the truth, she knew that would hurt and humiliate her parents, as well as cause a scandal. Rumors already abounded in the small town. She made a decision, one she hoped she wouldn't regret.

"I don't know for sure," she said, hoping that being thought promiscuous was better than consorting with a Jew. Besides, she wanted to protect Simon.

Ludwig and Maria took a moment to digest the answer. They turned to each other, and Marile thought she detected a brief look of relief on their faces. Maria thought this was bad, but there was still a chance it would not be the disaster she feared. It was a straw they gladly grasped.

"Then it wasn't the Jew?" asked Maria, finally speaking up.

"I said I don't know."

Silence pervaded the space around the table as the implication sunk in.

"Oh my God. Are you saying it could have been?"

Marile's pause was too long. Ludwig and Maria suddenly understood that the straw they were grasping might still fall from their hands.

With a deep sigh, Ludwig spoke up. "Marile, my dear Marile. Your mother and I have decided to send you away to Bad Reichenhall. Frau Gruenburger will take you in, and you will have the baby in the convent there. Beyond that, I cannot say. We are deeply disappointed with you, Marile. You have created a scandal. I am ashamed of you. You will leave next week."

Having delivered the sad and painful message, her parents got up from the table, turned their backs on their oldest daughter, and walked away.

With those words, young Marile Häusl's world changed forever.

The next week was difficult for Marile. Her sisters Bette and Rosie were not told why their older sister was leaving, but they sensed their parents' obvious rejection of Marile.

"I'm just going away for a short while," Marile told Bette. "I'll be back soon," she lied. In fact, she was unsure when and if she would be welcomed back. At work only Kuni had an idea of what was happening. Captain Greene had been informed that the young woman, one of his best staff members, was leaving. He made sure the department presented Marile with an official commendation for the work she had done in the department going back to well before the war had ended. On her last day he told her he was sorry to lose her and wished her well.

DACHAU CONCENTRATION CAMP, MARCH 1947

While Marile Häusl was preparing herself for her new life in Bad Reichenhall, the Americans had been preparing war crime cases against the SS and other personnel who had run the so-called Mühldorf concentration camp group. Fourteen defendants had been named, including Franz Auer, the procurer of slave laborers for the camp, which included Waldlager IV and V, Thalheim, Mittergars, and Gendorf. In addition, eight SS personnel, three Organisation Todt (OT) personnel, and three civilian employees of Polensky and Zollner (PZ) were to go on trial, which was to take place at the Dachau concentration camp site.

MÜHLDORF/BAD REICHENHALL, GERMANY, APRIL 1947

With a suitcase and a barely perceptible "bump," Marile Häusl waited at the Mühldorf *bahnhof* for the train that would take her to Bad Reichenhall. Only her father was there to see her off. Ludwig looked snappy in his dark-blue railroad uniform, now stripped of its symbols of the Nazi era. He stood with his daughter, his heart heavy, a tear in his eye. He did not hug her nor show any sign of affection. The train arrived and squealed to a halt. He had dreaded this moment for the last few days and often wondered if he and Maria were being too harsh on their daughter, but Maria was steadfast in her determination to send her daughter away, something to which Ludwig had reluctantly agreed.

Ludwig lifted the suitcase to the conductor and helped his eldest daughter up the stairway of the car. Marile turned to face her father, but he had already walked away. Leaving his precious Marile that day was the hardest thing he had ever had to do.

With tears in her eyes, Marile made her way to an empty seat by a window. The conductor stowed away her suitcase and asked, "Are you well, Fraulein?"

Quickly wiping her eyes, she said, "Yes, thank you."

"Do you have your ticket?" he asked.

Marile fumbled around, found it, and gave it to the conductor.

"Ah, Bad Reichenhall," he noted. "Very nice this time of year. Are you visiting family?"

Not wanting to explain her exile, she simply answered, "Yes."

The conductor smiled and moved through the train and soon disappeared into the next car.

The train traveled through the beautiful Bavarian countryside, but Marile stared unseeingly through her window. After an hour or so, the conductor tapped Marile on the shoulder. "Fraulein, you must change trains." He helped Marile with her suitcase, and she carefully deboarded the train. "It will be along in thirty minutes," said the conductor with a concerned look on his face.

Marile sat down on the bench on the platform. Things were happening very quickly, and she thought about what to do next. She liked Frau Gruenburger and was thankful that at least she had a friend in Bad Reichenhall. She could not believe her parents had sent her away and hadn't yet realized the extreme consequences of her relationship with Simon. Now she was an outcast from her family. She hoped the letter she sent to Simon at his Mühldorf Stadtplatz address had reached him, but she wasn't sure how he would react. She still had feelings for him but sorely needed some kind of reassurance from him.

The train arrived and she boarded. Again, the conductor was helpful but not as talkative. She settled in for the last few kilometers to what awaited her.

As the train pulled into the station, Marile saw Paula Gruenburger waiting on the platform. Apparently, her parents got word to the woman to meet their estranged daughter at the station. The train lurched to a stop with the usual squeal. "Bad Reichenhall," sang the conductor as he moved to help Marile with her suitcase.

The gray-haired, matronly woman approached Marile as she deboarded the train. "My God, girl, what have you done?" asked Paula Gruenburger, a serious look on her wrinkled face. The young woman's anxiety grew as she fought back tears. The seconds ticked by, but her anxiety was quickly allayed as a mischievous smile broke out on the older woman's face.

"Come on, come on, my dear. It will be fine. We have been expecting you, and you are very welcome here."

The Häusls had previously contacted Frau Gruenburger and explained the situation. They wanted their daughter away from Mühldorf to have the baby. They feared the child's father was a Jew and hoped something could be worked out after the child was born. They would have to wait and see. Perhaps they could hide her from the Jew. In the meantime, they had provided some money to pay for food and lodging.

The pair walked from the station to the Gruenburgers' small hotel. It was approaching evening as the sun began to set behind the breathtaking Bavarian Alps.

MÜHLDORF, GERMANY, APRIL 1947

Simon Ruder had returned from a trip to Munich to find a letter from Marile. He hadn't seen the young woman for several weeks and was anxiously anticipating their next meeting. He thought their relationship was blossoming and was looking forward to a future with her. He hoped her mother's attitude toward him had changed but had no reason to be optimistic. He climbed the stairs to his second-floor apartment at Stadplatz 44, unlocked the door, entered his rooms, and with a sigh, sat down in his favorite chair. He looked around the room. The half-finished suit still draped the sewing dummy. He would have to hurry to finish it soon. He wondered if he should open the letter now or wait. He was tired after a long day and wanted to clean up, but curiosity and the desire to hear from his beloved Marile took precedence. He looked at the envelope closely and noticed it had come from Bad Reichenhall. He thought that was strange and, suddenly worried, tore open the envelope and slowly read its contents.

"*Oy gevalt, oy gevalt,*" he exclaimed, reverting back to Yiddish. Panic rose and he had trouble breathing. His mouth went dry. He threw the letter to the floor and paced the room, mumbling her name over and over. After a time, he bent down to retrieve the letter. He held it as if it were aflame.

After a schnapps, or two, he calmed down, rubbed his eyes, and thought about what the letter had said and tried to determine what it meant for his future, for their future. He had learned she was pregnant with his child. That complicated matters, but while surprised, he was not unhappy. He learned her parents were terribly upset and that she was in Bad Reichenhall, probably because her diabolical mother wanted to spirit her away and hide her, especially from him. The child would be born sometime in September. After that, she didn't know what would happen. She also asked him not to contact her until she got settled.

A child, he thought. Visions of Anna and little Artur intruded into his consciousness. He thought of Lola. All gone, another lifetime ago, or so it seemed. They would understand. At least he hoped so.

After a night of pitiful sleep, he was determined to send word to Marile, to let her know he still cared for her and the child that grew within her. Simon considered the child a rebirth of sorts, a reaffirmation of his humanity, the final step in a long and painful ascent out of the hell he had endured for almost four years.

Later the next day Simon composed a passionate letter, confirming his love for Marile and for the child and promising his financial support. When he was satisfied with what he had written, he realized he didn't know where Marile was staying in Bad Reichenhall and wasn't sure why she hadn't mention it in the letter. That little detail did not stop Simon, however. He made the trip to Bad Reichenhall and asked around for the Gruenburger place and soon learned its location. He left on the next train, barely able to fight the intense desire to barge in on Marile.

He carefully reviewed the letter, made a few changes, and mailed it from the Mühldorf post office the next morning. Ironically, Maria Häusl, who worked at the post office and who had sent her daughter into exile, noticed a letter addressed to Marile in Bad Reichenhall. She looked around and hid the letter in her coat. She knew she would not be happy with its contents.

In Bad Reichenhall, Marile had settled in the small room in the Gruenburger home. She liked Frau Gruenburger and her husband. They were so unlike her parents, especially her mother, and she began to feel more comfortable with her surroundings. Puzzling her, however, she had not heard from Simon and wondered if he had gotten her hastily written letter. Or had he forgotten her.

That thought dragged on her mind, and in spite of the Gruenburgers, she felt alone and abandoned.

Simon was getting worried. He had not heard a word from Marile and was hoping, praying, she hadn't forgotten him or that her mother hadn't somehow discovered their relationship. He was in Munich on business when he composed his next letter. He repeated his declaration of love for her and asked why she hadn't responded. He mailed the letter while in Munich before he returned to his Mühldorf apartment.

"Marile, you have a letter," shouted Paula Gruenburger. "It's from Munich."

Marile wondered who it could be from. She had no friends in Munich, a much bigger city than her Mühldorf. Taking the letter from Paula, she immediately recognized the handwriting. She tried unsuccessfully not to look surprised or anxious as she excused herself and went to her room.

She read Simon's ardent letter. To her relief, Simon had not forgotten her; in fact, he still professed his love for her and the child she was carrying. His words comforted her. At least he still cared and hadn't abandoned her. However, when Marile learned about Simon's first letter that was never received, she became alarmed. Her mother worked at the post office, and if what she feared had happened, her mother now knew the full extent of the relationship, including the identity of the father of her child. That would be a disaster.

"Is everything all right?" asked Paula, sticking her head in the doorway.

"Paula, there is something I must tell you. Come in and sit down."

The older woman sat down on the bed next to her young guest. "Yes, my dear. I wondered when we would talk."

Marile began her story, leaving out very little. Paula listened intently without interrupting. She showed no surprise and made no judgments, for which Marile was thankful. Unlike her mother, Frau Gruenburger and her husband seemed to bear no particular animosity toward the Jews. In the resort town of Bad Reichenhall, Jews had been frequent guests until 1939. Paula remembered many Jewish families from Munich enjoying the facilities of the town and nearby Salzburg. But that was before the war, and much had changed. She did not expect many of the old guests to return.

"So the father is Jewish," began Paula. "What's he like?"

Marile sighed. "I've only known him since late 1945 when he was sick in the Mühldorf hospital. He's very smart, very kind, not anything like I was taught to believe about the Jews. We started as friends, and one day, you know."

Paula smiled. "Yes, I know. But now I understand why your parents sent you away." She paused, looking at the letter on the bed. "So what news comes from your Simon?"

"He is very worried and upset. He is probably worried that my mother fears he is the father. I'm not sure they know, but if they do...."

"So what does this Simon tell you?"

"He is happy about the baby and says he will send money to support us. Beyond that, I think he wants to get married, but I don't know. It's so complicated. They don't like Jews, especially my mother. She would never accept Simon." Paula smiled understandingly.

"He says he wants to come here to see me. I'd like you to meet him."

Paula took a moment to mull this over. "All in good time, little Marile. I think it's too early right now. If he is your friend, I would love to meet him. He sounds very kind."

Throughout the next few months, Simon visited his dear Marile several times. The Gruenburgers were at first surprised at Simon's age, some twenty-one years older than Marile, but as they became better acquainted with him, his charm and charisma won them over. True to his word, Simon sent money every month to pay for Marile's stay at the Gruenburgers' home.

In August, as the delivery date approached, Paula Gruenburger decided it was time to finalize the arrangements with the nearby St. Zeno convent where Marile was to have the child.

DACHAU CONCENTRATION CAMP, MAY 1947

On May 13, the court announced its findings and related sentences. Two defendants were acquitted. Five were found guilty and sentenced to death. Among them was Franz Auer, who had been responsible for procuring the slave laborers to feed the death machine located around the quiet town of Mühldorf. The remaining defendants were found guilty and were given sentences from fifteen years to life. The death sentences were later commuted to life sentences, except for Auer, who would be hanged at War Prison Number One in Landsberg, Germany.

BAD REICHENHALL, GERMANY, SEPTEMBER 1947

As dust motes danced in the light shafts slanting through the convent window and the last gold, purple, and orange rays faded behind the majestic Bavarian Alps, Marile Häusl gave birth to a baby boy. It was a short, easy labor on this Sunday, the seventh day of September. A good omen, she thought. Surely this child would be special. A tired nineteen-year-old Marile held the small bundle to her breast. She named him Rudolf after no particular family member. The sisters scurried about in quiet dignity, caring for the mother and her new infant.

The young mother rested for a few days, during which time she had no visitors. Paula Gruenburger came by soon thereafter to visit her young charge. Marile was asleep. Paula gently tapped her on the shoulder. "Hello, Marile, how are you feeling today?"

Blinking the sleep away, Marile focused on Paula, and after a short pause, she said, "I'm well, but a little tired." She looked around. "Where's little Rudy, where is my son?"

A sister entered the room with the baby in her arms and gently placed the infant in Marile's waiting arms. Paula smiled and stroked Marile's hair. She cooed over the little boy, nicknamed Rudy.

Taking a deep breath, Paula said, "Marile, you are to stay here for a few months. I will come by to see you and give you news, but you are not to have any other visitors. I have not heard from your parents, but I've sent them a letter notifying them of the birth of their grandson."

"Thank you, Paula. Have you heard from anyone else?"

"Not yet, but I suspect I will," she said knowingly. "You get some rest. I'll be back in a few days. Tell the sisters if you need me. They will come to get me."

Simon did not know about the convent when he left Mühldorf and traveled to Bad Reichenhall to see Marile. Upon arrival, he quickly made his way to the Gruenburger home. He was nervous. He could count to nine as well as anyone and was concerned he had not yet heard any news of the impending birth.

"Good day, Frau Gruenburger," he announced on her doorstep. "I have a little present for Marile."

"And a good day to you too, Herr Ruder. Please come in. I'm glad you came. We must talk. I have news."

Simon took off his hat and entered the home. Paula motioned him to sit. "Would you like some coffee?"

"Yes, please. That would be good." He knew only too well the cost of coffee and nervously wondered what manner of special occasion this would be.

Simon took the offered coffee. He blew on it and took a careful sip. "Ah," he said. "Thank you," and awaited the news. Paula sat down, aware of the man's barely concealed tenseness.

"We have good news, Simon. Marile has given birth to a healthy baby boy. She and the child are well. They are resting at a convent."

Simon was visibly relieved. "A convent? Which convent? May I see her and my son?"

"Simon, I…we think it best that you allow Marile time to recover. This has been a difficult ordeal for her."

Simon considered this. "Does the child have a name?"

"Yes, Marile has named the child Rudolf."

Though Simon heard Paula say Rudolf, he thought in terms of a Hebrew name, Rueven, a good Hebrew name, firstborn son of Jacob and Leah and father of one of the twelve tribes of Israel. In Hebrew, it meant "Look, a son." He marveled at the appropriateness of this. Unfortunately, it was not at all what Marile had in mind.

Again, he asked, "When can I see her? When can I see my son?"

"All in good time. We must give Marile time to recover and time to think. You must be patient."

In spite of Paula's assurances, Simon was suddenly plagued by doubts and fears. His stomach knotted. Time to think? Think of what? He feared the child would be taken away from Marile at the convent. He feared that now that she had given birth, Marile would be spirited away, and he would never see her again. He realized he still faced an uphill battle on his quest to create his new family and their future.

"Thank you, Frau Gruenburger. I will check with you in a few weeks. Please give Marile my love."

"I will, Herr Ruder. Please be patient. Marile is young, and she needs time." She took the package. "I will bring this to her. Thank you. Good-bye."

Simon turned and left the house, disappointed but not discouraged. He walked briskly to the *bahnhof* and waited for the train that would take him back to Mühldorf. He still had suits to finish and products to sell. All part of a plan—one that would take a bit longer than he had anticipated. Marile, he hoped, would be the central part of it. He knew what he had to do.

AMPFING, GERMANY, SEPTEMBER 1947

The rabbi was aghast. "Impossible!" he exclaimed, pounding his fist on the small table to add emphasis to his statement. The pair sat in the rear of the small synagogue in Ampfing, Germany. "Are you mad? This is inadvisable. I cannot be part of this."

Simon sat across from the small, intense holy man, watching his face redden. "Please Rabbi, let me explain."

"There can be no explanation. Simon, you are a member of this congregation. You helped rebuild the temple, for which I am grateful. But you were a victim of the Nazi oppressors like all of us. They killed your wife, your children, and more than likely, your parents. How can you possibly think about marrying one of *them*?"

Simon shrugged at the all-too-familiar tirade. "She is a good woman, Rabbi."

"Bah, a woman, indeed. I understand she is but nineteen."

"Twenty," corrected Simon, as if it would make a difference to the rabbi.

"What?" asked the rabbi. "Never mind."

"Rabbi, I love her. She has borne my son. I must do what is right and honorable. If I cannot get your blessing, I then ask for your permission."

The rabbi closed his eyes, lapsing into pensiveness. After a pause, he said, "You realize this will be difficult for both of you. I think more so for her. Our customs are different. She has grown up in a poisonous society. The

Hitler Youth. We know what they taught their children about Jews. The *Untermenschen*, they call us. Subhuman. How can she overcome this, the very fabric of her upbringing?" Silence, as both men realized the question was rhetorical, neither having nor deserving an answer. The silence persisted for several more heartbeats that seemed like an eternity to Simon.

The rabbi looked across the table at Simon and sighed. "Does she care for you? Does she love you?"

"I believe so, Rabbi."

"Will she make the deep commitment required to a complete a conversion? Will she learn and accept our ways? Does she possess the dedication essential to become one of us? Does she really understand what will be expected of her?"

"I hope so, Rabbi. But I must know the way is open to her should she accept."

"Simon, you know one does not become a Jew by merely declaring he or she is a Jew. This will be a difficult, rigorous process. She must convince three elders of her sincerity to become one of us. Myself, I am not so sure. But, Simon, if this is truly what you want and she completes her conversion, I will consider it a sign from God, and who I am I to question that?"

"Thank you, Rabbi," said Simon as he started to realize the immense challenges that lay ahead on the path upon which he had just placed his first steps.

BAD REICHENHALL, GERMANY, NOVEMBER 1947

A letter arrived from Mühldorf addressed to Frau Paula Gruenburger. The woman opened the letter. It was from Ludwig Häusl and bore bad news. It announced the death of Maria's Häusl's son Alois Kiermeier on November 1, finally succumbing to his wartime wounds.

Paula dreaded telling Marile the bad news but realized there was nothing to gain by delaying, and she soon made her way to the convent. Marile smiled as Paula entered her room. Paula did not smile back, and Marile sensed something amiss.

"Marile. I have some news." Paula paused, then sighed. "Your brother Alois has died from his wounds. I'm so sorry."

Marile was shocked and despondent by the news. Alois, her half brother, had been her favorite, and now he, too, was gone, as were her uncles, Leonhard and Max. A myriad of emotions played out in her heart and her mind. The war had been over for two years, yet the damage, both physical and emotional, was still evident. She wondered about Donei, her young friend who had yet to return. Hope was fading as no word on his fate had been received from the government. So many people gone. Her half brother and uncles. Her friends at the church. Was it all worth it? Ugly thoughts intruded. She thought of Simon. Angrily, she wondered if he and his people were the real cause of the pain that had been inflicted on her Germany. Slowly, however, the anger faded, and she realized it was frustration turning her thoughts in that destructive direction.

Yet these thoughts worried her, and she wondered why she was so quick to cast blame. She understood Simon was a victim, as were his people. She looked at little Rudy happily gurgling at her side and smiled. It helped.

As Marile left the convent at the end of November, the sisters wished her well. They were unaware of the identity of the father, and Marile had often wondered if that made a difference. It was an interesting question, one to which she would never know the answer. Happy to finally leave the confines of the convent, she returned to the Gruenburger house. Simon had continued to provide money to the Gruenburgers, and Paula was happy to have the young woman and her child staying with them, at least until things could be sorted out.

BAVARIA, GERMANY, DECEMBER 1947

Simon Ruder dreaded this time of year. The Jewish holiday of Chanukkah was approaching on the eighth of the month and went on for eight days. It was called "the festival of lights," a time for family, and it inevitably brought back memories he had hoped to lock away in some far corner of his mind. Not to forget. No, he would never forget, but he wanted to remember in his own time, not be so painfully reminded by the coming holiday. Memories of Anna came unbidden, the girl laughing when her mother lit the candles, one more each day. Little Artur, not understanding the significance of the ceremony, giggled with delight, especially when all the candles blazed. Little gifts were presented to the children. It was hard to believe that was only eight years ago, in another lifetime, it seemed.

While he attended the small synagogue in Ampfing, he did not celebrate the holiday at home. He did not even have a Chanukkah candelabrum, called a *menorah*, in his Mühldorf apartment.

His thoughts shifted. He thought of Marile in Bad Reichenhall and their infant son Rudy. He had not seen Marile since before the birth and had not yet seen his son and feared that he never would. He prayed to God, but would God understand? His Jewish friends certainly didn't, and this continued to be a source of frustration and friction, but he knew what he had to do.

Putting the holiday behind him, Simon vigorously conducted his business activities in Mühldorf, Munich, and Ampfing, but his fears over the future of his newborn son continued to haunt him. While he had been assured that he would be able to see the infant, so far that had yet to become a reality. He surmised Paula Gruenburger was stalling, perhaps with cooperation from Marile. He was worried and more determined to see his son, so in mid-December, Simon made another trip to Bad Reichenhall. This time, he would not be put off. He would see his son.

"Herr Ruder," said the surprised Paula as she answered the door. "So nice to see you," she continued, lacking sincerity. "Come in, please. It's cold outside."

Simon stepped into the house and looked around.

"I assume you came to see Marile. I'm not sure she is up to visitors right now."

Simon had been readying himself for the expected excuses and was about to protest as Marile made her way down the stairs. Simon turned his gaze toward the young woman. His heart soared, and he quickly met her at the bottom of the stairway.

"Marile. I have missed you so. How are you? How is our son?"

Marile looked over to Paula, who merely shrugged as the young woman considered her answer.

"I am well, Simon. Thank you for asking. Little Rudy is well also. He is growing."

Simon took a deep breath. "May I see my son?"

Paula was about to speak, but Marile interrupted. "Yes, Simon. It is time. Please follow me."

Against her better judgment, Paula acquiesced. "Follow us, Herr Simon."

Simon followed the two women upstairs into what had been set up as a nursery of sorts. Simon walked up to a small crib and finally saw his new son. Just over three months old, Simon thought the baby boy was beautiful, a miracle. Tears clouded his eyes. He recalled the close calls with death he had encountered. Had the good Dr. Mengele not inadvertently herded him into the other line at the Auschwitz train platform, he surely would not be standing here now. Had he been a step slower on the frantic midwinter death march from Auschwitz, he might have been just another corpse littering the trail in the snow. Had the uncharacteristically sympathetic SS guard Lichtner not saved his life, this scene would never have happened. As Simon peered at the infant, an image of Artur superimposed itself on the visage of young Rudy. How ironic, he thought. From Lemberg to Bad Reichenhall. Quite a journey. A miracle indeed.

Simon looked at the two women. They nodded in unison, and he picked up his new son. The infant made happy noises and Simon kissed him, and in that instant, he made a vow to God and himself that he would see this child grow to adulthood. One woman smiled, a tear running down her cheek, the other, only managing a grin, was hoping they hadn't made a terrible mistake.

BAD REICHENHALL, GERMANY, DECEMBER 1947

It was Christmas in Bad Reichenhall, and the inhabitants of the snow-covered town celebrated the holiday with cheer and hope that a brighter future was in the offing. Paula Gruenburger, Marile Häusl, and her infant son Rudy attended a Christmas Eve mass. They sang on old song called *"Stille Nacht, Heilige Nacht,"* composed in 1818, just across the border near Salzburg, Austria. American soldiers across Germany were singing the English version called "Silent Night."

1948

It was a cool, sunny day in the Mühldorf area of Bavaria as the aftermath of the war continued to sort itself out. Food was becoming somewhat less problematic, though still rationed. Private businesses were being opened, and more consumer goods were becoming available. Postwar politics raged as the American Military Government debated over how, when, and to whom the new German government should be entrusted.

It was into this cauldron of postwar activity that Anton Becker found himself released from his three-year captivity in a Russian prisoner-of-war camp. A three-week journey by rail across the frigid vastness of Russia and through the Ukraine deposited him and several thousand other released prisoners into a defeated Germany. Gaunt and slightly limping, the twenty-three-year-old was not sure his own family would even recognize him after years of backbreaking hard labor for the hated Russian victors. At least he was alive. Two-thirds of the German POWs had perished, died of exposure or disease, or were simply executed.

A difficult transition awaited the young man, but he was anxious to begin. First, however, he needed to return home in Oberbergkirchen, near Mühldorf.

He and many of the released prisoners were transported by the Americans from the Russian-held border to Munich. Becker and a few others were sent on to Mühldorf. He was almost home. The final sixteen kilometers were courtesy of an American GI in a jeep. Becker thanked the soldier who had dropped him off on the edge of the small town, and he walked the last kilometer or so toward his home. As he walked through the small town, people stared at him as he passed by. A few thought they recognized him, but weren't sure. This couldn't be the proud nineteen-year-old youth who had left for the *Wehrmacht* four years ago, could it? He was dead, they thought, no word had reached them for almost four years. Becker moved on, not looking at the people looking at him. He approached the small farmhouse and saw his mother hanging wet clothes on a line in back of the house. He stared at her for some time, not saying a word. He thought she looked much the same as he remembered, but older. After a short time, she turned and noticed him standing there, staring at her. She dropped the oft-mended shirt as recognition set in.

"*Mein Gott!*" she exclaimed. "Donei, Donei. You are back!" Gertrude Becker ran to embrace her long-gone son. "We thought you were dead. We heard nothing except that you were captured. Now you are back."

The young man, too, had aged. His mother noted the gauntness, the wrinkles, and the slight limp. She let go of him, as if afraid she was hurting him. She had heard rumors of the treatment of German POWs in Russia. Most had spent time in Siberia, a favorite location, isolated and brutal. She could only imagine the suffering her son had endured. Becker would not volunteer details, and she knew better than to ask.

Anton Becker spent the next month resting and gaining strength and weight. He was healing physically, but Gertrude worried about the emotional state of her son. Slowly, however, Donei began to express an interest in what had happened in Germany during the preceding four years. He seemed to be looking forward, not back. He talked about becoming a forester again, a career he had imagined during his early years in the Hitler Youth. His thoughts drifted toward his childhood friend, Marile Häusl. She would be twenty now, a grown woman. He wondered what had happened to her during the years he was gone. As teenagers, they had talked about getting married one day, and while amused, their relatives had assumed they would eventually. The war had changed all that.

One morning Anton Becker was finishing a meal in the small kitchen of the farmhouse. Not sure he wanted to hear the answer, he nonetheless screwed up his courage and asked his mother, "Do you know what happened to Marile Häusl? I think I would like to see her. It's been four years, and we were good friends."

Gertrude Becker had been dreading the question she knew would eventually be asked. Though she truly didn't know the details, she had heard that young Marile Häusl had moved to Bad Reichenhall last year sometime. Rumors abounded about some scandal but had settled down since then.

"Donei," she began. "I don't know much about the circumstances, but we heard Marile is now living in Bad Reichenhall. I think she moved there last year. Beyond that, we know nothing."

Becker didn't believe it. He thought there was more but decided to let it go. "I was just curious. It is not important, Mother." But it was. He decided once he felt up to it, he would travel to nearby Mühldorf and visit the Häusls and find out about his friend Marile.

DEGGENDORF DP CAMP, GERMANY, MAY 1948

On a warm, cloudy day, Simon Ruder had to personally attend to a special delivery of black market items to the Deggendorf DP camp. While he had conducted business with his camp contact, Rubin Gelman, this would be his first visit to the camp proper. Simon's Ukrainian runner had returned from a previous delivery with a stack of so-called Deggendorf dollars, valid only at the camp, so he was determined to set that straight. Simon wondered at the wisdom of his decision to hire the Ukrainians, especially after having been swindled by them, but the relationship had worked out so far. To the Ukrainians, this was Germany, not their homeland, and it was a job.

These particular black market items, oranges, were scarce and hard to come by, and Simon wanted US dollars for his troubles. After disciplining the Ukrainian, he set off on the ninety-five-kilometer trip from Mühldorf north-east to the Deggendorf camp in his well-worn Adler. The oranges were safely hidden in the trunk of the car, and three hours later, Simon was at the camp entrance. After meeting Gelman, the two men quietly made their way toward the kitchen area of the camp. On the way, Simon noticed a group of adolescent boys in smart uniforms marching around the grounds. Gelman noticed Simon's interest in the group. "Those are troublemakers. They are from a group called Betar. From what I hear, it is a Revisionist Zionist movement for youth. They want to go to Israel. Maybe soon, they will. Good riddance." Simon continued watching the boys as he and Gelman finally reached the kitchen building.

"So, let's have them," demanded Gelman. "We are looking forward to enjoying them. We don't often get oranges."

"And you won't ever get them again if you keep passing off those worthless, what do you call them, Deggendorf dollars?"

Gelman laughed. "Is that why you came personally?"

"Of course. That idiot I sent didn't even know the difference. I want American dollars!"

"Simon, such a hard bargain."

"If you don't want them, I have other customers."

"No, no. I want them. Just wait, I have the dollars."

"Then get some more. You can have these, whatever they are," said Simon, sliding the stack of Deggendorf dollars over to Gelman. The man sighed deeply and left for a minute. Soon he returned with an envelope containing US dollars. Simon took the envelope and made a count of the contents. Smiling, he removed the hidden sack containing the two-dozen oranges and handed it to Gelman, who took a deep sniff of one of the oranges. "Ah," he said. Deal concluded, the men shook hands.

"Simon, why don't you join me in the dining area for a cup of coffee? The good stuff, may be some of yours. Something to eat too?"

Simon checked his watch. "Maybe for a few minutes. I have to get back to Mühldorf before dark."

The dining room was sparsely populated as Simon and Gelman sat down across from a small group of men who seemed to be having a heated discussion. Simon noticed one small, balding man frequently lifting his right hand to his ear as if trying to hear the discussion. He said something to the man seated next to him, nodded, and then rejoined the conversation. Simon recalled a similar scene played out countless times with his younger brother Mendel. Curiosity piqued, Simon looked at Gelman. "I'll be right back."

Simon tried to act inconspicuously as he walked over to the table where the group sat to get a better look at the small man. A look of surprise formed on his face.

"Mendel! Is that you?"

The small man heard something, a puzzled look on his face. The man next to him poked him and pointed toward Simon. Mendel turned slowly to come face-to-face with his older brother. He blinked several times until recognition registered on his face. "Simon!"

"Mendel. It's you. My God, you survived."

Soon after the surprise and shock of the reunion had subsided, the two brothers sat alone at a corner table wondering what to say, what to ask, and afraid of the answers. They had not seen each other for ten years.

Simon decided to break to silence. "Any news of your family? Zofia and your son. He must be, what, ten years old?"

Mendel shifted uncomfortably. "Dolek is fine. He is here with me. He is a strong boy."

Simon waited for more, but with his brother's continued silence, he understood.

Mendel finally cleared his throat. "Zofia is gone."

"I'm sorry to hear that."

"Thank you," said Mendel. "And you?"

"Lola and the children perished in Lemberg."

After a long pause, Simon changed the subject. "How long have you been here?"

"About two years. We are waiting for any word about our emigration application. Dolek and I want to go to Canada or the United States. It's very frustrating, and not many people have been able to leave. What about you?"

"I'm living in a town near Munich, Mühldorf. I have an auto chauffer business, and I do some tailoring, among other things."

Both men paused to consider what was happening. A silence hung in the air, and it became obvious that neither man was ready to tell his story, at least not yet. While the physical scars had mostly healed, the psychological wounds would never completely be restored. Simon understood this and had moved forward with his life. He thought his brother, too, needed to move on. He looked around at the room and the others seated at the nearby table. He knew Mendel couldn't be happy here, just as he had eschewed the Feldafing camp two years ago. Then, on the spur of the moment, he said, "Mendel, why don't you move to Mühldorf? I could help you get settled, maybe help with some money or a job."

Simon reached into his coat pocket. "Here, this is my address in Mühldorf. I think it would be good for you and your son to leave this place while you are waiting to leave Germany."

Before Mendel could respond, a young boy in a snappy uniform quickly entered the room, looked around, and ran toward the table at which Simon sat.

"Papa," said the boy, turning to Mendel while ignoring Simon. The boy had traces of blood on his face.

"Dolek, what happened?" an anxious Mendel asked his son.

"I got into a fight, Papa. Just like always." Mendel looked from his son to his older brother. Shaking his head, Mendel said, "Yes, Simon, this is Dolek." Hugging the boy, he said, "Dolek, this is your uncle Simon from Lemberg. You are too young to remember him. Go over and say hello."

Hesitatingly, the boy disengaged himself from his father's embrace and stepped over to Simon. "I'm glad to meet you, Uncle Simon," he said as the two formally met. Simon thought about his own son Artur who would have been the same age.

"Hello, Dolek. I'm very happy to meet you too."

Mendel decided that now was the time to bring up some good news. Mendel sighed. "At least Izak survived. I saw him in Lodz a few years ago, but I haven't heard from him since."

"Izak? You saw him? My God, that's wonderful. We must find him."

Mendel nodded. "Yes, I agree." Then, with a frown on his face, he scrutinized the blood on his son's cheek and nose and with a deep sigh said, "Simon, what you said before, I think you are right. We will make plans to leave this place."

OBERBERGKIRCHEN, GERMANY, MAY 1948

Two weeks later the weather turned sunny, and Anton Becker traveled by bicycle to nearby Mühldorf, some sixteen kilometers to the southeast, and made his way to the small farmhouse at Xaver-Rambold Strasse 7. He arrived in front of the farmhouse well before noon, but now, looking at the white-washed building, he suddenly had second thoughts about what he was about to do. Would the Häusls recognize him? Would he be welcome? He thought of Marile, her pretty face in his mind. She was fifteen when he had last seen her. He wanted to see her and would not give up easily.

Thus bolstered, he approached the front door of the small farmhouse and knocked solidly with a sense of confidence. He had met Frau Häusl several times as a youth and remembered being intimidated by her, especially by her stern manner. He waited patiently as he heard some muffled voices and what sounded like dishes being handled. A few minutes went by, but seemed like hours, and soon he could feel his confidence starting to evaporate. Suddenly, the door swung open, and he was face-to-face with the elder Maria.

She, too, had aged, much more than his mother, he thought. The woman looked up at him, recognition not quite illuminating her face. He was about to greet her when she finally said, "Anton Becker. Donei. Is that really you?"

"Yes, Frau Häusl. I'm finally back. How are you? How is Herr Häusl?"

"Come in, come in, Donei," said the woman. "We were fearing the worst, but it's good to see you."

Anton entered the farmhouse and was motioned to a small table in the kitchen. He sat down as Frau Häusl set a pot of tea boiling. Soon the pot whistled, and a cup of tea appeared in front of him. The woman prepared another cup and sat down. She looked at Anton, remembering the youngster and his friendship with her eldest daughter in happier days. "My husband Ludwig is fine," she began. Then, as her face contorted with sadness, she continued. "I'm sorry to say the rest of the news is not so good. My son Alois died last November from his wounds in the *Wehrmacht*."

"I'm sorry to hear that," said Anton. "He was like an older brother to me." He knew there was more and tried to prepare.

After a nod, she said, "My brothers Max and Leonhard also died in the war in 1944. Josef survived and is living in Oberbergkirchen."

Anton realized that much of the propaganda he had been subjected to in Russia, especially the glorious victory over Germany, had turned out to be implausibly true. He knew the German army was in retreat when he was captured in the summer of 1944, but the dimensions of the defeat were just beginning to sink in. Silence pervaded the room as the full impact of the news began to find purchase in his mind.

"My God," he exclaimed. "What a tragedy. So many lives." Frau Häusl simply nodded in agreement and waited for what was surely to come next.

After a suitable silence, Anton finally asked, "And where is Marile? How is she?"

The woman stared at the young man, her mind racing. What should she say, how much should she reveal? After some time, she began. "My daughter is no longer living with us. She has moved to Bad Reichenhall."

Anton digested the news. He noticed the reference to Marile was "my daughter," not using her name. That struck him as unusual and a bit ominous, and though he remembered Frau Häusl as not being particularly warm, he sensed this was somehow different, a much angrier or sad tone.

After sipping his tea to stall for more time, he asked, "Why did she move there? Did she get married?"

Frau Häusl let out a sardonic laugh. I wish, she thought, but caught herself. That would have been a bigger disaster if she had married the Jew.

"No, Anton, she is not married. She had a child, a boy almost eight months old. We thought it best that my daughter be sent away to have the infant."

Anton was shocked by the news but not surprised. His years in the Hitler Youth had taught him the duty to have as many children as possible. He knew this from conversations with Marile based on her teachings in the girls' Hitler Youth. Besides, he thought, everyone knew Frau Häusl's son Alois was born out of wedlock and he was accepted into the family. Yet, in spite of this logic, he felt a pang of jealousy.

"Who is the father?" he asked too quickly and too forcefully.

Though she knew the truth, she lied. "That is not known. We have not seen the child, though we heard it is a boy."

Anton merely shrugged at the implications he didn't want to consider. He took another sip of the tea as he considered how to respond.

Across the table, an idea began to form in Frau Häusl's mind. Perhaps the situation could be saved, or at least made tolerable, if the former relationship between her daughter and the young man sitting across from her could be rekindled. That could solve the issue with the child, and especially her Jewish problem, once and for all.

She saw the thoughts race across the face of the young man and knew this was her chance to put her plan in motion, so before he could respond, she began, "My daughter spoke of you often. When you didn't return from the war, we feared you were dead. She was anxiously waiting for you to return, but after a time, we assumed you were dead and sadly, moved on."

Anton considered her words. "My daughter" again, he noticed. She can't bring herself to say her name. It must really be bad. Still, he and Marile had been close, even pledging to get married someday. Those feelings had not been diminished. He had thought of Marile often, especially during his three-year Russian prisoner-of-war experience. If she was in trouble, he would try to help her.

"Frau Häusl, I would like to see your daughter. Can you tell me where she is in Bad Reichenhall?"

"I don't know if that's such a good idea, Anton," she began while thinking she had him.

"Please, I would really like to see her again. It's been four years since I saw her last."

After a long pause, she seemingly acquiesced. "She is living with Frau Gruenburger in Bad Reichenhall."

"Thank you for telling me and for the tea." The young man pushed his chair back, stood up, and headed for the door. "I must be going now. Thank you again."

Anton Becker then made his way back toward the town center and the *bahnhof* to inquire about train schedules to Bad Reichenhall.

Although dead to her parents, or so she thought, Marile Häusl was still very much alive. She had grown accustomed to living in Bad Reichenhall, first with the Gruenburgers, then for several months in the St. Zeno convent to give birth, then more recently back with the Gruenburgers. Still, she missed her parents and family, whom she hadn't seen in over a year. Yet she still refused to give up her baby, little Rudy, who was now eight months old. She had just turned twenty without word from her parents or celebration, although she received a small gift, a long letter, birthday wishes, and some money from Simon Ruder, the father of the child, who had made it clear that he wanted to marry Marile and support her and Rudy. The young woman had thus far resisted, not out any lack of love for the man, but because he was Jewish and had insisted that she convert to Judaism, a line she was not willing to cross. She understood that doing so and marrying this good man would forever alienate her from her parents, would certainly result in excommunication from her church, and would perhaps even cause her to lose her beloved Germany. There would be no going back. Paula Gruenburger had continued to give her support and counseling, hoping to find a way to reunite the family. The older woman had become a surrogate mother to Marile and had taken a liking to the infant child.

Having finished nursing the infant, Marile put him to bed for the night and went into the kitchen area where Paula was preparing dinner. Paula was a very good cook, skills she learned while running the hotel before the war. She and her husband planned to rebuild the hotel and try to make a go of it soon.

Paula looked up. "Hello, Marile. How are you feeling?"

"Very well, Frau Gruenburger. Maybe a bit tired. Is there anything I can do to help?" Paula smiled. "Why, yes, it would be helpful if you could peel those potatoes."

Marile promptly began washing and peeling the stack of potatoes. She wanted to help as much as she could to pay back the kindness of the Gruenburgers.

As Paula watched the young woman work, she remembered the little ten-year-old with the braids who had visited them almost exactly ten years ago, before the war. She remembered Marile's parents who had come along on the trip. She thought of her own son, Helmut, and his friend, Leonhard, Marile's uncle who had perished in the war. A bad ten years for Germany and the Germans. Hopefully, better times were ahead.

A few days later a visitor arrived at the Gruenburgers' home. Paula answered the door and regarded the nervous young man standing there. He was blond and handsome but had an all-too-familiar haunting look on his face. She surmised he had likely recently returned from the war, probably from Russia, but he appeared in reasonably good shape.

"Hello," he said. "My name is Anton Becker from Oberbergkirchen. I am a friend of Maria, ah, Marile Häusl from Mühldorf. Her mother said I could find her here."

Paula tried to hide her surprise. She knew the Häusls did not advertise their estranged daughter's whereabouts, so this had to be something different altogether.

"Herr Becker," Paula began, only to be interrupted.

"Please call me Donei. Everyone does."

"Donei, then. Marile is very tired. I will tell her you are here, but please give us some time. Could you come back in perhaps thirty minutes?"

"Yes, certainly. Thirty minutes then."

The young man left, a nervous smile on his face and a wildly hammering heart in his chest. He checked his watch and began walking around the resort town, appearing to take in the sights but not really noticing. He was dreading the thirty minutes, yet wishing the half hour would pass by quickly.

"Marile, Marile," exclaimed an excited Paula Gruenburger. "A visitor came for you. A handsome young man. He says he is from Oberbergkirchen and you two were friends before the war. He said his name is Donei. Becker I think he said."

Marile was stunned and speechless for a moment. Finally regaining her composure, she managed, "Oh my God, is he here now?"

"No, I told him to come back in thirty minutes. I wanted to check with you first. He should be back in thirty minutes. Do you want to see him, or should I send him away?"

"I don't know what to do. I haven't seen him in four years. I, we all thought he was dead. He was my best friend. We even talked about getting married after the war." The young woman shook her head. "I have made a real mess of things."

"Nonsense, Marile," said Paula. "You have no reason to think that way. You have a beautiful baby and a bright future ahead, as does our Germany. Go meet your friend. He seems like nice boy. Renew your friendship. He deserves that much after what he's undoubtedly been through."

Marile sighed. "Maybe you are right. I'll go get ready, but I'm very nervous."

A short time later a very anxious Anton Becker stood at the door and knocked. He had no idea what to expect but had imaged this scene many times in the last half hour. Paula Gruenburger answered the door. "Come in Ant... Donei. Marile will be right down. Please, sit down for minute. I'm sure this is not easy for you." The young man sat down, looking around at the room. The grandfather clock in the corner tick-tocked, softly breaking the silence. He heard a baby crying, then being shushed.

Marile Häusl took a deep breath and made her way to the stairway. Slowly making her way down the stairs, she tried to image how her friend would look now, four years after he had left for the war. At the bottom of the stairway, she turned and entered the small room where he and Paula stood. She looked at Anton and thought how much older he appeared, no longer the nineteen-year-old she had last seen. He saw Marile and smiled at her. He walked over to her and hugged her.

"Marile Häusl," he exclaimed. "You look wonderful. How are you?"

Before she could answer, the baby started crying. Anton turned his gaze toward the stairway. "Ah, I'll be right back," said Paula as she turned and climbed the stairs.

An awkward silence ensued, neither Anton nor Marile knowing what to say. Finally, Anton said, "I hear you have a child, a boy."

"Yes, he's a beautiful little boy, almost nine months old. His name is Rudolf. We call him Rudy."

"Come, let's sit down, Marile. Let's catch up."

Relieved, Marile sat down and looked at her childhood friend, noting the lines on his face and how much weight he appeared to have lost. "So, how are you, Donei? I'm so glad you are alive and well. We all thought you were dead. What happened to you?"

Anton thought about how to answer her question. He knew Marile's two uncles Max and Leonhard had been killed in Russia in 1944 and her half brother Alois had died last November from his battlefield wounds. Unlike them, he had been captured and had spent over three years in a Russian prisoner-of-war camp. How could he explain the suffering to his friend?

He sighed and began. "I was captured in June of 1944 and taken to a camp in Siberia. A terrible place. There were thousands of fellow prisoners, and we were made to do hard physical labor. It was miserable in the summer and unbearably cold in the winter. Many died. I never thought I would return to Germany, but one day a few thousand of us were sent on a truck and then a train westward. It took about three weeks. I returned about three weeks ago and came here as soon as I found out where you were. But enough about me. Tell me what has happened with you. I talked to your mother, and well, she acted very strangely when I asked about you. I sensed something was wrong."

Marile knew this was going to be difficult. "Come, Donei, let's go for a walk." She looked over at Paula, who was standing in a nearby doorway. The older woman nodded slightly.

Marile got up and, with Anton in tow, walked out into the bright Bavarian sunlight. It was a beautiful day, white-peaked mountains glistening in the distance and a few tourists taking in the sights. The young woman sighed. "Donei, my parents sent me here to have my baby. She pointed toward a building to the left. I stayed at the convent over there where the boy was born. The father is a very nice man I met several years ago, an *Israelitisch.*"

Anton tried unsuccessfully to hide his surprise. He had not heard the term before but understood this was the now politically correct term for *Jew.* An uncomfortable silence ensued as Marile waited for her friend to digest the news. Instead, he appeared to be choking on it.

Finally, he said, "I see," with a slight undertone of, if not outright, disgust, certainly a strong hint of disapproval. He remembered the teachings of his Hitler Youth training, especially the hatred of the Jews. How could his little Marile do this? A Jew, no less. Now he understood her mother's reaction to his questions. Marile was dead to her family. An outcast.

Marile remained silent, waiting for her childhood friend to react.

After a while, realizing the harshness of his statement, he tried to soften the mood. After all, this was still his childhood sweetheart whom he had pledged to marry one day. "Do you love him? Will you marry him?"

Marile tried to blink away her tears. It was very personal and complicated and she resented the intrusion, but she realized she owed him some sort of an answer. "I do care for him. He is very kind and supports little Rudy and me. As for marrying him, I don't know. That's all I can say. I, we all thought you were dead. Now I am very confused. I need time to think."

Anton nodded to himself. "I think we all do," he said as he turned away and headed back toward the train station.

Marile wanted to chase after her childhood friend but decided against it and instead made her way back to the Gruenburger house.

Paula was waiting. "How did it go?" she asked.

"Oh, Paula. I'm so confused. Donei and I were supposed to get married. Then he disappeared for four years. Now he's back, and he didn't seem very happy to see me. I still care about him, but things are so different now. He's different. He's not the carefree, happy boy I knew. I think the war changed him. Besides, Simon is trying so hard to convince me to marry him. I care for him very much, but I'm afraid that's impossible. If I marry him, I feel like I'm turning my back on my parents and my religion. I don't know if I can do that. At least I have little Rudy."

Like a mother hen, Paula Gruenburger hugged Marile and stroked her hair. "We will get through this somehow. You just take your time thinking about things. Your friend Donei will be back, I'm sure of that. He just needs some time to think about things. Remember, he just came back from the war."

The train trip back home was like a nightmare for Anton Becker. He was a mass of conflicting emotions. While he was away at war, his childhood friend Marile had grown into a beautiful young woman, and now she had a child by some Jew. A Jew! After all the Hitler Youth training and warnings about those people. Then he remembered. They are not really people. He was shocked and deeply disappointed. And he was angry. Mercifully, he soon dozed off as the train made its way back toward Mühldorf.

As he entered his home, his mother sensed something was wrong. "Donei, how was your trip? Did you see Marile?"

Donei said nothing as he walked into the kitchen and sat down at the small table. Head in his hands, he looked up at his mother. A concerned look on her face, she sat down across from her son and waited.

"Mother," he began. "Yes, I saw Marile. She is all grown up. She is as pretty as I imagined every day in the prison camp. Thoughts of her kept me alive, gave me hope, something to live for. Now she has a child."

"Donei, that's not the end of the world. It's no secret that her mother Maria had Alois before she married Ludwig. Why does that upset you so?"

Donei looked at his mother, his eyes red. "The father is a Jew, Mother. The father is a Jew."

Gertrude Becker sighed. So that was it. Now she understood the situation. She could imagine the outrage and embarrassment Maria Häusl felt and why Marile had been so suddenly spirited away. A silence hung over the small table as Donei and his mother tried to find words that could articulate their thoughts.

"Have you seen the child?"

"No, I heard the little bastard, but I didn't see him. I wonder if he has little horns?"

Gertrude felt the pain her son was feeling but didn't like the direction it was heading. Reaching over, she put her hand on his arm. "Donei, I understand how you are feeling, but you must not become bitter over this. Marile was your friend. I think maybe she still is. Maybe she made a mistake, or maybe she cares for the father. She is a grown woman, not the little girl you grew up with. I know it will be hard for you, but if you care for her, you must give her a chance." She patted her son's arm and rose from her chair and left the room. Donei sat there for a long time thinking about what his mother had said.

"A Jew," he kept repeating. "A Jew."

OBERBERGKIRCHEN, GERMANY, JUNE 1948

Anton Becker felt lost, adrift, and floundering. He had been back from his Russian captivity for three months but realized fitting into postwar Germany was proving much more difficult than he had ever imagined. He could not just step back into his prewar life. Too many things had changed. The bitter German defeat, the Americans running things, so many of his friends gone, but most disturbingly, his disenchantment with Marile was taking a particularly heavy toll on his outlook. He brooded around his mother's house in Oberbergkirchen and expressed little interest in moving forward.

Gertrude Becker was growing more concerned about her son and decided to take matters in her own hands.

"Donei," she began one afternoon. "Have you thought about finding a job? Maybe you could become a forester, just like you always wanted. I think that would be good for you."

Annoyed, Donei let out a sardonic laugh. "Mama, right now I don't know. Maybe soon, but not right now. I do think about it sometimes, but I have much on my mind. Maybe I will try next year."

Obviously frustrated, Gertrude tried a different approach. "It's Marile, isn't it? You've been preoccupied with what she's done, haven't you?"

Donei looked at his mother as if she'd slapped him. "What do you mean?" he asked accusingly. There was no answer. He sighed and after a long pause said, "Yes, I'm not happy. No one is. On one hand, I'm very sad to lose a good friend, but I can't find it in me to forgive her for what she has done."

Gertrude shook her head and looked at her son with a sharp eye. "Donei, what makes you think you have the right to forgive her? I'm not taking her side, but she made a decision and will have to live with it. There's no forgiving; either you accept the fact or you don't. If she is still your friend, maybe you should try to understand. I know you are hurt and you think she betrayed you. I remember the two of you growing up together. But you were gone for four years. None of us knew your fate and assumed the worst. We went on with our lives. We didn't forget you, but we moved on. Donei, you must move on as well. If you still care for Marile, go, try to make peace, not with her, but with yourself."

His mother's words were painful, but he sensed the truth in them. He nodded his head. "I don't like it, Mama, but I understand what you are saying. Maybe I should try to do as you suggest. I promise to think about it. Maybe...."

Gertrude smiled as she patted her son's arm and got up.

Slowly, Anton's sense of betrayal began to recede as old memories intruded and feelings of friendship and even protectiveness for Marile began to reemerge. Perhaps his mother was right after all. Perhaps there was hope yet, in spite of the circumstances that so alienated him.

BAD REICHENHALL, GERMANY, JULY 1948

Anton Becker traveled to Bad Reichenhall on a bright, sunny day, a multitude of thoughts flashing through his mind. As he watched the countryside passing by his window, he tried to order his thoughts into what he would say to Marile. He tried to anticipate how she would respond and have an answer at the ready.

Becker arrived in Bad Reichenhall and immediately made his way to the Gruenburger house. He knocked on the door quickly before his resolve weakened. Paula Gruenburger answered the door, and as if expecting the young man, bid him to enter.

"Good day, Anton. I assume you are here to see Marile."

"Yes, Frau Gruenburger. Is she here?"

"She is, but what is it you want?"

"I would like to talk to her. That's all. Maybe for just a few minutes."

At that moment, Marile descended the stairway holding the infant Rudy. She looked radiant, Donei thought. "Who is it, Paula?" asked Marile, looking toward the doorway. She was surprised to see her childhood friend standing there.

"Hello, Donei. How have you been?"

The young man tried unsuccessfully to recall, much less articulate, the thoughts in his head. He was speechless. Marile waited patiently for an answer, but Becker merely stared at the small infant in her arms, forgetting everything he had so carefully practiced. Marile put the baby down in his little crib and excused herself. "I will be right back," she said as she gave Paula a knowing look.

Paula smiled at Donei. "Would you like a cup of tea?" she asked.

"Yes, thank you. That would be very nice."

Paula left the room, and Donei could hear the kettle fill with water. From behind a wall, however, Paula watched the young man slowly, furtively move over next to the crib and bend down to examine the infant. She almost laughed aloud as Becker looked around and, thinking himself alone, felt little Rudy's forehead. Confused at first, she wondered at the man's strange actions. Momentarily, however, she realized he was feeling for what he must have assumed were horns. She was astonished at how the Nazi Jewish propaganda persisted, even after the war. Several more quick passes over the infant's head apparently convinced Becker that no horns would sprout from the baby's head. In fact, Becker was relieved that the infant appeared normal, even Aryan-like.

The whistle of the teakettle startled Becker out of his thoughts, and he quickly hustled back to his chair.

"Here we are," said Paula as she handed a steaming cup to the young man. "Be careful, it's very hot."

"Thank you, Frau Gruenburger," said Becker as he gently placed the cup on a saucer with a reassuring clack. After a moment, he picked up the cup and blew across the top and gingerly sipped. "Ah, chamomile."

At that moment, Marile returned. She had combed her luxurious dark-brown hair and had put on a fancy dress. Becker quickly clacked the cup back to its saucer. Mouth open, he gazed upon Marile as if she were a goddess. She favored his gaze with a radiant smile.

"Well, you two have much to talk about, and I must get busy with making dinner," said Paula, winking at Marile as she returned to the kitchen.

Marile checked on her infant son and, satisfied, took a seat across from Becker. "So why did you come, Donei?"

Becker struggled to retrieve his carefully constructed lines. After a pause, he somehow managed to find his voice.

"Marile," he started nervously. "I have been thinking. Thinking about us, how it was before the war. Remember how we promised each other, you know, to be married one day?"

"We were children, Donei. What did we know?"

"We knew how we felt about each other. Do you remember how we used to ride our bicycles into the woods to pick berries and mushrooms?"

Marile rolled her eyes but let the young man continue.

"I know much has changed." His head turned ever so slightly in the direction of the infant, now giggling happily and waving his tiny fists in the air. "The war really affected everyone. I was locked up in Russia, in Siberia. Those dirty, barbaric, illiterate Russians. Almost as bad as the Je—" Donei did not see Marile's eyes flash for the briefest second as he continued. "Well, very bad. Many of my fellow soldiers died. I don't know if I will ever get over that."

"Is that what you wanted to talk about, Donei?"

"No, no, Marile. I'm sorry. I wanted to talk about us." Becker tried to swallow in a dry throat and took a quick sip of the tea. "I'm going to apply for a job as a forester. Remember how we talked about that? Marile, when I get the job, I think we should get married. Just like we dreamed of. Like we promised each other. We will be happy, and you and little Rudy can come home again."

Marile's eyes glistened with tears. Becker came over and put his arm around her. "You will see, Marile. We will be so happy, the three of us."

"We'll see, Donei," said Marile as she got up and went over to the crib to pick up her son. "Anything is possible."

Becker looked at his watch. "I must be going. The train leaves soon." On his way to the door, he patted the infant on the head and hugged Marile. "Please think about what I said. I've always loved you, and now is our chance to be together forever."

A romantic notion, thought Marile, but it didn't feel quite right. Not yet.

"Donei, I do care for you. I always will, but I need time to think about this. It's not as simple as when we were younger. So much has changed." She subconsciously glanced over to the crib, Donei following her gaze.

"I understand," he said. "But I know it will be fine. The child will be ours. He is perfect, Marile. A beautiful baby."

"Thank you, Donei. Let's talk about this after I have a chance to think it through. Thank you for coming. I enjoyed seeing you again."

The young man got up to leave. "Good-bye, Marile. Good-bye, Frau Gruenburger. Thank you for the tea."

Both women heaved a sigh of relief as Anton Becker left.

Anton Becker returned home to Oberbergkirchen but soon found himself back in Mühldorf to speak to Marile's father Ludwig. As an engineer, Ludwig worked irregular hours, and Becker found him at home on this afternoon. The brisk, sixteen-kilometer bicycle ride gave the young man time to organize his thoughts and practice his speech to Marile's father. His arguments were perfect, his logic sound, or so he convinced himself. He parked his bicycle in front of the farmhouse and strode up to the door. Taking a deep breath, he knocked on the familiar door. Shortly, Ludwig Häusl answered. He was wearing his uniform trousers but not the jacket, apparently either coming home from or getting ready for work

"Good day, Herr Häusl," began Becker. "How are you and Frau Häusl?"

Ludwig eyed the young man. "Anton. I heard you had returned. We are well, thank you." A pause. "What do you want?"

Undeterred by the apparent bluntness of the question, Becker continued. "I would like to talk to you, Herr Häusl. It's very important."

"I'm on my way to work at the rail yard. I have much work to do today. Now is not a good time. What do you want to talk about?"

"Marile."

As if jolted, Ludwig turned his head toward the open doorway and looked into the house. All was quiet. He turned back toward the young man. "There is no Marile here. She is gone."

"Please, Herr Häusl. Please listen to me. I visited your daughter in Bad Reichenhall. She is well. I have seen her child." After a long pause, Becker screwed up his courage and said, "I want to marry her."

Ludwig sighed, wishing it could be so simple. "Becker, you must understand, she shamed us. We sent her away. She is no longer part of our family. Frau Häusl has practically disowned her daughter. You are a nice young man, and I know you were her friend, but I cannot give you my blessing. If you want to marry her, I cannot stop you, but I do not think Frau Häusl would welcome her back. You must understand this."

Becker frowned but persisted. "Maybe Frau Häusl will listen. After all, she told me where Marile was staying. Why would she do that if she didn't want me to see her? Perhaps something could be arranged. If you could just talk to her."

Surprised, Ludwig thought about what the young man had just revealed. He had been unaware of his wife's conversation with the young man and grew curious, if not suspicious. Perhaps her unyielding attitude could be softened. Maybe the young man had a point.

"Anton, I cannot promise you anything, but I will speak to Frau Häusl. Now, I must finish dressing and leave for work. Good day."

As the men went their separate ways, they both had much to think about. Ludwig Häusl, a loving father whose daughter had brought shame on the family, realized a glimmer of hope for a solution that might resolve or at least ameliorate the tragic situation with his daughter.

Pedaling back home, Anton Becker was euphoric and felt he had made great progress toward his goal. When he reached his mother's home in Oberbergkirchen, Gertrude noted her son's upbeat demeanor as soon as he entered.

"Hello, Donei. Where have you been?"

"I went to Mühldorf to see Herr Häusl. I wanted to talk to him about Marile."

"Did you see him?"

"Yes. He was on his way to work, but we talked for a few minutes before he had to leave. He was very polite, but he told me Marile is not welcome at their home. I think he was sad about that."

"Is that all you talked about?"

"I told him I wanted to marry Marile, just like we promised each other."

Not wanting to discourage her son, Gertrude tried not to sound negative. "How did he react?"

"He said there was nothing he could do to stop us, but Frau Häusl probably would not welcome her back. Mama, that is confusing to me because it was Frau Häusl who told me where to find Marile. Apparently, Herr Häusl didn't know that. What do you make of that?"

Gertrude considered that for moment, then said, "That sly old woman! Excuse me, Donei, but a thought just came to me."

Becker looked at his mother, a puzzled look on his face.

Gertrude gathered her thoughts and continued. "Have you really thought about this? Why are you so anxious to marry Marile?"

"Mama, we love each other. We promised to be married one day."

"Yes, but does she feel that way? What about the child?"

"I think she does. She said she needed some time to think. I know Marile will come around." He thought about the child. "Mama, the child is beautiful. Not Jewish-looking at all."

An interesting comment coming from her son, Gertrude thought. As if you could tell. The only Jews the inhabitants of Oberbergkirchen had probably ever seen were those poor souls on long marches to nearby work camps, and those were mostly emaciated walking skeletons in striped rags.

"Why do you say that, Donei? This thing about the baby not looking Jewish."

"You know. No one wants any Jews around here. If I must accept the child, I will, but he must never know he is half Jewish."

Gertrude understood her son's logic. She had heard that often Aryan-looking young Jewish children were sent to German families to be raised as Germans, the children never aware of their true origins. But those were the lucky ones; most were murdered along with their parents. Like most adult Germans, Gertrude Becker had been forced by the Americans to view firsthand the atrocities committed by her Third Reich. That was three years ago, and the gruesome images continued to haunt her. She wondered about her son's attitude about the Jews and the Russians but had been afraid to ask. Now she needed to know, especially after some of their recent conversations.

"I understand what you mean about the child, and I think I agree if it comes to that. But you seem to have some strong opinions about the Jews and Russians. I understand about the Russians, but the Jews?"

An incredulous look on his face, Becker glared at his mother. "Mama, everyone knows about the Jews. I learned all about them in my eight years in the Hitler Youth. My God, Mama, they caused all this. They are responsible for Germany losing the war, again, just like in the first war. Don't you know they pull the puppet strings across the world? That they are all Communists? Why did you ask me this question? You should know all about them. Mama, I hate them. We should have killed them all. They are *Untermenchen*, not even human!"

He thought of the child. "At least Marile gave the boy a nice German name so I don't have to change it. Don't worry, Mama, I examined the baby, and he has no horns. The superior German traits would not allow that."

Gertrude heaved a heavy sigh. "The Russians?"

A sardonic laugh escaped Becker's lips. "The Russians are pigs, but they defeated us. I know Marile's two uncles were killed fighting the Bolsheviks. The damn Jews again! Her half brother Alois died too. I liked him. The Russians treated us badly, made us work too hard. Many German prisoners of war died. I was fortunate to survive and be released after three years. As you can imagine, I hate the Russians too."

Ach, so full of hate, thought Gertrude, but she let it pass. Maybe it would fade with time.

"So what are your plans now?"

"I'm going to continue to convince Marile to get married. I'm hoping her parents agree. You will see. Everything will be fine."

MÜHLDORF, GERMANY, JULY 1948

A flicker of hope kindled in Ludwig Häusl's chest as he worked through his shift at the Mühldorf train yard. His wife Maria would be coming home from her post office job about the time he awoke in the morning. He needed to talk to her about what Anton Becker had revealed to him. My God, he thought. Maybe there was a way out of this complicated mess. He would always remember the heartbreak he had felt as he had turned his back on his daughter as she boarded the train to exile in Bad Reichenhall. That was the hardest thing he had ever done.

Ludwig arose early the next morning after a pitiful night's sleep. Maria Häusl had just come home from work and was tired.

"You're up early," she exclaimed to her husband.

"Maria, we need to talk."

"I'm tired, Ludwig. What is it? Can it wait?"

"No, it can't wait. I've been up most of the night thinking about something."

Annoyed, she said, "All right. What is it?"

"Maria," he began as he looked into his wife's vivid blue eyes. "Anton Becker, you remember young Donei, he came by yesterday. He told me he visited our daughter in Bad Reichenhall. I was shocked to learn that you had told him where she was. I thought we agreed no one was supposed to know this. Then he asked my permission to marry her. What do you know about all this?"

With difficulty, Maria suppressed an uncharacteristic smile. "Ludwig. The young man came by a few days ago. He was very polite and wanted to see his childhood friend. At first, I did not tell him where our daughter was, as we agreed, but then he pleaded with me. In the end, I relented and told him she was in Bad Reichenhall living with the Gruenburgers. I didn't think he would find her."

"I see. Well, he did find her. Now he thinks he wants to marry her. What do you think we should do?"

Maria thought about her own son Alois, who had also been born out of wedlock. Maybe she owed him something.

"I don't know," she lied. "Maybe we should see what develops. What did you tell him?"

"I agreed to discuss this with you, but I made no promises." There was a long pause as Ludwig debated if he should continue. Finally, he said, "Maybe this is a blessing in disguise. Perhaps this could turn out well after all."

As Maria turned her back to her husband, a sly grin formed on her face.

"Maybe, but I have to think about it."

BAD REICHENHALL, GERMANY, JULY 1948

"Marile, you are like a daughter to me. You know I want to see you happy. What does your heart tell you?"

"Paula, it tells me many things, but not very clearly. It would be so easy to marry Donei. That would solve a lot of problems, but may cause more, even worse ones in the future. It just doesn't feel right to me. I need more time to think."

"Take all the time you need, my dear. You are welcome here for as long as it takes. So what about Simon?"

"I do have feelings for him. He is the father of my son, and that means a lot to me. But it seems impossible. Yes, Simon wants to marry me. He is doing quite well with his businesses. He is charming, sweet, and very intelligent. He is also Jewish and would insist that I convert before he would marry me. Can you imagine that? Me, a good Catholic, turning into a Jew. My parents would never let me come back. Simon wants to leave Germany. But, Paula, I love Germany. There are so many things to consider. This just doesn't seem like a very good choice. But I do care for him very much."

"Is that all?"

"What do you mean?"

"You know."

"Yes, I saw what the Third Reich did to his people. I tried to forget what I saw, but it is impossible. I just can't shake feeling responsible, guilty, for the crimes of my people."

Simon visited Marile and his infant son several more times, each time pushing Marile toward making a decision on marriage. Each time Marile professed the need for more time. It was a big decision, she would say, one not made lightly. Of course Simon could guess her real reasons, but he would continue to persist. He was convinced God would make sure he would prevail.

Anton Becker also continued to visit Marile and her infant son. He became more tolerant of and even charmed by the little boy in spite of his initial reservations about the boy's origin. His desire to marry Marile continued to burn, and he resolved to bring his quest to a successful conclusion. Once again he found himself back in Bad Reichenhall.

"Marile, I think we should get married as soon as possible. I'm sure your parents would approve. We can move to Oberbergkirchen and live with my mother, at least for a while. I applied for a job as a forester, and I'm sure I will get it soon. Remember when we talked about it? When we talked about us? Now we can make all that come true. Please say yes, Marile."

Marile exhaled a deep sigh. "Donei. It's not so simple. There are other things to consider."

"What other things? There's nothing that can stop us."

Marile's gaze turned toward the infant.

"Oh, I see," said Becker, following her gaze. "But that's not a problem. I actually like the little boy. I can adopt him, give him my name, unlike...."

Marile understood Becker's meaning but resented the implication. Her half brother Alois had never taken the Häusl name, instead adopting the Kiermeier maiden name of his mother. Becker had meant it as a noble gesture, but it had the opposite effect.

Trying to ignore the comment, she said, "That's not it, Donei. Name or not, I will keep Rudy regardless of what happens."

Becker considered where the conversation was headed. "You mean the father? The Jew. I thought he was out of the picture, that he was gone."

"What ever gave you that impression? Simon is very supportive. He sends us money to stay here. He, he wants to marry me."

Becker's face contorted with barely suppressed shock and rage. "What are you saying, Marile? Are you actually considering marrying the Jew? It's bad enough that...." Becker realized what he was starting to say and with extreme effort managed not to.

"Donei, he is the father of my child, and that counts for something. Yes, I care about you, but I also care about him."

Having recovered from his initial shock, Becker tried another approach. Trying to sound understanding, he said, "Marile, I understand how you must feel. But we love each other too. Think of the boy. Do you want him to grow up half Jewish? How would he feel? Think of your parents. Would they be happy? Would they welcome you back? Of course not. You might even have to leave Germany. Is that what you really want?"

Marile had heard all this before. She and Paula had discussed these issues at great length. Simon had an understanding of the challenges but merely considered them obstacles to be surmounted, not dead ends. Marile wasn't so sure.

Becker moved over to Marile and put his arm around her. "Please, Marile. Listen to me. You know in your heart I'm right. We will be happy. It will be a new start for all of us. Forget about the Jew. He will bring you nothing but heartache and grief. Let him go, Marile. There is no place for him and what's left of his people in Germany. You know that."

Marile was overwhelmed and began to cry. She knew Becker was right and she would have to make a painful decision soon.

Marile looked at her childhood friend and former Hitler Youth colleague. "Maybe you are right."

Becker embraced the young woman. "I am sure of it, Marile."

The pair embraced for a few moments. Becker looked at his watch. "Marile, I must leave to catch the train. I love you and trust you will do what is required."

Marile merely nodded. As Becker left, he almost ran into Paula Gruenburger, who had just returned from doing her errands. "My God, what got into Donei? I've never seen him so excited."

"Sit down, Frau Gruenburger. I have something to tell you."

Anton Becker pedaled his bicycle back home to Oberbergkirchen in record time. His life was about to change, and he wanted to share the news with his mother.

As he arrived at the farmhouse, he literally threw down his bicycle and ran into the small building. "Mama, Mama! I have great news."

Gertrude Becker came out of the kitchen wiping her hands. "Donei, calm down. What is this great news? Did you get the job?"

"No, Mama, much better. Maybe you should sit down."

Gertrude waved her arm, as if dismissing the suggestion. "Just tell me."

"Mama, Marile Häusl has agreed to marry me."

Gertrude Becker sat down. "My God, Donei, do you understand what that means?"

"Yes, we both do. We discussed it for a long time. We even discussed the baby. The child need never know his true father. We will raise little Rudy as our own."

"Do Marile's parents know?"

"Not yet. Marile wants to tell them. We must wait until that happens. Marile was insistent."

"What about the father of the child?"

"Mama, I don't know, but Marile said she would take care of it. Hah, the Jew will certainly not be happy."

Gertrude finished drying her hands with the towel and wiped her eyes.

MÜHLDORF, GERMANY, JULY 1948

Simon Ruder became increasingly discouraged and wondered why God had not yet delivered Marile Häusl. He understood only too well that challenges remained, unsurmounted.

A letter arrived from Bad Reichenhall. He recognized the handwriting as Marile's. He remembered the last letter from the young woman informing him of the impending birth of their son and wondered what the contents of this letter would portend. His mind raced, and a sense of foreboding overcame him. He tried to remain calm and resist the temptation to tear open the envelope, and instead, he used a letter opener to retrieve the contents. He nervously unfolded the letter, and to his horror, realized his worst fears were being played out in Marile's carefully handwritten words. Her words repeated her feelings for him but explained the impossibility of a marriage between them. The obstacles were just too great to overcome, even for love. She reiterated her feelings and deep respect for him and thanked him for his kindness and the many things he had taught her. In closing, she mentioned that little Rudy would be adopted by her childhood friend whom she planned to marry.

Simon was devastated. He sat down and wept. "Why, Lord? Why? Haven't I been a good father? Haven't I suffered enough?"

He traveled to Ampfing to meet with the rabbi. "What can I do, Rabbi?"

Trying not to project an "I told you so" attitude, the old man said, "Simon, it must be God's will, and you must accept it. It is probably for the best."

Simon realized he was utterly alone in this quest. None of his Jewish friends supported this idea, and no genuine sympathy would be forthcoming. He was on his own.

Returning to his apartment in Mühldorf, Simon began to pen a letter pouring out his feelings and despair. He reaffirmed his love for Marile and the child, promising to be a good husband and father. He complained about Marile's mother, whom he surmised was the root of all of their problems. He asked how she could allow her mother to control her life so completely. He spoke of betrayal and how he would never allow his son to be raised by another man. He promised to make her happy and take her away from Germany.

What else could he say to convince her? Simon was and had always been a proud man. His faith and strength of character had helped him survive years of Nazi atrocities. While not trying to sound like a hapless victim, he ended the letter with a statement hinting that something was due him for his suffering and loss and hoped that perhaps interjecting a bit of guilt might help his cause.

Simon made several revisions to the letter and was finally satisfied with the message. Motivated mostly by a profound sense of urgency and in no small part distrust of the postal system, he drove to Bad Reichenhall and, unseen, delivered the letter directly to the Gruenburger home and left immediately.

BAD REICHENHALL, GERMANY, JULY 1948

Later that day Marile had the letter in her hand. While she was expecting a response to her letter, she was nonetheless apprehensive as she slowly opened the envelope and removed the contents. Her hands were shaking as she read Simon's impassioned writing. She reread the letter several times, tears blurring her vision so much she had to put the letter down on several occasions. Paula Gruenburger walked into the room, looked at Marile, and immediately surmised the situation.

"What does he say?" she asked quietly.

Marile picked up the letter and held it up for the older woman to retrieve. Paula took the letter from Marile's still shaking hands and slowly began to read it, soundlessly mouthing the words. With a sigh, she asked, "What will you do now?"

Eyes red, Marile tried to answer. "All I know is that I am hurting a good man, but what else can I do? I promised Donei we would get married. He was so sure it was the only proper thing to do, that it would solve a great many problems."

"For now, maybe yes. But are you sure? Tell me, Marile, what does your heart say to you?"

"Honestly, I'm not sure I have the luxury of following my heart. My head tells me marrying Donei is the right thing to do. I think he would make a good father for little Rudy."

Paula let out a sarcastic laugh. "You know, I saw your Donei examining your son. I think he was checking for horns. Can you imagine that?"

Another sardonic laugh, this time from Marile. "So did I right after he was born."

Both women chuckled at the thought.

Paula recovered first and asked, "How is Donei? Has he gotten used to being back home?"

"I don't think he's getting better. It's only been a few months. I hear many returning soldiers are having problems adjusting. He's still filled with a lot of hate, especially against the Jews." Marile looked around, and in a quiet voice, whispered, "I think it's the Hitler Youth training. I don't think he ever forgot it. In fact, I think it's worse now."

"I see, though I'm not surprised. What does surprise me is how he has taken to little Rudy. He seems to have gotten over the father being Jewish."

"I hope so. I thought he was going to have nothing to do with me when he first found out. I really don't know what changed."

"I'm glad it did, but I must tell you I feel very bad for Simon. He is a good man, and I know you still have feelings for him. It's just the wrong place and the wrong time."

"I know you are right, Paula. I must think with my head."

"I'm proud of you, Marile, and I'm sure your parents will be as well."

There was a pause as Paula considered how to phrase her question. "How will you handle Simon? I'm sure he will not just give up."

"I owe him an explanation, Paula. He is an honorable man, and I've learned a lot from him. I know I will never forget him."

Back in Mühldorf, Simon waited impatiently for any response from Marile. Surely she must have read his letter by now. He wondered if the rabbi had been right after all.

Maybe he should have stayed in Bad Reichenhall after he surreptitiously delivered his letter, but he knew that would have most likely ended disastrously.

While Marile was relieved to have made the decision to marry Anton Becker, she agonized over how to handle the situation with Simon. She thought back a few months ago when Simon had first seen his son and how happy he was. Now he would never see the boy grow up. She recalled the schmaltz and salami sandwich he had offered her and how horrified she was. Not funny at the time but somehow memorable now. Surprisingly, she remembered how he had taught her that the Jewish holiday of Chanukah was not the Jewish version of Christmas despite the timing and that Passover wasn't really the Jewish Easter, though there was a historical and religious connection. She began to understand how difficult this ending was going to be. She could take the coward's path. That would be the easiest way, and no one would blame her. But Simon deserved better than that. And, she realized, so did she. And while she wasn't sure exactly why, Marile decided that her parents could wait until she met with Simon. That evening Marile composed a short note to Simon.

For Anton Becker, the euphoria of Marile Häusl's promise to marry him quickly evolved into an impatience he could barely control. "Mama, what is taking her so long?" he asked Gertrude. "She tells me to be patient; she needs to take care of some things. What things?"

Gertrude shook her head. "Donei, she's right. You must be patient with her. She must have much on her mind. Has she told her parents yet? I haven't heard anything. Besides, what's the rush?"

"I don't think she's told her parents yet. I think she wants to take care of whatever it is she is so bent on doing first. I suppose there is no rush, but I'm just nervous, that's all, Mama. We always planned on getting married, and now, after the war, it's finally going to happen. Not exactly as we planned, but still, I'm happy. I just hope nothing goes wrong."

"What could possibly go wrong, Donei? You two were meant for each other. We always knew that."

"I don't know, Mama. As I said, I'm nervous. Marile and I talked a lot. She said I've changed."

Gertrude considered her son's comment. She, too, had noticed a change, and it worried her. The war was over, but he still seemed at war with the world, especially the Jews and Russians. "Well, with what you went through, I'm not surprised," she said, trying to comfort her son. She hoped his disparaging attitude would ameliorate quickly once he married Marile and finally got the forester job he so coveted.

A few days later Simon found a letter from Marile waiting for him at his Stadtplatz apartment. He certainly didn't like the last one and nervously wondered what the contents of this one boded for him. Though not optimistic, nonetheless he was glad he had waited before doing anything drastic. Maybe she'd had time to think about the situation, and though he realized he was at a disadvantage, he still held out hope. He calmly opened the envelope and read the short note. It said simply

Simon,
I feel I owe you an explanation. I would like to talk. If you could come to Bad Reichenhall, I will be waiting.
Marile

Not exactly what Simon was expecting, but at least it represented a slim glimmer of hope. He would travel to Bad Reichenhall the next day.

Anton Becker grew ever more uneasy about the situation with his marriage to Marile Häusl and determined the time was right to push things along, so on a cloudy morning, he found himself at the Mühldorf *bahnhof* waiting for the first train that would take him to Bad Reichenhall. Once on the train, he thought about the approach he would use to convince Marile that the wedding should take place as soon as possible. They were in love, and she would surely agree to move forward quickly. He could think of no reason to delay. Confident of the outcome, he drifted off into a nap and soon dreamed about how wonderful life would be with his childhood sweetheart.

On the same cloudy morning Simon Ruder was preparing to make the trip to Bad Reichenhall when he was delayed by a client asking about a new suit. The man, a Dr. Ernst Loske, lived in the same building and had learned of Simon's tailoring business. Though Simon was in a hurry, he nonetheless agreed to take the necessary measurements and quote a price to the doctor. The two men talked briefly and shook hands. Dr. Loske noticed Simon's old Adler and proudly pointed to a new vehicle parked outside. It was a new black Volkswagen. The doctor explained how fortunate he was to obtain one of these cars as postwar production had just recently begun. Simon made the perfunctory comments about the marvelousness of German engineering and suggested the two get together at a later time.

"I'm glad to meet you, Herr Ruder," said the doctor as he climbed into the small car and slowly drove away.

An hour behind his planned schedule, Simon finally made his way to Bad Reichenhall.

Anton Becker arrived in Bad Reichenhall shortly after noon and quickly made his way to the Gruenburger residence where he would surprise his fiancée Marile. This he accomplished to a degree he could not imagine. As he stood at the entranceway, Paula Gruenburger was barely able to hide the "What are you doing here?" look on her face as she answered the door. "Why, hello, Anton. How have you been?"

"Fine, Frau Gruenburger. Is Marile here?"

"Yes, she is upstairs. I'm afraid today is a busy day for her."

Taking note, but momentarily ignoring the statement, Becker said, "I must talk to her. It's important."

"Would you like to sit down, Anton? Marile should be down right away."

As Becker sat down on a comfortable chair, Marile walked into the room and made her way to Becker. He stood up, and as the pair embraced, Marile peered over Becker's shoulder as she and Paula exchanged worried looks. With a shrug, Paula left the room on some pretext to give the couple some privacy.

"Hello, Donei," said Marile, a contrived smile on her face. "What a surprise. I wasn't expecting you."

Becker's eyebrows furrowed. "Well, my little Marile," he began softly." I was thinking about our wedding and thought we should discuss when it will take place. We love each other, and I see no reason to delay."

"Soon, Donei, soon. Please be patient."

"Have you told your parents yet?"

Marile sighed. "No, Donei, not yet. I'm not ready right now. I have a few things I must do first. Then I will. I promise."

Anton Becker was a smart boy who had excelled in his Hitler Youth training, especially marching and taking orders. Like a sponge, he had readily absorbed the teachings and propaganda of the defeated Third Reich. Now, as an adult, he found there were few things at which he excelled, but unfortunately, quickly jumping to conclusions was at the top of his list. Sensing the tension between the two women and what he thought were continued excuses and evasions from Marile, he reacted. Driven by paranoia and fuelled by lingering hatred, Becker exploded.

"It's the goddamn Jew, isn't it? What does he want?" Becker's face reddened as he began to lose control. "Why can't he leave you alone? Haven't he and his people done enough damage?"

Marile was shocked by the outburst. She tried to calm Becker down, but he would have none of it.

"What does he want, Marile? Does he want the little bastard back? Fine, he can have him, German name and all."

Paula had been nearby, listening to the exchange. As the conversation became heated, she returned. Both women were shocked by the diatribe from the man who had so fervently professed his love for Marile. Her eyes flashed fiercely, displaying the intensity of emotion engendered by the hateful tirade. Too slowly, Becker realized the effect his outburst had caused as he tried to take a more reasonable approach.

"Be reasonable, Marile. Once we are married, all this will be long forgotten."

Marile now looked at her suitor with different eyes. "Will it?" Marile paused as she carefully considered her next words. "Go!" she exclaimed, pointing to the door.

Becker tried to protest, but the young woman was firm. "Just go, Donei. I don't want to see you right now."

Abashed, Becker tried to apologize but realized it was futile. "Good-bye, Marile. I hope I will see you soon. Good-bye, Frau Gruenburger." Head hung, his face contorted into a scowl, the young man muttered something as he left the home and headed back toward the *bahnhof.* In his disturbed state of mind, he did not take notice of an old Adler automobile that almost hit him and then stopped near the Gruenburger house.

Apparently awakened by the noise, little Rudy began to cry. Marile rushed upstairs to comfort her son. She picked him up and gently rocked him back and forth. "Don't worry, my sweet Rudy," she cooed. "You're not a little bastard."

Marile looked at her son and thought about his future. The infant looked back at his young mother as if he understood and smiled. In that instant, Marile experienced an epiphany. She realized that her betrothed, Anton Becker, could never be the father that she and her son needed and deserved. His deep-seated hatred had not fundamentally changed and would continually rear its ugly head during the pledged marriage. She understood that, to Becker, little Rudy's very existence would be a constant reminder of Germany's defeat and the people he blamed, a hurtful weapon that could be used to inflict emotional pain. She determined that would never be allowed to happen.

Outside, Simon sat in his car, his hands shaking on the wheel. The sun had finally appeared, and the rest of the day looked splendid. He looked in the mirror and laughed. *I look as bad as that young man who just ran past me*, he thought, recalling Becker's retreat from the Gruenburger house, but not realizing the irony. He wondered what Marile wanted to talk about, and on the drive down, he had carefully crafted a response for any conceivable turn of the discussion, or so he thought.

Realizing the potential impact on his future that could result from the events of the next hour, Simon took a deep breath, left the Adler, and nervously made his way toward the house. A few minutes later, standing in the doorway, he knocked. Paula answered the door. "Good afternoon, Herr Ruder," she said politely, looking around. "How have you been?"

"I've been well, thank you," Simon lied. "Is Marile here?"

"Yes, she's resting. Come in, I will get her."

Simon tried not to let his anxiety show as Marile entered the room. He noticed her red eyes and guessed she had been crying. He wondered if it was for him or because of him.

"Hello, Simon," she said. "I'm glad you came."

Simon walked over to her, and the pair embraced. On cue, Paula left the room, this time sans any pretext. Unsure of what was happening, Simon motioned over to the small couch.

"Please, Marile, sit down. We have much to talk about."

"I have a better idea," said Marile. "Let's go for a walk. I see the sun is finally out, and I could use fresh air. Paula will take care of the baby."

Surprised at the turn of events, Simon quickly agreed. "I have my car if you want to go somewhere."

"No, Simon, let's just walk."

Simon agreed, and the pair left the Gruenburger house and began walking in the bright sunshine. Simon noticed the sign first. A smile lit up his face. "I have an idea. Let's go on the *Predigtstuhlbahn*, the cable car up the mountain. I've never been there."

"Oh, Simon. A wonderful idea. It's so beautiful there."

Marile and Simon made their way to the base of the cable car station. The *Predigtstuhlbahn* had been in operation since 1928 and took the passengers in a cable on an eight-minute ride up the mountain to the mountain station some 1,614 meters away. As a young man, Simon had spent summers in the Carpathian Mountains in Rumania, south of Lemberg, but these Bavarian mountains had a different charm. The pair looked down at Bad Reichenhall as the cable car made its ascent to the top of the mountain. The scenery was breathtaking, and Marile enjoyed the ride every time she made the trip. Simon, however, almost regretted making the suggestion, but pushed aside the thought as he saw Marile's mood improve, though he was still apprehensive about the conversation he knew was coming. The car soon slowed and came to a swaying halt as it reached its terminus at the mountain station. Simon and Marile exited the car and slowly walked to an area where they could gaze out at the awesome panoramic view.

After a few moments of silence, Marile became pensive, but forged ahead. "Simon, you know I care deeply about you. I read your letter many times and thought hard and often about how a marriage could possibly work. I just don't know how it ever could." Then, borrowing a line she had heard from Paula Gruenburger, "It's just the wrong time and the wrong place." Gauging the impact, she continued. "Just think how unlikely our chance meeting was. In normal times, none of this would have happened."

Simon tried to embrace Marile, but she squirmed away. "I'm serious, Simon. I wish there was a way, I really do, but I don't think it's possible."

Simon looked out at the view as he collected his thoughts. He looked at the mother of his child. "What a beautiful view," he started, "but nowhere near as beautiful as my Marile." The young woman rolled her eyes, but they soon teared over as she looked away.

With a deep sigh, Simon continued. "My dear Marile, I agree with much of what you said. Our meeting was improbable and certainly would never have happened without the war, but I'm convinced it was for a purpose. I'm sure the Lord, yours and mine, meant for this to be. Otherwise, why would it be so difficult? Why would we be so tested? The important thing is that we did meet, and now we love each other. We have a beautiful child. This was all meant to be. You are my destiny, and I am yours."

Marile wiped the tears from her eyes. "But how would this work, Simon? My parents hate you. We are in Germany, the land I still love, and a land you are anxious to leave. And then, there is the religion…issue. Tell me how to make this situation work."

Simon let out a sardonic laugh, perhaps to lighten the mood, or because he was stalling for time. "A few obstacles, to be sure, but nothing our love can't conquer. As for your parents, I will try to talk to them, introduce them to our son. They won't be able to resist. I hope to get their blessing. There are two things that will be hard for you, but if your love is strong enough, I know you can do them."

Marile tried to prepare herself for what was coming. She had thought about these issues, and the moment of truth was about to unfold.

Sensing the import of the moment and trying his best to avoid sounding as though delivering an ultimatum, Simon began. "Marile, you know how much I love you. I have thought about this for many months, and this is what I feel is what we should do. First, the religion issue. I think little Rudy should be raised Jewish as his grandparents would want. That means you must convert. It will be an involved process, but I know you will be accepted. Then, after we are married, I think we should immigrate to the United States or Israel. We both know Germany is not the place for us, but I promise to make a good life for us wherever we go."

Well, there it is, thought Marile, and even though it was not unexpected, it was now out in the open, and she had hard choices to make.

"Simon, my dear Simon. I do love you dearly, and now I know the price I must pay, for myself, my people, and maybe for my country." Unforgotten, yet unbidden, images of her passage through the grisly camp three years earlier flashed through her mind, and she instinctively understood why. "Simon, this is the most important decision of my life. Give me a few days to think this through. I will send you my answer then."

The ride back down on the small cable car took on a somber mood, as Simon and Marile were each lost in their own thoughts. They made their way back to the Gruenburger home, where Paula met them at the doorway and, with a knowing look, said, "Good-bye, Herr Ruder. It was nice to see you."

"Thank you, Frau Gruenburger," and as he left, he said, "I hope to see you again."

Once back inside, Paula gave Marile a questioning look. "So, what happened?"

"Oh, Paula. I must make a very difficult decision. I'm afraid Donei helped me make it, or at least he helped make it a little easier." Marile shook her head and continued. "Donei is not the answer. I understand that, and though I'm saddened by the reality of it, I have accepted it. I know Simon loves me and little Rudy. He wants to marry me, but there are a few conditions that concern me."

Paula listened intently. "Of course, there always are."

"Simon wants to raise our son in the Jewish faith. That means I must convert. I suspected that, but now it's official. I don't know what I'm getting into, so it's a little frightening. Simon also wants to leave Germany. You can't blame him for that, I suppose. He wants to go to America or Israel. I don't want to go to Israel. I will not go there."

Paula rolled her eyes. "I can understand that."

"I also want a civil marriage ceremony. I want to invite my parents. Is that too much to ask?"

"No, no, my dear. I think that is perfectly reasonable, and if Simon loves you, he will surely agree. But the important thing is how do you feel about this Jewish thing? Is this what you really want?"

"Paula, I'm not sure at all. I would have never dreamed of becoming Jewish. None of us could have imagined it. I've learned a lot from Simon, and the Jews are not the evil people as we were taught, but they are so different. So are their customs. And then there's, well, you know, the Jesus thing."

Paula sighed deeply as she considered Marile's words. "In the end, Marile, do you love him enough to go through with this thing? That is the real question."

"Yes, I have come to love him. He is the father of my child, whom he loves. He says, given all that, everything else is merely a series of obstacles to be surmounted."

"A positive attitude, especially for someone who went through the horrors we learned about." Paula paused for a moment and looked into Marile's eyes. "But I think there is more you are not telling me."

"You know me too well." Marile paused, considering if she should reveal her deeper thoughts and feelings. "Paula, I keep seeing the images of the camp the Americans made us go through. It's been three years, and the ghastly images keep coming to me, and even though I had little to do with it, I feel guilty. Not just for Germany, but for me personally. I know it sounds ridiculous, but that's how I feel. Maybe marrying Simon will bring some redemption. Maybe that's my atonement. Or my punishment."

"Ah, Marile. If you consider this punishment, maybe it's the wrong thing to do. I think we all feel some level of responsibility for what was done. But we also paid with the lives of our sons, our uncles and fathers. That doesn't balance what history will record, but you can't take on this responsibility yourself."

"But that's how I feel, Paula."

"Well, it would be good for your son to grow up with his father, whatever faith. I think you should follow your heart."

"Thank you, Paula. I promised to give Simon an answer soon."

Driving back to Mühldorf, Simon reflected on the day's events. He realized that something happened to dramatically change the direction of the conversation with Marile, something that had changed both their lives. As to what it was, that was a sleeping dog he would gingerly tiptoe around, not wanting to wake. He arrived at his Stadtplatz apartment full of hope and promise for the future. Now he would wait.

As promised, Simon received his answer two days later. It read simply

Simon, my answer is yes, but I insist on two things. I assume you want a Jewish wedding, but I also want a civil wedding ceremony. We can be married here in Bad Reichenhall. Then, if I must leave Germany, I want to go to America. I will not go to Israel.
Marile

With that note, young Marile Häusl embarked on an inconceivable passage to become part of that which she had been taught to loathe.

Simon read the note several times to make sure he had not missed some important point or hidden meaning and concluded he had not. He considered Marile's requests and quickly decided they were merely accommodations he was happy to make. *So it was to be America*, he thought and made mental plans to change his emigration form.

Simon drove the short distance to the small synagogue in Ampfing to meet with the rabbi to discuss Marile's conversion. He found the rabbi's skepticism unchanged from his previous meeting.

"Good morning, Simon. How have you been?"

"I'm fine, Rabbi. I have good news. My Marile has agreed to marry me, and she has agreed to convert to our religion. When can we start the process?"

The rabbi looked intently at Simon. He shook his head but continued. "I told you it would not be easy for her. You may coach and teach her, but she must prove to us she is truly dedicated to becoming Jewish, that she is worthy to join us." The rabbi sighed. "She must really love you to do this, and I wish her well, but we will not shortcut the process. I know you are probably thinking of ways to do just that, but I will not allow it."

"I understand, Rabbi."

"Make sure you do, Simon," he chided.

"When can we start?"

The rabbi made a show of checking a calendar. "I will meet with your Marile in two days. What kind of name is Marile anyway?"

"It's her nickname. Her formal name is Maria."

"*Gevalt*," muttered the rabbi under his breath."

"What?" asked Simon.

The rabbi rolled his eyes and said, "Nothing."

If young Marile Häusl had the expectation that the Jewish community would welcome her with open arms, she would be proven wrong in short order. Simon had warned her that the process would take significant time and that it would not be easy. Her first hurdle was to convince the rabbi in Ampfing, where Simon was a member of the small congregation there. Simon had coached her, not in Jewish history, but in what to say to the rabbi when he questioned her motivation.

"Simon, I know what to say. I'll do fine."

"I know you will, my Marile."

Marile had never seen, much less been, in a synagogue, unless of course those burning in the Third Reich newsreels counted. In fact, she really hadn't met any other Jews besides Simon and wondered if the rabbi would be like him. As the pair made the trip from Bad Reichenhall to Ampfing, they made small talk about the beautiful countryside and the mountains, but avoided discussing the rapidly approaching meeting with the rabbi.

As they reached the small synagogue, Marile was unimpressed by its size and condition. She was expecting something more along the lines of the churches in Mühldorf or even Bad Reichenhall.

Simon noticed her frown. "We completed the first repairs, but as you can see, we have work yet to do. This is a small congregation."

Simon donned a yarmulke upon entering. Marile looked at him. "It's called a *yarmulke*. The men wear it while in the synagogue." Marile nodded, but as she took in the temple, her initial impression was reinforced. It was not at all like a church. Could their God really live here?

They made their way to the small office at the rear. The old bearded rabbi was sitting at his desk and looked up as Simon and Marile entered.

"Welcome, welcome," he said, a smile on his face. "So this is Maria." He had apparently gotten over the name. "I'm glad to finally meet you, young lady. Simon tells me good things about you."

"Thank you, sir. I'm looking forward to moving ahead."

"Please, sit down," he said, pointing to a more comfortable chair near the desk in the corner. "Call me Rabbi. I'm not a sir."

As Marile moved to the chair, the rabbi turned to Simon. "You may wait outside. I wish to talk to Maria alone for a while."

Simon wasn't sure that was a good idea, but reluctantly turned to leave the room after reassuringly squeezing Marile's hand. She turned and smiled nervously as he left.

The rabbi took his duties seriously, reflecting the Jewish notion that a covenant with God was established when one became a Jew. He remained skeptical about Marile's motivation for wanting the conversion, and he wanted to be sure it was for the right reasons.

"So, my dear, we finally meet. I would like a chance to get to know you better and to ask a few questions."

"I look forward to answering them, si…Rabbi."

The rabbi remained at his desk and looked intently at Marile and steepled his hands. "Do not be nervous, my dear. We are just having a conversation."

"Yes, Rabbi."

"The first question I must ask is perhaps the most important, and I want you to think carefully before you answer."

Marile nodded and thought she was ready for the question that Simon had predicted.

The rabbi asked, "Tell me, why exactly do you wish to convert to Judaism?"

Marile paused, as if to think, but she and Simon had already rehearsed an answer they thought would be acceptable.

"Simon and I plan to be married, and I have agreed to convert as a condition of the marriage," said Marile, satisfied that she had acceptably told the rabbi exactly what he wanted to hear.

The rabbi listened to the response, and a barely perceptible frown formed on his bearded face.

"I see. Is that the only reason? Would you feel the same way if you were not to be married to Simon?"

Unprepared, Marile felt ambushed. An answer came to her, though she knew it must remain unspoken, at least for now.

The rabbi knew he had asked the right questions and that they needed the right answers before the next step in the process could be undertaken. He knew the young woman could never convince the elders in Munich if she couldn't convince him.

"Thank you, Maria. I think you must consider this course of action more thoroughly. I'm sure Simon appreciates your efforts here, but for now, I cannot approve. When you are ready, please come back, but first think about your answer."

Marile was stung by the perceived rejection. A dark thought came to her. *I am a member of the master race and these Untermenchen will not accept me?* Though she immediately chastised herself for the thought, she was nonetheless shocked by its vehemence.

The trip back to Bad Reichenhall seemed much longer than it actually was. Simon glanced at his future wife from time to time trying to judge her mood. "Marile, please don't be discouraged." He understood that it would require several attempts to finally pass the test but tried not to discourage Marile. "I blame myself for not preparing you, but now we understand what needs to be said to convince the rabbi. When we do this, I'm sure he will contact several other elders in Munich to continue the process."

Marile turned to Simon, a look of frustration on her face. "How can I convince them if I can't convince myself? If it wasn't for you, I would never have dreamed of becoming Jewish. I'm doing this for you, only for you, and maybe little Rudy. I can't lie to them, Simon, they would know. What do we do now?"

Two weeks later Simon and Marile were back in the small synagogue in Ampfing to meet with the rabbi. Marile had time to gather her thoughts and feelings and was confident she could answer the rabbi's questions.

"It's good to see you again, Fraulein Häusl," said the rabbi, motioning her to sit. He looked at Simon.

"Rabbi, if you don't mind, I would like Simon to stay. I want him to hear what I have to say."

His gaze went back to Simon and motioned him to sit as well.

"So let's get started," said the small bearded man as he paused to think. "Ah yes, Maria. I will ask you again. Why do you want to convert to our religion?"

The young woman sighed, and in the steadiest voice she could marshal, she began. "Rabbi, please consider my circumstances. I am Catholic. I have been in the Hitler Youth. I have been taught to hate you and your people. Since then, I met Simon who has survived inhuman treatment by the very hands that taught me. Because of Simon, I now understand and respect the Jewish faith. I love Simon, and he is the father of my child, a child who should be raised in the Jewish faith like his father. I ask you, is that not good enough reason?"

The rabbi stared at the twenty-one-year-old woman with a new respect. He glanced over at Simon and nodded slightly and, turning back toward Marile, said, "Yes, my dear, that is a good reason. But is it enough? Is it powerful enough to see you through this? I'm not so sure." The rabbi looked at Simon. "I'm sorry, but I must do what is right, but I will send you to you see my associates in Munich. They will decide."

This time the trip back to Bad Reichenhall proved to be less somber. Simon was satisfied with the outcome of the meeting. His love for Marile grew enormously as both he and the rabbi were moved by her heartfelt answer to the singular question. He was sure she would do well in the meeting with the rabbis in Munich and that the third time would be successful.

Simon smiled at his young passenger. "I have given this much thought, Marile. After the meeting in Munich, I would like you and Rudy to move to Mühldorf. You will be traveling to Munich for your teachings, and Mühldorf is much closer."

"I will think about it, Simon, but I hate to leave the Gruenburgers and Bad Reichenhall. And then who will take care of little Rudy while I am gone?"

"I'm sure we can work something out, Marile. I'm very proud of you, and I promise you will never be sorry."

Marile and the author, sometime in 1948.

418

Marile and the author at a lakeside amusement park in 1949.

MÜHLDORF, GERMANY, SEPTEMBER 1948

A letter arrived for Simon from the Deggendorf DP camp. In it he learned his brother Mendel and Mendel's young son Dolek had finally decided to leave the camp after two years and join Simon in Mühldorf. While happy to hear the news, Simon wondered how he was going to handle Marile's move from Bad Reichenhall and help his brother relocate at the same time.

The small red-and-black 1933 Adler Trumpf automobile approached the Deggendorf camp main gate and turned toward two diminutive forms, their suitcases resting on the ground beside them. It was noon, and the sun was shining down on Mendel and Dolek as they waved to their brother and uncle who had driven from Mühldorf to pick them up. The car squealed to a halt and Simon got out. "Hello, Mendel. I see you and Dolek are ready to go."

"Yes, Simon. It will be good to leave this place," said Mendel as he reached for the handle for the backward-opening door.

"Here, let me have your suitcases," said Simon as he walked to the back of the car and opened the trunk. He placed Mendel's case in first, followed by Dolek's smaller one.

"How are you, Dolek?" asked Simon. The young boy smiled but said nothing. He looked as though he had been in another fight, but Simon didn't inquire. Dolek squeezed into the rear seat as his father took his place in the passenger seat. Simon slammed the trunk lid and got into the car, and the trio drove off.

Simon and his brother were quiet as they made their way back to Mühldorf. Finally, Simon spoke up. "I found a small apartment for you in Mühldorf near the *bahnhof.* Nothing fancy, but it should be adequate, and it's cheap. It's only a few minutes from my apartment on Stadtplaz."

"Thank you, Simon. I'm sure we will be comfortable. We are not planning to stay long in Germany. We are hoping to go to America soon."

Simon snorted. "So am I, as are thousands of others. I think it may take some time, and we may be stuck in Germany longer than we planned. The Americans are arguing about when and how many of us to take." Unknown to Simon, his statement was to prove prophetic, especially in his case.

They soon arrived in Mühldorf and made their way to Simon's apartment on the main street of the small town.

On the way, Mendel noted, "Simon, this town is much smaller than Lemberg."

"Well, it's not Munich, that's for sure, but this is where I've been for three years, and it's not so bad. I think we are the only Jews here, at least in the town. There were others in the hospital, but I don't know what happened to them."

Simon parked the car outside the stately building that contained his residence. Mendel and Dolek expressed amazement at the spaciousness of the apartment, especially the high ceilings and the large windows looking out over the main street.

Simon laughed at their reaction. "Yours will be a little smaller."

"Why can't we stay with you, Uncle?" asked Dolek.

Simon looked at Mendel and laughed. "You can stay a day or so until you get settled. I can help you with that and send you to some assistance agencies. I hope you got rid of those damn Deggendorf dollars. They are no good here, you know."

"Yes, they are all gone. It took a while, but I have some German marks, but not many. But, you know, I may miss the camp. I made some good friends there, but it was time to leave, especially because of Dolek's fighting."

Simon poured two glasses of his favorite Drambuie as the two brothers sat in silence, lost in their thoughts. Mendel smacked his lips in appreciation for the rare drink.

Finally, Simon announced, "I'm getting married soon."

Seeing no immediate reaction from his brother, Simon remembered Mendel's hearing problem. He looked directly at Mendel and, louder this time, said, "I'm getting married."

Mendel heard this time. He blinked as the news set in. "My God, Simon, that's wonderful. But I thought you said there were no Jews in this town. Did you meet someone in the camps?"

"Mendel, it's a long, complicated story, and I don't want to explain right now. She is a wonderful woman, and she will be moving into this apartment in a few days. I think you will like her."

Over the next few days, Mendel and Dolek moved into their small apartment near the *bahnhof* and began a new phase they hoped would be merely another step on the way to their final destination of the United States.

For young Dolek Ruder, however, Mühldorf was to be yet another in a series of languages, cultures, towns, and schools. The school children of Mühldorf had not grown up with Jewish children, and most had never seen a Jew, yet suddenly one was in their midst. The older boys quickly decided to test Dolek, to see what this Jewish boy was all about. Having survived three years hiding under a stable, several years in Russian-dominated Poland, and a further two years in the Deggendorf DP camp, Dolek could more than hold his own. After a number of bloody noses and black eyes, none of them his, the German boys left him alone, and a few even became his friends.

BAD REICHENHALL, GERMANY, SEPTEMBER 1948

A note came to Simon inviting Marile to meet with two rabbis in Munich to discuss her conversion. Simon drove immediately to Bad Reichenhall to convey the message to Marile.

"Soon, very soon, Marile, we will be married," he said excitedly. "I'm sure you will do very well in this meeting, and then, you will become one of us."

Marile smiled at Simon's energetic enthusiasm, but the smile did not reach her eyes.

"What's wrong, Marile? You seem sad. You should be happy."

"Oh, Simon. I'm not sad. I'm just thinking of all I am leaving behind, my religion, my parents. But I know in my heart it's the right thing to do. I'm just nervous."

Simon sighed deeply. "I promise you again, I will make you happy. You will never regret your decision."

Simon made arrangements to meet the rabbis the next day. He thought he and Marile would drive to Munich via Rosenheim, avoiding Mühldorf. Marile looked relieved at the plan. "I haven't been back to Mühldorf in over a year, and maybe it's too soon to even drive through."

As expected, Paula volunteered to watch little Rudy. Early the next morning the pair prepared to leave. Marile kissed the sleeping boy good-bye and, with a quick wave to Paula, said, "We should be back later this evening. Thank you."

They drove westward for less than an hour before Simon decided to stop at a small establishment on the south shore of the beautiful Bavarian lake called Chiemsee for a quick *Fruhstuck*, breakfast.

"I love this lake," said the excited Marile. "We used to come here when I was young." Then a frown formed on her face. "But that was before...."

The pair ordered a meager meal, at least by prewar standards. The server brought two soft-boiled eggs, a whitish sausage, and some cheese. Not a feast, but adequate given the times. The view, however, more than made up for any culinary shortcomings.

So beautiful, so peaceful, thought Simon, his memory going back almost two years ago to the shore of Lake Starnberg when he had first visited the Feldafing DP camp. He idly thought of Julius Kaplan from Lemberg with whom he was reunited and wondered what had happened to his friend.

Simon was shaken out of his reverie when Marile said, "I hate to leave here, but maybe we should go." He looked at his watch, motioned for the bill, and made ready to leave. The pair got into the familiar red-and-black Adler and continued past Rosenheim and Bruckmuhl before turning north toward Munich. In an hour or so, they were in the capital city of Bavaria. Traffic was surprisingly heavy, but Simon negotiated it with aplomb and arrived at the synagogue on time for the meeting with the rabbi and another elder. The synagogue had been repaired from the damage it suffered before and during the war, but it still showed some of the effects. This was a Conservative congregation, not as strict as an Orthodox congregation would be. Simon did not want to press his luck. He had previously contacted the synagogue and discussed his plans. Satisfied that they had done their due diligence in exploring Simon's sanity and rationale and bolstered by the Ampfing rabbi's recommendation, they were amenable to talking to Marile.

An hour later the meeting with Marile concluded with the rabbi and elders impressed by and satisfied with Marile's story, and they agreed to start her conversion as soon as possible. They indicated it would take a year or more to complete and would consist of Jewish history, culture, prayer, holidays, Hebrew language, and other lessons culminating in a *Mikveh*, a ritual bath.

Simon was extremely pleased with the progress Marile had made and was thinking ahead to her move to his Mühldorf apartment. However, before returning to Bad Reichenhall, Simon had decided to show Marile his Mohlstrasse operation in the Munich Bogenhauser district. They drove across town to the nondescript building that housed his black market activities. Izak Goldblatt, Simon's business partner, greeted them at the door. Surprised at the unexpected visit, Goldblatt looked at Simon, then his gaze lingered on Marile. Then, after a not-so-discreet interval, he silently mouthed "*Zaftig*," and smiled. Simon scowled and, feigning annoyance, said, "Goldblatt, this is Marile. We are to be married next year."

"I'm very glad to meet you, Fraulein. Simon has told me very good things about you."

Marile blushed at the man's gaze. She had seen him say something but didn't hear the word, and even if she had, she would not have known what it meant. Yet she correctly assumed it had something to do with her and her appearance.

Simon cleared his throat and interrupted. "Marile, this is Izak Goldblatt from Lemberg. He is my business partner. This is where we do our business." He considered what to say next. "I'm afraid business is declining, and maybe we will shut it down in the near future."

Marile looked around at the shelves stocked with items like sardine tins, chocolate, bags of what looked like coffee beans, some oranges, and many white packs of cigarettes with a red circle on them. The latter she recognized as those her father had smoked. She even saw a few dark-brown, red-capped bottles of liqueur with a gold-and-red label called Drambuie. Now she understood where Simon had gotten many of the items that were otherwise difficult to obtain.

FELDAFING DISPLACED PERSONS CAMP, SEPTEMBER 1948

For the last two years, Izak Ruder had successfully blended into the Jewish community at the Feldafing displaced persons camp near Munich. As a tailor, he repaired and sometimes made new clothing for the other inmates, and his metalworking skills had come in handy for maintenance work around the camp. He had developed a network of friends and knew many more inhabitants by sight. The camp played host to some four to five thousand inhabitants, many waiting impatiently for emigration policies to loosen up. One day Izak was helping with a repair to the hospital building and came upon an inmate he had seen occasionally but had never met. The man's name was Julius Kaplan. The two men soon struck up a conversation.

"You are new here," said Kaplan, more of a statement than a question.

"Not really. I've been here for about two years. A group of us arrived from, well, let's see. We started in Lodz, then to the German border, only to find the Russians controlled the area. We left and entered what we learned was the American Zone, and we were sent here."

"How was Lodz?"

"It was tolerable for a while, but then the Soviets started taking control, and many of us were fearful of what was to come, so we decided to get out as soon as we could. Who knows what it's like now."

Kaplan nodded to himself. He had heard many such stories. People trying to return home only to find everything gone, everyone gone, and that they had no place to go. The Poles and the Ukrainians certainly did not welcome them back, with many returning Jews outright murdered. "Did you live in Lodz for long?"

"No, I lived in Krakow for many years. Before that I lived with my parents in a small town called Obertin, and I moved to Krakow as soon as I could, maybe about 1923. What about you?"

A surprised look flashed on Kaplan's face. He had heard the name of that town before but couldn't place where at the moment.

"My name is Julius Kaplan. I was a pharmacist from Lwow. It was once called Lemberg. That seems like a long time ago."

"Lemberg?" asked Izak. "I know many people from Lemberg. In fact, one of my brothers lived there." A sad, faraway look formed on Izak's face. "Sadly, I know nothing of the fate of him or his family."

"You must check the lists we have. They contain names of survivors. They are sometimes updated. One list, called the *Sharit Ha-Platah*, has the names of survivors from the camps around Bavaria. Come, I'll show you."

"Thank you, Julius. I have checked some of the lists, but not the last one you mentioned."

As the men left the hospital building and headed toward the administration building to check the lists, Kaplan turned to his new companion and asked, "By the way, what's your name?"

"Ah, where are my manners? I'm glad to meet you, Kaplan. My name is Izak Ruder."

Julius Kaplan tripped and almost fell down. "My God. Can it be?"

"What?"

"An old friend of mine from Lwow is Simon Ruder. Do you know of him?"

"My brother's name is Simon from Lwow. Is he here?"

"No, but I met him here several years ago. I think he said he was living in Mühldorf, a small town west of Munich."

"What did he look like, this Simon?"

"Well, Izak, he looked different than I remember in Lwow, but he should be better by now. He is of medium height, dark hair. He was on two crutches when I saw him last. He had a bandage on his neck. Oh, he had a number tattooed on his left arm. He told me his story about Auschwitz and Dachau."

An intent Izak listened to the story and considered his options. "I must go to Mühldorf to find this Simon. I think it may be my brother. I have another brother, Mendel, who left Lodz with his young son a little before I did. Maybe I can find them too."

BAD REICHENHALL, GERMANY, SEPTEMBER 1948

Marile stood in the doorway and looked around the Gruenburger home with fond memories as she prepared to leave for Mühldorf. This had been a refuge for her and her infant son for the better part of the last year, and she felt like she was leaving home again. Two suitcases at her side, she hugged Paula and took little Rudy from the older woman. Both women had tears in their eyes despite the knowledge that this was not a permanent good-bye, merely a transition into a new phase for the young woman. Yet Marile was apprehensive about the transition. She would be among strange people with different customs practicing a foreign religion, one she would soon be joining.

Paula looked at the suitcases. "Wait a minute. You forgot the crib for the baby. You may need it." She winked. She was back in a few minutes, the small crib neatly folded.

"Thank you for everything, Paula. I can never repay you for your kindness," said a tearful Marile.

"You don't have to thank me, my dear. Just be happy. Simon is a good man, and I'm sure he will do his best to make you happy."

"I'm sure too, but I'm still so nervous."

"I know you are, and I think you are the bravest person I know. I will pray that it will all work out."

A horn sounded and alerted the women to Simon's arrival. With a deep sigh, Marile opened the door as Simon came up to meet her.

"Good morning, my beautiful Marile. This is a wonderful day," he said cheerfully as he hugged his bride-to-be and kissed his infant son. He looked over Marile's shoulder. "A good morning to you too, Frau Gruenburger. It's nice to see you again."

Simon produced a bouquet of flowers for Marile and a small tin of chocolates, which he presented to Paula.

"Why thank you, Herr Ruder. That was very nice of you." There was a pause as the woman hugged her young friend again and kissed the infant goodbye. An awkward silence ensued as Marile finally spoke up. She looked at a not-so-patient Simon and, with a sad smile on her face, told Paula, "We must be going." And with little Rudy cradled her arms, she walked toward the waiting Adler that was to take her into a new life.

Simon dutifully packed the suitcases into the back of the Adler and came back for the crib. Marile watched with amusement as her husband-to-be scratched his head as he tried to discover the secret to fitting the crib into the car. She smiled to herself as he finally succeeded and, wiping a tear away, she heard Paula shout, "Take care of our Marile," as they prepared to drive off.

The trip to Mühldorf was uneventful, as even the small child sensed a change and remained quiet as the couple drove through the breathtaking Bavarian countryside with its forests and mountains.

"Are you nervous about returning to Mühldorf?" asked Simon, finally breaking the silence.

"A little," Marile lied, trying not to show her apprehension. "I haven't been to Mühldorf in over a year, and I don't know what to expect."

"I'm sure it's changed a little since you left." He avoided any mention of her parents, a subject he knew would upset her and was the source of her reservations. "You will like the apartment, right in the middle of town." He wondered if now would be an appropriate time tell Marile about his brother Mendel and his nephew Dolek who had recently moved to Mühldorf. Maybe it would help Marile adjust to her new life, a sort of surrogate family, he thought.

He looked over to Marile as she fussed with the infant when he began fidgeting. "One thing that has changed is my brother Mendel and his son have moved to Mühldorf a few days ago. They have a small apartment near the *bahnhof.* I know they will like you, and I think you will like them."

Marile continued quieting the fidgeting infant, more so to give her time to consider the news rather than attend to the now settled-down little Rudy. "That's good news," she said, not really sure it was. "You haven't really said much about them."

"There will be plenty of time to talk. We can invite them over for dinner once we get settled, maybe play some cards."

Marile turned to gaze at the passing landscape and rolled her eyes. Her new life was beginning to take shape. Simon drove the Adler through the light Mühldorf traffic and stopped in front of the Stadplatz 44 building. Marile had grown up in Mühldorf and was familiar with the area in the town center. Her school and church were nearby, as was the site where, a little more than ten years ago, she and several other young girls had presented bouquets of flowers to the Fuhrer. *Another lifetime ago*, she thought.

"Here we are," said a proud Simon. "I hope you will like it."

Simon exited the car and hurried to open the door for Marile and then unloaded the two suitcases. "This way." He motioned, holding the door open. "Just one flight of stairs."

Marile followed a panting Simon up the stairs. She laughed. "Take a rest, Simon. Don't overdo it. There's plenty of time."

Simon kissed the mezuzah on the doorframe and motioned the young woman inside. She did so cautiously at first. Once inside, she looked around and marveled at its spaciousness, high ceilings, and large windows. Simon chuckled to himself. He had seen the same reaction from his brother Mendel a few days ago. While items like furniture, drapes, and similar furnishings were still problematic, Simon had managed to procure a collection of functional, if mismatched, furniture, as well as plates and utensils. Marile inspected the rooms and determined the place lacked the homeyness of the Gruenburger home. It had potential, though, and she began making mental plans on how to correct the situation.

A week later, on a Sunday afternoon, a knock on the door announced the arrival of two visitors to the Stadtplatz 44 apartment. Mendel and his ten-year-old son Dolek were about to meet Simon's bride-to-be for the first time. Mendel was unsure of his feelings based on what his older brother had told him. He still questioned Simon's sanity but was willing to give the woman the benefit of the doubt, but to marry outside the faith, especially to a German, was difficult for him to fathom. Young Dolek, however, appeared unaware of the situation or didn't care.

A smiling Simon answered the door and bid his guests to enter. Mendel, too, kissed the mezuzah and slowly went into the apartment, not sure what to expect. Dolek followed reluctantly, more out of nervousness or shyness than apprehension.

"Hello, Mendel and Dolek. Welcome, welcome. I'm glad to see you again." The pair looked around the apartment and immediately noticed a change. The furniture had been rearranged, and a baby's crib now graced the center of the large room. A small form occupied the crib. At that moment, Marile entered, and the two guests immediately cast their gaze at the young woman. After a moment, Mendel turned toward his older brother with a sly look on his face.

Simon cleared his throat and announced, "This is Marile, my bride-to-be." Marile smiled sweetly and addressed her future brother-in-law. "Herr Ruder, I'm so glad to meet you. And your son too."

Mendel was momentarily speechless, trying to compensate for his hearing loss. Marile turned toward Simon, who discreetly tugged his ear. Marile understood and repeated the greeting, louder this time.

Mendel's face lit up. "Thank you, my dear. I'm so glad to finally meet you. My brother has told me so much about you." Marile turned toward Dolek.

"Sorry. This is my son Dolek. He is ten years old and will be going to school soon. He knows German, Polish, and a little Russian."

The young man stepped forward and addressed his future aunt. "Hello, Fraulein. I'm glad to meet you and hope we will be good friends."

The two brothers looked at each other in surprise but said nothing. "I'm sure we will," said Marile.

At that moment, the small form in the crib, awakened by the noise, began to cry. Marile rushed over to attend to her one-year-old son. She picked up the infant and gently rocked him, and soon he was quiet. With a proud, almost defiant look on her face, she said, "This is my, ah, our son Rudy." Mendel and Dolek looked at each other and slowly approached the mother and infant as if afraid of what the master race and Jewish union had produced. Marile proudly held up the infant so the pair could see him. "Look who it is," Marile cooed to the child. The infant turned his head toward Mendel, giggled, and smiled. He reached for the man who would be his uncle. Mendel gently grasped the tiny hand, and he, too, smiled at Marile.

"A fine son," he said. Dolek, too, became enthralled with the infant, who would soon become his cousin.

Mendel turned to Simon and said simply, "*Sehr gut.*"

MÜHLDORF, GERMANY, OCTOBER 1948

Izak Ruder and his new friend Julius Kaplan were working together on a maintenance job on the school building at the Feldafing displaced persons camp. They had become friends since meeting a month ago. As they were wrapping up the minor repair, Julius asked, "Izak, have you thought about finding your brother Simon? I haven't seen him in some time, but I hear he's still in Mühldorf."

"Funny you should mention, Simon. I've been thinking about him since you told me you saw him. I think maybe we should take a trip to Mühldorf. So tell me, what do you know about him?"

Kaplan considered how he should answer. He knew Simon had become enamored with a Gentile German girl but hadn't heard anything beyond that. He wondered if he should mention that.

"So," asked an impatient Izak. "Surely you know something."

Making up his mind, Kaplan began, "When I saw him last, he told me he had met a young German girl, not Jewish, and that she had become a friend of his. She worked for the Americans. Beyond that, I don't know."

"So he still acts irresponsibly. But I'm sure nothing came of it. Am I right?"

"Honestly, Izak, I don't know. I haven't heard anything, and it's been a couple of years now. I remember we went to Mühldorf, and he was living in temporary lodgings on Luddendorfstrasse, but he might have moved since then.

You know Simon, always busy working. He was like that in Lwow. He told me he wanted to leave Germany, probably to America, or Canada, or even Israel."

Izak sighed. "Well, I'm anxious to see my brother, so I suppose we should visit him in Mühldorf and see what he is up to before we all go our separate ways. I myself am waiting for word about going to England. I may even get married before then. What about you, Julius? Where do you want to go?"

"Whoever will take me. America, most likely, but even Israel."

It was a partly cloudy, mild day as Julius Kaplan and Izak Ruder made their way to the Feldafing train station bound for Mühldorf to find Simon. As they waited for the train, they could feel fingers of cooler air drifting down from the nearby mountains. Soon they boarded the partially full passenger car and stopped first in Munich and then were on to Mühldorf. Izak had never been here before as he looked around the small town. He would have been surprised to know that ten years earlier, the Fuhrer himself, accompanied by a large entourage, had stopped here to the adulation of the town folks, including little blond girls, their right arms raised high in boisterous salute. Such were the times. Hitler had stopped here on his way to important business in nearby Austria to announce the *Anschluss*, the annexation, subsuming that country into the greater Reich. Izak would never know or even guess that his future sister-in-law had presented the Fuhrer a pretty bouquet of flowers near where he now stood.

Kaplan recalled Simon's Luddendorfstrasse 6 address, and after asking directions, the pair made their way toward the destination. While both men judged the town quaint, inwardly, neither was particularly impressed, especially Kaplan, whose memories of prewar cosmopolitan Lvov kept intruding. Izak, too, remembered Krakow and how it was. A small sigh escaped him, and both men understood that those days and those towns, at least for them, would only be memories. After about a little over a kilometer, they found themselves in front of the Luddendorfstrasse address. Like many streets of a defeated country, especially those associated with the defeated villains, Luddendorfstrasse was to become Summererstrasse. A cautious Frau Weidermeyer answered the knock on the door and regarded the two men. "Yes, what do you want?" she asked, a not-so-well-disguised tone of annoyance in her voice.

Kaplan cleared his throat. "We are looking for an acquaintance of ours whom we believe lived here at one time. My name is Julius Kaplan, and this is the man's brother, Izak. We are looking for Simon Ruder."

"Ah yes, Herr Ruder," she said, the annoyance mostly gone as she remembered the coffee, oranges, and Drambuie. "Yes, he was such a nice, handsome, and clean man. Always well dressed. He left a little while ago, although sometimes I still get mail, you know, from the Americans."

Izak and Julius turned toward each other and nodded. "Do you have his new address?" asked Izak.

"Yes, somewhere on Stadtplatz, I think. I have it written down. Please wait just a minute." The woman returned quickly and handed Kaplan a piece of paper upon which she had written *Stadtplatz 44*. "It's only a kilometer or so past the hospital. Maybe ten or fifteen minutes. I think he said it was near a fountain."

"Thank you. You have been very helpful."

"I'm glad to help," she replied. "Please give Herr Ruder my regards."

She closed the door as the two men left, her back against it. *Jews,* she thought. *There are so many of them in town. When will they be gone?*

The two men began their short trek toward the middle of town. "That is a very nice lady," said Izak. Kaplan agreed absent-mindedly as he tried to focus on the route. After a few minutes of brisk walking, they noticed the hospital off to the left. "Not much farther," said Izak. "I'm a little nervous," he volunteered. "I haven't seen my brother in many years."

"I can understand that. The last time I saw him, he was on crutches and looked pretty bad. I'm sure he's better now. I'm curious about the young woman."

They continued walking, now lost in their own thoughts. When they reached Stadtplatz, they looked left and right, wondering which way to turn. "Look, there's the fountain," exclaimed Izak, pointing to the right. They turned in unison and quickly covered the last few yards and found themselves in front of their destination, a clean red-and-black Adler automobile parked in front. They entered the building and climbed the stairs, stopping in front of the door that bore Simon Ruder's name and a mezuzah attached to the doorframe. Taking a deep breath, Kaplan knocked on the door. They could hear an infant crying and then stop. A moment went by, and the door opened a crack.

"Who is it?" a soft feminine voice asked.

"Herr Ruder?" asked Kaplan in response. "It's Julius Kaplan from Lvov."

Simon looked up from his sewing machine. These days it seemed he was spending more time sewing than driving. "Who is it, *liebchen*?" he asked.

"It's someone named Julius Kaplan. Do you know him?"

Simon laughed, got up from the sewing machine, and headed toward the door. "Yes, *liebchen*. He is an old friend. You can let him in."

Marile opened the door, and Kaplan entered along with another, slightly taller and older man. Simon smiled when he saw Kaplan, but a look of confusion formed on his face as he tried to identify the older man with him. Simon's eyes widened as recognition set in. "Izak, is that really you?"

"Of course it is, you *putz*. It's good to see you after all this time."

The two brothers uncharacteristically hugged and slapped each other on the back. Izak was seven years older than Simon and had always tormented his younger brother while growing up in Obertin. Older brothers did that, but Izak watched over his two younger brothers until he left the small town and struck off to make his fortune in Krakow. There had been little contact between Simon and Izak and none after 1939. Until now.

"Come in, come in." He looked at Kaplan but said nothing. Turning back to Izak, he said, "My God. Where do we start?"

Simon motioned his two guests to sit and turned to Marile. "Please bring our guest something to drink. The Drambuie, I think, the best."

Izak regarded the young, attractive dark-haired woman. *Could that be his daughter?* he wondered. *Not Hannah. He called her Marile. And she looks to be a bit older than Simon's daughter would be.*

Marile brought out several small glasses and the brown bottle of Simon's favorite drink. He actually kept more bottles than he sold on the black market.

Simon poured the expensive liqueur into each glass, and the men toasted and made quick work of the contents.

Izak turned his head toward Marile, trying to be discreet.

"Ah," said Simon. "Gentlemen, this is my Frau, Marile." A white lie that he thought harmless and would avoid any unwanted questions. Izak noted the absence of wedding rings but said nothing.

"It's a pleasure to meet you, my dear. However, I find myself asking how my little brother came to be so lucky."

Marile smiled sweetly. Kaplan, too, added his compliments. Izak spoke up again. "*Nu*," he said, coaxing more from his brother, who understood and nodded in Marile's direction. She left the room and returned a moment later carrying an infant.

"This is our son, Rudy. He is a year old."

The two guests made the obligatory complimentary remarks about the baby. Marile smiled, politely thanked the men, and put the baby away. Soon the three men had another round of drinks as the conversation became more serious.

"What news of our family?" asked Izak. "I found Mendel two years ago in Lodz but haven't heard from him. I left while he was still there."

"Mendel is here in Mühldorf with his son Dolek. He lives near the *bahnhof*. We see them every week or so to play cards and feed Dolek, who has grown into a fine boy."

Izak paused, afraid to ask the next question, but continued anyway. "What of Lola and the children?"

Simon took a drink and shook his head. "They perished," was all he said. He looked over at Kaplan, who responded with a barely perceptible nod.

Izak sighed and took another sip. He understood no more would be said about this. "What of our parents and sisters?"

"We know nothing but heard that Obertin has no Jews left. I fear they all perished."

A hush descended over the small table as the somber reality sunk in, and while each man had a story, all remained reticent, especially Izak. Even after the war, they had seen the ghastly images, the piles of corpses being bulldozed into mass graves, and for now, it was enough to know they weren't among them. Many even questioned why that was so, and guilt began to prey upon them. No, it was better to say nothing and try to move on.

Kaplan noted the time. "Izak, we must be going. The train leaves soon."

Izak stood and faced Simon. "It's good to see you, little brother." He winked, adding, "But don't think I don't know about your little lie."

"Next year, Izak. Next year we will be married. Marile is starting her conversion, and it should be completed next year. She is a wonderful woman and is committed to seeing this through."

1949

A letter came from Munich addressed to Simon. It was written by William Weiss in longhand German and announced he, his wife Regina, and their young son Samuel were leaving for America. They would be sailing from Bremerhaven and were headed for a city in America called Detroit where they had relatives. William promised to write when they had settled in America and hoped they would reunite sometime in the future. Simon wondered how William had found him in Mühldorf and then remembered Julius Kaplan's suggestion to post his name and address at the Feldafing DP camp.

Simon reflected on the letter. He was happy for the young man and his new family. He lit a cigarette and sat down and reread the letter. With a sigh, he put the letter down, sat back in his comfortable chair, and soon recalled the day when William Weiss and his father David had first joined the group of tailors in the SS Loncki Prison in Lemberg. He remembered the young man, barely nineteen, and his father's penchant for cigarettes. They had been reunited at Auschwitz, William's tattooed number only thirteen higher than his own. A shiver shook him as he remembered that someone else would have borne his number had Dr. Joseph Mengele not intervened. Then came vivid images of a death march in the dead of winter that claimed so many of the prisoners, including David Weiss. Simon recalled a faltering David Weiss hoarsely imploring him to watch after his son.

Marile entered the room, suddenly shaking Simon out of his darkening reverie. She spied the letter lying on the floor. "Who is that from?" she asked.

"A friend from Lemberg," he said, not wanting to go into details. "It seems the exodus to America has finally begun."

MÜHLDORF, GERMANY, AUGUST 1949

A letter arrived at the Häusl farmhouse from the Gruenburgers in Bad Reichenhall. Ludwig was home at the time, and he carefully opened the envelope. He read its contents, a small card, and had to sit down. The card announced the wedding of his daughter Marile to Simon Ruder. The ceremony would take place in Bad Reichenhall on August 27. With a deep sigh, he sank deeper into the chair. His arms dropped over the arms of the chair as the card fell to the floor. He knew his wife Maria would be furious and considered ignoring the invitation. He would have to think about this, but in his heart he knew what to do and started making plans.

BAD REICHENHALL, GERMANY, AUGUST 1949

On a warm August day in Bad Reichenhall, a civil wedding ceremony was taking place in a small official office. Simon Ruder and Maria Katarina Häusl were married that day. Attending the ceremony were Paula Gruenburger and her husband and Dr. Loske and his wife and young daughter. Entering almost unnoticed and standing in the rear of the office was Ludwig Häusl. He had rearranged his work schedule to coincide with the wedding and would not leave for Mühldorf until the first train the next morning.

Marile, dressed in a white wedding dress, turned and noticed a tall man standing in the rear. She turned away, but then turned back to examine the man more closely. *Could it be?* she wondered. The man walked forward, and she finally recognized her father.

"Papa!" she exclaimed as she hurried toward him, but the pair stopped in front of each other, not knowing what to do next. They had not seen each other since Marile was sent into exile over two years ago. She remembered the pain of watching her father turn his back on her as she climbed onto the train. Ludwig, too, remembered his pain as he watched his eldest daughter exit his life and wondered if she could ever forgive him. He made the first move as he opened his arms and his daughter ran to embrace him. Marile looked around and then at her father. He shook his head. Her mother had not come.

Paula Gruenburger watched the interaction between father and daughter with tears in her eyes. "Herr Häusl, I'm so happy to see you. I know how much it means to Marile." Ludwig could only nod his head as he turned away, trying to maintain his stoicism without much success.

Simon entered the room, excited, though anxious to put this ceremony behind him. He greeted the guests but then noticed Marile and a tall man standing close together. He assumed it was her father and, steeling his nerve, made his way toward the pair.

Marile saw Simon approaching. *Oh my God, please help*, she thought and hoped for the best. "Papa, this is Simon," she said.

The two men faced each other and hesitantly shook hands. *So this is the man my Marile chose*, Ludwig thought. He studied the man closely and noted the well-made suit, the fine shoes, and the snappy look about him. They looked into each other's eyes as if to see into their hearts, and each man experienced a glimmer of recognition. But how could that be? They had come from vastly different worlds, yet the vague feeling persisted. They each tried to shake the feeling, but it grew stronger. Just then a train whistle blew not far from the hotel. Almost simultaneously, both men were back in March of 1945 in the aftermath of the air raid on the Mühldorf marshalling yard as Jewish concentration camp inmates were forced to make repairs on the tracks. Ludwig remembered the frail man with the piercing eyes looking at him and later wondering if he had somehow survived. The irony was not lost on him, and though neither man spoke of the encounter, they understood the bond that had been created at that moment.

After the short ceremony, the wedding reception took place at the impressive Hotel Bavaria at the foot of the *Predigtstuhlbahn*, the cable car to the top of the mountain. The hotel featured two large three-story structures at each end, sandwiching three large verandas running the length of the edifice, with an even larger patio on the ground floor extending in an L-shape around the right side of the building. The entire property was well landscaped with many bushes and mature trees. A myriad of tables and chairs for guests covered the patio and verandas. The majestic peaks in the background created a truly breathtaking scene as cable trams were making their eight-and-a-half-minute ascent to the top.

The party was small but festive as the group dined on a menu of *schweden-platte* (an appetizer), a main course of *kalbsschnitzel, salatplatte und bratkartoffel* (veal cutlet, salad, pan-fried potatoes), and *windbeutel m/sahne* (creampuff with cream). The meal was finished with *dohnkenkaffe m/torte* (coffee with cake).

Ludwig Häusl found himself actually enjoying the small wedding party, though he worried about what to tell his wife. He knew there would be hell to pay if she found out, but it would be worth it, especially in his heart. Besides, he wanted to see his grandson. He approached his daughter, now the official Frau Maria Ruder. "My dearest Marile," he began. "Congratulations. I'm happy if you are happy. Simon seems like a good man." Then, with a not-quite-disguised tone of apprehension, he said, "I would like to finally meet my grandson."

Marile smiled and looked toward Paula. She made a rocking the baby motion, and quickly Paula left the room. A few moments later, the older woman returned with the almost two-year-old child.

"Papa, this is Rudolf Ruder, ah, Rudy, your grandson."

A fine name, thought Ludwig. He had been uneasy about seeing the child, this fusion of the master race and a Polish Jew. Old prejudices were hard to overcome, and he silently chided himself for the thought as he bent down to regard the child without being overly obvious. To his relief, the toddler looked what he considered German, or German enough, even down to his blond hair.

"This is your *Opa*," said Marile to her son. "O...Opa," the toddler repeated. Ludwig smiled and tousled the child's hair. "Hello, my little Rudy," he said with genuine feeling. *At least now the little fellow has a last name.* He thought of his stepson Alois who never carried the Häusl name and was glad this two-year-old would not share the same fate, though for a very different reason.

Simon had discreetly kept his distance from his new wife and father-in-law while they engaged in what was obviously a serious conversation. He was encouraged when Ludwig seemed to have accepted the child and hoped he, too, would finally be welcomed into the family. He was tempted to join them, but a look from Marile told him *not yet.*

Ludwig was expecting the question from his daughter, and as he feared, it quickly confronted him. Marile looked at her father. "Papa, where is Mama? Why didn't she come?"

Ludwig had tried to prepare an answer, in fact, several, depending on the circumstances, but he knew only the truth would serve them both. The father and daughter locked gazes for a long moment.

"Marile, my little Marile. You know how stubborn your mother can be. Once she makes up her mind, there is no changing it. Her feelings toward the Jews, all Jews, are unchanged. She absolutely refused to come and doesn't even know I'm here. As far as she is concerned, you are no longer part of the family, and she will not allow you into our house."

"Opa," said the toddler, interrupting the conversation. Ludwig laughed, but not for joy.

Eyes wet with tears, Marile merely nodded. "Isn't there something you could do, Papa? You've seen little Rudy. She's his Oma, her first grandchild. Can't she understand and accept that?"

"Marile, I will try to talk to her, but she is going to be very upset with me when she finds out I'm here. Beyond that, I don't know."

"That's all I ask, Papa. I'm so glad you came and am very proud of you." She looked over at an anxious Simon, who recognized the signal to come over. He promptly approached the pair and saw the tears in his wife's eyes. He could only imagine the depths of the conversation that had transpired.

Ludwig spoke first as he regarded his new son-in-law, a mere ten years his junior. "Simon, I think you are a good man and that you will take good care of my Marile and grandson." He paused and, with a deep sigh, continued. "God, both mine and yours, certainly works in mysterious and indecipherable ways, but who am I to argue? Did they conspire, laughing at us now, or could they be one and the same? I'm sure I will never understand the way of it, but I accept it."

"Thank you, Herr Häusl."

Marile smiled at the two men, unaware of the irony and deeper meaning of her father's statement.

With a more serious look on his face, Ludwig addressed his son-in-law. "Simon, you must understand that I cannot welcome you to the family. Not yet, maybe never. And Marile, since you now live in Mühldorf, maybe something can be arranged, but for now, I'm sorry, you must stay away. Your mother is adamant about this. I'm sorry."

"What about little Rudy, Papa? Doesn't he deserve to see his grandparents?"

"We will see, Marile. Time will tell. He seems a fine lad, but we will have to see."

The party was drawing to a close as Ludwig said, "I must return to the hotel. My train leaves in the morning, and I am very tired." He hugged his daughter one last time and kissed her on the forehead. He faced Simon and shook his hand, this time without hesitation. "Good-bye, Simon, and good luck."

As Ludwig started toward the door, a small voice called out. "Opa." Ludwig turned to his grandson and patted the toddler on his head. "Good-bye, my little Rudy."

Marile watched her father walk away, but this time, he turned, smiled, and waved as he left. Marile smiled too.

Simon came over to his new wife and waved a paper in front of her. It was the marriage license. Marile gently took it from her husband and scanned it. She saw her name and his, both indicated *Israelitisch* as the religion. It was official, and she knew there was no going back.

HEIRATSURKUNDE

Copy of the original marriage certificate issued in Bad Reichenhall on August 27, 1949.

Simon and Marile Ruder in a 1949 wedding picture taken in Bad Reichenhall.
Pictured are Dr. Loske, his wife and daughter, Simon and Marile,
Paula Gruenburger, Herr Gruenburger, and Rudy, the author.

MÜHLDORF, GERMANY, SEPTEMBER 1949

After returning to Mühldorf in September, the married couple had another ceremony to perform, this time in Munich. While just married in a civil ceremony, Simon was determined to perform the ritual in the traditional Jewish manner. Having recently completed her year-long conversion to Judaism, Marile agreed, and on September 18, the Jewish ceremony took place in Munich with the rabbi from Ampfing and several elders taking part. Simon's brothers Izak and Mendel and Mendel's son Dolek were also there as well as a reluctant Izak Goldblatt.

"*Mazel tov!*" shouted the crowd after Simon shattered the traditional wine glass, an old Jewish custom. Even Goldblatt joined in. So now it was done, and the couple could get on with married life. As the party was breaking up, Izak Ruder took his younger brother aside. "Simon, I had my doubts about this, but now…well, I think it is a good thing. Marile is a fine woman, and I adore little Rudy." Then, after a pause, he said, "I think Lola would approve."

Though Izak Ruder's comment was intended to reassure him, Simon nonetheless experienced an unexpected pang of guilt. *Would she*, he wondered. But that was in the past, and he was, after all, starting a new future with a new wife and young son, who would not be happy with his impending appointment with the *Moyel*.

The Ruder family, circa 1950. From top row, left to right, Simon, brother Mendel, brother Izak. Second row, Maria (Marile), Dolek, Izak's wife Alice, third row, Rudy, the author.

Old habits die hard, if at all, and Simon frequently had company over to his Stadtplaz apartment to play cards. Brothers Mendel and Izak, Goldblatt, and other Jewish friends would sit around the table, drink coffee or schnapps, and play. If the mood suited him, Simon even brought out his bottle of Drambuie to which he had taken a liking from his black market days. Often the discussions centered around the slow pace of emigration and various views of the Americans still governing this part of Germany. The discussions often turned animated as each man voiced his opinion. Throwing down a card, Mendel spoke up. "I have filed an application with the authorities to go to England, Canada, or America. I prefer America, but we will go to whoever takes us first." With that pronouncement, he firmly set down his glass as if the news were earth shattering.

Simon looked around the table and snorted. "I have done that as well, but now my situation has changed. I have a wife and son, and they will go with me, so I must let the authorities know this." He motioned to the kitchen where dishes were being handled, maybe a bit louder than necessary. "Israel is no longer an option, so we will try for Canada or America. I hope it doesn't take too long. I know the Americans have allowed a number of what they call displaced persons to immigrate, so maybe soon, our turn will come."

Simon became pensive for a moment. "I know of one person in particular, an acquaintance from Lemberg. William Weiss was the young man's name. He and his father were in the Lemberg prison with me. His father perished when we left Auschwitz." Simon became quiet as images of the death march flashed through his mind.

"William survived, and the Americans took him to a DP camp near Munich, Feldafing, I think. There, he married another survivor, Regina, in 1946, and they immigrated to America just a few months ago. They moved to a city called Detroit where they make automobiles."

Simon got up and shuffled through a stack of papers and retrieved an envelope. "See," he said, holding it up. "From America. The young man sent me his address."

"Yes," said Goldblatt. "I also know of several people who have gone to America, but I think they had relatives there. We should agree that if any of us manages to go to Canada, England, or America, we promise to speak for or sponsor the rest of us."

The group loudly toasted the comment even as they each wondered if it was really possible. At any rate, they all knew they had to leave Germany, and soon.

Officially, things had finally begun to move. The Displaced Persons (DP) Act of 1948 enabled people displaced by World War II to start immigrating. This act authorized some two hundred thousand Europeans and seventeen thousand orphans to immigrate. President Harry S. Truman signed the first DP act on June 25, 1948. A second act, one that would be signed on June 16, 1950, would allow entry of a further two hundred thousand.

MÜHLDORF, GERMANY, DECEMBER 1949

Life went on for the newly married couple much as it had for the last few years. They became close friends with Dr. Ernst Loske and his family, who lived in the same building, and Dr. Loske became their family doctor. Simon's auto chauffer business prospered, as did his tailoring activities, so much in fact that he was able to severely curtail his black market dealings. Yet, in spite of his success, he remained almost desperate to leave Germany. He had heard nothing regarding their emigration status, and this caused him many sleepless nights. He had hoped that his updated International Refugee Organization (IRO) application showing his new status with a wife and child would facilitate the process, but it had apparently made no difference. Soon, however, world events affecting the United States would add another course of bricks atop the already significant wall blocking his road to immigration.

During the Chanukah holiday, Marile had a surprise for her husband that would once again require him to update his IRO status. Little Rudy giggled with delight as Simon lit the candles on the eighth day of the celebration. Marile smiled at her son's reaction but then became more serious.

"Simon," she began. "I have something important to tell you."

Now what? thought Simon as he turned his attention to Marile.

"Dr. Loske says I am pregnant. Next year we are going to have another child. The baby is due sometime next May."

Simon blinked as he digested the news. He struggled for words as he tried to process his feelings. Certainly he was happy with the news, but he had hoped to be out of Germany when another child came. Still, that was over five months in the future, and perhaps they would be allowed to emigrate before the child was born.

"That's wonderful, *mein liebchen*," said Simon.

"Are you not happy?"

"Yes, of course I am, *liebchen*. I was just hoping we would be out of Germany by now. I wanted the next child to be born in America."

Marile sighed. She had heard this too often but decided not to make it an issue. "Soon, maybe after the birth of this child, Simon. Then we will go."

"I hope you are right, Marile."

1950

MÜHLDORF, GERMANY, MAY 1950

Dr. Ersnt Loske had a serious look on his face as he examined the very pregnant Marile Ruder in his office. "The baby is due soon, but I am a little concerned. I don't like what I'm seeing and am afraid the birth may be a difficult one for you." He walked around the office and reviewed his findings. After a few moments, he seemed to have come to a decision. "Frau Ruder, I'm going to send you to the hospital in Schwindegg. I think they may have better facilities to handle the birth of your baby."

Anxiously, Marile asked, "Is it serious, Doctor?"

"I don't think so, but I'd rather be safe. I know some of the doctors there, and I'll discuss this with them."

"Thank you, Dr. Loske. I'll tell Simon, and he can take me there. Can Frau Loske take care of Rudy while I'm there?"

"Of course."

Marile left and returned to her apartment, just down the stairs.

Looking up from his sewing machine, a concerned Simon asked, "Is everything all right? What did the doctor say?"

"Just that he thought we should go to the hospital in Schwindegg to have the baby. He thinks the hospital there is better equipped to deliver this baby."

"Did he mention any problems?"

"No, just that he noticed something. I don't know what, but I trust him."

Two weeks later, Simon took Marile to the hospital in Schwindegg, some twenty-three kilometers west of Mühldorf. The next day Marile went into labor and gave birth to a daughter whom the couple named Elfriede, after Simon's mother, Chija Frima.

1951

As usual, a card game took place in Simon's Stadtplatz apartment, but this time Mendel seemed unusually animated. Marile brought out refreshments as the two children watched. One-and-a-half-year-old Elfriede soon dozed off, but Rudy continued to observe the scene as he clutched his stuffed rabbit. Shortly after everyone was seated, Mendel cleared his throat. It was a sign, and everyone knew something was coming.

"We are going to America," he said proudly as he passed around a document indicating the destination in the United States was to be Milford, Connecticut. He and Dolek were scheduled to leave on November 29 from Bremerhaven.

No one had ever heard of Milford, Connecticut, and the group had trouble finding it in an old atlas. Finally, Dolek spotted it. "There it is!" he said excitedly. "So far away."

MÜHLDORF, GERMANY, DECEMBER 1951

As Mendel prepared to leave Germany, he thought about the journey that had brought him this far. He had spent years in work camps, in hiding, then in a displaced persons camp, and though his fortunes had improved after reuniting with his brother Simon in Mühldorf, he was still anxious to leave Germany. It was now December 6, and the embarkation date was only two days away.

Marile had volunteered to help Mendel and Dolek pack. "I will miss you, Marile," said Mendel as he packed his few belongs in his small apartment near the *bahnhof.*

Thirteen-year-old Dolek agreed. "I will miss you too, Aunt Marile. "Thank you for everything, especially your cooking."

Marile smiled at the compliment. "I'll miss you too, Dolek." She and the boy had formed a bond of sorts, and she had mixed feelings about his departure. The young man had recently completed the Jewish *bar mitzvah* ritual bestowing manhood upon him, and he tried to remain stoic, but without much success.

Simon came by the apartment to check on progress. Mendel had sold many of his belongings, including a sewing machine and some leftover cloth, but nonetheless, he packed as much as he could to take into his new life.

"I'll take care of what's left," said Simon to his younger brother. "Don't worry. Things will go smoothly. You'll be in America before you know it. We will be there soon too, God willing."

Unknown to Simon, God was not listening that day, but the Americans had been.

After a tearful good-bye, Marile left and returned to her apartment. Little Rudy and Elfriede had been left with the Loskes, and she wanted to get back as quickly as possible. Packed and ready to go, Simon accompanied his brother and nephew to the nearby *bahnhof* to board a train to Munich and then another to the northern port city of Bremerhaven to board a ship bound for America.

As the bags were loaded onto the train, Simon and Mendel patted each other on the back. Dolek, too, now almost as tall as his uncle Simon, followed suit. No one knew when they would see each other again, but all assumed and prayed they would see one another sometime soon. Dolek boarded the train first, turned, and waved to his uncle. Mendel followed quickly. "Thank you, Simon. Good luck, and may God bless you and your family," he said and then disappeared into the passenger car.

The train whistle blew, and Simon watched as the train slowly puffed out of the station. He envied his brother and, while happy for him, lamented his own situation. Pensively, he watched the train disappear. On his way back to his Stadtplatz apartment, his frustration resurfaced. It had been several years since he had applied for immigration to America or Canada and had time and again been passed over, even after his marriage and the birth of his two children. Something would have to be done, but he was at a loss to know what.

Simon arrived at his apartment in a bad mood. Watching his brother and nephew leave Germany had merely added to his mounting frustration. He was frequently depressed as he watched more and more survivors immigrating to Canada, Israel, and America. The card games occurred less frequently until only Simon and Marile remained.

"What's wrong?" he asked Marile. "Am I cursed? Are we cursed? Why are we being left behind? Is God punishing me for something?" Unbidden, several reasons came to him, but he quickly brushed them aside.

"Simon, I don't know what can I say? Maybe it just was not meant to be. Maybe we were meant to stay in Germany."

The look on Simon's face frightened Marile. He paused, barely controlling his temper. "Marile, I will be damned if I stay in Germany. It is not an option for us. You must understand this."

Marile sighed deeply. She intuitively realized that she, too, must leave, that the path she had chosen inexorably set her course. She could never go home, even in her own country. "You are right, Simon. We must leave."

Mendel and Dolek Ruder watched the German countryside pass by as they headed north to Bremerhaven. The trip of some eight hundred kilometers took over ten hours, stopping in or near towns like Frankfort and Hanover before finally reaching the port city. They reached the debarkation point to find hundreds of other refugees already waiting in long lines. Papers needed to be verified, then a quick health check, and then, more waiting. Finally, on December 8, Mendel and Dolek Ruder were allowed to board the ship. Mendel noticed the name, the USS *General Stuart Heintzelman*. He was confused by the German-sounding name. Unknown to him, the ship was actually named after an American general. She was built in 1945 and had made many trips across the Pacific to Manila and Yokohama from San Francisco with homeward-bound American soldiers. Then, as part of the Army Transport Service, on October 30, 1947, she left Bremerhaven with 843 displaced persons from Estonia, Latvia, and Lithuania bound for Western Australia. Survivors William and Regina Weiss had crossed the Atlantic in 1949 on the busy ship. The US Navy had reacquired the ship in 1950, and it was put to work transporting troops supporting the Korean War. In late 1951, the USS *General Stuart Heintzelman* set sail from San Francisco to New York for transport duty in the Atlantic. Now, Mendel and Dolek Ruder were among the hundreds of refugees anxiously waiting for the ship to leave the German port and take them to uncertain, but undoubtedly new lives in America.

A week later it was to get even worse, at least for Simon. A letter arrived from his older brother Izak informing him that he and his wife Alice were immigrating to England and that they planned on visiting Mühldorf before they left.

Simon's mood grew darker, bordering on desperation. He showed the letter to Marile. Izak was not a frequent visitor, and Marile's relationship with Izak and Alice was not as close as her relationship with Mendel and Dolek.

"Simon, don't be discouraged. It's a sign that soon we, too, will have our chance. We cannot be far behind. You must be positive." Simon nodded absent-mindedly, lost in his dark thoughts.

Izak and Alice Ruder visited the Stadtplatz apartment a few days later bearing gifts. Four-year-old Rudy received a small toy fire truck, and his sister Elfriede was given a little plastic doll, though she was too young to understand and immediately tried to put it in her tiny mouth.

"England finally accepted us," said an excited Izak. "We sail across the Channel in two days. Alice and I are very excited and glad to finally leave Germany." Then, with a serious look on his face, he asked Simon, "Is there any word on your status?"

Simon frowned. "No good news yet, Izak. I don't understand. Every time I make inquiries, I am told it is 'pending.' It's been 'pending' for years."

"Well, I'm sure your turn will come. Things are loosening up and people are leaving."

"I'm happy for you and Alice."

"Thank you, Simon." Then, after a pause as if Izak was considering what to say next, he said, "Have you considered Israel? Many Jews are finally getting in."

The look on Marile's face answered Izak's question, and he quickly regretted asking. Simon just shook his head.

The two brothers shook hands as the women hugged. Soon Izak and Alice departed with a promise to keep in touch. Simon wondered about that and the many unanswered questions surrounding his older brother. Like many survivors, Izak had not volunteered his story, and Simon had not inquired. "We did what was necessary," was all Izak had ever mentioned, assuming his story was something better left a mystery.

1952

After the departure of his two brothers and nephew, Simon became more discouraged than ever. Moreover, the memory of the earlier 1949 immigration of his Lemberg fellow camp survivor young William Weiss and his new wife Regina to Detroit in America merely exacerbated his already intense frustration. He had high hopes that this year would be different, but so far, nothing had changed. In his mind, a pattern was emerging, and he was determined to find out why he and his family were being routinely passed over, so with a renewed sense of urgency, Simon traveled to Munich and asked around for advice. He was referred to a lawyer whom everyone said might be able to help. After getting directions, Simon made his way to the small office of Werner Winkler, a short, thin, bespectacled man of indeterminate origin and age. The rumor was that he was Jewish, but no one knew for sure, and neither he nor the contents of his office offered any clues.

"Please sit. What can I do for you?" asked Winkler as Simon entered the small, sparsely furnished office. Ever cautious, Simon studied the man sitting across from him and wondered, *If he is Jewish, why is he still here? Why is he helping Jews? Is it out of some altruistic need, or just money? If he is German, is he trying to finish the job of ridding Germany of the Jews legally?* He looked around the office and noticed a small rectangular area on the wall, slightly lighter in color than the surrounding area, as if a picture had been removed. *The Fuhrer?* Simon wondered, though he still couldn't be sure.

Regardless of the man's past, Simon decided that the man's motivation was irrelevant as long as it would facilitate his family's departure from Germany, so he calmly explained his situation, emphasizing the frustration it engendered. "Herr Winkler, can you investigate why this is happening?"

Winkler steepled his fingers as if in thought. "Are you certain this is not just taking the normal time going through the process? You understand there are hundreds of thousands of displaced persons applying to emigrate. It takes much time to process all of these people."

"I understand," said Simon, "but I think something is wrong, and I would feel much better if I knew for sure. My two brothers, a nephew, and other survivors have already left, and we are still here. Is there something you can do to help us?"

Winkler looked intently at Simon, who thought he perceived a brief flash of empathy on the man's face. After a measured pause, Winkler responded, "I have some contacts with the authorities that might provide some answers. It will take a few days, maybe a week. It will cost you for my time. I will call you when I have something. If that is satisfactory, leave me your information."

"Thank you, Herr Winkler. I will look forward to your call."

Business concluded, Simon felt better, but on the trip back to Mühldorf he worried about what the lawyer would find. He went back to work without telling Marile where he had been or why.

A week later the awaited telephone call came. Simon answered the telephone. "Yes...yes...in one hour," Marile heard her husband say.

Replacing the receiver, Simon responded to the puzzled look on Marile's face. "I have important business in Munich, *liebchen*. It's nothing to worry about. I will be back in a few hours." Simon kissed his surprised wife and said good-bye to Rudy and hurriedly drove back to Munich to Winkler's office. He was more than anxious to hear what the man had learned, and his anxiety level only increased as he got closer to the city.

Taking a deep breath, Simon entered the office, and Winkler motioned him to sit down. He removed his spectacles and cleaned them with his handkerchief, taking far longer than Simon thought necessary. Satisfied, Winkler nodded and fished around for some notes. "Herr Ruder, I have news, some troubling, but some good." Simon said nothing but motioned for the man to continue.

"Your wife and children are not considered 'displaced persons' because they were born here in Germany. They will be considered for immigration, but under the German quotas established by the United States, if that is where you want to go. The Americans spoke highly of your wife Maria when she worked for them after the war. However, the German quota is small, so the wait may be somewhat longer."

Simon considered this for a moment as a sense of relief washed over him. *So that's it. A complication, but nothing major,* he thought. "What's the good news?"

"Herr Ruder, that is the good news. The bad news concerns you and your political leanings."

Simon went suddenly pale, and he slumped heavily back in his chair, almost overturning it. *Here it comes,* he thought. *Please don't let it be my worst nightmare.*

After a moment, Winkler continued. "I learned that the Americans listened to your speeches several years ago and remain uneasy about exactly where you stand politically. And now, it's even worse. I'm told the US Congress passed a new law, the Internal Security Act, and among a number of other restrictions, it does not allow entry to America to any foreigner who is a Communist or who might engage in activities that would be prejudicial to the public interest, or would endanger the welfare or safety of the United States. They suspect that maybe this describes you. I believe these restrictions are in response to the worsening situation with Russia and the war in Korea. Your status is 'pending,' but with so many applicants, they do not have time to clarify your status. By then, who knows?"

A dispirited Simon Ruder sat at the table, his head in his hands. "*Oy vey iz mir,*" was all he could manage to say over and over.

Winkler shook his head. "Herr Ruder!" he said loudly to shake Simon out of his lamentation. "If I may ask, what were you thinking when you spoke so harshly against the Americans? They may not have been perfect, but they provided great comfort to the Jews."

"Herr Winkler, you must understand, it was right after the war. Things were not so good. I thought the Americans were moving too slowly. It wasn't clear to me what was really going on. Yes, I was critical of their handling of the situation, and I thought I could help my people by speaking out. So I did. Many people came and listened to me. I now understand that I was wrong. When I was younger, I even thought Communism was good for the Jews, but those days are over now."

"So now what will you do?"

"What can I do? Do I have any options? I absolutely must leave Germany with my family. I cannot stay here."

"I understand, Herr Ruder. Maybe something can be done. It was said that if you could have someone in America advocate on your behalf, someone who has known you for a long time and can vouch for your moral character, that would be a positive thing. Also, it would be good to have someone who could sponsor you, or at least provide some financial aid so the Americans are satisfied that you and your family will not be a burden. These things would likely improve your situation."

Simon's face lit up. "Thank you, Herr Winkler. You have been a great help."

Driving back to Mühldorf, Simon carefully composed a letter in his mind. When he arrived at his apartment, he immediately penned the letter still lingering in his head. After careful revisions, he was finally satisfied and placed the letter in a new Air Mail envelope. He retrieved the letter from America and carefully copied the address in Detroit, Michigan, USA.

Simon awoke early the next morning. "Marile," he shouted. "I'm taking care of some business and running a few errands. I should be back in a few hours."

"That's fine, Simon. I'm going to see Dr. Loske and do some shopping. I'm taking Rudy and Elfriede with me. Should I pick up anything special from the butcher shop?"

"No, *liebchen*, nothing special. I will see you later."

Simon hurried to the post office to mail the letter. He paid the price of the *Luftpost,* Air Mail postage, handed the letter to the clerk, and hoped for the best.

Marile and the children were still gone from the apartment when Simon returned from the post office and his errands. A note on the table indicated that Marile was at Dr. Loske's office and would be back soon. Simon decided he would surprise the family by making an early lunch, but Marile had a surprise of her own. With four-year-old Rudy and two-year-old Elfriede in tow, Marile entered the apartment and excitedly announced, "Simon, I have good news. We are having another baby in September."

DETROIT, MICHIGAN, AUGUST 1952

It was a bright, sunny summer day on August 5, 1952, as a letter was being notarized in an office building in Detroit, Michigan. The letter, meticulously written in longhand German, attested to the outstanding character, industriousness, and loyalty of one Simon Ruder and pledged financial support if he and his family were allowed to immigrate to America. The letter was signed by William Weiss.

1953

It was time. Simon had been avoiding it for some eight years, and now, with a renewed sense of optimism about immigration, he gathered up his wife and two of his children and drove to Ampfing, about ten kilometers away. The six-month-old infant boy, Manfred, was left in the care of Frau Dr. Loske. Simon had made the trip to Ampfing dozens of times over the last eight years, but this time the destination was different.

"Where are we going, Papa?" asked Rudy.

"A place I must see again. And something you, your mother, and sister must also see. Maybe you will not remember, but one day, I hope you will understand."

It was a sunny, cool day as they approached what appeared to be a large field, and as they drew nearer, they saw it was encircled by a high metal link fence. Simon stopped the car nearby and slowly exited. He stood there for a moment as a shiver shook him in spite of the sunny weather. Marile came up beside him and took his hand, shaking him out of his dark reverie.

Simon walked toward the fence as memories called to him and ghostly tendrils seemed to reach toward him through the rusting metal links in a welcoming embrace. He could make out decayed ruins of guard towers that had once stood overlooking the former camp. The field was mostly overgrown, but he could imagine the partially submerged primitive huts that had served as pitiful shelters. He closed his eyes and could hear the dogs. His nostrils were assaulted by the ungodly stench that had clung to everything in the camp like a blanket. He remembered lying there, more dead than alive, the camp Capos, fleeing after having administered what they intended to be fatal slashes and leaving him to die. Yet Simon had survived, just barely, as the US Army liberated the camp on that day in May of 1945.

"Let's walk," he said quietly. He called Rudy over and took the young boy's hand and began walking toward the fence. Marile took Elfriede's little hand in hers and followed her husband. The three-year-old girl tried to keep up, but Marile had to pick her up once in a while. They walked slowly around the outside perimeter of the former camp for another twenty minutes, the children's gaze focusing intently on the passing scene.

"Papa, this place is so ugly," said Rudy, as if sensing its sinister past.

Simon let out a sardonic laugh, surprised at his young son's comment.

"Yes, it is, my little Rudy. It was and it always will be."

Marile came up behind her husband, the toddler Elfriede in tow. "What is this place?" asked Marile, though she already suspected.

"Hell," said Simon.

The Ruder children in early 1953, Elfriede, age three, and the author, age five.

MÜHLDORF, GERMANY, MAY 1953

The good news finally came in May 1953. The Simon Ruder family was finally cleared to leave Germany and come to America. The documents indicated the family was bound for Cleveland, Ohio.

"Why are we going to this Cleveland?" asked Marile. "Isn't that where Mendel went two years ago?"

Simon wondered about that too. He assumed it was because his brother had done well there and had sponsored him. In fact, the truth was somewhat different. Cleveland, Ohio, had developed into one of the largest garment manufacturing centers in America, rivaling even New York. Most firms were family owned, predominately Jewish, and most had been established by immigrants from Germany and Eastern Europe. There were also several large firms, such as Richman Brothers and Joseph & Feiss, at which Mendel Ruder had found employment. Jews had been in Cleveland as early as the 1830s, and by 1860, there were twelve hundred Jewish families living there. For Simon Ruder, however, one firm in particular would shape his professional fortunes. Established in 1939 on Cleveland's West Sixth Street in the Bradley Building by Maurice Saltzman and Max Reiter, Ritmore Sportswear produced a comprehensive line of women's wear. The firm became Bobbie Brooks in 1953 when Saltzman bought out Reiter. Simon would find steady work on West Sixth Street for the next twenty-five years, building his unimaginable and unlikely American dream.

"Yes, that's where Mendel went, but what does it matter? We are finally leaving Germany. That's what is important." Marile just shrugged and began making plans for the long-awaited move.

Now that a departure date had been set, there was much to do. Simon sold his two automobiles. The trusty Adler went first. Marile packed items that she thought the family of five would need in the new world but soon realized everything could not make the trip. Pictures, selected dishes, cutlery, and clothes were all selected and prioritized, even five-year-old Rudy's pair of *lederhosen*. Unfortunately, Simon's stock of cloth and his sewing machine would have to stay, but his Jewish religious items, such as his prayer shawl, books, and menorah were all packed with special care. In all, the Ruder family packed what they could, their worldly possessions tightly packed in a large wooden box. Finally, the Opel left for its new owner, and the family prepared to leave Mühldorf for Munich and on to their new lives.

Marile said a tearful good-bye to her sisters Bette and Rosie. Although she tried, her parents refused to see her off. "Tell Papa I love him. Mama too. I'll write when we get to America." With final hugs, the sisters parted.

Early Tuesday, June 30, the five members of the Simon Ruder family boarded a train to Munich. Simon made sure the precious wooden box was securely loaded onto the baggage car. He checked and double-checked the American Joint Distribution Committee (AJDC) emigration service papers and placed them in his suit pocket. These documents would show that Simon Ruder, Maria Ruder, and children Rudolf, age five, Elfriede, age three, and Manfred, nine months old, were bound for Cleveland, Ohio, in America.

In Munich, the family was taken to the Munich Flughafen (airport). Simon supervised the transfer of the wooden box, making sure it stayed within his sight. After the usual checks and verifications, thirty-three so-called "migrants" boarded the Seaboard and Western DC-4 charter flight bound for

Idlewild Airport in New York. The Ruder family represented "migrant" numbers twenty-seven through thirty-one on the AJDC emigration service papers. Since none of the family had ever been on an airplane, this was a new and sometimes frightening experience for them. Fueled, baggage loaded, and passengers aboard and situated, the captain pushed the throttles, and the silver, four-engine DC-4 with an American flag, red and white stripes, and bearing number N1221V on the stabilizer lumbered down the runway and took off into the sunny Bavarian sky headed north.

The flight to America would take them first to Shannon Airport in Ireland, some 952 miles distant, then another 1,983 miles across the North Atlantic to Gander Airport in Newfoundland, Canada, and the final 1,101 miles to Idlewild Airport (now JFK) in New York.

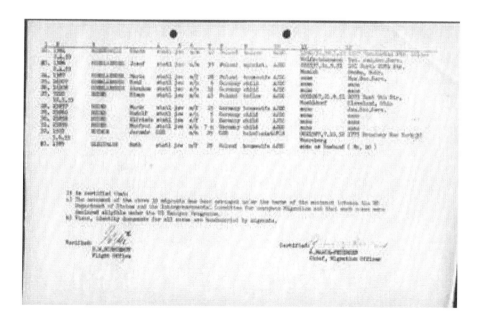

Copy of another manifest showing the Ruder family as "migrants."

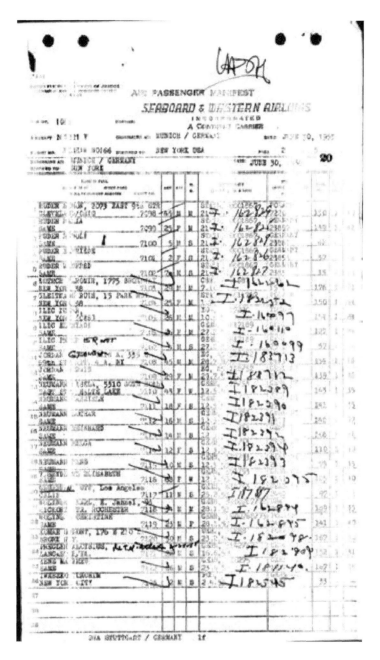

Copy of the original Seaboard & Western Airlines passenger manifest.
Members of the Ruder family are listed first on the document.

This is the actual aircraft that transported my father, mother, sister, brother, and the author to our new life in America on June 30, 1953. It carried registration number N1221V.

Less than twenty-four hours later, after two refueling stops, and some tomato soup with crackers, the Simon Ruder family finally found themselves in America. Having flown some 4,036 miles, the DC-4 landed at Idlewild Airport located in the borough of Queens in the city of New York at 8:12 a.m. The family was met by a representative of the United Services for New Americans (USNA), an organization formed in response to the influx of Jewish immigrants, providing assistance with the port entry process, financial aid, shelter, and travel arrangements. A young, pretty Jewish woman introduced herself. "My name is Rachel Feldman," she said in Yiddish, assuming Simon would understand. "I will help you get through the process here, then you will travel to your final destination." Simon nodded as though this was obvious to him. Rachel took the group to immigration to verify their documents and to customs to search their luggage and the wooden box Simon had been so relieved to see coming off the airplane. He watched as the customs officials sifted through their belongings and then, satisfied, resealed the box. After several hours, Rachel arranged to transport the family and their belongings to overnight lodging some twelve miles away in Lower Manhattan. Feeling more comfortable, Simon asked Rachel about the details of the plan. She explained, "Mr. Ruder, we have arranged transportation to Cleveland for you and your family for tomorrow evening. You will go by train. But first, tomorrow morning, I will take you on a quick tour of the city. This will begin your 'Americanization' process. Now we will go to the hotel for the night. You and Mrs. Ruder must be tired. It looks like the children are already asleep."

The USNA vehicle, loaded with the Ruder family and their possessions, left the airport area and headed toward the hotel. Crossing onto Manhattan Island, Simon marveled at the sheer number of cars and the constant cacophony of honking horns, squealing brakes, and an occasional siren. Simon seemed overwhelmed by the city.

"Look at the buildings. Look how high they go into the clouds."

Rachel laughed. "They are called skyscrapers. Tomorrow you will see more."

The group reached the hotel and entered the lobby. "Wait here," she said as she took care of registering the family. Marile notice a red Coca-Cola vending machine into which someone had just inserted a coin and then pulled out a familiarly shaped bottle containing a brown liquid. Marile remembered GIs in Germany carrying around these bottles and had always wondered what it would taste like. Having completed the registration, Rachel noticed Marile's interest in the vending machine.

"Would you like a Coca-Cola, Mrs. Ruder? Maybe one for Mr. Ruder too?"

"Well, maybe," said Marile. "If it doesn't cost too much."

Rachel laughed. "It's only five cents, a nickel. It's been the same price forever." With that, she walked over to the machine, inserted a nickel, and withdrew a cold bottle. She popped off the cap with a reassuring *whoosh* and handed it to Marile. "Mrs. Ruder, try this." She repeated the process and handed the bottle to Simon, who took a drink as he would a beer. The fizz quickly went up his nose. Marile sipped hers with much better results. "This is very good," she said. "I like it."

By now Simon had recovered and drank more slowly. "Very sweet," was all he said.

The next morning Rachel and the Ruder family walked down Forty-Second Street. Simon was surprised to identify various languages, including Polish, German, Russian, and Yiddish. He even saw a group of Hasidic Jews, dressed as he remembered from his past. Then an observation struck him. Everything moved quicker here: the people, the cars. People laughed in the streets. They spoke Yiddish openly, and no one looked over their shoulders. *My God*, he thought. *What a country.*

Marile followed along with the three children. Even with infant Manfred in a borrowed stroller, she managed to stop and peer into every shop window, gazing at goods she never knew existed. Rachel smiled at the reaction of these new immigrants. She had seen the looks of awe many times before, and this would certainly not be the last time.

"Time for lunch," said Rachel as they stopped in front of a small restaurant. The family followed the woman inside, and they sat at one of the tables. Rachel handed Simon and Marile a menu that neither of them could read. Intently, Simon scanned the menu and thought he recognized the words "frankfurter" and "hamburger" but wasn't sure what they meant. Showing his menu to Marile, he pointed to those menu items. Marile motioned toward their guide. Rachel noticed the look of confusion on Simon's face and chuckled.

"A 'frankfurter' is a kind of sausage in a long roll. It is very American." Simon nodded and asked about the 'hamburger.'

"It is also very American. It is ground beef shaped in a, how do you say it, a patty and fried or grilled. It is placed in a round roll. The Americans love them. Sometimes they put cheese on them, and then it is a 'cheeseburger.' We will not do that, though. You will become accustomed to these and other foods, but where you are going, there are many Jews, and you will recognize the foods there as well. It is all part of the process to become Americans."

Later that afternoon Rachel arranged transportation for the Ruder family, their luggage, and the precious wooden box to Grand Central Terminal located at 89 East Forty-Second Street. She would stay with them until the train left later that evening. It was still light as they arrived several hours early for the 10:10 p.m. departure of New York Central railroad train number 59,

The Chicagoan, scheduled to arrive in Cleveland at 9:30 a.m. on the following morning on its way to Chicago.

Simon had lived in Lemberg for several years and had visited Munich on many occasions, so he was familiar with good-sized cities, but New York seemed so big, so vibrant, as if the war had never affected it. Even Munich still bore scars from the war, but this city, it was so different, so modern. As they arrived at the huge building on Forty-Second Street, Simon was unprepared for the grandeur of Grand Central Terminal. As they entered, he gazed in awe at the high vaulted ceilings, the marble floors and walls. Simon thought back to his old friend from Lemberg, Jacob Lansky, the architect, and knew he would have approved. Marile, too, had traveled to Munich and loved that Bavarian city, but she was also overwhelmed by New York City. It did that to people, especially the first time.

Rachel settled the family on a bench and went to the large ticket counter to collect the tickets for the family's trip to Cleveland. Simon followed her and asked about the luggage and wooden box. Rachel nodded and said, "Simon, everything has been taken care of. Even now your luggage is on a large baggage cart waiting to be loaded, and your box is located next to the cart. I know how important these things are to you, but you have nothing to worry about. Everything is safe." She handed him several tags. "These are for claiming your luggage and box when you arrive in Cleveland. Someone from the Jewish Family Service will meet you at the terminal. Here are your tickets."

Rachel checked the large clock in the middle of the terminal. "We have two hours until the train leaves. There is a place inside where we can have a quick meal before the train leaves."

Gathering up the family, Rachel took them to a small diner inside the huge terminal. Simon opted for another beef frankfurter. He had learned a new phrase: hot dog. He had also developed a taste for potato chips. *I am on my way to being an American,* he thought. Marile ordered a hot dog as well and shared it with the two children. The infant Manfred was still asleep, oblivious to the dramatic events of the last few days.

"Do you have any questions?" asked Rachel as the group ate their food. "You should be in Cleveland by nine thirty tomorrow morning."

"How far is this Cleveland?" asked Marile. Rachel consulted the timetable she had picked up at the ticket counter.

"About six hundred miles. Maybe 972 kilometers."

"Do we have to change trains?"

"No, this train will take you all the way there. Just stay on it until you hear the conductor announce 'Cleveland.' In fact, the train will continue to Chicago, which is another three hundred forty-one miles, five hundred fifty kilometers. Remember, this is a very big country."

"Have you ever been to this Cleveland?" asked Simon.

"No, I have not, but I know there is a large Jewish community there. I understand your brother and his son live there. I have sent several Jewish families there in the last few years. Many came from Germany, some by ship, others like you, by airplane. Many were displaced persons, and I think they were originally from Hungary and Poland." Rachel looked at Marile. "Maybe your case is different."

Simon took a final bite of his hot dog. "Maybe not so different," he said thoughtfully.

Rachel unfolded the timetable and circled Cleveland. "If you have any questions, just show this to the conductor, but remember, when he calls out 'Cleveland,' that is where you get off the train. Your luggage and box will be taken off the train by the workers. Do not lose your baggage claim tags or your tickets. The conductor will collect your tickets shortly after the train leaves the station."

"Thank you, Rachel," said Simon. "You have been very kind," added Marile with a smile.

"Don't worry, everything will be fine," said Rachel reassuringly. She checked her watch. "We must be going. They will be boarding your train in thirty minutes. I will take you to the waiting area."

Rachel paid the bill and left a tip. The family followed Rachel to the waiting area. She walked over to a railroad employee and, pointing to the family, had a short conversation. The man nodded and smiled.

Soon the train loudspeaker announced the boarding of train 59, *The Chicagoan*, to Chicago with intermediate stops at Croton-Harmon, Buffalo,

Erie, and East Cleveland before reaching Cleveland. The rest of the stops after Cleveland didn't matter to the Ruder family. That last stop is where their future life would take root.

Rachel took the family to the line ready to board the train. She handed a brown sack to Marile. "Something for the journey."

"Thank you," said Marile, without looking inside the sack.

Rachel looked at the family. She understood their anxiety. "Good luck to you. Have a safe trip, and welcome to America."

The man Rachel was talking to motioned the family to follow him, and he led them down to the underground platform to a long row of shiny passenger cars. Though he knew the family spoke no English, he nonetheless, perhaps out of long habit, said, "This way, folks."

They understood and followed the man into the cool, lighted car. He pointed to four seats, and Simon, Marile, Rudy, Elfriede, and Manfred sat down and tried to make themselves comfortable. The children were asleep almost immediately, taking the events in stride. Simon took Marile's hand. "This is what we have been waiting for. A new land, a new life. Whatever it holds for us, I will work hard, and I promise to make you happy."

"I know you will, Simon," said Marile, trying to sound optimistic. "I know you will," she said as she leaned over and kissed her husband on the cheek.

The train left precisely at 10:10 p.m. and accelerated smoothly out of the terminal. It came out of the tunnel, and Simon gazed at the myriad of lights of New York City. *Amazing*, he thought, but soon he, too, dozed off.

The train came to a smooth stop at the first stop, Croton-Harmon, some thirty-two miles from New York City. Simon awoke and looked out the window, trying to see what was happening. *A long stop*, he thought. He didn't know that the electric locomotive that had taken the train this far had been switched for shiny diesel locomotives that would take the train the rest of the way. Shortly, after an almost imperceptible bump, the new locomotives were coupled to the train, and it was off again, rolling into the night. Sleep eluded Simon as he tried to watch the scenery pass by in the dark. He could catch glimpses of water on his left as the waning gibbous moon reflected off the smooth surface of the Hudson River. He heard the sound of the train's horns and the railroad crossing bells. He saw car headlights waiting for the train to pass. Then there was darkness again as clouds obscured the moon. He heard the horns again and marveled at how different they sounded from the shrill whistles of trains in Poland and Germany.

As the New York scenery ghosted by, he had time to think. Now that the family had finally left Germany and had actually arrived in America, he worried about the future toward which they were hurtling. *Could he support his family? Would the family be accepted? Would they fit into this new country?* Only time would tell, but he promised himself he would do everything to be successful. He looked over at his young wife, already asleep in the seat to next him, still cradling the infant Manfred. Rudy and Elfriede shared a seat across from him. He wondered what the future held for his children. *What opportunities will be available to them? How can I ensure their success in America?*

Sleep finally overtook him, but it was far from peaceful. Suddenly, he was back at Auschwitz, the stench of death, the starvation, the beatings tormenting his thoughts. No amount of Coca-Cola could erase that. Then the death march in the dead of winter, the trail of corpses. Then Dachau, more death, more starvation, more beatings. He moaned in his sleep. A stifled scream awakened Marile. She had heard this before and immediately took steps to calm her husband.

"Shh, shh, Simon. It's all right. It's only a dream. You are safe. We are in America."

Simon blinked himself into wakefulness. He looked around and finally remembered where he was. He sighed. "I wish I had a schnapps."

Marile laughed. "Go back to sleep. Everything will be fine. Soon we will be in this Cleveland."

Manfred stirred, hungry again, so Marile tended to his needs. Soon the infant was asleep again. She checked her husband and took his hand. "Sleep now."

And he did, this time mercifully, much more peacefully. Now, as the Ruder family slept, the train passed through towns like Albany, Schenectady, Utica, Rome, Syracuse, and Rochester. As the sun slowly crept up behind them, the train slowed and pulled into the Buffalo Central Terminal in Buffalo, New

York, on time at 5:50 a.m. They had traveled 431 miles. Only a scant 187 miles separated them from their new lives.

Life in the coach began to stir as other passengers began to awaken. Drawn shades opened to let in the rosy dawn. The two older children stirred and began to fidget. "I'm hungry," complained Rudy. His sister chimed in as well. Marile looked at her husband, who motioned toward the sack provided by Rachel. "Ah," said Marile as she reached for it and looked inside. Neatly packed were four oranges, a bag of potato chips, several cookies wrapped in a clear covering, and two packages of what looked like fingers of cake. Curious, Marile withdrew one of them. Wondering what American creation this might be, she smelled the package. Nothing familiar came to her nose. She looked at the writing emblazoned on the package. It read "Twinkies." She mouthed the unfamiliar word and hesitatingly tore open the package. She touched one of the golden fingers and found it moist and a bit sticky, but it smelled good, and she was hungry. She tentatively took a small bite and a smile came to her face. The two older children watched their mother and soon had their little hands out. Marile took out the second finger of moist cake and carefully divided it in half. White cream oozed out slowly, another surprise. Rudy and Elfriede reached for the offered morsels and devoured them. Marile laughed at the mess they made with cream on their faces. She took out a handkerchief, wetted it with her tongue, and wiped their faces.

Simon was lost in thought, wondering why the train hadn't moved. He was oblivious to his wife and two children as they consumed another American icon.

"Simon. Try one of these. They are delicious." She unwrapped the second package and handed one of the cakes to her husband. Absent-mindedly, he accepted the offering and took a bite. "It is good," he said and quickly finished it off.

Presently, the horns sounded, and the train began to move. Marile dug into the sack and retrieved an orange, a luxury but not unknown to them as Simon had sold them on the black market in Germany. Marile peeled the fruit and handed Simon several sections and one each to Rudy and Elfriede. Again, she had to wipe their lips as juice escaped their little mouths.

A woman walked down the aisle and noticed the two children. "What adorable children!" she exclaimed with a smile. Marile smiled back at the compliment and quietly said, "Thank you," drawing on the meager English vocabulary she had picked up while working for the Americans some eight years ago. The woman nodded and continued down the aisle.

Marile look over to her husband. "Simon, what are you thinking? You look worried."

"Maybe a little worried. I have many questions, *mein liebchen*." He looked at his children and smiled. Marile took his hand and, with all the enthusiasm she could rally, said, "Everything will be fine. I just know it." She had almost convinced herself.

The train sped through the rest of New York State past Dunkirk and Westfield. Soon the conductor walked through the train, calling out, "Erie, next stop is Erie, Pennsylvania." Having traveled a further ninety-two miles, the train glided smoothly into the stately Erie Union Station at precisely 7:45 a.m. Several passengers got up, collected their belongings, and exited the train as several more climbed on board. Simon watched intently through the window as the baggage was unloaded onto waiting carts and taken into the station. Presently, with the now familiar blast of the horns, the train began moving again, seemingly restless to carry the Ruder family the final ninety-five miles to the new life that awaited them.

The train gathered speed and made quick work of the Lake Erie shore segment of Pennsylvania and moved into Ohio. This time Simon took Marile's hand. "Soon we will be there." Marile discreetly rolled her eyes at the obvious truth Simon had shared with her, but she did not allow her anxiety to show. "Yes, Simon, I'm looking forward to it," and in a reassuring gesture, she squeezed his hand.

Simon peered out the window as the more rural countryside sped past. The train thundered through Ashtabula, and soon, the conductor came through again. "East Cleveland. The next stop is East Cleveland."

Hearing "Cleveland," Simon perked up and was about to get out of his seat when the conductor came by. He shook his head and motioned Simon to sit. "Not this stop. One more after this." Meager as it was, Marile understood enough English to translate the conductor's statement. Simon sat back down as the conductor smiled, nodded to Marile, and continued through the car. Soon the train came to a stop at the East Cleveland station, less than ten miles from the final destination that would be the new home of the Ruder family. It was a quick stop, and as the train began to move, the conductor came by again. Then came the announcement Simon had been waiting for. "Next stop in ten minutes will be Cleveland. Cleveland, Ohio, is the next stop." He paused in front of the Ruder family and nodded.

Marile gathered up their belongings and made sure the children were ready. The infant Manfred stirred, blinked, and went back to sleep. Rudy and Elfriede both yawned and, sensing the excitement, were soon wide awake. Simon looked out the window and could frequently catch a glimpse of a tall building in the distance that was rapidly getting larger. He tried to point it out to his family as it drew ever closer. He didn't know it at the time, but he was looking at the Terminal Tower, its fifty-one stories making it the tallest building in North America outside New York. As the stately limestone-clothed building became larger and larger, the conductor came by again and made his announcement. "Cleveland, Ohio, in five minutes."

Upstairs in the main terminal, Natalie Abrams prepared to meet the new Jewish family that was scheduled to arrive from Germany by way of New York. She checked the emigration services document one more time to make sure. Then she heard the announcement. "Arriving, *The Chicagoan* from New York on track...." She hurried to meet them, just another family among the influx of Jewish refugees flowing into America.

The train slowed and coasted into the bowels of the huge building. It was 9:30 a.m. as the train came to a smooth stop. The conductor helped the exiting passengers and took extra time to help Marile with the children. Simon nodded to the conductor and pulled out the baggage claim tags. The conductor pointed upstairs. Confused, Simon was about to protest when a woman approached the group. "It's all right. I'll take care of this," she said to the conductor. Relieved, he quickly got busy helping other passengers. The woman turned to Simon and, assuming he spoke Yiddish, said, "Hello, Mr. Ruder. Welcome to Cleveland. My name is Natalie Abrams. I am from the Jewish Family Service."

Natalie, thought Simon. *Russian for sure. But this is America. It doesn't matter here.*

Natalie slowly took in the rest of the family. Her gaze lingered a moment too long on Marile. *She doesn't look Jewish.*

Simon quickly gathered his thoughts. He spotted the ring on her finger. "I'm glad to meet you, Mrs. Abrams," he said as he watched baggage being unloaded and piled onto the waiting cart. Natalie turned and guessed at the cause of Simon's anxiety. "Don't worry, your baggage is safe." Finally, he saw the precious wooden box being removed from the baggage car and gently lowered to the concrete platform and heaved a sigh of relief.

"See, nothing to worry about. We should get going to the office. By the way, you are just in time for the holiday tomorrow," said Natalie.

"Holiday?" asked Simon. He looked at Marile, who just shrugged.

"The Fourth of July is tomorrow. It's America's one hundred seventy-seventh birthday. You will learn all about American history."

The horns blasted again, and the train accelerated out of the terminal to continue its trip to Chicago.

Simon smiled. "Then a year from today will be the Ruder family's first birthday in America."

Natalie smiled as she led the Simon Ruder family out of the terminal and into an uncertain, yet optimistic new life in Cleveland.

EPILOGUE

It is a cold January day in 2006 as a small group of people huddle under a blue canvas shelter in a Jewish cemetery south of Cleveland. The day is uncharacteristically devoid of snow, and though sunny, the winter sun contributes little in the way of warmth. With a shiny black hearse and a line of cars with little purple flags in the background, the rabbi conducts a short ceremony after which workers slowly lower the casket into the freshly excavated hole. Time has finally accomplished what the Nazis, SS and vicious camp Capos failed to do. Six months shy of his ninety-ninth birthday, Simon Ruder passed away peacefully in his sleep exactly sixty-one years after the brutal death march from Auschwitz began. As she promised Simon a time long ago, his wife of fifty-seven years, Maria (Marile) was at his side until the end. She now sits quietly under a warm blanket surrounded by her five children and watches her husband's burial.

The rabbi picks up a shovel and begins the symbolic filling of the hole. David (Dolek) Ruder picks up a shovel and is immediately joined by Simon's children, German-born Rudolf, Elfriede and Manfred, and his two American-born daughters, Jeanette and Doris. As they take turns shoveling the dirt, they each instinctively understand that they are taking part in the final act of a remarkable play in which Simon Ruder played a leading role. As the group begins to break up, they pause to study the nearby graves. A few yards from Simon's gravesite is an older one bearing Simon's younger brother Mendel who passed away in 1979. They pass another nearby gravestone bearing the name Eugene Weissbluth. Mr. Weissbluth moved to Cleveland with his son Tomas and was, for many years the Ruder family insurance agent, often admonishing the author for his teenage driving record.

The somber group hugged each other and headed for their cars, not realizing that a scant four months later, they would be here again, this time on a much sadder note. Maria Ruder, nee Häusl, the young girl who had presented Adolf Hitler with a bouquet of flowers sixty-eight years ago, would succumb to complications during heart surgery at the Cleveland Clinic and be buried next to Simon.

THE AUTHOR

Mr. Ruder has spent over thirty-five years working in a corporate environment for companies including General Motors, IBM, ATT, Nissan, Electronic Data Systems and several others before finally achieving a lifelong goal of writing this book. While Mr. Ruder has written articles for diverse magazines about auto drag racing and model railroading, this is his first full-length novel.

Rudy attended the Ohio State University, holds a Bachelor's Degree from Cleveland State University and spent time as Associate Professor teaching computer programming classes.

His family emmigrated from Germany to the United States in 1953 and at the age of five, he began his rapid assimilation into the American culture. He participated in various sports including baseball, football, track and tennis. He frequently dabbles in road and drag racing, flying and owns a classic car restoration business focusing on American muscle cars. Rudy occassionaly engages in Information Technology and Management consulting activities and has traveled extensively throughout the United States, Europe and Japan.

[i] *"Der Untermenschen"* in Hofer 1960 p.280. Originally published by the Reichsfuhrer SS, SS Headquarters (Berlin, 1935).

[ii] This section is based on information from an article by Michael B. Shimkin, titled *"An Incident at Ampfing"*, RG-09.005*03, United States Holocaust Memorial Museum, Washington, DC

Made in the USA
Charleston, SC
24 January 2015